"*Pieces of Silver* is a story straight from the author's heart that will leave readers pondering the characters and their lives long after the final page is turned. Excitement, intrigue, and romance! If this is the type of book to expect in the future from Ms. Lang, I can't wait for her next one! Bravo!"

—Tamera Alexander
Author of *Rekindled*, Book One in the Fountain Creek Chronicles

"*Pieces of Silver* is an intriguing story set in America during World War I. Fear and betrayal, coupled with love and patriotism, parallel the characters and our nation during tumultuous times. A twist of an ending adds up to a great read."

—DiAnn Mills
Author of multiple books including *Footsteps*,
At the End of the Bayou, and *When the Lion Roars*

"Talented author Maureen Lang brings the World War I era to life through vivid description, endearing characters, and a thread of intrigue. Simply put, *Pieces of Silver* shines."

—Kathleen Fuller
Author of *Santa Fe Sunrise*

"Maureen Lang has masterfully recreated the dangerous days of intrigue surrounding the United States' entrance into World War I, the Great War, and has given us true-to-life characters who seem to walk off the pages and into our hearts. *Pieces of Silver* is a thrilling story about a long-neglected era in our history."

—Louise M. Gouge
Author of Ahab's Legacy Trilogy

"A powerful story of love, betrayal, espionage, and faith that will keep you spellbound to the last page. I loved this story."

—Wanda L. Dyson
Author of the critically acclaimed
Johnson-Shefford Case Files suspense series

PIECES *of* SILVER

MAUREEN LANG

Kregel
Publications

To my mom.
Thanks for asking God to bless my writing with
a contract. Who knew that was all it would take?

Pieces of Silver: A Novel

© 2006 by Maureen Lang

Published by Kregel Publications, a division of Kregel, Inc., P.O. Box 2607, Grand Rapids, MI 49501.

The persons and events portrayed in this work are the creations of the author, and any resemblance to persons living or dead is purely coincidental.

Unless otherwise indicated, all Scripture quotations are from the King James Version of the Holy Bible.

Scripture quotations marked NKJV are taken form the New King James Version. Copyright © 1982 by Thomas Nelson, Inc. Used by permission. All rights reserved.

Library of Congress Cataloging-in-Publication Data

Lang, Maureen.
Pieces of silver : a novel / by Maureen Lang.
    p. cm.
    1. Prejudices—Fiction. I. Title.
PS3612.A554P54 2006
813'.6--dc22   2005036166

ISBN 0-8254-3668-0

Printed in the United States of America

06 07 08 09 10 / 5 4 3 2 1

ACKNOWLEDGMENTS

FIRST, thanks to my family for not minding too much every time the computer called to me when I should have been tending to other matters. I'm especially grateful to my husband for his encouragement along this rocky road back to publication.

And to my dad and Grandpa Howard, who inspired my fascination for war and history.

I am indebted to Paul Ingram at Kregel for showing interest in my work, which led to the publication of this book. Thank you, Paul! I'm also grateful to editor Becky Durost Fish for her attention to detail and in general making me look better than I am. And of course to the rest of the Kregel staff that turned dreams of this manuscript into the reality of a book.

A huge thank you to Special Agent Diane Rivers for her friendship, expertise, insight, and inspiration.

I am also grateful to my first readers—trusted friends and family who might have cringed over early rough spots but gave me encouragement anyway: Laura Palmere, Grace Schmidgall, and Marji Schmidgall. And to my writer's group who helped me polish: Julie Dahlberg; her husband, Scott; and her mom, Judy Knox. Also April Witkowski, Dawn Hill, and Joanna Bradford. Thank you all for traveling this writing journey together.

I'd also like to thank Jeff, Paul, and Rusty . . . wherever you are. You saw this project before God took me through the fire. See what can come out of the ashes?

"What are you willing to give me if I deliver Him to you?" And they counted out to him thirty pieces of silver.

—Matthew 26:15 NKJV

CHAPTER *One*

Washington, D.C.: February 28, 1917

With the telephone ringing amid the machine-gun staccato of a dozen typewriters, Liesel Bonner didn't hear her name. But when she saw the frown creasing Mr. Hodges's brow as he headed her way, she knew he must have called her more than once. Beyond him, Henry Miller, the senior clerk of the large law office, sent Liesel an anxious glance from behind round spectacles resting on his nose.

"Please join me in my office in five minutes, Miss Bonner." Mr. Hodges was typically polite despite the annoyance on his fair-skinned, jowly face.

"Yes, Mr. Hodges," Liesel replied. "I'm sorry I didn't hear you."

"Quite all right." He left Liesel's typing table to go with Mr. Miller to the clerk's rolltop desk at the end of a row of similar workstations in the center of the office.

Hurriedly, Liesel proofread the letter still rolled in her Remington typewriter. She had just five minutes to finish; the letter was due back to Senator Burle in ten. Reading forward first for content, then backward for misspellings, Liesel found the letter without error and pulled it from the carriage. With familiar ease, she quickly typed an envelope and slipped it along with the letter into a larger packet and sealed it. Standing, she retrieved her pencil and pad from its slot on her rolltop desk and headed to Mr. Hodges's office, stopping only once to ask the mail boy to deliver the letter immediately to the senator on the floor above.

The senior partner's office was an island of calm compared to the hubbub of the stenographic pool. Liesel waited just inside the door, fully expecting Mr. Hodges to enter behind her, but a breeze from a barely opened window stole her attention. For the last day of February, it was uncommonly warm, and she welcomed the hint of spring. She heard the honk of a motorcar from several stories below, followed quickly by the neigh of a horse. The two ways of transportation seemed at odds sometimes. With the popularity of motors growing, she wondered if the old hay burners were beginning to feel unnecessary. She certainly would if she no longer had good, hard work to keep her busy.

Mr. Hodges entered the office, and Liesel took her seat opposite the oblong mahogany desk. Sitting at attention, pencil poised, gaze on the pad, Liesel waited. She heard Mr. Hodges close the door and walk across the carpeted floor to his desk and sit in his cushioned leather chair.

At last she looked up. It was unusual for Mr. Hodges to hesitate. By the time he was ready to dictate, he normally had the entire letter formatted in his mind.

"Were you adopted, Miss Bonner?"

Had he asked if she might consider testing the law of gravity by jumping out the window, she could not have been more shocked. Never in the two years of her employment had Mr. Hodges—or any man except perhaps the elderly janitor Mr. Brindley—spoken on a subject remotely personal. And to ask such a question without preamble made her gape, too surprised to answer.

"Well?"

Shaking her head, she said, "No, Mr. Hodges."

He frowned, mumbling words barely loud enough to hear. "I doubt it would make a difference." Then he shifted in his seat, leaning forward, resting his elbows on his desk, and letting his fingertips meet just below his soft chin. "How long have you worked here?"

She told him, growing more curious by the moment.

"Were you born in Washington, Miss Bonner?"

"No, sir. Annapolis." The collar on her starched white blouse began to prickle.

"And your parents? Were they born there, too?"

"No . . . they were not."

"Germany?" He asked reluctantly it seemed, and the sense of foreboding that had begun at her collar spread.

Nodding, she put down her pencil.

"Everyone says you're the fastest and most accurate stenographer here, Miss Bonner, and of course I agree."

"Thank you." In spite of the compliment, Liesel did not relax. Mr. Hodges never engaged in personal conversation.

"You understand the sensitive nature of our work here, Miss Bonner. Undoubtedly you've seen any number of confidential reports pass between this office and the senators and embassy personnel with whom we work."

She felt no need to reply.

He cleared his throat. "Recently a decision has been made that affects this office." His voice became gruff. He picked up, then replaced a pencil on his tidy desk; folded his hands, then unfolded them; picked up the pencil once more. Liesel watched the unusual fidgeting with growing unease. "I see no reason to hide the truth when you're no doubt smart enough to figure it out yourself. There are those here who feel—justified or not—that it is poor form for us as an agency so closely connected to the direct government of the people to keep in our employ anyone not . . . shall we say, of Allied blood."

His rambling sentence sounded like no more than campaign speech rhetoric. But when she was sure, without doubt, of what he was saying, she met his scrutiny stare for stare. To his credit, he did not flinch, though in the end he was the first to look away, clearing his throat again.

"There are those who feel," he went on, "that though our two countries are not yet at war—"

"Excuse me, sir," she said, barely aware she was interrupting a senior partner, something she'd never done before. "But we both represent only one country, you and I. My blood is as American as any other born here."

"Miss Bonner . . ." She had tested his patience, or perhaps he was embarrassed because her words were true. Perhaps he simply didn't agree with her. Liesel had no way to tell. "Believe me," he continued, "I shall be sorry to see you go. I do believe you *are* the best stenographer we have and this firm is losing an excellent worker. But there is nothing I can do." He sighed deeply and leaned forward. "The news is not good today. It's been released for tomorrow's paper that the German ambassador to Mexico received a telegram from the German war secretary promising to give Texas to Mexico if they join the war against us. Imagine that! Texas—our own Texas—given to Mexico as spoils of war! Incredible as it sounds, Miss Bonner, we are headed for war. *War.* It's unavoidable now. In a matter of weeks, we may be mobilizing the biggest united army this country has ever seen."

War. The word reverberated in her brain. Mr. Hodges said the word again, as if he couldn't believe it himself. Yet another thought battled for attention in Liesel's mind: she was without a job. What was she to do? Wait out the war in hiding until it ended? Ludicrous.

Didn't she believe, like her parents waiting for her at home, that everything happened for a reason? That life—and everything in it—was no mindless accident, it was part of a scheme, a plan. A plan within the full knowledge and sovereignty of no less than God Himself. But what about things that made no possible sense, like this? In the absence of logic, of reason, what was she to think?

Just now, nothing made sense.

But she did understand this session, like her job, was at an end. Mr. Hodges stood, reaching to take her hand. Standing, she found her knees surprisingly steady, though barely a moment ago she wondered if they would support her leaden weight. Liesel accepted his hand, amazed that her own did not tremble when inside she felt like the branch of a willow in a storm. She heard him say something about how she would be missed. She even thought she heard him mention she was not the only one leaving. Could that be true? Were all German-blooded Americans involved in government work being fired? She couldn't believe that.

The walk back to her desk from Mr. Hodges's office had never been so long. Once there, she stopped. What was she to do now? She couldn't very well sit down as if nothing had happened. This was, in fact, no longer her desk. No longer her spot to claim, a spot at which to become so immersed in hard work that she forgot everything else in the world. . . . This was where she was needed. Until now.

She took her purse from the bottom drawer of her desk. Glancing around, conscious it was her last view of an office that had at least offered duty and challenge if not identity, she turned. The others she'd worked with for the past two years were busy with their work. How normal they all seemed, how oblivious that her world had suddenly turned upside down. What was she to do?

She eyed the door. That familiar door. Would she leave, just like that? Couldn't she fight for her job, raise the obvious objection that she'd been nothing but a loyal employee, a loyal citizen? They had no real reason to fire her.

But Liesel knew she wouldn't fight. Suddenly she scorned the life she'd enjoyed for twenty-three years, a life of such comfort that it hadn't taught her how to properly fight for anything.

She left her desk, heading to that door. Just as she neared her destination, she heard footsteps close behind. "Miss Bonner . . ."

Liesel turned to Henry Miller, the senior clerk who had hired her two years ago and had never since looked her in the eye.

"Yes, Mr. Miller?" Liesel said, prepared to defend her departure an hour before quitting time.

As soon as she looked into his eyes behind those round glasses of his, his gaze left her face in favor of the floor. "I . . . just wanted to say I'm sorry things have gone this way. I, of course, had no vote in what happened."

Instantly surprised, she said, "You knew . . . before today?"

Mr. Miller flushed a splotchy red. "I—I'm sorry, Miss Bonner. There was nothing I could do."

Shaking her head at her own confusion and anger, she knew any sensible conversation was outside her grasp. She mumbled a brief, "Thank you," to the fretful clerk, then looked once more at the door waiting for her ahead. On the other side, she would no longer be Liesel Bonner, stenographer. She would be Liesel Bonner . . . what?

BALTIMORE

He ran a hand down the tattered lapel of his tweed jacket. He knew the item his fingertips sought was still there; he felt it against his chest as if it had a life of its own, pressing into him with warmth and weight. He smiled. Some people wouldn't like to carry such a thing so close, but to him, it was like riding a roller coaster at the World's Fair. Controlled danger, safe yet daring.

A breeze from the harbor made a stray strand of blond hair tickle his forehead, and he pushed it back out of his line of vision. He needed a haircut but had little time for mundane things anymore. He had to make two more drop-offs like this one at different docks along the East Coast.

A sailor approached. They knew enough to trust each other, even though neither knew the other's real name. He himself had chosen to be called Patria, a Latin word that connected him to the Fatherland. Under normal circumstances, there would have been almost no chance of his path crossing an Irish sailor's, but this man hated England almost as much as Patria loved Germany. Their two passions had been intricately enmeshed ever since the outbreak of the European war back in '14.

The sailor he knew as Caffer took a look around before approaching, but between the darkness and the closed seaside shops lining the shore, there was little chance they were being observed. Patria had made sure of that already.

He handed Caffer the cigar-shaped object from his pocket. It had neither protection nor camouflage; he simply handed it over in its open and deadly state. Not that anyone with an untrained eye would recognize it for what it was.

Caffer shook his head and gave an off-center smile. He was a strapping young sailor, with his Gaelic black hair and fair skin, and Patria knew he was anything but a coward. Yet Patria also knew Caffer had hated these little cigars since the day one started to burn in his pocket. The Irishman liked it better when they were handed to him in a cargo box.

"Don't worry," Patria whispered, a tease in his tone. "I checked the copper myself, and it's thick enough to last ten days. Plenty of time for you to place it aboard ship and get back home tonight."

The small lead cigar was the clever invention of a German chemist now serving time in an American prison. But it hadn't taken Patria long to find another chemist, one who had taken up where the imprisoned German left off. Into a hollow pipe was placed a copper disc to divide the cylinder in two. Each end was filled with acid, one picric, the other sulfuric . . . or any inflammable liquid if sulfuric acid was in short supply. The ends were plugged with wax to make the pipe airtight. Variable thickness of the copper disc decided the timing of the fire, acid eating through a thin disc more quickly than a thick one. And once those acids mixed, fire shot out from both ends like a firecracker before it exploded.

Though Caffer said nothing, his gaze went to the docks as he placed the object beneath his jacket. Patria followed the line of the other man's stare.

"It's the *Olimpiada*, Caffer," Patria whispered softly. "Not that one."

Caffer nodded, then scowled. "Those Russian ships . . . I get tired of goin' after them, is all. Now let me at that one . . ."

"It's a passenger liner, Caff."

"And you'll not convince me it carries only passengers, so don't even try."

Patria joined Caffer's morose stare at the English vessel scheduled to sail the following day. Everyone knew what lay hidden underneath boxes marked "flour" and other such innocuous labels. Munitions bound for English guns. English guns that killed Germans and subdued Irish.

"No matter," Patria said, pulling his gaze from the vessel. "The *Olimpiada* carries far more cargo than that one, and a fire aboard it will stop more bullets from reaching Allied guns than any other ship down there."

"Give me one of these for an English ship, and you'll see where I place it." Caffer turned on his heel and walked back toward the dock.

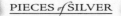

Patria watched him go. The plan was to place the incendiaries in the cargo holds of ships carrying munitions to the Allies. They weren't placed with the ammunition; that would cause too much harm to the ship too quickly. Their aim was to cause the captain to flood the holds in order to put out the flames, giving the crew enough time to evacuate if necessary. The final goal: render the ammunition either soaked or sunk and therefore useless.

But Caffer, he was a bold one, and Patria knew the man didn't care about the measures they took to do their job without loss of life. That was precisely why Caffer wouldn't be trusted aboard an English vessel. They weren't doing this to take lives; they were doing it to save lives—German ones.

WASHINGTON, D.C.

Mrs. Lindsey walked to the end of the row of plain, identical wooden desks with a cup of coffee in one hand and a new file in the other. David de Serre, one of the young agents for whom she worked, stood at the window of the office, studying another file in his hand. The natural light probably made the reports easy to read, despite the fact it was past five o'clock. The row of desks, casually referred to as the bullpen, was nearly empty. Most of their co-workers were gone for the day, replaced by the skeleton night crew.

"No more hot coffee after this," she said as she placed it on the single bit of free space left on David's desk. That corner was always left free; around it could grow a jungle of paperwork, boxes of files from both past and present cases, an assortment of books and maps. Both David and Mrs. Lindsey could find the corner with their eyes occupied elsewhere, as Mrs. Lindsey did just now. She studied David's handsome, young profile. As usual, he was absorbed in the work before him and didn't acknowledge her. He probably knew she had neared and he'd eventually get around to the coffee—perhaps even before it grew cold. But David never acknowledged the obvious. His words were as sparse as dew in the desert.

"Weber brought in his latest on Luedke," said Mrs. Lindsey.

David eyed her. Without being asked, she told him what he wanted to know. "The German he's been seen with so many times—Roch—sailed yesterday from New York on a ship headed to Switzerland. Weber's addendum makes it clear he thinks Luedke is taking over for Roch. Weber added a list of names of possible candidates as Luedke's new 'staff.' Known agitators mostly."

David took the file she offered, setting aside the one he'd been studying from another case. David went straight to the list of names. He was the case agent on Friedrich Luedke, a German alien suspected of "seditious behavior." While Weber didn't exactly report to David, it was David who coordinated all the information gathered from every possible direction—from other agents running leads as well as from zealous civilian groups like the American Protective League.

"Tell Weber to keep his distance with Luedke more than ever now. If he's moving up the ranks, he's not alone anymore. And remind Weber not to let the APL know too much. They have all the subtlety of a teenage boy judging a beauty pageant at the county fair."

"You can tell him yourself tomorrow," Mrs. Lindsey reminded David. "You have a meeting with him at ten o'clock."

"Cancel it. I have what I need right here. What I've just told you is all I have to say about it. You can forward that to him."

"That's fine," Mrs. Lindsey said, pleased. "Now you're free for brunch at Senator Cardulla's."

One look from David, and Mrs. Lindsey knew the jest had been caught. Of course David would not attend a senator's brunch or anyone else's social event. Even though he was one of the most dedicated investigation agents in Washington, David was not accessible to someone with a social agenda.

"Better be careful, David," said Mrs. Lindsey with her after-hours maternal tone. "This agency hasn't been around long enough to assume it's permanent. They may very well switch you to VIP protection in the Secret Service. President Wilson has three daughters and a new wife. You may have to escort them to every tea party in Washington."

David went to his desk, reviewing the list again as he retrieved his coffee. "That will be the day I resign, Helen."

Mrs. Lindsey smiled at the young man affectionately, although he didn't notice the look. She certainly hoped David would never be moved from the spot he filled so well. When the European war began back in '14, David had been reassigned to his present position in the Bureau of Investigation, tracking down possible espionage within U.S. borders. Before that, he had been a field agent pursuing bankruptcy fraud with his systematic, methodical investigative style.

He was no different with this assignment, except Mrs. Lindsey noticed something she'd taken for granted when he was just chasing bamboozlers. She wouldn't have thought it possible, but he became even more meticulous. While others at various levels of government police scurried about arresting

Germans or German sympathizers nearly every day of the week, David went about his job carefully—more slowly, without doubt, but with assurance and determination and something a bit harder to find these days: restraint. As concerned and eager citizens leaped into the American Protective League to help equally eager agents, convinced they'd find a spy on every corner, David tempered his investigations with objectivity and caution. As a result, David's cases were wrapped tight at delivery and remained strong all the way through to conviction.

"Well, I'm not sure some of the other agents around Washington enjoy these social engagements any better than you would, but they haven't the boldness to refuse as often as you do."

That made David look up, though he did not seem offended. "Often, Helen? Often suggests I've accepted at least once. I like to think I'm consistent."

"You really ought to start considering some of them, David," Mrs. Lindsey said, making her way back to her desk at the opposite end of the room. "You'll be thirty years old next week, and soon you'll be too old to think about marriage."

"I'm only twenty-eight, Helen," he called after her, and she turned around to look at him, shaking her head.

"David de Serre, you fit this job as if you were born for it. But you can't even remember your own age. This is 1917. You're going to be thirty."

If he had a retort, he held back. David de Serre was never one to defend a lost point.

"Just when did you stop keeping track of the years?" Helen wondered, although she didn't expect an answer. David rarely engaged in conversation that didn't serve an obvious or immediate purpose. So with her question unanswered, Helen left the office, saying good night on the way.

David watched Helen leave. Her words conjured up unexpected memories. He may not have been born for this job, but he'd wanted it since his tenth birthday. Not detecting frauds—although he'd found that more interesting than he'd expected—but *this*, what he did every day now that international tension was at yet another peak. This was what he was meant to do.

He looked again at the file in his hand, not really seeing it. What he saw instead was a boy who'd just turned ten, a boy who ran so hard he felt a stitch in his side.

He kept going in spite of the pain. He ran until he came to the rows of tiny houses that led to the sleepy fishing village nestled at the foot of what most people called his family's "castle." He'd heard the jokes plenty of times about the

Potomac being the moat to the famous de Serre seaside mansion. His father was the shipping king who married the fancy Belgian heiress with ties to Belgian royalty. It was only fitting they should have a moat.

David crept up silently to one of the cottages, stopping below an open window. Sea air pulled the curtain's hem beyond the ledge.

And then he heard it. A deep, erratic breathing, choked by a sob now and then. David came around to the porch, where he found Emilio, ten years old like himself, but crying like a little baby.

Emilio didn't even wipe his eyes when he saw David. "They took him. Just . . . just took him."

David scooted toward Emilio and sat next to him. "It's why I came. I overheard your mother tell my dad what happened. Don't worry, Mio. My dad'll get him out." He made the promise even though he didn't really know. David's dad could be powerful when he chose to be, but it was the choosing part David couldn't depend on. His dad only did what he wanted, nothing more.

Emilio shook his head. "It doesn't matter. Papa will die if they lock him up. He doesn't like closed-in places, especially since he's been sick. It'll kill him. I heard my madre say so."

"They can't hold him there. They can't just make up lies about somebody. This is a free country—my dad says so all the time."

Emilio shook his head again. "Free for some. For you."

Then they saw her. Rosa Ramirez was a small woman. Sometimes when she laughed she looked more like Mio's sister than his mother. But just then, walking in the moonlight with a dark scarf over her black hair and a strange look on her small, triangular face, she looked far older. She didn't seem to see the two boys run from the porch to meet her. She stared ahead as if blindly finding her way home.

"Madre!" Emilio said quietly but desperately. He took her hand in his and squeezed, and at last she looked down at him. Tears burst from her like from a broken vessel of water, pouring from great pools in her eyes.

"He'll be home, Madre," Emilio promised, sounding braver than he had in front of David. "David's papa will make sure. He'll not let his very best gardener be gone for long. Just wait and see, Madre. David says—"

"No, Mio," she said as she wept. David could not understand her after that, for she wept fiercely and spoke so quickly in Spanish that he could not keep up. He made out only a few words, "Padre . . . muerte . . . coraz—n . . ."

When Mio turned to him at last, the tears on his face were dry, and he looked somber, different all of a sudden. Supporting his mother, Mio led her up the stairs to their house. "Adios, David." He spoke in a voice that sounded courageous and tremulously timid all at once, "I take care of Madre. I have no Padre now."

David's feet stopped. He wasn't conscious of stopping; he just did because he didn't know what else to do. He watched his friend nearly carry his mother up the stairs, wanting to help but afraid he'd be rejected, as if just by being an American, he was somehow partly to blame. David let his feet take him away, knowing he had no place to go but home.

How was it, he wondered, that a man could be arrested for being Spanish?

David now knew how that had happened. At ten, he'd been confused and frightened, but he'd learned later on that very day exactly what went on during the war with Spain.

That was nearly twenty years ago. David looked around the empty bull-pen. That night had led him here, and now another war raged. As in '98, the country was ripe for people to act on fears and prejudices.

Although he hadn't known how God would use that terrible night, David now knew it had spawned in Mio a deep and lasting faith, one he'd introduced to David.

And that faith had put David exactly where he was today.

CHAPTER *Two*

LIESEL jumped off the trolley when it stopped at her street, and she walked at a brisk pace despite her fatigue and the lovely April weather. Nearly another week gone, each day spent job hunting with nothing to show for it except sore feet and discouragement. She longed to go home and forget that most of Washington wanted nothing to do with someone who possessed a name as German as her own.

You want me to work, Lord. Your Word is filled with those who are blessed with righteous work. Help me to trust You.

Then she remembered. This was Thursday. In addition to Sunday afternoon, Thursday was the day of the week Mama gathered her family for dinner: all eight of them, not including Papa and Mama herself.

Liesel's steps slowed. She felt the fatigue more than ever, realizing she would have to face not just her parents and younger siblings after another day of failure, but Ernst and Karl and their wives as well. Liesel was already late, and dinner was probably on the table. With a sigh, she climbed the steps of the front porch to the modest brick home. There was nothing to do but go in.

"What happened to the notion that it wouldn't be constitutional to join this fight?" Liesel heard her older brother's voice from the dining room. Karl was filled with ardor, a recent change since America had declared war on Germany and the clash now threatened to touch everyone through conscription, even her formerly lackadaisical brother.

They were already seated at the table, where Liesel's place awaited her. Her sister-in-law Katie shot her a welcoming smile. Mama passed her a plate of hot *Rouladen*. Her brothers Karl and Ernst continued without inviting her into the conversation, for which Liesel was grateful. She didn't want to talk about America preparing for war any more than she wanted to talk about her lack of employment. The two topics were undeniably meshed.

Liesel took a drink of water from the same glass she used every night. She could tell it was hers because it had an *L* scratched into the bottom, the same way each of the Bonner children had an initial etched into the bottom of their glass. It was a ritual each one performed on their tenth birthday: etch their glass with Papa's glass tools. Everyone except Greta had an initialed glass, and she would get to etch hers on her next birthday. The last of the Bonner glasses to be marked.

"Oh, that was a protest, all right," said Ernst, the oldest, derisively. "It was loud, anyway."

"But people listened!" Karl insisted. "We have no business over there! 'No foreign entanglements.'"

"That's just what all the German warlords wanted America to think," said Ernst, calmer and less impassioned than his younger brother, yet confident. "They don't want us against them, our numbers—or our wealth. But it won't be long before we've gathered and trained an army big enough to get over there and win this thing."

"You've none other than the kaiser to thank for helping people forget the argument about not getting involved in foreign strife, Karl," said Karl's wife, Katie, who was never afraid to speak her mind even if she held a different opinion than her husband. As usual, her tone was clipped with a British accent, which, to Liesel anyway, made her sound all the more authoritative. "He made this war far more America's business when he offered Texas to Mexico."

Karl turned to his wife with the same angry scowl he'd aimed Ernst's way a moment earlier. "Okay, then, if this is a war for democracy, how is it that you force such a thing by way of war? Force freedom on Germany? It has to be won for itself by its own people."

Ernst beat Katie to a response. "The Allies aren't forcing Germany into democracy; they're just protecting other governments like France and Belgium from losing *their* choice."

Karl groaned, obviously buying none of it. "All I know is that Papa was born there. We have cousins over there. All of you sound like the rest of the city out there, hating everything German. Hating *us*. Look how Liesel lost her job for no good reason."

Liesel didn't have to lift her gaze to know everybody was looking at her; she could tell by the sudden silence. Evidently her verbose family decided not to so much as breathe until she acknowledged the statement. So she shrugged but kept silent. She wasn't going to join Karl's bandwagon or Ernst's, either. She wished they would move on to some other topic. Everywhere she turned, people talked of the war. Sometimes she felt others knew of her German heritage even without knowing her name. She wasn't as blond as her brothers nor heavy-boned like her mother, yet somehow it seemed others just *knew*.

"Yesterday I heard about a dachshund being stoned. Even German American dogs aren't safe."

"That's enough, Karl," said Papa, and Liesel saw her father's gaze wasn't on his outspoken son; rather he looked with concern on the youngest at the table, nine-year-old Greta. Obviously Papa thought the discussion had gone far enough.

The rest of the meal was comparatively quiet. Mama tried to make small talk, but no one cooperated. The room was filled with a pall, like a miniature cloud of the war that had already darkened Europe's skies for almost three years.

Liesel rose to help with the dishes, but Mama shooed her away, telling Liesel she looked tired and to go upstairs and rest. Liesel welcomed her concern. Obviously Papa or Mama had warned everyone in advance not to ask if she'd found a job that day. She would be eager to talk—once she finally had good news to offer.

She left the dining room for the stairs in the hall, imagining a hot bath and the softness of her bed. Yet before she reached the top, someone knocked at the front door.

"Liesel," shouted Rolf, one of the twins, "it's Josef!"

Ignoring her throbbing feet and tired legs and back, Liesel retraced her steps at her younger brother's call. Thoughts of going straight to bed disappeared with the pleasant realization that Josef had returned to town.

"Josef! You're back!"

He greeted her with a hug, and Liesel welcomed the embrace. If she was too tired to look her best, he certainly didn't have that problem. Always vigorous and healthy, his slightly tanned skin gave him a vibrancy that never failed to appeal to her. Josef stood several inches taller than her own five foot seven. His thick blond hair waved naturally away from his perfectly symmetrical face—hair that was the color she'd always wished for herself, of sand lightened by the sun. Instead her hair was somewhere between blond and brown and her eyes far less interesting than the bright blue of his. Hers were neither blue nor gray but rather a pale shade of each. Though she had hardly felt like smiling just moments ago, resisting Josef's grin was difficult in spite of her fatigue and slightly dour temper.

Behind Josef, Liesel's father and older brothers appeared. For a few minutes, they stood and chatted, welcoming Josef back into town after his lengthy business trip. Before long, Papa retreated into the parlor, signaling Ernst and Karl with all the subtlety of a factory manager ordering his employees around.

"Welcome back," Liesel said to Josef once they were alone.

Josef's ever-so-blue eyes stared into hers, and she felt familiar affection take its place in her heart. She must have missed him more than she thought.

"Let's go outside," he invited.

She followed, and they took seats on the wooden swing hanging on chains from the porch rafters. A few late birds flitted as they settled in their nests in the maple out front, and from somewhere below a cricket started to sing. Liesel leaned back on the swing, slipped her tired feet out of her shoes, and rubbed them against one another.

Josef put an arm about her shoulders, and Liesel welcomed the contact, resting her head against him.

"Will you be in town for a while?" Liesel asked.

She sensed sudden tension in the way he held her and pulled away to look at him.

"I'm taking the midnight train to New York." Before she could respond, he added, "I have to be there bright and early, but only for a day or two this time."

She put her head back on his shoulder. "At least you won't be gone a month and a half again."

He stroked her hair. "Was it that long?"

She laughed. "Don't you know?"

"I lose track of time, especially when I'm sitting here with you. Nothing else matters."

"Hmm," she said with some chagrin. "Then why must you go away again?"

He put his other arm around her for a complete embrace. "I will miss you and think of you every day, as I always do."

"Right." She didn't believe a word.

He caught her chin in his hand and looked at her in his uniquely intense way. Even in the dimming light, the look pierced her. It made her feel like they were alone in the world. Sounds from inside of the house faded away.

"Don't ever doubt that I miss you when we're apart, *Liebling*."

He kissed her, not a long kiss, but warm and promising. His lips tenderly claimed hers with a gentleness that seemed nearly reverent, as if he held something back out of an esteem that made her precious to him.

"Perhaps we better not sit here together," he whispered, although he still held her against him as he spoke into her ear. "With you near me, I can't resist stealing a kiss. And that one doesn't count as a good-night kiss, because I plan to claim another later. Right here on your mama's favorite swing."

Liesel laughed and pulled away. He was joking, of course, but at any moment someone might come outside, and that would be the end of any such snuggling. So they sat on the swing a little bit apart, still holding hands.

"I called on your father soon after you left, weeks ago," Liesel said, "wondering if he might be able to contact you. He didn't know how to find you."

"My customers are farther reaching all the time. Business is good."

"But isn't it dangerous for us not to know how to contact you? What if you have an accident? Or what if your father has an accident? How could we get hold of you?"

He shrugged casually. "I call home from time to time. The telephone is a wonderful invention. Your parents should invest in one. They're becoming quite common in the homes around New York."

"You're changing the subject."

"Nonsense." He squeezed her hand. "I appreciate your concern, Liesel, but my work keeps me going. I don't have time to check in with my father on a daily basis."

Nor with a wife. Despite the thought, how tempting marriage seemed. To no longer care about her missing identity from a lost job, to have a new identity, to have a job right in her own home—one that society so obviously honored. Katie had quit working as a stenographer without a backward glance once she married Karl.

"So why did you want to contact me? It must have been serious if you went to my father. You usually avoid him."

Ottovon Woerner's stern visage came instantly to mind. As a child, Liesel had wondered if his monocle might fall out of place if he laughed, and she was still waiting to find out. "'Avoid him.' Such words, Josef. He's Uncle Otto to me and everyone in my family."

Josef only shrugged, not recanting his words. "Why did you want to find me?"

She hesitated. Telling him she'd been fired was no easier now than it would have been weeks ago when it happened. "I lost my job."

"Oh? How come? I thought that law firm was doing well."

"It is," she said. "I was fired because . . . because they no longer want Germans working there."

"What!" The word spewed from suddenly taut lips.

"I wasn't the only one," she assured him. "And as unfair as it is, I'm afraid it's not uncommon these days. Justified or not, everyone is against the Central Powers."

Josef let out a breath that sounded like the slow hiss of a deflating tire. "It's all madness. America has no business over there."

Liesel gave him a little smile. "You sound like Karl."

"American merchants protecting their interests are forcing Wilson to get involved in Britain's war. If bankers hadn't loaned Britain all that money to finance their war, we wouldn't be involved now."

"Britain's war? Not Germany's?"

"*Deutschland* has only done what it believes best."

"But they invaded Belgium," she reminded him softly. "Britain didn't start this."

"And *Deutschland* did?" Josef asked, incredulous. "All we did was go to the aid of Austria when the archduke was shot down. And protect ourselves from France and Russia—two sides waiting to divide us up, suck us in."

She put a gentle hand on his shoulder. It was corded with tension. "'Us,' Josef?"

He leaned forward on the swing, resting his elbows on his thighs and rubbing his face in his hands. "I don't want this country and Germany at war. With all the Germans living here, it's like two members of the same family feuding. It's ridiculous."

"I agree entirely," said Karl from the front door. He stepped out on the porch, with Katie behind him.

She looked exasperated. "Out here, at least, I hoped we could get away from talk of war."

"You can," Josef said, suddenly smiling as if he hadn't a single concern. Liesel saw the smile and marveled. Josef's ability to control his emotions was far more advanced than that of anyone else she knew, especially herself.

"Jolly," said Katie happily as she took a seat on the banister nearby. "It's the one topic Karl and I cannot come to terms on."

Karl laughed for the first time since Liesel had arrived home. "It is? The *only* one?"

"Of course, my love!" she said as she stroked his face. "Now that America is finally preparing to step in, what else do we talk about?"

Liesel watched with affection, knowing their marriage was as solid as any she'd witnessed. She'd been trying to figure out what Katie saw in Karl ever since she'd introduced them to each other several years earlier. Whatever it was, Katie had loved Liesel's brother almost from the moment she'd met him.

"What we should talk about instead is my poor *Liebling*," said Josef. "I just found out she lost her job." He turned to Liesel. "You know, my father could easily offer you a position."

She'd thought of the two businesses Josef's father owned, a glass factory on the edge of Washington, D.C., and a coking company just outside of Baltimore. He'd employed her father and two brothers for as long as Liesel could remember, first back at the stinking, coking coal plant (that's all she remembered, that her father and brothers always stank like sulfur), and now at his glass factory. They no longer stank; in fact, she hadn't smelled sulfur since they'd moved outside of D.C. a half-dozen or so years ago. Her brothers didn't seem to mind working for their rigid "uncle," who preferred to work every day of the week instead of doing anything else . . . and seemed to expect at least Josef to do the same.

But Liesel wasn't sure she could adjust to working for Uncle Otto. She remembered a time when he'd corrected her for wanting to play a game when there was still work to be done in the kitchen. Surely she would feel like a child again if she worked for him.

Besides, Uncle Otto already employed half of her family. She wasn't ready to let him do the same for herself. She could find a job on her own.

"Did you read the paper yesterday, Josef?" she asked.

He nodded.

"Didn't you see how President Wilson asked every one of us to be part of the great service army? To speak, act, and serve together?"

"A noble idea," he said. "To do all, give all for the nation. Like Germany."

"As I see it," Liesel continued, "once people start acting on that presidential request, I'll have a job in no time. I want to be part of that great service army—it's the least any of us can do. You're already a part of it. Everyone is who works to support the industries of this nation. So are Karl and Papa and Ernst, down at your father's glass factory."

"Don't leave me out of it," Katie quipped. "Housewives are to end all extravagances and practice strict economy." She nudged Karl's midriff, which looked a bit softer than it had on their wedding day months earlier. "Looks like a diet for you, dearie."

"Yeah, well, if I get drafted, the army will put me on a diet of its own."

"You see, Josef?" Liesel asked. "Nearly everyone was mentioned in that proclamation, everyone of any value to society. I'm young and healthy, and I have qualifications. I want to work. More than that, I need to work. I can't let the rest of the nation be part of it all while I sit back and watch."

He smiled and lifted one of his sun-browned hands to gently stroke her cheek. "Sounds like you need a job."

"Liesel," said Katie in a voice that sounded tentative, unsure. "I know you want to find a job on your own—"

Karl interrupted his wife. "Now, Katie, we agreed not to get involved. Besides, Mama told us not to talk about jobs because it only depresses Liesel."

Katie shook her head. "The topic was already brought up, and I'll wait for Liesel's objection, thank you. And *we* did not agree on anything, Karl. You told me not to get involved, but if we had discussed things, maybe we would have agreed to tell her."

"You'll just give her false hope."

"We don't know that. It could work out splendidly."

Liesel spoke before Karl could reply again. "What could?"

Katie looked prepared to speak to Liesel but hesitated with one final look at her husband. "Karl, how strongly do you feel about this?"

He shrugged, equivalent to permission granted. Liesel silently took note of the little exchange. As opinionated as her old school chum was, Katie really did respect Karl's wishes before launching plans of her own.

"I had a note from my former boss yesterday. He knows I'm married, of course, and as such not available. But he wondered if I knew of someone— someone exceptionally good—and in need of a job. He's putting together a new department at the railroad and needs someone to work long hours. Of course I immediately thought of you. Shall I ring him back?"

"You bet!" Then Liesel glanced with surprise at her brother. "Why wouldn't you want Katie to tell me about this?"

His lips pursed together before speaking. "Because his new department has to do with government work. Your law firm had to do with government work. They fired you. What makes you think you'll be hired if they don't want Germans working for the government?"

Liesel took a deep breath. That did cast a shadow over her sudden hope. "Oh."

Katie stood, stepping in front of Liesel. "But I *know* this man, Liesel. Seamus Quigley would never refuse to hire somebody just because of a name. He's a good man."

Liesel lifted one brow, reserving a bit of that soured hope. "It's worth a try, anyway."

Josef patted her back. "Of course it is. With Katie to recommend you, he'll snap you up the minute he sees you. We'll be celebrating your new job any day now!"

CHAPTER *Three*

NEW YORK

DAVID de Serre bit into the peach he'd purchased from the street vendor. Leaning against a lamppost, he knew he presented the classic picture of a loafer: baggy corduroy pants well worn at the knees, a wrinkled cotton shirt, a brown fedora hiding only some of his dark, wavy hair.

If only his father could see him now. He'd castigate him, no doubt, for his casual appearance—if his father recognized him at all. David couldn't recall how many years it had been since he'd seen his father. When David had graduated from Harvard almost seven years ago, neither of his parents had attended. They'd been living in Belgium at the time and probably weren't aware of the occasion, though in a moment of weakness, David had sent them an announcement via the mail. They'd sent a motor car as a belated graduation gift a year or so after—a sporty, bright yellow Packard Runabout that would have been the last model David, with his sedate, cautious tastes, would have chosen. But he still owned the wretched thing and told himself it was because of economy and convenience, nothing more.

Casually viewing the growing number of people filling the street, David finished the fruit and threw the pit in the general vicinity of a collection bin sitting on the edge of an alleyway. Above the barrel was a sign with the plea to eat more peaches. He knew the government reduced the pits to a charcoal powder for the lining in gas masks for the soldiers, and with all the new recruits, that need grew every day. Evidently the flies were also grateful, judging from the swarm that welcomed David's contribution.

David continued walking, following the flow of people toward the park. Soon he reached earshot of a rally. The speaker interested David, and the man was just warming up, enumerating the great potential, prosperity, and purpose of the country that presumably all present called home. Soon the real message began: a gathering of patriotic citizens promoting the protection of its youth. David knew enough of the jargon to guess what that meant: anti-conscription. Resist the draft.

David passed through the crowd, assessing the mood and the reception of the message. The speech effused patriotism of a sort, obscuring the rebelliousness of its true message. Love our great and youthful country, love its purple mountains' majesty, but protect it from the mercenary warmongers who would send our young boys to their death over nothing more than monetary interests invested overseas. Love our country; hate war. A noble speech, but a dangerous one since the only way to resist conscription nowadays was evasion or insurrection. And that meant prison. Then how much would they love their country?

Cheers and adulation rang through the park as the speaker drew to a close. Even those on the rim, who probably had not heard much of the speech, joined the shouting. David clapped, too, if only to fit in, while he made his way closer to the improvised platform. Many others pressed in, perhaps hoping to shake the speechmaker's hand. Two large men in middle-class business suits pushed the rest of the group back, as if they wanted to be first in getting to the speaker for a word. From David's vantage point outside the thickest part of the crowd, he saw the orator hustle away as the two men made his escape easy.

David didn't follow, just watched the man go. He'd seen enough—a face with the name. He folded the leaflet he'd received and put it in his pocket, noting the name emblazoned on the top: Andrew Nesbit.

David wanted nothing more than to arrange for the locals to arrest the man. Gut instinct told David that Nesbit was guilty of sedition at least, if not treason. The man may have sounded like a patriotic American, passionately concerned over American blood. David almost sneered at the thought. If this man wanted an insurrection against the war, he was anything but a pacifist. And if he had hooligans to protect him from a cheering crowd, he no doubt had other people around him with similar loyalties.

Getting this man for sedition wasn't good enough. For now, David had what he needed. A face. He could wait until he had Nesbit on charges that would stick for however long it took to keep him out of business, at least until the war ended. Whenever that might be.

———

Patria stuck a hat on his head and hurried from the crowd, looking over his shoulder and gratefully, if silently, acknowledging the work of his two compatriots who held back the crowd so he could get away.

So much for another speech by the popular pacifist. Andrew Nesbit had all the potential of becoming quite a celebrity if not for the extreme caution Patria took. He'd made sure no one had ever taken a photographic image of Andrew Nesbit, or if they had, the photo never found its way to development. Nonetheless, if Andrew grew more popular, people might start recognizing him on the street. Patria knew when enough was enough, and that moment was now. Pocketing his clear glasses and using his hand-kerchief in a feigned sneeze, he removed his false mustache, as well. He also took off his jacket, completing his new image as he walked along the busy city sidewalk.

Speechmaking had been fun when he'd started out a few years ago but had grown lackluster. Of course, the newer assignments he'd been given must be responsible for that. Greater responsibility, greater excitement.

But next week's assignment from the German businessmen Patria worked with would not be exciting. He was to start at yet another factory to stir a strike. Strikes sometimes took months to settle, leaving factories idle and hulls empty instead of supplying ample goods to the Allies.

Such a result was worth the time he spent among the poor, though he hated every moment of it. No matter how inventive he'd become at leaving food for some of the families he inevitably met or how ingenious he was to anonymously deliver clothes or toys to the grubby little children belonging to the fathers he worked with, there were always too many to serve. More faces. More needs. More pain . . . far too much for one person to alleviate—especially since he was the one who inspired the strike to begin with, the very thing that heaped more impoverishment upon such families.

While Patria didn't relish going back into the slums of factory life, he didn't question the order nor did he resist. For the Fatherland, he thought—for the Fatherland. A land of poets and thinkers blessed by a God who had given them the power and discipline to deserve their turn at a historic empire.

And Patria was only too ready to see that day come. Once Germany won this war, it wouldn't matter if he went to Germany or stayed in America.

German ways would spread everywhere, more quickly than before. How proud he would be that day to see that his efforts had made a difference.

———————

The Baltimore and Ohio Railroad lobby was spacious and impressive, with marble floor, muted lighting, and high windows draped with elegantly sweeping fabric. Brocade armchairs beckoned respite next to a fireplace that offered warmth in winter. Someone had placed a bouquet of flowers where the flames would have been, so even with the arrival of spring it served to inspire comfort. In the center of the lobby sat a large desk with a smiling receptionist. It was precisely five minutes before Liesel was expected at one o'clock.

"I have an appointment with Mr. Seamus Quigley," Liesel announced, secretly hoping the woman didn't inquire for her name. Those smiles always disappeared when she introduced herself.

The receptionist didn't ask, and her smile didn't waver. "Mr. Quigley is on the third floor, just opposite the elevator. You can go right up."

"Thank you." Liesel hoped her queasy stomach settled soon. She hadn't been able to eat a bite of lunch. This might not be her last chance at a good job, but it appeared to be her *best* chance.

The young elevator attendant asked her the floor, and Liesel told him. Her unsettled, empty stomach dropped as the elevator rose.

She carried an envelope containing her application, the one Katie had hastened to give her last night. Katie had done nothing but praise the virtues of Mr. Quigley, so much that Liesel found herself wanting this job more than any other. She imagined Mr. Quigley as all Katie said: fair minded, hardworking, kind, while demanding the same high standard from others that he set for himself. Liesel had graduated near the top of her class at business school; she relished the idea of being able to prove herself. This chink in her identity from having lost her job at the law office could easily be repaired with the help of a new, better job.

She looked down at her tailored yellow suit. The jacket reached her waist and was trimmed with a row of tiny white flowers matching each buttonhole. The skirt itself traveled mid-calf, and her white shoes gleamed. With a gentle touch, she lifted a gloved hand to be sure the little yellow hat still sat squarely upon her head.

"Job interview?" the elevator attendant asked, giving her a glance.

Liesel nodded.

"The B&O's the place to work, and ole Quig's a swell fellow. He'll like you fine."

The doors opened smoothly, and the attendant unlatched the inner gate, grinning all the while. "I bet I don't see you till the end of the day."

"Thank you," Liesel said and stepped out of the elevator. The wide hallway offered little by way of direction; no plaques or signs hung upon the freshly painted walls. But she heard voices, many of them, coming from an open door nearby.

Standing at the threshold of a huge, high-ceilinged room, Liesel thought she had never seen so few people making so much noise. Less than a dozen workers appeared to be setting up an office, while another half dozen worked diligently in their midst. One sat with only a telephone and a pile of papers in front of him on the floor, scribbling information. A trio of men stood before a huge map, one with a long pointer and another with tacks, the one aiming and the other marking while the third stood talking all the while. Near them huddled another set of conferees poring over a different map, this one not yet hung. It was laid out on the floor, and one man on his knees had a pencil he used to make various marks.

Just then, a man neared her. He was one of the three who had been by the map on the wall. He stood at Liesel's height, with brown, receding hair, a sturdy build, and what appeared to be an easy smile on his rather pleasant, round face.

"Are you the friend of Katie Harris?" he asked quietly despite the noise around them.

Liesel nodded. "Yes, I am."

"I'm Seamus Quigley." He offered his hand in a firm grip. "It may not look like it, but you've come to the right place. As you can see, we're just setting up. If we can find you a chair, we'll talk about the job right now."

She followed Seamus Quigley to a storeroom down the hall, where he found two chairs. Rather than bringing them back to the busy office, he sat in the small, dimly lit room where it was quieter, inviting Liesel to do the same. The diversion of their odd surroundings took her mind off her eagerness. She glanced around at the unused file cabinets, chairs, and desks.

Mr. Quigley took her application. Liesel stared at him as he read it over, knowing if Katie hadn't already told him she was a German American, he surely would know once he glanced at her name.

"You went to the same school as Katie," he noted aloud. "That's good."

Liesel did not reply; she let him finish his perusal. Either he read quickly or he skimmed the majority of the information provided, for a moment later, he set the application aside with a frank look upon his face.

"We're working with the government," he said.

That opening statement washed Liesel with caution. Maybe Karl had been right.

"I'm sure you've read the papers lately," Mr. Quigley continued, "how we're all doing our part to mobilize for war. You can bet the railroad is playing one of the most important roles, if not *the* most important. We'll be moving men and equipment as fast as we can, not just from here in the East but from all over the country. That means new track, new engines, new schedules, more manpower. Communication is vital. I'll need a stenographer who can make sense out of the jumble I try to pass off as handwriting—and do it quickly. I need somebody who will be here every day, who isn't afraid of hard work or staying late. I need somebody to read me, to understand what I'm trying to get across and make sense of it even if *I* can't figure out a way to say it. In short, I need an extension of myself, one who can write down my words and transcribe them for everybody else."

He paused long enough to glance away, then eye her again. "I warn you right now: I'm tough as an old dog. I work hard, and I expect everybody around me to do the same. But it's like this, miss. We've gotten ourselves into a war, right or wrong. I'm too old to join the fight, so I'm gonna do it right here on my own territory. I'm gonna mobilize this country to be the best it can be, to get those boys from training camps to the navy and shipped outta here. And I can't do it alone. I need help. You want a part of helping your country? If you do, then I've got the place for you right here."

Liesel listened, spellbound. Hard work never frightened her. Helping her country excited her. This man's energy inspired her. Here was purpose in a way she'd never really felt before. She nodded, then shook herself out of the spell. "But don't you want to see if I can type?"

He laughed. "Katie says you can. Her recommendation is enough for me to hire you right now. I've got a stack of letters on my desk. There's a typewriter down there, too, if we can find it. What do you say, then? Want to try it?"

They both stood at the same time, and Liesel held out her hand before he could. "I'd like to, Mr. Quigley. I'd very much like to work here."

"That's the way we like to hear it around here!" Then a frown crossed his face, and he looked toward the open door as if to make sure they weren't overheard. He pushed the door closer to the jamb, though it didn't close altogether. "There's just one thing. I noticed your name on the application."

Liesel remained composed, though she felt like taking a step back as if preparing herself for a blow.

"This is a sticky one, miss. A sticky one to be sure. I need someone with your qualifications, and you need to work. It should be simple, but the truth

of it is we're dealing with the government in a time of war. That's not to say the government can't treat people fairly. What I am saying is that companies like mine need trustworthy employees." He ran a hand over his sparse hair. "I can see I'm making a mess of this, so I'll just say it outright. I want to hire you. Based on what Katie said, I know you'll do a fine job. But for me to do that, I'm going to have to pull a little wool over my boss's eyes. I think we can work it out, though. You graduated the same year as Katie, didn't you? Same school, same year?"

She nodded.

"Then this'll work fine, just fine. They do background checks, and I noted you put your school on the application. They check for Katherine Harris, and it's there, see?" He offered a short laugh as if enjoying himself and inviting Liesel to do the same. "Of course, it means taking off your prior work history, since we don't want them checking that avenue, do we? We can jot down Katie's past work so there won't be any long gaps in your career, and I'm the only one they'll ask about that, so it won't be a problem."

"What exactly are you saying, Mr. Quigley?"

He looked around again and continued to speak in a hushed tone.

"I'm saying I'll switch the name on your application. Put Katie Harris's name on it. Nothing to it. You get the job; I get the help I need; the bosses don't have any reason to question why I've hired someone with—"

"A German name?"

He nodded.

She sucked in a deep breath, looking away from his eager gaze. "I see." She may as well have been fired.

"You have to understand something, miss. Everybody's edgy these days. Things aren't like they used to be. That war started in Europe almost three years ago, and they're thinking of ways to kill people that have never been used before. It's an ugly war, uglier than ever. If the government and companies like the B&O are being unfair to German Americans, it's only because they're afraid. It's not a good reason, miss, but it's a reason."

"I agree with you, Mr. Quigley. Only I don't think I can work using someone else's name."

"What's the harm?" he asked, open palms entreating her. "You work; you get paid. What does it matter if somebody else's name is on the check?"

"I don't know . . . it doesn't sound legal—"

"Think it over, at least. If you're anything like me or like Katie, you're not happy unless you're busy. Why not work here where we need you? By golly, I always get the job done in the best way I know how. That means getting a topnotch stenographer. Details don't matter. Don't matter a fig."

Liesel said nothing.

"I can tell from your application that you're used to working," he went on quietly. Her silence must have inspired the salesman in Mr. Quigley. "What are you going to do, go home and sit? If the B&O isn't hiring Germans, I doubt anyone else will, either. Oh, maybe you can get a job at a bakery; they probably don't care if you're German. But everybody else does. And with a name like Seamus Quigley, I've felt me own share of bigotry, don't ya know," he added with a suddenly acquired brogue. "Maybe that's why I'm willing to go out on this limb to hire you in spite of the risk."

"Why take a risk, then?"

His gaze held hers. "Because Katie Harris recommended you. Because the attitude of excluding *all* Germans stinks. Like I said, they used to feel that way about the Irish; some still do, since half the Irishmen I know back home and here hate the English. I could name a long list of reasons, but the real one is that I need somebody, and I need somebody good—now. They know I can get the job done and they won't ask too many questions, especially if they don't see anything on the application to flag it down. There's really nothing to worry about. So how about it? It's just a name on a check; that's all."

She could think of nothing to say. Part of her wanted to retrieve her purse and leave, but somehow her feet stayed firmly in place. *Purpose.* More words reverberated in her head. *Meaning. Value. Contributing something that actually mattered.*

"I won't say we can't find another person to hire because chances are we will eventually. But if you prove everything Katie said about you, I'd be sorry to see you go over a trivial matter like this. It really is nothing to worry about, like I said. I trust Katie's word on you; they trust me; they'll trust you."

He approached the door and opened it wide again, turning to her with a paternal smile. "Let me show you the typewriter, at least."

Liesel's head spun as she followed him out of the storeroom and back to the large, noisy office. He produced nothing less than a brand new Remington typewriter along with a stack of work just awaiting eager fingers for transcription. Sweet temptation, nearly overwhelming.

"Why don't you stay the rest of the afternoon?" he suggested. "Get a feel for how things are around here. Don't make any permanent decisions until the end of the day. How about it?"

She found herself nodding before she considered all of her objections. Was she wrong to want to work? Was she wrong to want to contribute to the war effort? To want to be needed? Was she wrong to go about doing it in a way that was less than honest? The questions came fast and furious, but Mr. Quigley left her alone with all the typing, and she sat down and did what came naturally—she worked.

Everyone was so busy in the office she had little time to talk. That was best, since she wasn't sure how to introduce herself anyway. She attacked the pile of typing and never looked up, and after a few hours, she was as exhilarated as she was exhausted.

Mr. Quigley's astonishment over all she'd accomplished confirmed the kind of boss he would be. Most of the other co-workers were gone, and he followed her to the elevator.

"I'll see you tomorrow, then?" he asked.

In his friendly enthusiasm, it was all too clear he wouldn't give a second thought about using alternative methods to get a job done. If he was conscientious about anything, it must be about hard work.

"I . . . don't know."

The elevator opened, and the same boy who'd brought her up hours earlier greeted her warmly as he pushed aside the gate.

"Take Miss Harris to the lobby, will you, Sam?" Mr. Quigley glanced at her as he referred to her by the name, as if testing her reaction.

A ripple crossed Liesel's brow, but not a single objection passed her lips.

When the door closed, the young attendant turned to her with a smile. "That was either the longest interview on record or you got the job."

Liesel nodded. She lost her stomach again when the lift glided down to the first floor. The job had indeed been offered to her, but could she accept it?

For the next three mornings, Liesel was dressed and ready for work a half hour before she needed to leave. Despite her reservations, only one thought kept her up most nights: she could hardly wait to get back to work.

Surely it wouldn't be long before she'd proven herself too valuable to lose, even with her real name. A couple of weeks at most.

By Sunday, her first day off, she marveled at how easily she'd accepted the idea. Mr. Quigley hadn't needed to say much to convince her the job was too important to jeopardize.

At church, she prayed over the deception, but when the pastor spoke about patriotism and duty, hard work, and giving all energy as if to the Lord, she knew God understood the motives behind her decision. Surely He must.

Later that day, she felt nearly tranquil sitting beside Josef on a rare, lazy afternoon. He'd been home for three days, and they had been together every evening since. They'd shared dinner at an Italian restaurant on his first evening home, just the two of them. The next night, they had dined with the entire Bonner family amid all its cacophony of sound. Last night, they had eaten at Karl and Katie's. And this afternoon, they had picnicked on the banks of the Potomac. Josef had planned and provided the entire meal. Granted he hadn't packed it himself as Liesel would have done, but the fact that he'd taken the time to instruct one of the von Woerner cooks to prepare the meal had been touching enough to bring a smile to Liesel's face.

A smile she lost now and then throughout the day. He was leaving tomorrow.

They sat close on a park bench, the picnic goods packed away and stored in the back of Josef's Bearcat motorcar. The wide Potomac stretched before them, water lapping along its way.

"Do you think they're out there?" Liesel pondered aloud.

Josef glanced from his place beside her. "Are *what* out there?"

"German U-boats. That's what they say."

He chuckled. "Never listen to the 'theys' of the world, Liesel."

"So . . . you don't think they're there?"

He shrugged. "It's a big ocean. A big coast. Even if Germany wanted to send U-boats over here, what good would they do? The boats are serving Germany better against British ships or the ones carrying munitions."

She nodded, letting go of the topic. She didn't really want to talk about the war anyway.

She ran her thumb over the top of his hand, where he held hers. "It's been nice having your company these past few evenings, Josef."

"Yes, even in the little bit of time you've spared for me." He sighed and looked out at the water. "I'm almost sorry you were able to get this new job you love so much. It demands much of you and takes you away from me."

"It's the best job I've ever had. I've never felt so needed."

He smiled, stroking the palm of her hand. "I can see you love it. We're happiest when we're doing what we were made to do, aren't we?"

"Are you happy, Josef?"

He gazed at her curiously. "Yes. Why do you ask? Don't I seem so?"

"Yes . . . only I see you so rarely it's hard to say anymore."

He laughed. "We've just spent the last three days together."

"Evenings," she corrected.

Putting both hands on her shoulders, he captured her gaze. "I would spend every waking moment with you if I could, Liesel. When I'm with you, I'm at peace. I don't feel that anywhere but at your side."

He kissed her then, though it was barely more than a graze since they were not only in public but it was broad daylight. She welcomed the kiss as much as the words.

They sat in silence on the bench for a while after that, still watching the sun's reflection on the water.

"Do you know it's only the most intimate relationship that tolerates silence with complete ease?" Josef asked after a moment.

Her heart pounded at his comment. "Like old married couples, you mean?" Now was as good a time as any to make it official. Was he going to ask her to marry him at last?

He pulled her close, putting an arm around her shoulders and pressing her head against his shoulder. "Exactly. There's comfort envisioning a life like that."

She waited a moment longer, but Josef said nothing more. Evidently he wasn't finished enjoying their intimate silence.

Liesel let her breathing go normal again. She thought about what he'd said, telling herself she'd been foolish to think he would ask her to marry him under such ordinary circumstances. Besides, it was understood they would marry . . . someday. Everyone in her family expected it, and she guessed Uncle Otto did as well. Why did she need the formality of Josef asking her?

So she let her head rest against his strong shoulder, trying to enjoy that silence he'd observed. She wanted to voice her hope that they would always have things to share even when they were old. Josef kept far too much to himself, especially lately, especially when she asked questions. He told her so little about his travels, his business meetings, his clients. And while she was anything but a chatterbox herself, she would have liked a little more exchange than Josef was willing to give these days.

But even as she had such thoughts, she had to admit her own recent reticence. As much as she enjoyed working for Mr. Quigley, she hadn't shared everything with Josef. She hadn't told him, or anyone, that she was using Katie's name in place of her own.

"See that boat out there?" Josef asked after a while, pointing to a lightly sailing skiff. "We'll sail something like that from here up to New York, where we'll get on one of those long, fancy passenger liners. And then we'll go to Germany. Together."

Liesel watched the sails billow from the wind, carrying the boat along the choppy water. She'd long been aware of Josef's wish to go to Germany. If the war hadn't broken out, he would be there already doing graduate work at one of the universities his father recommended.

Seeing where her parents had lived appealed to her. "But . . . just for a visit?"

He stroked her arm. "I don't see why we couldn't spend part of every year there. Live here *and* there for months at a time."

She shook her head. "Your business would never allow you such a life-style. You can barely be away from it for a few days, let alone months."

"Once the war is over, Liesel, things will be different. You'll see."

She sighed. She certainly hoped so. At least she wouldn't have to go by another name.

CHAPTER *Four*

PATRIA lifted the cup of whiskey for another swig, fighting a shudder at the taste. Despite being a member of a prominent church, Patria was not averse to drinking and opposed the prohibition efforts of women and churchgoers. But this whiskey was the lowest grade of the stuff he'd ever tasted. That they charged a nickel a glass was outrageous, the way it burned his throat. Those seated around the scarred wooden table at the workingman's pub didn't seem to notice, or if they did, they didn't complain.

Patria looked like one of them. He was willing to wager no one would recognize him even if by an odd quirk someone from his other, respectable life entered this very pub. He had done what he always did when he wanted to fit in to the role of an impoverished factory worker. He wore an old suit he stored in a locker at the train station, a suit that to his knowledge had never been cleaned. He wore that suit for the day leading up to his assignment so the rest of his body could acquire a similarly worn look: no washing or shaving, no combing of hair. He even found some rust to rub into his skin, his knuckles and nails, and behind his ears. And he slept on a park bench, which enhanced the whole look by adding more wrinkles to an already puckered suit. It never took long to smell just like the rest of the unwashed masses.

"The way they speed us today, even Paco couldn't keep up, and he's the best."

General assent followed that comment, even though Procopio Rodriguez, known as Paco, wasn't there to say one way or the other.

"But tomorrow, we not stand for it," Miroslav said after naming a litany of offenses the bosses had foisted on the workers. "The bosses, they not so bold to do away with us now, heh? If we don't keep up, what they do? Not so many men waiting for job anymore."

Patria liked this kind of talk. During the days he'd spent at this metal casing factory, he'd searched through the workers to collect the most discontented among them. And there were plenty to be found. From seven in the morning to half past twelve, then from one to half past five, they labored under a boss forcing them to work harder, work faster, without a break except dinner.

The foremen tried to sound patriotic, telling the workers how the boys being trained for war would soon need the casings into which ammunition would be stuffed. But everyone knew that wasn't the only result the bosses looked for. Arms companies made the most money these days—not that they passed any of that on to the workers. They were still paid eighteen cents an hour under conditions harsh enough to make a strong man old before his thirtieth birthday.

It was almost too easy to find a reason to strike.

"Miroslav is right," Patria put in, adding the hint of a Polish accent to his words. "Their power is not so great now. If we don't work, they not find replacement so fast, not anymore. They hope to sell more metal than ever because of the war. But do our wages go up with more work? No, we are pushed harder!"

"You come to the meeting tomorrow night," Miroslav invited those at the table. "We walk from the job, and others do, too, because we are in union. We stand up together against them."

One or two looked interested; another pair looked every bit as skeptical. "We walk," one said, and the other interpreted because the first one spoke only Russian, "and they find more men like in the past."

"No, no!" Patria assured them. "See for yourself tomorrow morning. Miroslav is right. The men looking for work are not so many. They go to join the army, more and more every day."

"But there are still men," the interpreter said. "Enough."

Patria shook his head. "We are union now. Other unions walk, too, and there are not enough men to replace all if we walk together."

The words inspired what sounded like a cynical laugh. "And how do we feed our families if we walk?"

Patria frowned. It was the question he always heard, for which there was no good answer.

He looked the man squarely in the eye. "We help each other."

"You? Feed me? Look at you! Look at everyone here. We cannot feed ourselves right now except at these pubs!"

He was right, of course. The food at these pubs, while cheap, came at a price. Cheap food as long as patrons drank.

The man tipped his glass, then smirked at Patria. "You won't help me. Gather ten men with nothing, and you still have nothing."

"The union will help," Patria pledged, though he guessed their union wouldn't give the men a cent. Even in peacetime, strike funds weren't guaranteed, and money often ran out long before the strikes did. "We pay dues. They will help. If not," he added, knowing he always had an ace in the form of the German banking group backing him, not to mention his own considerable funds, "we join a new union, one that pays. There is a man talking about it at the meeting."

The man seemed to lose some skepticism. His brows raised, he said, "We will come to this meeting. But we promise no more than that."

"Good," Patria said. "There they will tell you to strike. And if not," he added, his eyes scanning those at the table, "there are other ways."

Even Miroslav looked at him curiously at that statement. "What other ways?"

Patria leaned forward. "The Chinese have a way of it. Maybe you heard. They say, 'Small pay, small work.' We can learn from them. We do less—less of what we do now. We jam machines, meddle at docks to have the men ship crates to wrong place. Easy mistakes to cover. If we do enough, they not track it so well. Either way, we make them pay for the way they use us."

No one objected to Patria's plan. Years of harsh conditions were enough to make even a righteous man bitter. Workers caged in jobs that paid barely enough to feed themselves and their families, barely enough to live in the hovels they called home—they had no place else to go. It was the same everywhere. The elite of the cities made sure of that.

As Patria looked at their smudged faces, he knew it would be different one day. *One day*, he thought, *when Germany wins the war and our ways spread, the rest of the world will see that our ways are best. A world in which the strongest men live in dignity.*

David de Serre sidestepped a hole in the middle of the paved road. Evidently new road construction left little equipment available to repair the old. Every corner of Washington echoed the labor of new work, even in the front yard of the Justice Department building where David walked. Men shouted orders over the clatter. Hammers pounded nails into place, and rhythmic saws cut fresh wood. Buildings sprang up overnight to house a new committee or agency; dormitories emerged to contain freshly hired government workers.

David entered the Justice Department, a modest old structure by Washington standards, at least in comparison to the Treasury Department across the street. There was talk about constructing a new Justice Department building now that its staff was increasing in number if not in power. But David had grown up in something similar to a palace. He didn't need to work in one. He liked the old place, even if he did sometimes complain about a lack of tight security.

David took the stairs up to his office. The elevator might be an invaluable invention, but for four stories, it was too slow for David. He often mindlessly raced those who waited at the bottom of the elevator platform and frequently reached his office more swiftly. Besides, he liked the exercise.

He found Helen at her desk on the far end of the office. As usual, she greeted him with a folder and his first cup of coffee. He received both without a word and, once he reached his own desk, pulled out a financial file he'd received the day before. Public records of donations received from wealthy businesses to all sorts of German institutions. From the Bundt and German schools to less reputable German newspapers and clubs. Familiar names of prominent business owners were listed alphabetically.

"Oh, David," said Helen, as if she'd forgotten an important message. "Weber stopped by this morning. That girl he saw with von Woerner a while back was spotted here in the city."

He glanced at the list, spotting Otto von Woerner along with another name: Josef von Woerner. Two men whose money spoke loudly of their belief in spreading German ways.

At least one of those names was on an agitators list for picketing against the sale of arms to belligerent countries. Josef von Woerner.

"Anything new on her connection to von Woerner?"

"Just what you already know. Her father works for von Woerner's father—evidently has for quite a number of years, starting back when he just owned von Woerner's Coking Coal in Baltimore. We also checked her name and education. No criminal record. Nothing unusual at all."

"What was she doing when Weber spotted her?"

"That's what's so interesting. She was going into the B&O building."

"So?"

"Sooo," she repeated, drawing out the word, "Weber followed her inside and she stayed on the floor reserved for work coordinated with the WIB."

David's interest piqued. "The War Industry Board?"

Helen nodded.

"Is he sure it's the same woman?"

"Well, he's seen her twice, and he has a graduation picture of her from her stenographers' academy. It's not an individual shot, but he's pretty sure."

"Have him check with the APL. They may have something on her. And," he added as an afterthought, "get in touch with the Burns people."

Burns Detective Agency, founded just a few years before by a former Secret Service chief from the Treasury Department, had all sorts of tidbits David used if the information could be wrangled out of them. He'd learned Helen was particularly adept at doing so, and David had come to depend almost entirely on her to deal with them. Ever since the beginning of the war, Burns had taken it upon himself to watch and tally any activity that smacked of espionage. As rumored, David found that Burns had compiled German info for the Brits, and British info for the Germans. A true entrepreneur. David might not approve of the means through which Burns got his information or what he did with it, but he had to admit he was effective. David wouldn't like using him at all if he thought he was still giving information to the Germans, but all that had stopped when the U.S. entered the war. At least that's what Burns said.

David returned to his work, resolving to keep at it until he had something. If there was anything on this latest subject, he would find it.

Liesel straightened the stack of finished work on her desk. After just a few weeks at the B&O, she felt more satisfied than she ever had at the law office. To understand the contrast, she looked no further than Mr. Quigley himself, who set the tone for the railroad office. He was hardworking and demanding yet fair and approachable. He never failed to encourage those around him, praise those who did well, support those who needed it. He was all business, yet played the father role to everyone, modeling, directing, correcting, inspiring. In a short span of time, Liesel had developed a great respect for him—in all areas but one.

It was the end of yet another day, and still he'd said nothing about being free to use her own name. She'd told him she would stay but only with the agreement that he would tell his superiors her real name once she'd proven herself a trustworthy employee. Hadn't it been long enough? She couldn't go on indefinitely as Katherine Harris.

Liesel found Mr. Quigley behind a stack of boxes in his new office. Placing the finished letters in his outstretched hand, she waited until he looked up. He did so at last with a smile on his face.

"These are excellent, as usual, Katie. I don't know how you read my writing. I can't read it myself half the time."

She noted the name he called her so easily, letting it pass without comment. "You may not win a penmanship award, but at least you're consistent in your style. Once deciphered, it's no longer a challenge."

"Glad to hear it. If you can pull up a chair, I'll dictate something for you to do . . . no, let's see, it's almost six o'clock. You go on home. I'll write it out, which may help me organize it a bit better anyway. I'll leave it for you to do in the morning."

"That's fine, Mr. Quigley. There's just one thing I need to talk to you about before I go."

"Oh?"

She nodded. "I'm sure you know the subject, sir. I was wondering . . . you call me Katie so easily, as do the others. I've grown quite used to it, yet—"

"Good, good!" He smiled broadly. "I was hoping you'd feel that way. Your background check returned without a question. Everything is perfectly fine, just as I thought. All they did was call the school, and your name—Katie's, that is—came up just fine. Not a problem to be found." Mr. Quigley leaned back on his chair, folding his hands behind his head. "Things are as uneasy as ever out there, you know. The false name on your application was a necessary step." He leaned forward and lowered his voice, although Liesel knew no one else was still in the office. "I've always considered myself an excellent judge of people, Katie. On the inside. I don't care a fig what a person looks like; it's what's on the inside that really matters. And you're true blue. I knew that the moment you walked through the door. But others don't seem to trust their own instincts these days. It's the war, I guess. Makes 'em jumpy."

Liesel was sure he was right about that but still railed against the situation. She didn't want to have to juggle a lie much longer. She'd never been part of a deception in her life and was fairly confident God didn't care about her excuses.

But now the thought of leaving was intolerable. She'd slipped into this job as easily as a mother taking care of her baby. Some might call it instinct, and maybe it was. Certainly it was instinctive to want to survive, and having this job seemed to provide that. A place.

But she couldn't entirely ignore her concerns. "I'm really not comfortable with this . . . situation." Her voice was almost a whisper. She didn't look at him.

"But you just said you've gotten used to it. Why, you're answering to the name as if it were your own." He laughed. "There's really nothing to it, you know. It's not a crime to work and collect a paycheck, which is all you're doing. When things settle down overseas, we'll have no trouble whatsoever setting things straight. You'll see. This war will be over before both of us know it."

Liesel sucked back her uneven breath. "You . . . you want me to keep Katie's name until the end of the war?"

He raised his brows as if it were a good idea but then, addressing her obvious alarm, added, "Well, of course that'll depend on how long this drags on. Just wait a little longer. Things will get back to normal, probably well before the war ends. In just the couple of weeks you've been here, you've already become irreplaceable."

"I'm glad for that, sir. Only it's the deception. It goes against everything I believe in." She couldn't catch a sigh before it left her lips. "I expect it's my own fault, though. I accepted the position."

"I don't think we need to assign fault anywhere," he said, adding gently, "You know, I'm a church-going man myself, wouldn't have it any other way, for the kids of course."

Relief coursed through her. "You do understand, then!" She felt the burden tumble off her shoulders.

"But it's like this. We're stuck with the way it is. If I open up the truth now, it'll probably mean your job. Maybe even mine. When Katie called me with your recommendation, I couldn't pass it up. There was a risk, and we took it because we see the big plan. I've got to stay with this job because I'm the best one to do it. This country is at war, and it needs me. You see how it is?"

Feeling the burden slip back into place, she looked away.

"We're getting this nation ready to fight," he reminded her. "If we don't get them boys in and out of them training camps, keep the supplies moving along, it could stop the whole blasted army. You may think typing a few letters and helping to keep my silly head straight is a harmless job, but let me tell you, it isn't. If I had to worry about every letter I wrote or what's scheduled in my day, I'd be pretty useless to the old B&O. Could we replace you? Not easily, that's for sure. But I'll tell you right now I don't want to. We're a good team. I can think easy around here, knowing you're here to clear up the details."

"Thank you," she told him quietly.

He grimaced. "No need to thank me. Selfish, that's what I am. You make my life here easier. I make the B&O work easier. We're making a difference, Katie."

Liesel nodded, her heart heavier as she left the office than it had been when she entered. All the way to the trolley, she considered the situation, as she'd been doing the past two weeks. Katie had been right. Working for Seamus Quigley was proving to be the most valuable experience of her career so far. He gave her more authority than she'd ever received at the law office, even after so short a time in his employ. He was the kind of man who got the job done in the most efficient manner, no matter if he had to try unorthodox methods—hiring her being a prime example. He believed in what he was doing. He believed in her, too: in her abilities and intelligence and dependability. Leaving now wouldn't just take away the best job she'd ever had; she'd be letting him down, as well. Maybe even jeopardizing his job, the way he claimed.

More excuses?

Surprisingly, through most of each day it hardly bothered her that she was part of a deception. She was so busy she had little time to talk to any-one, and the issue rarely came up. It was only at the end of the day that she thought of it, another day gone without resolution.

Every way of a man is right in his own eyes: but the LORD *pondereth the hearts.* The proverb sang through her mind. *God does know my heart.* Yet why was it she'd never told Josef or her parents the details of how she'd gotten this job?

On the trolley, Liesel leaned back and set aside the newspaper she'd brought to read. The car usually emptied by the time her stop came up. Turning her attention to the window, she saw her own reflection in the fading light of early evening. Outside, the street looked busy as usual, and she watched with mild interest all the people scurrying about.

Ready to close her eyes and rest as the trolley nudged to a start again, something in the window caught her eye. Not out on the sidewalk, but a reflection just above her own. Turning quickly, she sought the owner of the serious expression, but even as she pivoted in her seat, the man who had been across the aisle stood and exited the car altogether, landing easily on the street behind and walking briskly away.

Liesel couldn't help herself. She swiveled to watch his departure. She considered what had caught her attention. Something in his manner had seemed odd. He hadn't been looking out the window; he'd looked directly at her as if studying her. And while it wouldn't be the first time Liesel had felt the lingering glance of a man, this one was different. So serious, as if memorizing her.

She looked around, wondering suddenly if she'd developed some sort of phobia. Rarely was she in public without overhearing someone condemning

the Germans, and sometimes she felt as if she wore a tag identifying herself as such.

No one seemed to notice either the man's hasty departure or her perusal of those left aboard, so, somewhat abashed, she settled back and waited for her stop.

All memory of the encounter faded when she arrived home to the excitement of Mama and Greta. On the kitchen table was the largest bouquet of flowers any of them had ever seen. Roses, carnations, chrysanthemums, and orchids graced Mama's favorite vase. At the base was a card they couldn't wait for her to open. From Josef.

David de Serre didn't stop to watch the trolley disappear down the street. This was the closest he'd come to Liesel Bonner, but he wasn't quite ready to make himself known. Not yet.

Liesel Bonner. Katherine Harris. One and the same. One worked for the B&O in connection with the Railroad War Board. The same woman but with a different name cavorted with a man who was a known German loyalist, one who at the very least had picketed against armaments being sent overseas. Just who was this woman who lived with one identity and worked with another?

The deception had been easy enough to figure out. When David first saw her, he knew she was the same woman he'd seen with von Woerner. Although he hadn't been able to study her at close range, at least not more than her profile, he knew she possessed a wide smile and large eyes. When he'd looked up the graduation picture, he'd seen her face right there in the middle of the class of 1914. He decided her eyes must be blue or gray because they were light in the photograph. And her smile, even in the relative anonymity of a group shot, was wide, the kind most people noticed.

The list of names at the bottom made no attempt to identify all the girls in the class; it was alphabetical. Both names had been there: Katherine Harris and Liesel Bonner. So David went to the school itself. At first the dean had been reluctant to talk at all. Yes, she remembered Liesel Bonner. A fine student—the daughter of German immigrants. Was she in some kind of trouble? David had assured the dean she was not. He quickly learned the woman had fond memories of Liesel Bonner. Such a considerate girl. Katherine Harris had been there as well. The dean thought the girls would have stayed in touch after graduation; they'd been close throughout their two-year program at the academy. They even attended the same church, she recalled. They graduated near the top of the class and were popular among students and faculty alike. David wasn't surprised by that information. The face he saw in the picture seemed to represent a happy, hopeful young girl from a stable, secure family.

When the dean pointed out the two girls in the graduation picture, David made very sure which was which. Liesel Bonner was the woman he was interested in. But despite her apparent good looks and respected reputation with the dean, she was a woman working with a false name for a government war board. Interesting indeed.

And of course, he couldn't let that continue.

CHAPTER *Five*

"THIS will be the last time we meet face to face," the man told Patria. Even in the dim moonlight Patria saw the corkscrew-shaped scar on the man's broad chin, the one feature that stood out from his otherwise unremarkable appearance.

At two in the morning, it was unlikely anyone saw them in the remote cornfields along the Piedmont hills. Yet Patria had taken precautions, traveling by train as far from the city as he could and going on foot the rest of the way. He was sure Luedke had done something similar; no vehicle was in sight to attract attention or be identified.

"These orders should carry you through the next four months," Luedke said, handing Patria an envelope. "Best study them tonight. It'll take a while to decode them. They were drawn up by von Bernstorff himself before he left."

The German ambassador had been deported just before Wilson went to Congress for a declaration of war. But so far, Patria had noticed little change within the network in which he was so intricately involved. Until tonight.

"Where are you going?" Patria asked.

"Best if you do not know. Watch your back. They don't care whom they arrest these days."

Patria shook the other man's hand, swelling in the knowledge they were comrades bonded in dream, devotion, and danger. "And you as well, *mein Freund*."

Luedke turned and walked away, disappearing beyond the young corn-field into a line of trees. Patria knew enough not to stay in one place too long. He waited a few minutes, then went on his way, as well.

When he'd first been approached by a German businessman back in '14 about "working" for the German government, Patria had never dreamed it would take him as far as it had. He was responsible for several factory strikes, had personally gummed up the works at two munitions plants and a rubber factory, had delivered enough cigar bombs to sink or damage a dozen English and Russian ships, and had given at least as many public speeches, which he hoped had made some young men hesitate about joining up to fight against Germany.

His only regret in the work he did was that he was unable to tell his father about any of it. Yet.

———————

Seamus Quigley ran a hand over the top of his head. He'd started losing his hair almost ten years ago, yet every time his palm rubbed against his nearly bald scalp, it never failed to surprise him that most of his hair was no longer there.

"Eight o'clock in the morning," he said to himself, "and I'm already stuck."

He didn't care if anyone outside his office heard his auditory thought process. He wasn't the only one talking to himself these days.

He couldn't avoid the facts. The old B&O was as much a problem as every other railroad in this country. *Obstinate. Every last one of them.* Seamus sighed. What he'd hoped to accomplish so easily with the authority of the government behind him was proving more difficult than he'd imagined. This office didn't need him. What they needed was a general with an army, one who could force private industry to comply with a plan that suited the country as a whole. True, it wouldn't suit each individual company, but this was hardly the time to worry about market shares and monopolies. If the railroad industries didn't comply with the WIB, Wilson was bound to step in and take control. That would be a sad day for democracy, but maybe there was no way around it.

A tap at the door distracted Quigley. Not Liesel, as he expected, but Miss Gardener, another stenographer recently hired to help Liesel.

"There is a gentleman here to see you, Mr. Quigley. Mr. de Serre."

"Who is he?"

She peeked over her shoulder, then turned back and whispered, "Special Agent de Serre. From the Bureau of Investigation."

Quigley lifted his brows. "Show him in. Oh, have you seen Miss Harris yet this morning?"

"No, Mr. Quigley. Not yet. Should I send her in when she arrives?"

"No, no. Thank you, Miss Gardener. Show in Mr.—what did you say his name was?"

"De Serre," she said as she left the small office.

Quigley closed the file on his desk, took his seat, then rose again a moment later when a young, dark-haired man entered the room. *Pleasant looking fellow,* Quigley assessed in that first moment. Eyes as dark as his full head of hair. A square jawline and broad shoulders. Quigley extended his hand, noting a firm handshake from the man who stood a half head taller than Seamus himself.

"What can I do for you, Mr. de Serre?" He indicated the chair opposite his desk and dropped into his own. He liked working from a sitting position with somebody so much taller.

"I'm from the Justice Department's Bureau of Investigation," the visitor stated, displaying his badge. "We've assumed some of the duties of the Secret Service, namely looking into domestic espionage activities."

Espionage. The word stood out like a peasant in a palace. *What could he possibly want with me?* "And how can I help you?"

"You have in your employ a Miss Katherine Harris."

Quigley felt something land in the pit of his stomach, something the approximate size and weight of an anvil. "I do," he said quietly. *They can't possibly know about the name business, and why should they care even if they do?*

"Mind if I ask you a few questions about her?"

He shook his head, even though it was a lie.

"I understand you hired Miss Harris?"

Quigley calmly folded his hands on top of his desk, feeling heat collect under his collar and at his armpits. "That's right."

"What do you know about Miss Harris?"

"She's an excellent worker."

"Is that all?"

"What do you mean?" Quigley asked. *Did my voice just shake, or am I imagining things? Did he notice? What's this all about?*

"Do you know anything about her outside of the office?"

"Very little," he admitted. He clutched at that, he liked sticking to the truth as much as possible. Especially now. "I know she lives at home with her folks. She attends church quite a bit. As I said, she's a hard worker, and that's all that matters around here."

"Is that so?"

Quigley found himself avoiding the bold stare of the man across from him.

De Serre leaned back in his chair. "I'd like to speak to Miss Harris when she arrives. Mind if I wait in here?"

"Be my guest," Quigley said, hoping he sounded sincere. He tried to smile. "I can't imagine why a government agent would want to talk to our sweet Miss Harris, though."

The man across from him offered nothing more than the turned-up corner of his mouth, not exactly a smile.

Quigley cleared his throat. Obviously this guy wasn't giving any information. "You don't mind if I get on with my own work, do you? I have a department to run."

"I'll just wait right here. Ignore me."

Oh, sure. Quigley tried swallowing the lump in his throat. He left the office, going directly to Miss Gardener's desk as he searched the room for Liesel.

He glanced back at his office, seeing the government agent at the threshold. He knew the man couldn't hear him if he kept his voice down. "Miss Harris arrive yet?"

"No, Mr. Quigley."

"Listen, tell her to wait for me in Benson's office downstairs if she arrives while I'm gone. If she arrives after I'm back, knock on my door but don't say anything." Turning his back on the watchful agent to conceal any action, Quigley searched her desk frantically and pointed to a fistful of pencils. "Bring me those pencils. *Don't* let her go to my office. Are we clear on that?"

Obviously curious, Miss Gardener nodded. If she was about to ask any questions, Quigley didn't linger to find out. Wishing Liesel had a telephone but knowing her family didn't, he went to the lobby of the building, where he could usually find a hoard of boys waiting to earn a nickel for delivering a message or package.

Stopping at a bench just inside the door, he retrieved a discarded newspaper, pulled a pencil from his pocket, and scrawled his message on the corner of the printed sheet: *Stay at home today. Will contact you later. Respond to this message by writing down the date you started working for me, so I know you've received it. S. Quigley.*

Folding it and wishing he'd had the foresight to take some paper and an envelope with him but unwilling to return and risk detection, Quigley picked one of the boys for the mission: an eager kid with a torn pant leg and a streak of dirt on his chin.

"This has to be delivered right away, boy. Here's two nickels for the trolley, one for the way there and one for the way back. I'll give you another three if you get back within the hour. Understand?"

The boy nodded eagerly, and Quigley gave him the address. "Don't dally, kiddo, or you won't see any more nickels when you get back."

The youngster dashed out the door, and Quigley watched him go. Quigley didn't know if he was doing the right thing, but without time to dwell on it, he didn't see any other option. If Liesel was somehow in trouble because of using her sister-in-law's maiden name, then Quigley was to blame. If he could just warn her, maybe they could straighten this whole mess out before too much came of it.

David stood by the window looking at the unattractive view of the garbage collection at the back end of the two-story building across the gangway. From the open door behind him drifted the usual sounds of an office: a typewriter clanking away, telephones ringing, voices at a low, businesslike tone. He also saw the empty stenographer's desk just outside the door, one he assumed belonged to the mysterious Liesel Bonner.

There was no doubt in his mind: Seamus Quigley was hiding something. A casual perusal of the office revealed nothing unusual. David found the whole situation increasingly interesting. He hadn't come here expecting a conspiracy, yet he had little doubt Quigley knew something he was unwilling to share. Exactly what that could be both baffled and intrigued David.

Just then, Quigley appeared at the door and went to his desk. "It's surprising for Miss Harris to be late like this," he said without looking David's way. "Her family doesn't have a telephone so she might be unable to contact me if she's sick. I'm wondering if perhaps she won't be in at all today."

"I'll wait a bit longer. Then if she doesn't show, I'll be out of your way."

"Yes, well, I'd be happy to tell her you were here and have her telephone you later. If you just want to leave the number where you can be reached . . ."

David turned back to the window, letting his action speak for him. He heard Mr. Quigley take the seat behind his desk and was certain he detected a sigh.

"I hate to have you wasting your time like this."

David glanced over his shoulder. "No waste at all."

Quigley shifted in his seat and shuffled papers on his desk. Oh, yes, he definitely wanted David out of here.

A glance at his wristwatch told David it was past nine thirty. Quigley could be right; perhaps she wasn't coming in today.

Before much more time elapsed, David decided he would go out to the Bonner house himself.

"I hope you don't mind if I return later, Mr. Quigley. Only if necessary, of course."

They shook hands, and David made for the exit, leaving what appeared to be a relieved man behind.

He could take the trolley, but his Packard would be quicker, even allowing for the two-block walk to where it was now parked.

Barely twenty minutes later, David pulled to the curb at the Bonner house. At the door, he raised his hand to knock just as he heard hasty, light footsteps behind him. Turning, he saw a rather unkempt boy march past him and boldly finish the knock David had just prepared to launch.

"Who are you looking for, young man?" David inquired.

"I got business, all right," the boy defended himself proudly. He held up a folded piece of newsprint. "A message for the lady who lives here."

"Do you know her name?"

"Course I do," the boy replied, as if such a question challenged his whole mission.

"And what is it?"

The boy turned to face David squarely, folding his arms in front of his scrawny chest. "Do *you* have business here, mister?"

David couldn't help but grin at the boy's gumption.

"Yes, as a matter of fact, I do."

The boy knocked again, and after a few moments the door opened. Through the screen, David saw for the first time up close the face he'd only seen from a distance so far. That face, he noted, even through the mesh, was far more attractive than the one in the class photo, even with a curious frown touching her forehead just now. Skin so pure and fair it could belong to a child—but there the resemblance to a child ended. Before him was a young woman, and a beautiful one at that.

She glanced from the boy up to David. "Yes?" she inquired, looking straight at him with those wide eyes. Eyes that were such a pale blue, it was as if she could see more than what others could with just ordinary eyes.

David felt like shaking himself but settled for clearing his throat instead. Practically the only woman he spent time with these days was Helen at the office. His lack of expertise and ease around the opposite sex obviously needed attention. "We arrived at the same time but have separate business," he explained. "I believe this young man's errand is rather urgent."

"I got a message for you," he said.

The girl opened the door and took the folded paper, turning it around to read it. On her face gathered a myriad of emotions, but David noted confusion most of all.

Before she had a chance to reply, the boy spoke again.

"I got to bring an answer back right away, miss. Can you give it to me so I can get along?"

She disappeared behind the door, and David leaned just a bit to follow her movement with his gaze. She stopped at a table beneath some hooks on the wall. Pulling a pencil out of a small drawer, she scribbled something, then refolded the note, also taking a small pouch from the drawer and extracting a coin, judging by the sound. She returned to the door and opened it long enough to hand the paper and a nickel to the boy.

"Thanks, lady!" he said with a crooked, toothy grin, and he raced down the front steps.

The young woman's gaze returned to David. "And what can I do for you?"

She looked every bit as troubled now as she had confused a moment ago. Just what had that note contained? Some sort of warning?

"My name is David de Serre," he began. Then he pulled his badge out of his pocket. "I am Agent de Serre. From the Justice Department's Bureau of Investigation."

Eyeing the badge, she made no move to allow him inside. When she looked back up at him, he saw the concern on her face multiply. She took a noticeably deep breath. "What can I do for you, Agent de Serre?"

"I'd like to speak to you for a few moments. May I come in? I have a few questions I'd like to ask."

The woman looked back into the house, as if deciding. David filled the hesitation with a suggestion. "We can talk here on the porch if you prefer."

Without a word, she slipped through the barely opened door, closing the inner door behind her.

"What sort of questions do you have?" Her voice sounded a little better outside, not so timid.

"Perhaps you can tell me, Miss Bonner, why you found it necessary to take on a second identity?"

A surprised blue gaze shot his way. "A second identity?"

"Katherine Harris."

If she had any notion of denying what he already knew, he saw it leave with the sag of her slim shoulders. She took a seat on the swing, not looking at him. Her eyes looked suddenly tired and perhaps just a little afraid. He found that reassuring; fear was as good an impetus as any to get people to tell the truth.

"I go by my sister-in-law's maiden name at work," she said. "It was the only way to get a job."

"Why don't you tell me all about it?"

She looked up at him, clearly assessing him. For a moment, he wondered what she saw: The enemy? A police officer? Obviously someone unpleasant, for she looked away with a hint of distaste in that frown.

"Not long ago, I was fired from my job at a law office in the city." She stood as if, having tapped a new well of strength, she could face him better on two feet. Her voice grew bolder as well: not loud but more firm and confident. "I am the daughter of German immigrants, Mr. de Serre. I was born here, though, which makes me as American as anyone else who claims citizenship. Yet the office for which I worked viewed me as a German. They informed me they didn't wish to keep on anyone not of 'Allied blood,' as they termed it." She folded her arms, and he found himself momentarily distracted by her long fingers and tapered nails.

"I looked for another job and couldn't get so much as an interview. This was around the time President Wilson asked Congress for a declaration of war. It appeared no one wanted any part of a German, a Liesel Bonner. They didn't see me as an American. They saw only a German."

She paused a moment, unfolded her arms, and placed one hand around the chain of the swing. She still looked at him. "So I did what I thought necessary, what I thought the times demanded." Her gaze broke from his for the first time but returned steadily a moment later. "I couldn't get a job with my own name, Mr. de Serre. What does that say about tolerance in this country?"

He did not reply. Indeed, she looked as if she didn't expect a response. He had to respect her, though. Here he was with the power to have her arrested, and she acted as if the government he represented was the one headed to trial.

She must have noticed her tone of voice sounded rather challenging, for the next moment she looked away.

"I know I shouldn't have used someone else's name." Then she looked at him again. "But I've done nothing wrong. I work each day and collect an honest paycheck. That's all."

"Under a fraudulent name in a job gained through fraudulent means."

Her eyes widened, and concern doubled to worry. "What has fraud to do with working for a living?"

"Using a false name on an application counts," he reminded her. "If you were working for a grocer or a hat shop, I might think no harm has been done, though even there I would insist you tell the truth. But you are working closely with the United States government, Miss Bonner. At any time, that is a great responsibility. But in wartime, it's quite a bit more serious."

Standing stiff, hands at her side and chin elevated, she asked, "What do you plan to do, Mr. de Serre? Are you here to arrest me?"

From the little he saw of her, from the background this house and family and neighborhood represented, she must have no idea what it would be like if he actually did have her arrested. Yet she looked as if she was ready to face that challenge.

"No, Miss Bonner. As a matter of fact, it's not in my jurisdiction to go about arresting people; I gather evidence. But there is one way for you to avoid an arrest by the proper authorities, and I will accompany you to make sure it's done. You will resign from your job."

CHAPTER *Six*

LIESEL stared at the man who stood not two feet from her. Quit her job? Is that what he'd just said?

"I don't understand." Even to herself she sounded obtuse. But she didn't care.

"Let me help, then," he said congenially. "I don't know the motives behind what appears to be a rather desperate attempt to land a government job. Therefore, I cannot in good conscience allow you to keep that job, considering our state of war. Either quit the government job, or I'll see that you're fired. And that," he added, looking at her steadily, "is the least I will do."

Once again, Liesel sank to the swing. Though she felt his stare, she ignored the government agent.

She considered explaining how she felt about working. Would he understand that she *needed* to work? That she felt as useless as a livery horse in their nearly horseless society if she didn't work? What about the great service army? The president this very agent served had called for that civilian army. All she wanted was to be part of it.

But she couldn't form the words. Even to herself, such arguments sounded feeble. Eyeing him, she told herself she should be glad he wasn't ordering her arrest. He appeared as cold as early spring rain. He wouldn't understand.

A silent prayer, a plea for wisdom. She hadn't fought to keep her last job, and that had ended all too quickly. That's why she knew she must say *something* to have any hope of keeping this one.

"Why couldn't I just make sure they set my records straight? About the name, I mean? And let things continue as they are?"

His gaze didn't waver. "As I said, Miss Bonner, this is a time of war. For me to let you continue as is, I would have to trust you, wouldn't I?"

She looked away.

"Do you think the B&O would keep you on if they knew about the means you used to get the job?"

He didn't have to say those words. She'd thought of that even as she'd spoken and knew there was no hope now that the truth was known beyond just herself and Mr. Quigley.

She stood, squaring her shoulders in an effort to look as if she had the strength she would need to leave this job she'd so quickly come to love. "There is no need to accompany me back to the railroad office, Mr. de Serre. I will do as you say."

"You don't have a choice, Miss Bonner. I plan to see this through."

"Very well. Will you excuse me a moment?"

"I'd rather keep you in sight. At least for the time being."

Liesel's lips tensed to a frown. "I need to get my purse."

He gave her an unfriendly smile. "Just don't slip out the back door, Miss Bonner. I have no intention of letting you go."

Liesel let herself inside, glad he'd allowed their discussion on the porch. Mama was no doubt still upstairs tending Greta, who was home sick from school. With a hand to her own tumultuous stomach, Liesel wished she could stay home under Mama's care, too.

She trotted upstairs, telling Mama she was setting off for work since Mama had returned from the drugstore and could tend Greta herself now. Thankfully, Liesel's mother knew nothing of the whole situation, and Liesel wasn't about to try explaining it all now. Then she retrieved her purse and joined Mr. de Serre on the porch.

"If you're comfortable riding in a car, I can save you the trolley trip," the agent said, indicating the sporty motorcar parked at the curb. "If not, I'll accompany you to the trolley."

True to his word, he wasn't about to let her out of sight. At the moment, she didn't care about trolleys or motorcars or anything else. She didn't want to do what this man demanded but knew she had no choice.

Liesel slid into the front seat of the motorcar. She'd never ridden with anyone but Josef. It seemed odd to ride with someone else, even if he was a government agent.

He drove easily, neither fast nor slow, cautious at each intersection and when passing trolleys. Liesel viewed him from the corner of her eye when they stopped to let a trolley pass on the adjacent street. Dark hair waved in perfect layers even as the wind tried to break the pattern. His smoothly shaven jaw jutted out at a rugged angle. His nose might seem large on another face, but on his it sat in perfect proportion. Lips neither too full nor too thin, eyes set deep and shrouded by brows that matched the chestnut of his hair. His hands, as they effortlessly guided the steering wheel, appeared long and lean like the rest of him. He was handsome, she determined in that moment. Not in a flicker-stardom style like Josef, who would turn any head. No, this man was someone you might miss on the street, but if you didn't, your gaze would unquestionably linger.

When he looked at her with the beginning of what appeared to be a smile, Liesel abruptly turned away. What was wrong with her, assessing him as if they were out on some sort of date? He very nearly had her arrested not ten minutes ago. He was forcing her out of a perfect job with a perfect boss and he had admitted he didn't trust her. Because she was of German heritage?

They reached their destination, and Liesel left the Packard Runabout without waiting for his assistance. She walked into the building, unhappily hearing his footsteps in sequence with hers.

When she stepped into the office, Margaret Gardener waylaid her before she reached her desk. With a glance at Mr. de Serre in the rear, Margaret whispered, "Quigley went to your house. What's going on?"

"Mr. Quigley will explain everything to you when he returns," said Mr. de Serre before Liesel could answer. "You'll excuse Miss . . . Harris while she tends to a rather urgent matter, won't you?"

At Liesel's desk, Mr. de Serre took up Liesel's pad and paper and wrote a few lines before handing it to her.

"Type that up, sign it, and leave it on Mr. Quigley's desk."

I regret to inform you of my immediate resignation, it read. *Due to circumstances beyond my control, I am unable to continue employment.*

Liesel slipped a piece of paper into the carriage of her typewriter. She typed quickly, adding one last line, Thank you for the opportunity to work here. She would have included something more personal about missing Mr. Quigley, but with the prospect of Mr. de Serre overseeing each word, she refrained. Then she signed it, folded it once, and laid it on Mr. Quigley's desk.

Her desk was full of personal items: a small framed photograph of her parents with Greta, a potted plant Mr. Quigley had given her, a box of beige stationery, a set of handkerchiefs, a tin of lemon drops. And her Bible, the one she read during lunch. She couldn't very well leave it all behind, since she doubted she'd be allowed inside the building again. Retrieving the tin of candy, she returned to Mr. Quigley's office and placed it on top of her note. She only kept them for him anyway. Now he'd have to keep track of them himself. Returning once again to her desk, she took the Bible, the handkerchiefs, and the picture, leaving Mr. Quigley's personal stationery for whoever took her place. She sighed at such a thought. Her replacement.

She turned and silently followed Mr. de Serre toward the office door. From the corner of her eye, she saw Margaret Gardener gaping from behind her desk.

Liesel reached no farther than the threshold when she nearly bounced into an obviously flustered Mr. Quigley. He was breathing heavily, as if he'd run up a flight of stairs, and the little hair he had was sticking out at odd angles.

"Miss Harris! Glad you finally made it in." He nodded an acknowledgment to Mr. de Serre at the same time. "I see you met up with our favorite Miss Harris."

Mr. de Serre did not reply.

"I left a note for you on your desk," Liesel explained. "I—I'm afraid I'm leaving the B&O."

"Well, let's all go back into my office and discuss it, shall we?"

"I really think—" Liesel began.

"Miss Harris is my best employee," Mr. Quigley interrupted, looking over Liesel's head at Mr. de Serre. "I think it would do you some good to hear a few things from me. Shall we step into my office?"

"Yes, Mr. Quigley," said a surprisingly affable Mr. de Serre. He looked every bit as interested in the discussion as Mr. Quigley. "I would like to hear what you have to say about all of this."

That evidently was invitation enough for Mr. Quigley, who led them quickly to his office, where, once they were all inside, he quietly closed the door.

If he was about to come to her defense, it was far too late. Liesel hardly wanted him to admit he had knowledge of the situation; it might lead trouble to his own door. As she saw it, once she agreed to the name switch, it had become entirely her own responsibility.

"Mr. de Serre—" Quigley began.

Liesel quickly cut him off. "I don't think there is anything either one of us can do to change the situation."

"Well, he can hear me out, can't he? Listen to what I have to say on the subject?"

Liesel turned her back on Mr. de Serre and stood in front of Quigley, capturing his gaze and staring at him hard. "Mr. de Serre is from—"

"I know all about where he's from, and that's why I think he should hear from me before he takes you away."

"But you didn't let me speak, Mr. Quigley. I am working here under a false name. A name I fabricated completely on my own. He has every right—"

Mr. Quigley shook his head. "It's no good, Liesel. If he's insisting on taking you from here, he may as well take me, too." He looked from her to Mr. de Serre. "Look, de Serre, I knew all about the name."

"I won't let you do this, Mr. Quigley," Liesel protested. She turned imploring eyes on Mr. de Serre. "He only helped me to get a job. It was all my idea."

David looked at her but addressed Mr. Quigley. "What is it you wanted to say?"

"It's this," he said. "Liesel may have a German name, but she's American through and through. I cooked up the scheme, not her. It's dumb to overlook a hard worker just because of a name. She's that and more—she wants to do something for this country. I as much as forced her into the charade because I knew she wouldn't be able to work here if she told the truth. And I didn't want to lose her. She's a crackerjack. Got that, de Serre? A crackerjack."

It was impossible to read Mr. de Serre's reaction; his face remained stoic. "It's good of you to come to her defense, Mr. Quigley. And if she proves to be anything other than a 'crackerjack,' I'll be back to talk to you about this whole thing. But the situation stands. I cannot allow her to continue in this employment regardless of your opinion of her or whose idea it was."

Quigley appeared about to say more, but Liesel shook her head. "No, Mr. Quigley. It's no use. But thank you."

He looked as if he'd just lost something, rather uncertain and defeated, perhaps a little frustrated. And he'd never been dearer to Liesel than at that moment. She wanted to give him a proper farewell—a hug or at the very least a warm handshake—but not with the hawk eyes of a government agent behind her. So she simply said good-bye, then turned and exited the office.

Outside the building, she hesitated when Mr. de Serre seemed headed back to his car. She couldn't very well thank him, yet some sort of acknowledgment seemed appropriate. After all, if he could have had her arrested, he hadn't gone through with it.

"I assure you I will be using my own name from now on," she told him, squinting from the sun when she turned her face to look at him. He adjusted his position to block the light entirely, and she might have smiled at the consideration except she couldn't muster one.

"I can take you home," he invited.

She shook her head. "No, thank you, Mr. de Serre. I've taken up enough of your time. And you needn't keep an eye on me. I won't be falsifying any applications between here and my house."

He laughed with what appeared to be complete ease. Evidently he didn't feel the same awkwardness she did.

He held out his hand, and she shifted her belongings to accept it. It was as if he'd done her a favor. As she turned to walk away, she thought perhaps he had.

"Miss Bonner," he called.

She faced him, surprised and expectant.

"That book under your arm." He glanced at the leather-bound Bible, and she nodded an acknowledgment. "When you get home, look up Proverbs 21:2."

She felt a smile erupt without effort. "'Every way of a man is right in his own eyes: but the LORD pondereth the hearts.' It's a verse that helped me decide to stay at that job, Mr. de Serre. God *did* know my motives."

She turned away, but not without feeling just a little bit vindicated.

———————

David watched her go. So the Bible hadn't been simply collecting dust in that drawer. Somehow that didn't surprise him.

Back at his office, he went to the telephone desk that a half-dozen agents shared. Only one other agent was there, Greg Donahue, and David acknowledged him with little more than a nod. Donahue was one of the eager young agents whose record for arrests was beaten by none—a fact that irritated David but for reasons few would find obvious. If competition had anything to do with the number of arrests each agent was responsible for, then Donahue won without dispute.

That was exactly what irked David about him. Donahue often let competition rather than reason rule. He never hesitated to interfere in others' cases, he "borrowed" records without returning them, he preened before the press, and more than once, he had been written up as a "hero."

The worst of it was David knew his dislike of the man could be mis-construed as sour grapes. Because of Donahue's eagerness for the head-lines, their department was gaining some notoriety, along with a bigger budget. But David would hate to count how many false arrests Donahue was responsible for because of his lack of caution, his disorganization, and his eagerness to draw another tick mark beside his name for putting yet another German behind bars.

David picked up the receiver when Donahue left the table. A moment later, a familiar operator answered, and he put through the request. This was one call to the American Protective League David preferred to handle himself.

Once he reached the party he normally dealt with, he went straight to the point. Charles Hackett, on the other end, didn't make any attempt at small talk. He'd spoken to David before.

David gave Hackett Liesel's home address. "It's a heavily German resi-dential neighborhood. There's a German evangelical church nearby; the pastor is Heimbrecht."

"Got it. Who are we looking at?"

"Liesel Bonner," David stated, then added, "And Hackett, don't squeeze this one too tight. Got that?"

When he hung up, he reconsidered his action to bring in the APL. He knew civilians in that organization could go overboard and often did, but in this case, he'd have to trust them. If anyone could gather surreptitious infor-mation in a timely basis, it would be Bonner's own neighbors.

David returned to his desk, sitting down to initiate a report of his own. *Profile: Liesel Bonner.* For a moment he stared at the nearly blank page. Just what was it about this one that made him so cautious? Instinct, he sup-posed. Some resurrection of Mio's dad, wrongly accused. Something about this woman refused to let him believe she could be involved in traitorous activities. Maybe it was everything Quigley had said and the fact that the man had been willing to put his own job in jeopardy to hire her—or at least come to her defense.

Or maybe it was just the color of her eyes.

Nonetheless, David wrote out the day's events. He wasn't about to let a pretty face keep him from his duties.

CHAPTER *Seven*

LIESEL sat on the front porch swing, her Bible next to her open to Psalms. She hadn't gone inside. Mama didn't even know she was home.

There on the porch, the very spot where Agent de Serre had confronted her, she relived the whole conversation. How had they learned of her identity? Even her own parents hadn't been privy to the escapade. Nor had Liesel told Katie for fear of having it seem as though Katie had given consent if somehow the scheme was found out. How had the government found out?

Liesel wished she'd had the gumption to ask some questions of the investigative agent, but she'd been on the wrong end of the legal system to be too bold. She doubted she would ever know now.

Sighing, Liesel looked around. Was she destined to spend the war unemployed? Staring at this porch day in and day out? The thought made her shudder. She wanted to work, but the idea of going from office to office and being turned away over and over again made her sick to her stomach. Standing, she thought she might finally try some of Mama's special tea that she'd made for Greta earlier.

When she opened the door and hung her purse on the nearby hook, Mama burst from the kitchen.

"Liesel! Mr. Quigley was here. He is most upset! What happened, child?"

Liesel couldn't think of an appropriate answer. She was reluctant to admit everything to Mama. However, just as Greta had had to admit her stomachache had been her own fault for eating too many green apples off a neighbor's tree, Liesel knew she must tell her mother she'd hung on to a job through less than admirable means.

"He is a good man, Liesel. So worried about you."

Liesel could only nod, not trusting her voice. She would miss working for Mr. Quigley. She walked past Mama into the kitchen, where she found Greta's tea still warming. Mama followed.

"It's a rather complicated story, Mama," she said at last, pouring a cup.

She told Mama almost everything about how she'd agreed to use Katie's name. However, she did not bring Mr. de Serre into the retelling at all, saying the truth of the name had been discovered and she had been asked to leave. Mama shook her head and frowned, but she was forgiving in her manner. The war, she claimed, had made the whole of Washington act in a most peculiar manner, and war, she'd added, touched everyone—on the battlefield or not.

Charley Hackett sipped a cup of coffee, purposely delaying what he had to say as he eyed the young man across from him. They sat at a table along-side the window at a small but busy café, one where two middle-class gentle-men would hardly be noticed even by their busy waitress. Charley almost smiled behind the steaming cup in his hands. The newest member of the APL sitting before him was fairly bursting with enthusiasm.

"I chose you for a reason, Mr. Miller," Charley said to the bespectacled man across from him. "You used to work with her. You live on the same end of town. You could easily join her church, no questions asked. They might think you consider yourself to be a prospective beau, but what's the harm in that? I hear she's a pretty lady, this Liesel Bonner."

"Yes, she is!" The young man nodded so vehemently Charley thought the round glasses might slip right off his nose. "I'll do whatever it takes, Mr. Hackett. Only one thing. Why does the government want to know anything about Miss Bonner? I can't imagine anyone more harmless."

Have you looked at yourself? Charley wondered. The eager fellow had prob-ably been rejected by every branch of the armed forces because he was under-weight and nearly blind. *No wonder he's so keen to prove himself in the APL.*

"All I was told was to use kid gloves with this one," Charley admitted. "Which either means she's the sweetheart of somebody important or they plan to use her themselves. So you've got to be subtle, Miller. And you can start right now by telling me everything you know about her."

"Well," he began, his face melodramatically serious, "she worked for Hodges, Pierson, and Deane for two years. Right out of stenographer's academy. I hired her," he added with what appeared to be a puff of pride. "She was an excellent worker—highly dedicated, never absent, very conscientious. Everyone respected her."

"Then why'd they can her?"

Mr. Miller frowned. "A . . . decision from the top. No Germans."

Charley grunted. Given her last name, he'd guessed immediately why she was being targeted. Did it have to do with being fired from this job with the railroad?

"How'd she take getting sacked? Resentful?"

Henry Miller shook his head. "Oh, no. Dignified. She just left, and we never heard from her again. Not even to pick up her last paycheck. I had to mail it, and I hate to send checks in the mail. Not entirely safe, you know. I hope she got it all right. I would have preferred delivering it myself—"

"Yeah, well," Charley interrupted. "What else do you know about her? You worked with her for two years."

"That's right," he said. "But I wasn't what you'd call a friend. Hodges, Pierson, and Deane discourages fraternization among the workers, especially the clerks and stenographers. I know very little about her outside the office except that she comes from a nice family."

"A nice family," Charley repeated. He hated nondescript words like *nice*. It was hard to respect the young pup, yet very often these young, eager ones did a good job. Charley would wait and see. "How do you know about this nice family?"

"I visited there once to deliver Miss Bonner's Christmas bonus check that first year. You see, she left without it, thinking she wasn't due one because she hadn't been there a full year. But she was such a good worker they—"

"Ah, so the family has met you. That'll make you less of a surprise when you start inquiring after her at the new church you'll be attending. Good, good. Anything else you want to say about her?"

The man was silent a moment, looking from Charley to the window and letting out a long, slow breath as he considered his response. Then he shook his head. "No, not a thing except she's a swell girl. That's all I'd like to add."

"Fine." Charley passed an envelope over the table. He detested the word *swell* almost as much as the word *nice*. "Here's the name of the church she attends and her address, although I guess you already know that. There's also a list of things we want to know: names of people she associates with, activities she's involved in. Anything you can find out about her right down to the food she eats. You'll have to observe her pretty carefully, Miller— subtle, so as not to be noticed about the whole thing. Got it?"

He nodded vigorously again, opening the envelope, then closing it with a nervous glance around the public café. "Should I look at this at home?"

"That's a good idea. There are a couple of forms in there for you to fill out on her; makes it all easy. You'll find your badge in there, too."

Charley saw Henry Miller's thin fingers pass over the middle of the envelope, where it bulged from the metal inside. Like Charley's badge, it was inscribed with *Secret Service*. He remembered when he'd gotten his, a memory marred only by the look on David de Serre's face when he saw the badges passed out. That was shortly after the government allowed the APL the prestige of official cooperation between the two organizations. De Serre had been sure the badges would cause quite a stir at the real Secret Service of the Treasury Department. Well, he might have been right about that, but it didn't matter to Charley. The term "secret service" fit what they did far better than it did any employee of the government.

"Look here, Miller. That badge is worth a lot more than the buck you paid for it when you agreed to work with us. Don't misuse it."

"Oh, I most assuredly won't, Mr. Hackett. It'll be an honor to possess it."

"Yeah, well, you've got my telephone numbers both at home and at the office, so you can reach me any time. That's it, then, Miller. Contact me as soon as you have anything."

The young man stood and hesitated before turning away. For one awful second, Charley thought the fellow was going to salute. Instead, he walked away, apparently without a thought to covering the cost of the cup of coffee he'd just consumed.

CHAPTER *Eight*

"THESE should just fit in the luggage trunk," Josef said to Liesel, going around to the solid, square box behind the rear-mounted gasoline tank of his Bearcat. In a moment, he tucked away a week's worth of work the ladies from Liesel's church had donated to the Red Cross, clean white bandages stuffed into neat, manageable sacks. When Liesel had told Josef just the day before that she was trying to find someone to transport their donation from the church to the Red Cross, Josef had immediately volunteered. So instead of attending his own church with his father that morning, Josef had joined Liesel at her family's church.

"I can drop them off tomorrow," Josef said as he opened the car door for Liesel. "I have to leave town again, but I should have time in the morning."

Liesel took the passenger seat, watching Josef round the car and get behind the wheel of the open roadster. "Why don't we drop them off now?"

"Is that how you want to spend our Sunday afternoon?" he asked. "Toting bandages? We have just enough time to make it to the neighborhood ballpark. Today is that game my father sponsored with the German American Boys' Club. After that, I thought we could drive outside the city and watch the crops grow."

The ball game was the favorite topic lately for the boys at church. Henry and Rolf were too old to participate, but they planned to attend anyway, as did almost everyone else Liesel knew.

She didn't utter the thought that had come to mind the first time she'd heard Josef's father had set up this game. *Why*, she wondered, *was he doing this sort of thing now?* While growing up, all Josef did was talk about or play sports, from bicycling to baseball, and Otto von Woerner had never shown the slightest interest. Not even enough to come to any of the games Josef had played. Now Otto was sponsoring a boys' game when Josef couldn't possibly reap any benefit. It simply made no sense.

"Wasn't that game scheduled at Potomac Park?" she asked.

"My father rescheduled it for the neighborhood. You know, friendly territory and all."

"Oh." Then she asked, "Couldn't we drop off the sacks on our way out to the country after the game?"

He patted her shoulder, then started the car. "You're forever the conscientious citizen, Liesel. No wonder everyone admires you." He slid one of his most charming smiles her way. "And I do, too."

His smile was too hard to resist. As they turned the corner, she happened to see Henry Miller emerging from the church. She waved a greeting.

"He's an odd little man," Josef commented as they drove beyond sight of him.

"I suppose."

"Strange that he showed up at your church given that you knew him before. Where did he used to go to church?"

"I don't know," Liesel answered. "I know very little about him, actually."

"From the way he acted after the service today, I'd have thought the two of you the oldest friends."

"He *was* rather friendly," Liesel said. "I suppose he's not as shy as I thought. Perhaps he's not so afraid to talk to me now that I'm no longer at the law office."

Josef glanced at Liesel, then back to the road. "Maybe he's glad you don't work there anymore."

Liesel looked at Josef's profile. "What do you mean?"

"Only that he seems interested in you. And why not? You're a beautiful woman, Liesel."

Liesel warmed to his compliment but couldn't agree with his opinion about Mr. Miller. "It's been months since I worked with him, and he never paid me the slightest attention other than in a professional way."

Josef shrugged. "Maybe you didn't notice him staring at you during the sermon."

She laughed. "You sound positively jealous, Josef!"

"Maybe I am." He took her hand in his.

Liesel felt his fingers squeeze hers, and she stifled the first thought that came to mind: *There is a way to stave off other men, even if it's only Mr. Miller who may be looking my way.* Without mention of a wedding or even an official engagement, why shouldn't other men consider her available?

Instead, she said, "So, you're going out of town again already—tomorrow?"

He nodded, still attentive to his driving.

"You're gone more and more these days, Josef. Where are you headed to this time?"

"Oh, here and there."

She looked at him. "Here and there?"

He nodded again.

"Josef." She paused, giving herself time to consider exactly what she wanted to say. "Why is it that you won't discuss your business with me? I'm not exactly ignorant of the business world, you know."

"Of course you're not," he assured her. "You have one of the soundest minds I know. But talking business is like talking politics. It's not something I like to do . . . you know, with . . ."

"Me?"

"Not you in particular, Liesel," he said quickly. "Just women in general. It doesn't seem logical since there are so few women in business—well, what's the point?"

"My father and I discuss business . . . and politics, too, even though I don't have a vote."

"I know." He sounded neither pleased nor displeased by that. Then he let out a long breath. "To be honest, Liesel, I talk about business all week, and I wouldn't think of burdening you with it."

"Maybe I wouldn't find it a burden. I've worked in business for more than two years, and I intend to work again, as soon as I can."

"I know! It's good for you, Liesel. I've seen how happy it makes you. I want what you want. How is your job search going?"

She was well aware he was eager to switch topics. Josef might be old fashioned, but he was already coming around to considering the idea of women having the vote. Surely, seeing the value of women in business wasn't far behind.

And since looking for another job was the one thing that occupied her time these days, she didn't mind the new subject. She told him about the half-dozen applications she'd filled out and the half-dozen rejections.

Josef had been sympathetic when she'd lost her job because her real name had been discovered. He hadn't seemed bothered in the least that she'd stooped to such measures to get the job in the first place. Liesel didn't mention that the Department of Justice had gotten involved. Not only did it add to the humiliation of being fired, but it also pointed back to the suspicion she was subjected to as a German American. And Josef would hardly welcome news like that.

"I think you should reconsider working for my father," Josef told her gently. "He would welcome you."

"He already employs my father and two brothers. What would he do with me?"

"With your skills? Put you in the office. Why don't you let him?"

She shrugged silently.

"I'm only trying to help, Liesel," Josef added. "You said a moment ago you want to discuss business matters with me. What better way to do that than for you to work at my father's most lucrative office? Besides, I know being turned away after submitting an application must hurt you. You can't keep it up; you're far too sensi . . . sensible."

She eyed him suspiciously. "Were you going to say sensitive?"

"You caught me." He smiled with apparent guilt. "Liesel, you *are* sensitive. You're a woman. You're supposed to be."

Liesel rolled her eyes. "There aren't any sensitive men in the world?"

"Not many," he admitted. "How sensitive do you think those guys are overseas? If they start out that way, they get it beaten out of them at boot camp. Just how long do you think they'd last if they thought about what they're doing?"

She nodded. "I understand your point, Josef, but I don't agree I'm being sensitive. This is a time of war! I want to use whatever talent God gave me to serve my country, but I'm being stopped because of blind prejudice."

He patted her hand. "It's *Deutschland* they hate, not you. And they're wrong. Blind and wrong."

She didn't reply.

He glanced from the road to her. "That's what makes this all so rotten, don't you see? Who would have thought America would be at war with *Deutschland*? Even though some people would like to be rid of us, do you know how many *Deutschlanders* are in this country? If all of us, not just Congress, had a vote on whether or not to go to war, do you think we'd have voted to go ahead? I don't think so."

"Perhaps."

"You're better off working for my father, Liesel. With Germans. We have loyalty to one another. At least with my father, you'll have job security."

She grinned. "Because he is the owner or just because I'm German?"

"Both." Since they'd come to the park where the ball game was being played, he pulled to the curb and cut the engine before turning to look at her. "So, will you be ready to report to my father's office first thing in the morning? Sticking with Germans?"

Liesel held back a sigh, knowing to show her reluctance would only hurt his feelings. Visions of how Uncle Otto ran his household came to mind. How many servants had he fired because he thought them lazy for wanting one full day off a week? Too, she recalled conversations she wasn't supposed to have heard between her mother and father—how her father thought Otto pushed the men too hard and, despite providing a good salary, offered little by way of gratitude for a job well done.

"I'm not sure, Josef. I have at least one more lead from the newspaper lined up for tomorrow."

"All right," Josef said with a smile. The smile that always melted her heart. "You follow your leads. But Tuesday morning if you haven't been hired elsewhere, then you'll go to my father?"

"Yes," she answered. Her lack of enthusiasm was apparent even to herself, but perhaps it didn't matter. She could hardly define for herself why she was so reluctant to work for Uncle Otto. How could she explain it to Josef?

"It won't be so bad. You'll like old Lucy. She's been with Dad for years. She'll make your job a breeze."

This time Liesel did sigh. "That's what I'm worried about. What would he need me for?"

He drew her closer for an embrace. "You won't regret this, *mein Liebe*. Before very long, you'll get along with my father as if he were your own. This will be good for you, Liesel. For us."

Is that what he's waiting for? For me to get along better with his father? She stared at their surroundings, the familiar park, the few cars she recognized, hearing cheers from the ball diamond just beyond the hill. Even as she considered the thought, she quickly banished such a notion. While she and Uncle Otto weren't exactly on friendly terms, they were always cordial to one another. Perhaps it was the way he talked about Germany. Apart from business opportunities in America, it seemed he regretted having left the land of his birth. He never visited Germany because the voyage over had made him so sick—and perhaps he wouldn't leave his businesses in anyone else's hands, anyway. She had the distinct idea nothing was as important to Uncle Otto as Germany and his business interests.

Liesel accepted Josef's hand, and they walked to the ball field. For the rest of the afternoon, Josef cajoled smile after smile out of Liesel. It was easy to watch him cheer on the players. His voice thundered above others, calling out encouragement and praise to the boys, whooping the loudest when someone scored. There was something innately positive about Josef that made anyone around him happy to be near. Liesel had never been immune to his charm. Few were.

But while she enjoyed the day, she worried over tomorrow. If this last interview didn't work out, she would have no reason *not* to work for Uncle Otto—especially since her options were considerably fewer in Washington. She had to keep clear of government jobs simply because of the Bureau of Investigation. Working for Uncle Otto might be her best option for a good job.

Besides, it was obvious Josef would be pleased by her working with his father. Perhaps it would prove all he hoped—allow her the opportunity to discuss business with him, get to know Uncle Otto better, and make it easier once the three of them were an official family.

Yes. Perhaps it will work out for the best.

David unwrapped the yellowish limestone chalk he'd borrowed from his friend Mio's eight-year-old son. He'd thought of the idea during a visit with Mio's family. The eight-year-old had been reprimanded by his mother for drawing a mustache above his five-year-old brother's upper lip with the dry, pasty stone. Afterward, David and Mio had quietly laughed to remember the mustaches they grew when they'd roomed together before Mio married Anna. Mio's had been sparse in comparison to David's, a source of considerable teasing.

David had searched the boys' toy box for the discarded chalk he now held in his hand. It would wipe off if the experiment proved fruitless.

Pulling out the picture of Josef von Woerner picketing against arms shipments to belligerent countries, David carefully drew a mustache on the handsome, clean-cut image. The color wasn't a perfect match to von Woerner's blond, but it was close enough.

And there he was. Andrew Nesbit.

Why hadn't he seen it before? Von Woerner and Nesbit were one and the same.

David again studied the list of von Woerner's financial contributions. His money proved his loyalty, and the picketing incident proved he was willing to do more than just contribute. Now this. An insurrectionist. David had heard with his own ears the kind of speeches Andrew Nesbit gave. Ever since America had declared war, his speeches could fall under the category of sedition.

David could easily bring him in.

Trouble was, there was something about von Woerner that made David believe sedition wasn't his most serious crime. He knew the man traveled quite a bit, and David had spread the word along the coast to keep an eye out for him. Twice now, strikes ensued in some company or another in the exact city von Woerner had last been seen. Not only that, three ships had sunk which had left harbors where von Woerner had been spotted. Coincidence?

David set aside the file on von Woerner to read another report, this one on Liesel Bonner. It contained everything from the outstanding grades she received throughout school to the clubs and activities she'd been involved in from her youngest years—mainly church groups when she was little, but as a teenager she'd been a Girl Guide in a new organization called the Girl Scouts. Then she was a counselor at the YWCA, a Sunday school teacher, a hospital volunteer. The single controversial item listed was that she belonged to a suffragette organization, and someone had clipped an old newspaper photo of her at a suffrage parade.

Not one German organization among them.

It listed the family's connection to the von Woerners that, on the surface, seemed innocent enough. Indeed, Liesel Bonner herself seemed innocent— an upstanding, patriotic citizen who had contributed far more to society than many others by the young age of twenty-three. A crackerjack.

So was that it? Between a federal investigator and the APL, they'd come up without a mark on the reputation of Liesel Bonner. Why was he so relieved?

Simple, really. If she was as above reproach as it appeared, she had no knowledge that her boyfriend might be working toward German rather than American interests. If she were as American as she appeared, she would have every reason to want von Woerner stopped before he did anything that could get him into serious trouble.

David had every intention of finding out just how deep her patriotism went.

CHAPTER *Nine*

LIESEL assessed her appearance for the last time before leaving for the day. From the tiny sprig of paper flowers on her lightweight blue felt hat to the trim blue of her prettiest suit, she presented a picture of both pure femininity and all business. Off-white gloves rose to meet the jacket's elbow-length sleeves, although, at the moment, she wore only one glove. The skirt had double box-pleats, two in front, two in back, and hung to the exact measurement of nine inches from the floor. Her shoes, also off-white, had a modest, sturdy heel and were tied at the instep with a lacy ribbon. Since it promised to be a warm spring day, she left the top mother-of-pearl button loose on her lightweight jacket, allowing the laced collar of her sleeveless cotton blouse to peek out from beneath.

With her ungloved hand, she touched up her face with a bit of powder. She'd be anxious enough at today's interview, and the last thing she wanted to worry about was a shiny face. Satisfied her appearance was the best she could manage, she left her bedroom for downstairs, preparing to call a farewell to Mama and then be on her way.

Just as she reached the dining room, she heard a tap at the front door, and Mama suddenly emerged from the kitchen, nearly bumping Liesel aside as she came through the swinging door to answer the mid-morning summons.

"I'll see who it is, Mama," said Liesel, "and then I'm off to the city again."

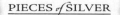

"Oh, Liesel, you look so pretty! You'll have a job for sure this time." Mama continued on toward the front door as she spoke. "It's probably another salesman for those brooms. I tell them I have a broom, but still they come back."

"I'll send them on their way," Liesel assured her, and Mama halted, letting Liesel pass her by.

"That's right. You young people, you know how to make your voice firm. You tell him, Liesel. Tell him so he won't come back." That said, Mama headed back to the kitchen.

Liesel opened the door wide and with force, entirely prepared for a showdown. But the person standing before her was no salesman. Her readiness to be combative altered instantly to surprise before settling back into preparation for another confrontation, albeit of an entirely different kind.

"Agent de Serre." There was no warmth in her tone; she sounded colder than she probably should have given the fact that they'd parted on somewhat friendly terms. But it was a parting she'd expected to be permanent.

"Good morning, Miss Bonner. I would have telephoned, but your family—"

"Has no phone," she finished for him. "Yes, my father doesn't like some of the new inventions. He'd rather talk to people in person, face to face."

"I tend to agree with him on that," Agent de Serre told her.

Liesel looked behind her. No sign of Mama. Looking back at her visitor, she asked, "What is it you wanted, Mr. de Serre?"

"I was hoping we could sit down," he said. "This may take a few minutes."

Liesel looked over her shoulder again.

"If you would like we could go somewhere else," he suggested, "perhaps a coffee shop?"

She hesitated, looking at him through the screen. In spite of calling herself a fool for even noticing, she was struck again by an attraction to Agent de Serre. He stood taller than her even though the porch was a step down from inside the house. He wore a brown serge suit, perfectly fitted to his lean form. He'd taken off his hat already, revealing his thick, dark hair. His eyes were every bit as dark, with little laugh lines just starting to form at the edges. *Brown eyes don't fade*, came a thought from nowhere. Briefly, foolishly, she wondered how he would look with graying hair. He would undoubtedly be just as handsome at sixty-five.

"Will you wait a moment?" she asked, and he nodded.

Leaving the door open, she went to the kitchen. She had no idea what to say to Mama. What could he possibly want with her? He'd said he wanted to talk. She'd quit her job and hadn't used any name but her own on the count-less applications she'd filled out. Besides, she hadn't inquired after a single government job. She couldn't possibly be in trouble. What did he want?

Peeking around the kitchen door, Liesel spotted her mother just coming out of the pantry. "Mama, it wasn't a salesman."

"Oh? Who was it, then?"

"Someone I met through my old job," she answered truthfully enough, not wanting her mother to worry. "He wants to take me into the city. Buy me a cup of coffee and save me the trolley ride. So I'm going, all right?"

"That's fine, dear," said Mama, rolling out cookie dough on the kitchen table. It was the twins' fifteenth birthday, and she always made a special treat on such family holidays. Treats were getting rare with the beginning of voluntary war rationing: meatless Mondays, sweetless Tuesdays, and wheat-less Wednesdays. Liesel could tell Mama was rolling the dough a bit thin even though this was meatless Monday and not sweetless Tuesday.

"You'll be home for the boys' birthday dinner, though?" Mama called as Liesel retreated.

"Yes, Mama," she said, then grabbed her purse and went out the front door.

Agent de Serre stood on the front stone walkway, under the shade of the maple in the yard. He appeared to be looking up into the branches as if searching for something.

"Maples are great," he commented, and she could barely hear him over the din created by the birds nested up there. "Birds love them."

Liesel looked up as well, and although she knew there were dozens of the winged creatures living there, she couldn't spot one through the thick, dark green leaves. "That tree is why Mama wanted my father to buy this house," Liesel said. "Mama saw it as a giant bird house. She loves it."

"They make a lot of noise early in the morning, though."

"I think she always hopes finches will take over, but usually we get spar-rows. She doesn't seem to mind. She's always leaving them plenty to eat."

Even now, leftover bits of bread crusts were scattered on the ground. Greta never ate the crust on bread, and Mama didn't complain since it all got eaten anyway.

"Would you like to stay in this neighborhood or go into the city?"

"To the city, if you don't mind," she said. "I was headed there anyway." The brief interchange about the birds had seemed so friendly it served Liesel well. Even to herself, she sounded—and felt—more relaxed. He couldn't have brought any trouble with him. Surely something in his manner would forewarn her of that.

"Do you have a new job?" he asked as he opened the door to his Packard Runabout for her.

She looked up, catching a purely inquiring look in his brown eyes. "Are you asking because you don't know, or are you just making conversation?"

He laughed. It was such an easy laugh she marveled that he seemed so relaxed when she suddenly felt so nervous. "I may be a federal investigator, Miss Bonner, but I do not have the resources to follow you about. And if you knew me better, you would know I rarely say anything just to make conversation. Not that I didn't do a good job with the bird thing just now."

Liesel climbed into the car. "I do not have another job yet, but I haven't given up. That great service army President Wilson called into action weeks ago is bound to find a place for me somewhere. I'm headed back out today."

He nodded, evidently familiar with the civilian "army" to which she referred. "Perhaps I can help you."

He'd flung the words so casually as he walked around the car to let himself in that she was unsure she'd heard him correctly.

"You . . . you've come to offer me a job?"

Starting the car and directing it from the curb, he looked at the road instead of at her. "Of sorts. Perhaps you'd better hear what I have to say before you come to that conclusion."

Confused but intrigued, Liesel settled back in the seat. They traveled the tree-lined streets of Washington, passing homes of the wealthy beyond Liesel's more modest neighborhood. Interspersed were tall, white church spires and, the closer they came to the center of the city, homes and buildings that had housed the famous and the infamous. They passed the marble obelisk of the Washington Monument and the parkland surrounding the Executive Mansion. On Pennsylvania Avenue, trolleys rolled down the center of the wide street while motorcars and carriages were relegated to the edges. As they passed the clock tower next to the new construction site where the Southern Railway Building had burned down the previous year, she looked ahead to see the colonnade of the Treasury Building.

"Did your mother ask who you were going off with?" he asked.

"No," she said, then added suspiciously, "How did you know my mother was home?"

"Oh, we spy chasers have our methods of finding these things out." He spoke with what appeared to be a very serious tone of voice. Too serious, for a moment later he was smiling. "I heard her ask if you would be home for dinner. Your 'Yes, Mama,' gave it away."

Liesel averted her gaze, hoping he couldn't tell just how hard her heart thumped in her chest. His teasing manner did little to dispel her discomfort.

"What I need to know, Miss Bonner, is if your family knows it was a federal agent who asked you to resign from your former job."

"*Asked* me to resign?" she repeated with a challenge in her voice, then wished she could recant the tone. What was she doing, calling on him to clarify his words? If she wasn't already in some kind of trouble, was she looking for some? All her life she'd done the right thing and been practically meek as a mouse because that was how she'd been raised. This probably wasn't the right time or the right person at whom to direct her individual revolution.

That smile again, with teeth that looked so straight and white he could have been any dentist's best advertisement. "Shall we say strongly recommended?"

She wanted to smile, how she wanted to, just to be able to do something so casual. But she couldn't. No smiles until she knew what he wanted from her.

"Are you feeling all right, Miss Bonner?" he asked after a moment. "I admit I haven't much experience in casual banter, especially with someone I barely know, but I have made a concerted effort to put you at ease, and frankly, I see it's not working."

"Perhaps if I knew what business you have with me—"

"Soon enough," he said as he pulled the car to a parking spot. "Here we are."

Mr. de Serre had stopped near a small café that had wide, striped awnings shading its windows.

Despite being the middle of a regular workday morning, the restaurant was busy. As they waited for a table in silence, all sorts of thoughts went through Liesel's head. He couldn't possibly have called on her to offer her a job. He was a government employee and had made it clear she was barred from government work, at least for the duration of the war. Without knowing what to think, she grew more curious by the moment.

"Your booth is ready," said a girl behind them. "I'll show you the way."

Liesel stood, woodenly following the waitress, who couldn't be much older than the twins. The table was in the far corner, a booth with high backs and sides that had to be opened like a train car door in order to slide onto the seats. An electric lamp hung on the paneled wall above the narrow table, but despite that, it was dimly lit, giving the aura of complete privacy. Once she sat down, Liesel could see only the confines of the booth.

After the waitress took their order, Liesel looked across the booth and folded her gloved hands. She waited for Mr. de Serre to speak.

"If concern over why I've sought you out is making you uncomfortable, then please be assured this has nothing to do with you personally, Miss Bonner." He leaned slightly forward. In the dim light, he looked younger than he'd appeared in the morning sun, and every bit as handsome. "You are in no trouble, and I haven't come back to make any for you."

"Then what is it you want with me?"

"I need your help."

Skeptical, she lifted one brow. She'd heard rumors of some civilian groups teaming up with government agencies to spy on people. Perhaps there was more to those rumors than just fright-induced imaginations.

"How?"

He let out a slow breath, looking her straight in the eye. "First, Miss Bonner, I will tell you I have done some checking on you. What I have learned is that you are a patriotic American citizen who, based on the type of groups you've been involved in most of your life, probably doesn't find it easy to lie." He cleared his throat and added, "In spite of the incident with the B&O application."

"Were you trying to learn what my motives were for that lie, Agent de Serre?" she asked. That hardly seemed important, not important enough for him to come after her and take time away from his job.

"Partly," he said. "And partly because if I'm going to ask for your help, I have to trust you. So I needed to know a little about your background."

"And what did you find?"

He told her, from the Girl Scouts to her Sunday school routine. "Of course, I'd like to know more before I work with someone, but it's a start."

Barely over the fact that he knew more about her personal history than she recalled herself, she asked, "Just what is it you'd like me to help you with?"

"The reason trust is so important, Miss Bonner, is because what I'm about to share with you can go no further than this booth." Hardly an answer to her direct question. "If what I'm about to tell you goes beyond this booth, charges of treason can be brought against you. Do you understand?"

Silently, she nodded. *Treason! Do I even want to hear what he has to say?*

Something must have caught his eye because he didn't continue. Glancing around, she still could not see over the booth; she simply wasn't tall enough. But a moment later, the waitress delivered two cups of coffee, and when she was gone, Mr. de Serre continued.

"Please be aware that I have no authority to coerce you into helping me, Miss Bonner. What I'm about to tell you is considered privileged information, and that is the only authority I have over you: to keep it confidential. I do not raise the term of treason lightly."

"I understand." A hint of excitement grew alongside her nervousness. She couldn't deny she had mixed feelings about receiving whatever it was he wanted to share. But even in the few moments she had to consider the situation, another idea began to form. This was a federal agent asking for her help. She might not be able to find a job, but maybe she could serve her country in some other way.

"I am after someone we've been watching closely for the past few years," he said. "Originally we termed him an agitator, someone adept at making trouble on a consistent basis. Picketing, handing out controversial propaganda, participating in parades and rallies that often went against the government—even against neutrality back when the war was young and we were trying to stay neutral. After that, this person was involved in a group that worked to establish an arms embargo—specifically, against the Allies, since they receive the majority of arms with the British blockade stopping Germany.

"The actions of this person were technically legal until we declared war a few weeks ago. At that point, sedition became a factor. Tell me, Miss Bonner, do you know anyone whom you would call . . . zealous about Germany?"

Otto von Woerner came to mind, with his insistence on speaking German, reading German newspapers, talking about the Fatherland as if it were his home instead of America, but Liesel said nothing.

Agent de Serre went on as if he hardly noticed her lack of cooperation. "German organizations right in this area have the goal to stir up trouble and prevent, or at least further delay, our involvement in the war. Our joining in may not have come as a surprise to our military, but to an army concerned only about our own shores up until now, it's taking some time to become a factor in Europe and still protect ourselves over here. We're going as fast as we can, but frankly, it's a bigger job than anyone really guessed. The last thing we need is interference. Some organizations loyal to Germany are financially backing strikes on companies vital to building up our arms. And while strikes are perfectly legitimate, someone getting a job at a company with the sole aim of inspiring a strike is not."

He paused, and she felt his steady gaze on her as if he were waiting for her to participate in the conversation.

He went on without receiving any input from her. "Then there are the more nefarious crimes: sabotage ranging from gumming up machinery to planting incendiaries on ships carrying war goods. We've targeted a few people we suspect of doing this sort of thing. Spies, Miss Bonner, right here on American soil."

"People talk about spies all the time," Liesel said, recalling more than one conversation at church or overheard on the streetcar. She didn't admit she thought the stories exaggerated, only made more interesting by people looking for gullible audiences. She thought such audiences were easily found considering the times but didn't believe there was much truth in many of the tales.

"Perhaps spies aren't lurking about every corner," he said as if he'd read her mind. "But I assure you, Miss Bonner, they're out there. And I'm sure you'll agree they should be stopped."

He was looking at her so closely. Did she need to state the obvious? "Of course."

"Tell me, do you think you might know anyone involved in such things?"

She held his gaze, refusing to cave in to the uncomfortable feeling creeping up as he continued to stare at her so intently. Being a loyal German was one thing; spying quite another. Otto von Woerner was simply not the type to go about inciting strikes or blowing up ships. "Of course not. I don't even know anyone who attends war rallies—either for or against the Allies."

"Really?"

He sounded so surprised she knew a moment of doubt. She herself had attended many rallies but only in favor of the women's vote, and those had become more rare as war rallies gained in popularity even among women. She remained silent under the surprised look on his face.

"I wonder, then, Miss Bonner, what is your opinion of this war?"

Liesel crossed her arms, tilting her head to one side as she attempted to study him. "Mr. de Serre, I fail to see what my opinion has to do with your pursuit of a traitor." Feeling her hands tighten ever so slightly upon her crossed arms, she asked, "Unless I am the person you suspect?"

He laughed. Such ease! How freely he breathed.

"Of course not, Miss Bonner. I just need a little more confirmation that we're on the same side if we do come to some sort of agreement about working together."

Liesel let her hands slide to her lap, where in spite of regaining a sense of calm, her fingers repeatedly entwined, then opened, and her palms felt damp. She was grateful that the table between them hid her restless movements.

"When war first broke out over in Europe, I thought it was sin. A total lack of respect for the life God gave us—killing one another over heaven only knows what. But I saw the reports, same as everyone else, of how Germany invaded Belgium after promising to let her stay neutral. And still Germany occupies her. I've seen Germany sink our ships—I remember the *Lusitania*, too, just like all the others still lifting their fists at Germany. But I also see the British blockade starving the people of Germany. I have cousins there who must be going to bed hungry. To be perfectly frank, I hate this war. But my father left Germany because he no longer wanted to be part of a monarchy. He wanted to raise his family—me, Mr. de Serre, and my brothers and sister—in a country where his vote means something. I am as American as you are, and so I stand with our government. Now we're in that great foolish war over there, and like it or not, I stand with our armies. Against Germany."

She leaned back, feeling her cheeks run warm with color. There was something about his manner that egged her into telling him in detail just what views she held.

He smiled, but he looked different somehow. Still at ease but so very somber.

"I'm glad to hear those words from your own mouth, Miss Bonner. That makes it easier to say what I must. I assume because of your loyalty to our country that you would stop anyone guilty of the crimes I listed earlier? Of the propaganda, the strikes, the incendiaries?"

Riveted by his expression, Liesel said, "If I knew anyone doing such things, of course I would help. But—"

He held up a hand, open-palmed, revealing long, slim fingers. A strong hand, really. She looked at it rather than at his face.

"Josef von Woerner."

The name barely sunk in through her study of the lines on his open hand. Then, when he slowly lowered that hand, she looked back at him, confused. She thought he'd said Josef's name! Why should he know Josef?

"Josef von Woerner," he repeated in a low voice. "We believe his loyalties are such that he would do whatever necessary to slow down America's participation in the war. Certainly he's guilty of sedition, organizing rallies to persuade conscientious young men and their families that it is perfectly acceptable, even noble, not to volunteer or even to avoid the draft. But we are beginning to suspect worse of him. Inciting strikes to stop production of war material, bombing ships to stop transport of war goods. We can prove he is a troublemaker, Miss Bonner. And we believe he is capable of going to dangerous lengths in the name of loyalty to Germany. If all I suspect of him is true, he is, to put it plainly, a traitor."

Liesel stared at the man across from her. A nearly total stranger talking about Josef, her Josef, as if he knew all sorts of malicious things about him—things of which she had no clue. None of it could be true, of course. It was all some horrible mistake.

"I don't know what to say to you," she whispered. Her excitement over a possible job that budded a few minutes ago disappeared. Even the anger she'd felt while defending her patriotism evaporated. She felt nothing. She was numb.

"You can say you'll help me get solid evidence on him." Mr. de Serre sounded as if it were the most logical notion in the world. "What we have now is a hodge-podge of suspicions and coincidences coupled with some people he knows who *are* guilty. He might very well have been singled out by Germany because of his staunch German loyalties and his generous contributions to organizations that promote German ways. Or maybe Germany considers Josef one of its own because his father never gave up German citizenship. Perhaps they felt justified in calling Josef into service."

An immediate defense of Josef came to mind, pushing aside that initial numbness as anger took a new stand. "Of course Josef would admit he is a member of the Bundt and other German organizations. Do you suspect all members of German clubs and groups?" She shook her head, letting out a quick breath of air. "I hardly think someone who wants to see a perfectly respectable heritage preserved is worthy of the suspicions you have about those bombings and such."

Mr. de Serre's brown eyes held hers calmly as if he saw her anger and wanted to dispel it. "Sitting in jail cells in the federal prison in Atlanta are several Germans and German Americans whose goal was to stop the shipment of war material to Allied countries. They had no problem designing incendiaries or setting up illegal unions to pay striking workers if those workers would stop the production of munitions. Those people are in prison, Miss Bonner, because they were guilty of interfering with this nation's best interests. I am at this moment tracking their trails to see if any one of them lead squarely to Josef's door."

"Josef knows a lot of people, lots of Germans, even chemists through his job. If he knows any of those men in prison, it will only be a coincidence."

"Like it is a coincidence that ships seem to sink when they leave a port at which Josef has been spotted? A coincidence that a strike has erupted in a town Josef has visited?" Agent de Serre shook his head without letting her speak. "There are too many examples to be simple coincidences."

"I'm sure that's all they are," Liesel insisted. "Josef von Woerner is a good man. Yes, he is of German descent and does want to see German traditions enjoyed. But he was born here in America, Mr. de Serre. He is as American as you and me."

"Precisely, Miss Bonner. Which makes him a traitor and not an alien spy like the others sitting in jail."

Liesel shifted in her seat, wishing it was easier to stand and leave this restaurant. But sliding to the end of the bench seat and unlatching the door that held her in would take a bit more time than she wished. She pushed aside her untouched cup of coffee and prepared to leave.

"Mr. de Serre, I have nothing to say. I'm sure you're mistaken about Josef. He isn't any of the things you suspect."

Mr. de Serre made no attempt to slide to his own edge of the bench. He watched as she fumbled with the silly booth door.

"This is a surprise to you, of course," he said, his voice still placid compared to what she felt inside. "Think it over, Miss Bonner. When you realize how you can help your country, I'm sure you'll come to the right decision."

At last she freed the door, and it flipped open with a thud when it hit the booth's wall.

"Please don't contact me again, Mr. de Serre," she told him. "I couldn't possibly be of any help to you."

She slid out in such a hurry to leave she nearly forgot her purse. She was two steps away before she realized something was missing and, ignoring her embarrassment, returned to the bench and leaned over to retrieve it.

"Good day, Mr. de Serre," she said mustering what composure she could.

"One thing to remember, Miss Bonner," he said before she could turn away again. "Everything I said today is strictly confidential. You don't want to forget that—for your own good."

Liesel wished she could think of something to say but couldn't. She merely nodded tight lipped, then went on her way. It was embarrassing enough for a woman to be seen leaving a restaurant unescorted. If Mama knew, she would be mortified. But breaching etiquette was far preferable to spending one more moment alone with Agent David de Serre.

―――――――

David watched her go as far as he could from the confines of the booth. He considered their conversation as he finished his coffee. Though some of what he'd intimated about von Woerner had been stretched beyond current evidence, David didn't regret his exaggeration. Gut instinct told him he was right; only caution held him back from arresting von Woerner right now. Certainly someone like Agent Donahue wouldn't have waited this long.

Her reaction wasn't a total surprise. What else had he expected? For her to say, *"Oh, yes, I've suspected my family's lifelong friend of being a spy for quite some time now. I'll be glad to help you turn in the man I've been dating. The man I love."*

While he hadn't expected that extreme, he had expected her to hear him out. He hadn't even told her how he wanted her help. Did she think he would ask her to report every little thing the man did? Did she think he would ask her to put handcuffs on him the next time she saw him? What *did* she think?

He had to admire her reaction to it all, though. Maybe it was her pristine past, but he believed she'd been shocked when he had said von Woerner's name. Despite her defense of the man, he believed her words about standing with America against Germany. In his line of work, David had been lied to so many times he'd lost count. But he was certain today would not be included in such a tally.

Liesel Bonner might not want to see David again, but unfortunately for her, he was already planning his next visit. He meant to keep his eye on her. She might not be a liar, she might even be a patriot, but he also knew people didn't always stick to their convictions when it came to matters of the heart.

He meant to make sure Josef von Woerner didn't get the best of her.

CHAPTER *Ten*

LIESEL jumped on the first horse-drawn trolley moving slowly enough for her to safely board. Shaking, she didn't take a seat. Instead, she leaned her forehead against the cool, iron bar supporting the trolley's green roof, and closed her eyes. An image of Josef setting a bomb, then heaving it onto the center of a ship full of sailors ran through her mind in frightening detail.

Pushing away the thought, she opened her eyes. It couldn't be. Josef would never do such a thing. He was far too . . . too what? Too loyal to America?

She finally took an empty seat on the trolley, uncertain and uncaring about her destination. Of course Josef couldn't be involved in the things Agent de Serre had said. Yes, Josef loved Germany and German traditions. But his father was far more vocal about such things than Josef, and they didn't suspect Uncle Otto, did they? Otto von Woerner wasn't even an American citizen, as Josef was. Josef was honest and hardworking, a loyal, lifelong friend to her and her family. He was kind and gentle. He loved people. He loved her. Surely he could not be involved in anything dangerous and illegal and . . . *treasonous*.

Liesel leaned forward on the seat, resting her chin in the palm of her gloved hand. She wondered why the government should single him out. Because he belonged to so many German clubs and organizations? Because of a few coincidences? In all of Josef's travels selling glass and coking coal, he was bound to be any number of places where there was trouble.

But that thought sent Liesel's spirits lower. Josef did travel all of the time. She hadn't the faintest idea where or why. Business, he always said.

She wished she could simply go to Josef and tell him about Mr. de Serre and insist Josef go to the Justice Department to straighten out the whole thing. He could even take some kind of oath, if they wanted. He was an American citizen, and it should be obvious he would never do anything against his own government. If they wanted him to take an oath, surely he'd do it. Then this whole thing would be over and Agent de Serre wouldn't waste his time following Josef.

But of course Josef was out of town, and Liesel couldn't reach him. Even if she could, another thought, just as serious, came to mind. How could she go to Josef and tell him to straighten out this whole mess? She would have to reveal everything Mr. de Serre had told her, and he'd made it very clear that for her to do so was to commit treason herself.

This is ridiculous! How can I help Josef without telling him what I know? Why, I'd even be helping Mr. de Serre by clearing all of this up. Saving him the time and energy of chasing an innocent man.

She should know far better than some government agent if Josef was capable of getting into such serious trouble. After all, she'd known him her entire life. Even when he and her brother Karl played rough boy games, Josef hadn't minded if Liesel tagged along. Over Karl's protests, Josef defended her. In spite of that, he and Karl were like brothers. Though Josef was a year younger than Karl, it had been Josef who taught both her and Karl to ride a bicycle. And when they'd made a secret fort in the woods a good half mile from home, it was Josef who overruled Karl and said Liesel, a girl, could come inside. That was the place where they had planned their war strategies. Josef was usually the general, but sometimes Karl was, too.

Even that memory clouded Liesel's mind. She remembered too much. When they played, it was never cowboys and Indians the way her oldest brother, Ernst, used to play. No, Josef insisted Karl play Germans and Turks or Germans and Russians or Germans and French, whatever war Germany had ever fought in history. And Germany always won, even if it meant letting Karl be the victorious general.

It had been a long time since Liesel had thought about such things. When had she begun thinking of Josef as anything but a brother? It was that day in 1908, late in the summer....

Labor Day. Papa said they lived in the best country in the world—for many reasons, but one of them was because not long ago America had set up a day just to celebrate its workers. Papa had the holiday off, and he'd taken them to stay

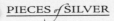

at a seaside home that Uncle Otto invited them to use. The mansion had been owned by a business associate who'd recently passed away. Without a family, the wealthy German investor had left it to Otto, who had been instructed to sell it and disburse the money to various German interests. In the meantime, the house sat empty, so there was no reason for him not to loan it to the Bonners. Josef had accompanied the family on their holiday out to the North Carolina coast, but Uncle Otto had stayed behind to work.

Though September, it was still hot. Josef had read about a six-day bicycle race going on in Berlin. That whole summer, he did nothing but ride his own bicycle. And since he was unable to bring it along on the train ride to the coast, he had the idea to run up and down the shore because he didn't want to miss a day of exercise. He'd read that was how the cyclists kept up their stamina, and he wanted to be just like them.

That was the first time Liesel noticed what a handsome boy Josef was turning out to be. He'd cajoled Karl into running with him, though Karl couldn't keep up. She had admired Josef's athletic grace and how the sun baked his hair white-blond, how his eyes reflected the blue of the ocean. Somehow, being away from home had made her see Josef in a new way. She was shy around him for the first time in her life.

That night after dinner, everyone wanted to take a walk by the beach. Karl and Josef had gone out first, going back to a spot down the shore that they'd discovered earlier. It wound around into a secluded inlet. When the rest of the family came out for their walk, Josef was all for showing Liesel their latest find. As usual, Karl was less eager. So Josef had taken her there by himself.

"This would be a great place to wait and ambush somebody," he'd said that night, pointing out the high hill just above the inlet. Then he turned to the water. "Or an enemy ship could let its best fighters swim ashore under the cover of night. They could stand where we are and hop up to overtake the unsuspecting villagers before they even knew what hit them."

"Unless the tide came in while that army stood here."

He laughed. She thought perhaps he might have found her statement witty. She hoped so.

Then he grabbed her hand and pulled her even farther into the shadows. "Look at these rocks over here. When we saw them in the daylight, they looked like somebody had put them here on purpose to hold back the water from this little cave. Maybe somebody tried to live in there once."

Liesel wanted a closer look and climbed onto the flat, smooth rocks. She could see the blackness of the cave's mouth.

"How high is it inside? Did you go in?"

"Come on. I'll show you."

They scaled the rocks with youthful ease and were inside the dark, damp cave in moments. Liesel could stand to her full height, but Josef had to hunch a bit. It was so dark Liesel couldn't see a thing and she wished they'd come during the day. Or perhaps it was better at night—at least she couldn't see what little bugs and other vermin might be squirming around her.

"I think we'd better get back. It's kind of cold in here."

Josef took her hand again and led her out. It was slippery, but he followed the same path they'd just traveled. This time, as they reached the last string of rocks, Liesel lost his steadying hand and slipped on a patch of moss. Landing flat on her back on the sandy shore, she was grateful for the darkness once again. Perhaps he hadn't seen how awkward her fall had been. Wincing more from bruised pride than anything else, she tried scrambling back to her feet before Josef could see how helpless she must look lying there.

But Josef was too quick for her. He was at her side before she could stand, and he helped her to a sitting position.

"Just stay put a minute," he told her, laying a hand on her shoulder to still any movement. "Did you hurt anything?"

Brushing her hands free of sand, she shook her head. She could see his face more clearly now. The moon had emerged from behind a cloud and cast its light all around them. The ocean drummed a rhythmic beat, and Liesel felt everything disappear at that moment except the moon and the ocean, Josef and herself. She was embarrassed by such romantic thoughts, thinking how handsome he was. And she felt so stupid for having fallen that she couldn't look at him.

"I'm all right," she assured him.

Rather than rising to his feet and helping her to her own, Josef sat beside her, obviously not caring that the sand was somewhat moist.

"I'm glad your family let me come along," he said. "Do you know why?"

She shook her head, unable to resist looking at him.

"Because I get to be with you."

Before Liesel knew what was happening, he bent his head closer and kissed her. She didn't know if she should let him. Even as his lips descended on hers, her first thought was of Mama and what she would think if she knew. But Liesel didn't care. She had wondered for a long time what it would be like to be kissed, and until that day, she hadn't imagined that Josef would be the one to show her.

Karl's call interrupted them. Liesel didn't know how long Karl had been calling. He sounded perturbed. So they brushed the sand off one another and found her brother. But Karl did not speak to Liesel for the rest of the holiday. After a while, she guessed he must have seen them kissing and thought she was wrong to have allowed it.

Her memory of those days was stark. She thought she loved Josef then, even though things seemed to return to the way they'd always been after coming home. But she'd never forgotten that night, and it seemed only fitting they would one day marry.

She shook away these thoughts and looked out the side of the open trolley. The breeze felt good; she was so warm and agitated. She was on the opposite end of Pennsylvania Avenue from where she wanted to be to check a job at a newspaper office in the heart of the city. Yet the mere thought of presenting a composed front now seemed lost. She wanted to go home. Even reluctance over working for Uncle Otto couldn't inspire the strength to present an application to one more place. At the next stop, she jumped to the pavement.

Making her way to another corner to catch a trolley in the direction of home, she considered Uncle Otto. He was the one the government should be investigating. Liesel bit back the sour thought.

Just why was working for him such a disagreeable prospect? He had a foreign look to him despite having lived in America for so many years. He looked just like Kaiser Bill with his mustache and monocle, except Uncle Otto wore no uniform. But if Liesel was uncomfortable around him just because of the way he looked, then she was certainly no better than anyone else with the flimsiest reasons for prejudice. No, it wasn't the look of him.

Uncle Otto was like a lot of successful men. Strict. Ordered. Inflexible. Someone who demanded his way. She was sure he ran his business the way he ran his household or worse, and Liesel had never wanted to go to Uncle Otto's as a child. She and her brother Karl had been allowed in only one room of that gigantic house, and even then they had to be quiet when they played their games with Josef. On the rare occasion they visited, Uncle Otto never seemed happy to see either her or Karl.

That was obviously it. Was she still seeing Uncle Otto through a child's eyes? Of course she was! And that was silly. Josef had as much as said he wanted her to know his father better so that when they were a family they could be closer. He was right, of course. She hardly knew Uncle Otto.

Perhaps now that she was no longer a child, she and Uncle Otto would learn to like each other. Getting closer to him would help strengthen Liesel's relationship with Josef. Maybe he wanted them to be a family in the broadest sense of the word—personally and professionally.

She wondered if she would know exactly what sort of business Josef conducted once they were married. All these trips he took were ostensibly to sell Uncle Otto's coking coal and glass to new markets. Lately he was gone for weeks at a time, and Liesel assumed it was because he traveled farther away, which demanded more time on the road. Just why was it so impossible for her to know where he was, what he was doing? Even his own father didn't know how to reach him. Josef could be doing just about anything.

Even stirring up strikes?

Stunned that the thought came so easily, she shook her head and breathed in the fresh air. A trolley approached, and she was glad to have to search for another nickel rather than dwell on the thoughts so eager to fill her mind. This day had brought no peace, and she longed for the solace and privacy of her own bedroom.

She would work for Uncle Otto.

Liesel found some small measure of peace that evening. She spent dinner with her family, glad everyone was so caught up in the twins' birthday celebration that they didn't seem to notice her unusually quiet demeanor. Everyone enjoyed Mama's cookies, even if they were spread a bit thinner than they used to be. After dinner, they played a game of quiz, something Papa had made up years ago. He read a passage from the Bible, then asked questions of each child, easier ones for the younger, more difficult ones for the older. It was sufficient to pull Liesel's mind from the day's events, so she didn't mind playing along.

Just before she intended going upstairs for the evening, she turned to her father. "Papa," she said slowly, almost reluctantly, "I'll join you on the trolley in the morning. I told Josef that if I didn't get a job today, I'd show up in his father's office on Tuesday."

Papa's brows raised as if he were surprised. Then he smiled. "That's fine, Liesel. I'll enjoy the company, and you'll do a good job for Otto."

"Yes, Papa," she said, not looking at him. She turned from the room, going toward the stairs. But when she heard her father's footsteps behind her, she stopped before she reached the first stair.

"*Mein Liebe,*" he said quietly. "This is not so bad, is it, that you go to work for Otto?"

Liesel turned his way without looking up at him, wishing she could tell him everything that was on her mind. But that wasn't possible. "No, Papa."

He put a gentle thumb and forefinger to her chin. "What is it, then? You've worked hard to find another job. You've done your best, haven't you?"

She nodded, her eyes still cast down.

"No one can find fault with that. It is a blessing that Otto can offer you a position. Perhaps that is precisely where God wants you, at least through this war. And I can keep my eye on you."

At last she looked up at him, wondering if he was serious. Though he was smiling, she knew he was only half-teasing. "Oh, Papa. I'm fully grown and don't need you to look out for me."

"Of course, of course. But that doesn't mean I won't if given the opportunity." He drew her close for a hug. "These are unsteady days, Liesel. It will do at least one of us good to have you close by."

Liesel hugged him back, closing her eyes, breathing in the familiar scent of him. She was glad he no longer worked in that coking coal factory where it smelled. The glass factory left no such distinctive residue except a faint one from the great gas furnaces, but Papa took an unheard-of daily bath to wash that away. Ever since he left the coking coal business, he never wanted to stink again.

"Good night, then, *mein Liebe*," he said and let her go.

———

Liesel rushed down the stairs, struggling with one hand to secure the last covered button on her beige suit while holding her shoes in the other hand. Papa came out of the kitchen, work uniform on and lunch pail in hand.

"Well, good morning! I was wondering if you were going to start your new career on time or not."

"I'm ready," she said slipping into her shoes.

"No breakfast?" said Mama from behind Papa. "You must eat something, Liesel."

"No, Mama. I haven't any time today."

"Well, take the apple from your father's lunch and eat that on the trolley. Oh, dear! I didn't make a lunch for you. And you don't have enough time to make one for yourself."

"That's all right—"

But her father interrupted with what looked like a smile of chagrin. "I'm sure your mother won't mind if I give you mine. She's eager enough for you to have my apple."

"Oh, Hans," scolded Mama with a little laugh.

"I can buy my lunch," Liesel told them.

"Buy lunch!" Papa hooted. "Whoever heard of such a thing?" He headed toward the door, calling over his shoulder, "You can have some of mine. Mama packs more than enough. Come along now. We'll miss the trolley if we don't get going."

———

If Otto von Woerner was expecting Liesel on Tuesday morning, Lucille Burnbaum obviously wasn't.

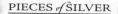

"Mr. von Woerner didn't tell me he was expecting you for certain," she said, looking down her nose through her spectacles at Liesel. She was tall and thin, even taller than Liesel. She might have been pretty once, for her brows were dramatically arched and she wore bright red lipstick as if accustomed to highlighting her best feature, which might have been that mouth if she smiled. Her hair had probably been another attribute at a younger age, for it was thick. But the strands that weren't already gray lacked any luster, as if preparing for the coming change. Colorless eyes seemed unnoticeable behind the silver-edged spectacles, except that if such eyes could hint at her thoughts, she obviously had no welcome for Liesel. She stood over her wide wooden desk like a bird of prey guarding its nest.

"Is he in his office? I'm sure if you simply tell him I'm here—"

"Of course he's not in yet!" Miss Burnbaum's tone was as harsh as her face. "If you will have a seat in the lobby, I'll send someone to fetch you when he arrives."

Liesel looked back toward the door of the office. The lobby, at least the only one she knew of, was on the other end of the factory. Eyeing the two cushioned seats just opposite Miss Burnbaum's desk, Liesel asked, "Couldn't I wait here?"

"Mr. von Woerner doesn't like people loitering in this office. Those chairs are for appointments during the day. Certainly not for the first thing in the morning before he's even arrived. Now if you don't know where the lobby is—"

"I know where it is," Liesel replied, then turned back to the door.

She waited a half hour before a boy dressed in the typical factory garb arrived to invite her back to the owner's office. He was a talkative young man, just at the legal working age of fourteen. He said he often ran errands for Miss Burnbaum, and that if Liesel were staying on, he'd be happy to do errands for her, too.

Other than her father's, his was the first pleasant face she'd seen thus far. However, when she stepped back into Uncle Otto's office, Miss Burnbaum presented an entirely different picture. She was smiling and laughing over something Uncle Otto had just said, who stood next to her chair behind her desk. And as Liesel suspected, Miss Burnbaum's face had the shadow of beauty when her dull eyes sparkled and her painted lips curved upward.

Uncle Otto and Miss Burnbaum turned to Liesel at the same time, smiling and welcoming.

"Well, here she is!" Uncle Otto greeted her. "Josef told me to look for you today, Liesel. Ah, I suppose in business we should follow the rules of decorum. No more Uncle Otto and Liesel here, is that right? It will be Miss Bonner and Mr. von Woerner during business hours. Can we remember that?"

She smiled. "I think we'll manage." She had never seen him quite as comfortable as he appeared just now. He held his monocle between the fingers of his left hand, allowing both of his eyes to look wide and friendly.

"Well, this is my own Miss Burnbaum. You have worked in offices before, Liesel—Miss Bonner. But Lucille here—that is, Miss Burnbaum—can no doubt show you a few tricks to office work. She's been with me for nearly twenty years, and I can say she has taught me a thing or two. We'll be like family. *Ja?*" He asked it of both women, who nodded simultaneously.

"Well, then," he continued, stepping away from Miss Burnbaum's desk and heading toward his office, which was just a few feet away, "I will let you get acquainted. Oh, and Miss Bonner," he said, as if the thought just struck him as he placed his monocle to his left eye, "perhaps you don't know. I like the office opened at precisely eight o'clock. You will be here by then tomorrow, won't you?"

Liesel glanced from Uncle Otto to Miss Burnbaum, who could easily vouch that she'd arrived a few minutes before eight that very morning. But Miss Burnbaum merely smiled, saying nothing.

"Yes, Mr. von Woerner. I'll remember that."

"Good, good," he murmured, then disappeared into his office.

Miss Burnbaum straightened a stack of papers in the center of her desk, something that hadn't been there earlier. Looking around the office, Liesel waited for Miss Burnbaum to speak. There was no place to sit except the two empty chairs by the door. A plain wooden typing table had been pushed aside, but the only chair near that was Miss Burnbaum's. Perhaps Liesel could pull up one of the chairs by the door and use that table for a desk. Suggesting as much to Miss Burnbaum, who seemed to be pointedly ignoring her, the older woman at last looked up.

"I don't think that's such a good idea," Miss Burnbaum said. "There isn't a lot of space behind my desk, and I'm moving constantly in between that table and right here. I'll see if we can set up a desk for you in there."

Liesel looked toward a room on the opposite side of Uncle Otto's office. Without waiting for an invitation since none seemed forthcoming, she went to the door and opened it wide, peering into the dimly lit room. The only light came from behind Liesel from the broad window next to Miss Burnbaum's spacious desk. But even that little light allowed her to spot the obvious: it was a storage room with barely enough leeway for the supplies

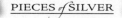

stacked along the walls. The majority of the room was taken over by a huge hectograph, an older version of the one she'd worked with at the law firm.

Over her shoulder, she said, "I don't think there's enough room for a desk in here."

Miss Burnbaum came up behind her. "Nonsense. We'll just move the hectograph back a little, and you'll have more than enough space."

"But these machines are terribly loud," Liesel pointed out. "And in such small confines . . ." Her words dwindled away. Clearly she was not getting through to Miss Burnbaum.

"I rarely use this old thing," Miss Burnbaum said. "I don't mind using carbons, and I keep myself well organized so that I don't need to make unnecessary copies of every little thing. And of course, we often use the printer down the street. I'm sure it won't bother you in the least. This room will be like having your own office, won't it?"

If that was supposed to sound inviting, it held little appeal. "Where should I sit until my desk arrives? Is there someone I can contact to see if it's on its way?"

"No. I'll send for the janitor, and he'll bring one from office storage downstairs." She glanced over her shoulder at Liesel. "If we'd known for sure that you would be here today, we'd have been prepared. Josef merely told his father it was a possibility."

Liesel told herself that sounded reasonable enough and resolved firmly that she would get along with Miss Burnbaum . . . no matter what. If Liesel's faith had taught her anything, it taught her God loved all.

That goal proved harder than she imagined. By lunchtime, Liesel's patience—and temper—were stretched to the limit. Yet she kept a firm, if sometimes desperate, lock on her lips, knowing while it might feel good to let that temper go, it would no doubt come back to haunt her. She wanted to work, and she didn't want to disappoint Josef.

When she met her father at midday to share the contents of his lunch pail, she was unusually quiet about the details of her morning. And Papa didn't press, for which Liesel was grateful.

The rest of the day, Miss Burnbaum handed out information as well as work as if it were the last of the family fortune. To each inquiry, Liesel was given only brief, vague answers. To each offer of help, she was rebuffed with the explanation that Mr. von Woerner only liked things a certain way and that way was Miss Burnbaum's way. By the end of the day, Liesel was exhausted, though certainly not from work.

But at least she had something to think about other than everything Agent de Serre had said. Every time those thoughts came to mind, she pushed them away as if they were poison to her mind. Josef couldn't possibly be involved in any of the things the federal officer suspected. It just wasn't possible that the man Liesel knew—and trusted—could live a life of such duplicity.

For the remainder of the week, little changed at the office. Liesel saw almost nothing of Uncle Otto, who was busy and brusque when she did catch a glimpse of him. Often Miss Burnbaum went into his office, coming out with a stack of work that she kept to herself. Once or twice, Liesel heard laughter from behind the closed door and wondered what they were talking about. She'd so rarely heard Uncle Otto laugh she wished she could have heard it better over the sound of Miss Burnbaum.

Hours went by, and Liesel could find nothing to do. The boredom was like a cruel punishment, making each day drag. It drove her by Friday to seek Uncle Otto himself. She waited until Miss Burnbaum left on a last errand of the day before tapping on Uncle Otto's office door.

"Come in," he said, his tone gruff. He didn't look up from his desk when Liesel entered. "Lucille, this report must be retyped. I meant for this second paragraph to follow the fourth—"

"I'd be happy to do some typing for you, Mr. von Woerner," said Liesel eagerly.

Uncle Otto looked up, surprised but noticeably displeased. "*Nein*, Lucille will handle it. She is familiar with the project already." He put aside the report and gave her his apparent attention. "Did you need something?"

Liesel came to the edge of his desk. She stood stiffly, having had plenty of time to rehearse exactly what she was about to say. "I feel I'm not earning the salary you are giving me, Mr. von Woerner. Miss Burnbaum is certainly very competent at keeping you satisfied, so I wonder if there is another aspect of office work that could become my responsibility. Bookkeeping, perhaps? Tallying accounts? Keeping track of billing? I'm good with numbers."

"I admire your willingness, Miss Bonner, but you are entirely in Miss Burnbaum's care. She mentioned you've had some trouble adjusting. Perhaps I keep her too busy to spend enough time with you. I'll speak to her about it."

He turned back to the papers in front of him, an understood dismissal, but she was loath to leave. Yet it appeared she had little choice. Near his office door, however, she made one more attempt, this time in a more personal vein.

"Have you heard from Josef this week?"

"No, Liesel," he said, still distracted by the report he was revising with his pencil.

"Do you know when he'll be back?"

"No, I do not."

She would have left feeling quite the all-around failure even at attempts to spark conversation with her possible father-in-law, but he spoke again.

"I do not discuss personal topics here in the office." His tone wasn't quite so gruff, merely factual.

She started to reply, but Miss Burnbaum entered through the office door at that moment.

"Anything wrong, Mr. von Woerner?" she asked, looking past Liesel to her boss.

"*Nein.* Miss Bonner was just saying good night."

"That's right," she agreed.

Miss Burnbaum stopped between Liesel, who was nearing the door, and Mr. von Woerner's desk. "I thought I heard something said about Josef."

Liesel wondered exactly how long Miss Burnbaum had stood just out of sight of the open office door, but she said nothing.

"Miss Bonner was just wondering when he would be back."

"Miss him, do you, dear?" Miss Burnbaum said, her voice thick with sympathy.

Liesel would have chosen not to answer except Uncle Otto looked up from his report as if he, too, wanted to know.

"Of course," she answered. "I would prefer to know how to reach him, to talk to him by telephone at least while he's gone."

"He moves around too much for that," Uncle Otto said.

"Of course," Miss Burnbaum reiterated. "Salesmen do, you know. He can't very well be tracking down a telephone line every day. He's very dedicated to his work."

"Yes, I understand that," Liesel said, not looking at either of them.

Miss Burnbaum approached, guiding her closer to the door by linking her arm with Liesel's as if they were chums. "The von Woerner men are very dedicated, Miss Bonner. You would do well to learn that about Josef and try to understand him rather than judging him for not calling."

"I wasn't. . . ." Liesel didn't finish the sentence. She doubted Miss Burnbaum's real interest and doubted even more that Uncle Otto would understand.

Sufficiently shooed from Uncle Otto's office, she stood near Miss Burnbaum's desk, which remained empty since Miss Burnbaum immediately headed back toward Uncle Otto. It was quitting time anyway, and her father would be waiting for her downstairs. As Liesel considered leaving, she heard Miss Burnbaum speak.

"Perhaps Josef doesn't call her for a reason, Otto," she said.

"What do you mean?"

Liesel couldn't help but stay put. She wanted to know what Miss Burnbaum meant, too.

"Only that he's had plenty of opportunity to ask that girl to marry him and hasn't. Perhaps he has no intention of doing so. She'll soon be quite the old maid."

Liesel heard Otto clear his throat and give a mumbled reply that she couldn't make out. In any case, Liesel had heard enough. Old maid, indeed. *I may well be at the shore, but Miss Burnbaum is on the other end of the pier.*

With that thought, Liesel retrieved her purse, then left the office, glad there was just one more day to the workweek and then Sunday. A day of rest.

CHAPTER *Eleven*

DAVID de Serre left the Treasury building and headed back across the street to his own office. Another three hours wasted. Three hours of looking through old evidence that had led to the suspicion of linking von Woerner to Luedke—but not one piece that would keep them in jail if David authorized their arrest. He'd have to come up with some solid evidence soon, or they might suspect they were being watched and flee.

The New York police called it pure luck that they had been able to arrest a number of Germans planting incendiaries on outgoing vessels. One of the devices had been placed on a ship set for a voyage to Archangel, but the ship had evidently been diverted to Marseilles, a shorter journey. When the hull was cleaned out, they found the incendiary rigged to set fire later in what was to have been a longer voyage. David chose to believe the hand of God had directed them to the devious device that could have caused such havoc.

What David needed was a break like that. The evidence they had on von Woerner was still nothing more than coincidence except for minor infractions like speaking engagements that could be construed as seditious. But if David sent Josef von Woerner to jail, he was determined to keep the man there until the end of the war.

So far, though, the ships that had suspicious fires or rudder damage either sank after the crew abandoned or were so badly damaged they left no trace of what caused the problem to begin with. But David was sure the devices were identical to the ones German spies had used more than a year ago.

Maybe his break would come through a new source. It had been nearly a week since he'd spoken to Liesel Bonner, more than enough time to have let the information he'd shared simmer. It was time to check the progress.

Saturday morning, the last day of the workweek. Perhaps Miss Bonner wouldn't mind an unexpected Saturday evening visit.

––––––––––––

Liesel set aside her purse, curiously viewing the stack of material dwarfing her desk. It was quite a heap, overflowing into boxes stacked on either side so that her chair had even less room than normal.

"Good morning," said Miss Burnbaum cheerfully from behind. She must have been in Uncle Otto's office, since her neat oak desk had been empty when Liesel had passed it a moment ago. Liesel turned to her with a question.

"What's all this?" She hoped she didn't sound quite as skeptical as she felt, this being the first work sent her way all week.

"Mr. von Woerner tells me you're looking for some extra work." Miss Burnbaum's thin face looked even more pinched this morning despite the bold red rouge and lipstick that stood out on her rather sallow complexion. "So I am only too happy to accommodate you."

Liesel's brows rose with unexpected delight. "Looks like quite a project. What am I to do?"

"I had the janitor bring these up from the basement. They're sales files. They need to be recorded. In here," she added, handing her a ledger.

"Closed accounts?" Liesel repeated as she saw one stamped in bold, red letters.

"That's right."

"But why—"

Miss Burnbaum, who had already backed away, spun around. "You asked for more work, Miss Bonner. I hardly think it's appropriate to question the type."

With that, she turned back on her heel and left Liesel's closet.

Liesel pulled on the cord to the single, bald electric light that hung just above her desk. It cast the same neat tent of illumination it always did except that with all the new stacks, quite a shadow fell on the workspace Liesel normally used in the center of the desk. Carefully rearranging the workload, she rummaged through the files. She looked for dates, common names, or cities to sort them into some semblance of order. That took some time, since the files appeared as though they'd never been sorted.

It was nearly the lunch hour before she was ready to start tabulating the information. The work was tedious and repetitious, something that any bright child of her sister Greta's nine years might accomplish quite competently. Nonetheless, Liesel offered no complaint. At least she was working. She went to lunch and returned promptly to her office, plodding through the afternoon and determined to work through the fatigue of such a boring task.

On the trolley ride home that evening, Liesel couldn't help but be thankful it was Saturday. Monday would come soon enough, but for the moment she would enjoy the prospect of not seeing a glimpse of Miss Burnbaum for the next twenty-four hours.

"Busy week?" her father asked, startling Liesel from her relaxed position. She lifted her head from its resting place on the back of the trolley bench.

"Not especially so," she admitted, then added hopefully, "I think it'll take some time before Miss Burnbaum shares any important duties."

Her father nodded. "*Ja.* That Miss Burnbaum has been with Otto many years. She's probably used to doing things her own way."

Liesel didn't elaborate on the accuracy of her father's statement, although any number of examples quickly came to mind. Her father himself had modeled giving others the benefit of the doubt, treating them with the charity Jesus Himself had practiced. So she remained silent.

Giving others the benefit of the doubt reminded Liesel of another topic warring to fill her mind. And that, of course, was even less possible to talk about. All week it had lurked behind her thoughts, waiting to be allowed attention. Such thoughts were hardest to elude during mundane moments, as during the monotony of that day's work or during a trolley ride. After a week of struggle, she now found it all inescapable.

Liesel looked at her father's familiar profile. What would he say if she simply blurted out that the U.S. government suspected Josef of being a traitor? He would laugh. It *was* ludicrous. There were times this week when she'd wanted to have a good laugh over the whole thing herself.

"I wonder when Josef will be home," she said.

"I'm sure you'll be the first to know," her father replied, his old blue eyes twinkling her way.

"What do you think about Josef, Papa?" she asked.

Her father looked at her, that teasing aura replaced by obvious consternation. "What kind of question is that? Josef is Josef!"

"But what do you think of him? I mean, what do you like about him? What do you not like about him? *Do* you like him, or should I say, would you like him if he wasn't Otto's son?"

Her father shook his head and held up the palm of one hand to quiet her barrage of questions. "What's all this? Do you miss him and just want to talk about him? Go find a girlfriend."

She laughed. "Oh, Papa. I don't want to talk girl talk. I want your opinion. After all, you're my father. Aren't you supposed to give your blessing if your daughter is going to marry somebody?"

His father looked at her with raised brows. "Has he asked you?"

Liesel broke her gaze from his. "Well, no. Not yet. But let's just assume he will. What would you think?"

He cocked his head to one side, as if considering her as someone he'd just met. "I don't know why you're asking such silly questions, Liesel. Josef has been like a son to me all these years. Even if you and he do not marry, he will still be part of the family. Although," he added, "I doubt he'll come around much if you marry someone else."

"Why do you say that?" she asked. "It's not as if anyone else has come calling."

Papa shrugged. "Only that Josef is taking his time about asking, that's all."

Miss Burnbaum's words came immediately to mind. "Papa, do you think I'm going to be an old maid?"

He fanned his palm her way as if to shoo her words away. "Now you need that girlfriend."

Liesel gave him a grimace, then looked out of the window. She knew she could have had opportunities other than Josef. Somehow, though, she'd assumed she'd be Josef's wife, eventually. He was good to her; he was fun to be with. He was comfortable. He was . . . well, *Josef.* And she trusted him.

For the first time, she found herself questioning that thought.

Her father patted her hand, drawing back her attention. "If Josef doesn't ask soon, maybe you should stop giving him your time whenever he's home. Maybe you should see someone else. You ask your mama what you should do. There are plenty of young men at church who would follow you around if you let them. That Mr. Miller seems eager."

Liesel looked away. Mr. Miller was hardly her idea of a prospective beau, and if she had to choose between him and Josef, she would wait a few more years for Josef. But she didn't welcome such a thought. Was she settling for Josef because there was no one else of interest in her life? Was she so comfortable with Josef that she would be content to share the rest of her life with him? Where was the romance in that?

Liesel frowned. She hadn't had doubts about Josef before. Why was she doubting her feelings for him now? All week, she'd maintained that the accusations of Agent de Serre against Josef were ridiculous. She still believed that.

She wished Josef were home. But in the same moment, she was relieved he wasn't. She knew she'd be tempted to tell him everything Mr. de Serre had said, and she couldn't. Agent de Serre's warnings had been all too clear.

As they came to their stop and stepped off the trolley, Liesel eyed her father again. How good it would be to hear him say Josef was a decent and honorable man. Of course he couldn't be involved in the underhanded ways of a traitor. She would take comfort in having such thoughts confirmed.

But she could only sigh and keep her thoughts to herself.

The sun was low but still warm and bright when they rounded the corner of their street. Liesel would be glad to be home.

Just then, she caught sight of a familiar yellow roadster. It sat at the curb just outside her family home. Empty.

Hurriedly looking around for the owner of that motorcar, Liesel's steps grew reluctant. What was he doing at her house? Had he the audacity to go into her home and inquire after her?

Despite the fact that she'd fallen a few paces behind, once her father reached the porch, Liesel raced past him and entered their home first. Without stopping to remove her gloves or discard her purse, Liesel burst into the parlor, where she found her mother, the twins, and Greta all sitting rather stiffly in front of Agent de Serre. He was ensconced in Papa's chair, lemonade in one hand and his other hand resting on his knee.

Upon sight of Liesel, Mama jumped from her seat with the suddenness of a woman far younger. On her face was a mixture of something akin to alarm, excitement, and curiosity.

"Liesel, your friend David de Serre has come to visit you."

Papa entered the room behind Liesel, who mirrored only curiosity.

David de Serre rose from the chair, a half-empty glass of lemonade still in hand. He looked to find a place for his glass, eyeing the small mahogany table that shone under the hard polishing efforts of Liesel's mama. But upon touching the bottom of the glass and finding it wet, he pulled back. The unsophisticated movement might have been a sweet insight to the man if it had been anyone other than David de Serre. He approached Liesel and greeted her with what appeared to be a rather shy smile.

"I'm sorry to have arrived unannounced," he told her, speaking as if no one else were in the room. "But I was hoping to take you to dinner tonight."

"Oh! A date!" Greta's childish voice was followed by a giggle, and Liesel wished she were close enough to silence her little sister. "What's Josef gonna say? I thought Josef was your tootsie-wootsie?"

"Ah, Greta!" said Mama. "Tootsie-wootsie! You listen too many times to the songs in the park."

Greta giggled and looked up at Agent de Serre. "Do you know what a tootsie-wootsie is?"

He rubbed his chin. "Let's see. Well, a tootsie is a toe, isn't it? Let's count all the little tootsies."

She giggled again. "No, silly. A tootsie-wootsie is a boyfriend!"

"Oh." He leaned over and half-covered his mouth, whispering loud enough for all to hear. "And your sister already has one of those?"

Greta nodded.

"Well, then I guess all I can be is a friend who happens to be a boy. Is that okay? But I like the sound of that word. What did you call it? Tooty-fruity?"

She laughed. "Tootsie-wootsie! You're funny."

"Come along, Greta," said Mama as she pulled the child from the room.

"What's wrong?" Greta asked loudly. "What did I say? I just think he ought to know she's already got a boyfriend. I *like* him." Her questions faded away as the kitchen door swung shut.

Mortified, Liesel looked up at David de Serre. His presence never failed to disarm her. Having her entire family suddenly present to witness that only added to her discomfort.

"Well," de Serre said, his gaze going from Liesel to her father, who stood silently. Then the agent shifted the lemonade to his left hand, wiping his right hand dry before extending it to Papa for a handshake. "My name is David de Serre, sir. I met your daughter through the railroad."

"Oh?" he asked, looking from David to Liesel. "Would you like to come in and sit down again, or have you had enough of this family already? I don't blame you if you have, Mr. de Serre. We're hard to take all at once if you're not used to a lot of talking. Liesel," he said to her, "why don't you take Mr. de Serre's lemonade? I think he's finished with it."

Mechanically, Liesel did as her father suggested, glad for the moment to slip into the kitchen to discard the glass. There she found Mama still holding Greta, who looked eager to get back to the parlor. Liesel didn't know what to say.

Mama let go of Greta and came to stand in front of Liesel.

"Do you know this man well, *Liebchen?*" Mama asked. "Do you want to go to dinner with him?"

Liesel looked down at Mama's concerned countenance, wishing she could tell her everything about him. No, she did not want to go to dinner, but she couldn't begin to explain all the reasons. She knew he wouldn't just disappear, though, and that she had little choice but to go with him. And since the last thing she wanted was for either of her parents to worry, she forced herself to sound cheerful.

"Yes, Mama. He's a nice man."

Mama's brows rose as if considering her words. Then she frowned anew. "Ah, but *Liebchen,* what about Josef?"

Liesel frowned. "What about him?"

"What will he think about this?"

"Yes, Liesel, what *will* Josef think?" Greta asked, eyes gleaming. She was at the door, already peeking out toward the parlor.

"Oh, nothing at all," Liesel answered, growing more irritated by the moment. "It's as Mr. de Serre said; we're friends."

"It's the best of friends who end up married." Mama shook her head, putting a palm to one cheek. Her eyes still looked worried as she pulled Greta away from the door. "I don't know, Liesel. If he's such a nice man, why does he ask to take you to dinner if he knows about Josef? You told him, didn't you?"

"He knows."

Mama then took Greta's place and peeked around the kitchen door, where, from over her head, Liesel caught a glimpse of de Serre still standing just a few feet from Papa. Closing the door, Mama turned back to Liesel.

"He's a nice-looking young fellow," she commented.

"I hardly noticed, Mama."

"Oh, really?" she said, taking Greta's hand once again, as if anticipating the nine-year-old scooting out. "Well, watch your heart, then. Some things we don't notice sneak up on us."

"Oh, Mama!" said Liesel, exasperated. She left the kitchen, and everyone looked at her as she approached the parlor archway. It appeared she was supposed to say or do something, although she hadn't the aplomb to know what.

"Well?" her father said after a moment. He hadn't taken his regular seat and still stood near Mr. de Serre just under the parlor entranceway arch.

Liesel looked at him expectantly, wondering to what he was referring. She knew she must appear the absolute dunce, but she hadn't the faintest idea what to do next.

Her father spoke again. "Don't leave the poor man wondering, Liesel. Are you going to dinner with him or not?"

Liesel could have smacked her own forehead. "Of course. Yes," she mumbled, realizing she still wore her gloves and her purse had never left her hand. "Yes, of course."

"Very well, then!" To Mr. de Serre, Papa said, "There's a nice little place just two blocks west of here. Mario's. I know, I know. What's an Italian restaurant doing in this German neighborhood? Go and try the food, and you'll find out. Besides," he added in a whisper that Liesel could nonetheless hear, "I know the owner and every waiter there. I don't often let my children go out with people who are strangers to me, Mr. de Serre. Short of accompanying you myself, this is the next best thing." He sounded friendly and firm all at once.

"I understand," Mr. de Serre said.

Papa walked them to the door, and in a moment Liesel was on the porch with Mr. de Serre. Papa watched them descend to the street, waving at them from the doorway.

Still bemused over the complete surprise at finding this government agent enmeshed in the center of her family, Liesel let him open the car door, and she slipped inside, waving at her father.

Mr. de Serre drove away from the curb, and Liesel stared at him, waiting for him to explain why he was here.

"Do you like Italian food?"

"What?" she asked.

"Italian food. Do you like it?"

She nodded, temporarily distracted by the question. "Of course. Who doesn't? What were you doing at my house?"

"I thought it was obvious," he said, looking at the road as he navigated a turn. "Let's see, two blocks west. I'm not as familiar with this neighborhood as you are. I've never been to Mario's."

"Mr. de Serre, what are you doing here?"

"Taking you to dinner. I'm glad you like Italian food. I don't think your father would take it very well if I took you anywhere else."

"And just how will he take it when he finds out the only reason we met to begin with is because you wanted to have me arrested?"

He laughed, evidently so comfortable he was enjoying himself. "I didn't, though, did I? He'd thank me for that."

"And will he thank you for trying to coerce me into helping you trap our family friend?"

He was already stopped at an intersection. The neighborhood was quiet as the sun began to set, and there was no other traffic around. Setting the car into neutral, he turned completely toward her with a frown on his handsome face.

"Is that what you think I'm doing?"

Liesel hesitated but only for a moment. "Aren't you?"

He turned back to the wheel, but he only put his hands on the leather covering, not shifting back into gear. "Yes," he said after a moment. "That's exactly what I came to do." Then he let out a slow breath, looking at her again. "That, and to remind you not to tell anyone what I told you the other day. I thought perhaps it might be something you'd want to discuss with someone. Someone in your family, or a friend, or Josef himself."

"I haven't seen Josef all week," she told him.

"I know. He's in New York."

It shouldn't have surprised her to learn he knew of Josef's whereabouts. Yet she deeply resented the fact that the U.S. government knew the location of the man everyone accepted as her boyfriend when she didn't know the first thing about how to contact him.

Mr. de Serre put the car back into gear and continued toward the restaurant. They were there in moments.

Several neighbors were enjoying a Saturday evening out, and Liesel acknowledged those who would not be ignored. Briefly, she wondered what they must think. She'd been to this very restaurant many times with Josef.

Giorgio, a waiter familiar to Liesel, took their order. Liesel was determined to regain the composure she'd lost the moment she'd spotted that sporty yellow Packard.

"Miss Bonner," Agent de Serre said when the waiter left, leaning close to the checkered tablecloth. He spoke low so that no one but Liesel could hear over the musicians in the corner. "I know that I'm the last person you want to see. But I can't disregard your help just so you can live in the comfort of ignorance. And you shouldn't want to."

Liesel folded her arms on the table in front of her, eyeing him. "Just what makes you suspect Josef, Mr. de Serre? I've heard about how eager the government is to catch spies even when they're not really spies. Guilt or innocence seems of little importance just so long as the people you're after are German."

He leaned back and folded his arms across his chest. "Do you think I've fabricated my case against Josef?"

"I'm sure it wouldn't be the first time." She sounded so sure, yet she knew her argument was tenuous even as she proposed it. She'd only heard the rumors, had no evidence of how common it was, and certainly no evidence that Mr. de Serre himself was involved in such cases.

He leaned forward again. "I will ignore your mistrust of me because you've been treated badly by others," he said. "The job hunt and all. It mustn't be easy these days for German Americans."

She looked at him in disbelief. The name David de Serre sounded every bit as Allied as Katherine Harris. He couldn't know the first thing about how hard it was.

"But I do have evidence against Josef. And in spite of what you might think, I do not go around arresting every German I see."

"Otherwise you would have arrested me?"

He shrugged just as their food was delivered.

When they were alone again, facing two steaming plates of spaghetti, Liesel spoke in a low but firm voice. "What kind of evidence?"

"Other than your friend's associates and the sightings of him near the docks—where he could have no possible legal business—and the fact that we recently found proof that he took a job in a company which ended up on strike, I saw him myself, posing as Andrew Nesbit. He gave a rather impassioned speech about every man's duty to live in pride, not die at the hands of mercenary warmongers who delight in war simply because it keeps the factories busy."

She shook her head at the news, ignoring her food even as Mr. de Serre dug into his own. "I'm sure you're mistaken, sir. Josef is a salesman, not a speechmaker."

He set aside his fork long enough to pull from his pocket a palm-sized photograph and hand it to her. "That's your Josef, isn't it?"

Liesel looked at the picture. It was Josef, all right, with other men she didn't know. They carried posters about stopping the flow of armaments to belligerent countries and other anti-war sentiments.

"They're picketing a munitions plant," David explained. "Two weeks later that plant was on strike, with strike funds fueled in from outside the union."

"Fueled in? By someone just wanting the strike to continue, you mean?"

"Exactly. And that's illegal."

Liesel handed the photograph back, seeing her hand tremble as she did. Mr. de Serre let the photograph rest beside his plate.

Liesel watched de Serre take up his fork and spoon again, expertly twirling the long strands of spaghetti around the fork. He smiled, allowing the utensil to pause on its way upward as if in an invitation for her to try her own. Liesel marveled at how outwardly calm he appeared. Of course, why

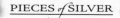
should he be the least bit nervous? This was just a case to him, a job. It didn't matter one bit that he kept chipping away at Josef's whole life, the Josef she thought she knew well enough to marry.

She looked down at her plate, and her stomach turned in aversion even as it growled with hunger.

"It's good," he said. "I grew up on all kinds of food, but my family never had an Italian chef."

"Your family had a chef?" The question slipped out between her waves of nervousness.

He nodded. "My mother didn't cook."

"Was she ill?"

He shook his head, taking another bite and chewing before answering. "No, she just didn't like to be in the kitchen."

Liesel felt her brows knit together. She couldn't possibly be interested in this man's personal life but couldn't seem to help herself from asking more questions. "Why?"

He shrugged. "I don't know. Actually, I don't know her very well. Let's just say we shared the same roof, but it was a very large roof, and I didn't see her much." Then he said, "I was in college before I tasted spaghetti for the first time, and it's been one of my favorites ever since. How is yours?"

She looked down at the unsampled fare before her; she knew Mario made the best spaghetti in town. Seeing Mr. de Serre relaxed and talking so casually about other subjects made the growl in her stomach stronger than the ache. She took a first bite.

"Do you like Spanish food?" he asked after a moment. "Rice and tamales and tortillas?"

"I don't know," she said. "I've never had it."

"If you ever get the opportunity, don't pass it up."

"So your Spanish chef was your favorite?" she asked.

He shook his head. "No, we never had a Spanish one, either. French, mostly. My mother is Belgian with ties to French traditions. We had an occasional Oriental chef when my parents felt like impressing someone with their flamboyance, and one Greek. Oh, and of course we had a German chef for a while. Hilda. She made excellent blintze."

That they sat discussing food seemed ridiculous as she caught sight of the photo of Josef. She put down her fork and said, "I'm really not very comfortable, Mr. de Serre. I'd like to go home."

He took up the photograph, setting aside his fork. Placing the picture in his inner pocket, he took a long swallow of water, wiped his mouth with his napkin, then sat perfectly still, looking at her.

"Miss Bonner, what do you think about all of this? Do you really believe I've made this up?"

Liesel wanted to proclaim that's exactly what she thought—how she wished she could. But she couldn't. She shook her head, looking away from him.

Peripherally, she saw him lean closer. "I know very little about you, except that this must be very painful for you."

Too confused to know what to say or feel, she only knew she could hardly commiserate with him.

"You love God and want to serve your country, don't you?"

She nodded.

"Then serve your country by bringing this man to justice."

Seeing how convinced he was only intensified her confusion.

"Miss Bonner." His voice was little more than a whisper. "We must stop anyone interfering with government work. If he's guilty of stirring up strikes and sinking ships, he's hurting our country's production when we need it most."

Liesel looked at him at last. "If you think he's sunk ships . . ." She stopped herself, then started again because she had to know. "Has he . . . hurt anyone?" She had to ask, even though doing so revealed the possibility of accepting Josef's guilt.

The importance of the question was not lost on de Serre; she could tell by the look on his face. Shaking his head, he gave her a small smile. "No. Not yet. But that doesn't mean it won't happen. It's bound to with the explosives he's using. With America's involvement going forward at full speed, he's bound to get bolder. If his loyalties are as strong as they appear, then we're now his enemy. He'll do whatever it takes to prevent us from helping the Allies."

Liesel rested her forehead on one of her hands, shaking her head. One feeble part of her clung to Josef's innocence. "It can't be. Not Josef."

"It is."

Liesel didn't know when she'd begun to doubt Josef and believe Mr. de Serre. Certainly she hadn't believed a word when Mr. de Serre first came to her. She thought him mistaken, the whole notion ridiculous. But day after day, the doubts would not go away. Tonight, there seemed no other explanation. Josef had been seen in person by Mr. de Serre, posing as someone else. And then that photograph. That and the loyalty she knew Josef had toward Germany pointed in the same direction. Mr. de Serre might have the right man.

"Josef is idealistic." She looked at Mr. de Serre. "Whatever he has done—if he's done anything—I'm sure he believes he is doing the right thing."

"That may well be true," de Serre said. "The German network has been successfully persuasive, especially among the German reservists in this country. They are far more organized than I'd expected. That's where you can help me."

Liesel shook her head and stayed him with her hand. "No, Mr. de Serre. I may accept that Josef could be loosely, remotely involved in something he shouldn't be, but that doesn't mean I've agreed to help you."

Mr. de Serre visibly stiffened, clearing his throat and looking away as if embarrassed. "Of course. But please understand this, Miss Bonner. What von Woerner is doing is illegal. It's no less than your duty to do what you can to stop him."

Liesel nodded, although she wanted to do anything but. She wanted to cry. She wanted to leave. She wanted to go to Josef and confront him, talk sense into him if that's what he needed. She wanted to believe in him again. To trust him again.

"Would you like to go for a walk?" de Serre asked at last. "I can leave the Packard here, and we can walk back to your parent's house."

She nodded again.

Outside, the air was warm but refreshing. She walked slowly. Home suddenly didn't seem the refuge it normally was. Knowing what she knew, unable to talk about it . . .

"Is it information you need, Mr. de Serre?" she asked at last. Perhaps knowing what he wanted would help.

"In some ways, yes. He's an elusive man. He has a talent for disappearing and reappearing after the trouble is in full swing. Now that you have knowledge of what we suspect, is there anything you've ever seen him do, anything he's said or referred to that may lend support to our case?"

"I haven't seen him carrying about any explosives, if that's what you mean." She couldn't disguise the caustic note in her voice.

"But you'll let me know if you do?" he asked, and his voice had a teasing lilt to it, as if he were trying to counter her resistance with charm. "What I need," he continued quietly, almost gently, "is knowledge about his banking habits lately. We think he's dealing mostly with cash to avoid creating additional banking records. But he must have a record somewhere, and we need evidence. Knowledge when he's carrying great sums of money, something along those lines."

Liesel stared ahead. "Josef never talks about business with me. Of course, he always has cash with him. . . . He comes from a wealthy family." That admission was just one more piece against Josef, but Liesel guessed it was nothing new to Mr. de Serre. Josef had the resources to do everything he was accused of. She glanced at Mr. de Serre, once again overwhelmed by the situation. "I'm sorry. This is all such a shock. It still is, even if I'm starting to believe it's true."

They stopped on the sidewalk, looking at each other. His dark eyes as he looked down at her were full of concern. "This changes your life, doesn't it, Miss Bonner?"

She was nodding before she knew what she was doing. Would she allow herself to be soothed by the man chasing Josef?

"When you left the railroad that day, you had a Bible under your arm," he said softly. "I remember because when I referred to a verse, you knew it immediately, even quoted it to me. Every time there's a bend in the road, the wisest thing is to look up. Look up first, Miss Bonner. God will direct you around the bend."

She couldn't help but smile, sad though she felt. She'd trusted Josef once, expected the truth from him. Maybe she hadn't looked up enough. Maybe she'd put her trust in the wrong place.

They started walking again. "Do you read the Bible, then, Mr. de Serre?"

"Yes, I do. As often as I can these days. Which regrettably isn't as often as I'd like."

"And do you pray?"

He nodded, putting his hands in his pockets as they continued down the street.

"Do you pray for the wisdom to go after the right suspects?"

"Yes, I do."

Liesel sighed. That was more than she could hope for. At least Josef wasn't being hunted by someone only after blood.

"Actually, Josef reminds me of two people in the Bible," de Serre said after a moment.

Liesel raised surprised brows his way, waiting for him to elaborate.

"Peter and Judas."

"Judas I suppose I can understand," she said reluctantly. "But why Peter?"

"They both betrayed Jesus, remember? Peter on the night of Jesus's arrest, when he denied knowing Him three times. He loved Jesus, yet he betrayed Him."

"How does that remind you of Josef?"

"Because Peter made a mistake. He betrayed Jesus out of fear and confusion. He didn't think through what he was doing. Perhaps something like

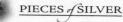

that happened to your Josef. Evidently he has been raised with loyalty to Germany, not America, even though he might love America."

"How do you know that?"

"By learning about his father. I assume he came here for his businesses, which reportedly thrive. But he never cared to apply for citizenship, which I assume is because he considers himself still German. Perhaps Josef does, too, even though by being born here he automatically became an American."

Liesel didn't want to admit just how insightful were his observations.

"So," he continued after a moment, "is your Josef a Peter or a Judas? Does he betray his lord—in this case not Jesus but America—out of loyalty to another lord—Germany—or simply because he's mercenary and the German pockets go deep for this kind of work? Both Peter and Judas felt guilty over their actions, Miss Bonner. But while Judas made the mistake of ignoring God, Peter repented and cried out for forgiveness that Jesus freely gave. And we both know how their lives turned out: Peter spread the gospel as a great apostle."

"And Judas went out and hanged himself," Liesel added in a whisper.

Liesel's thoughts crashed into one another like waves to shore, leaving nothing tangible to catch hold of, nothing with which she could draw any conclusions.

When her mass of thought was too much to entertain alone any longer, she spoke. "What can Josef do to get out of trouble, Mr. de Serre?"

He glanced down at her, a look of sympathy on his face. "I'm afraid if he's guilty of treason, there's very little he can do to avoid some kind of punishment. Some of it depends on how deeply he's involved. If he's just been a vessel through which the Germans have poured money to others doing the dirty work . . . well, that's one thing. If he's doing some of the dirty work himself or if it's his own money he's using, he may get off with a stiff monetary fine and a relatively light term in jail. That's the best he can hope for."

"Jail!"

"Believe me, that's his best hope."

"What is the worst that could happen to him?" she asked firmly.

He didn't look at her as he answered, "Oh, just a long jail term, likely."

Suddenly forgetting all semblance of propriety, as if she'd totally forgotten she walked with a virtual stranger, she grabbed his arm. She'd read enough books to know what happened to traitors in the Civil War not so long ago. One of their neighbors still talked about it.

"They can . . . they can kill him, can't they? The government, I mean! They can shoot him by a firing squad or hang him for treason."

Mr. de Serre put two steady hands on her shoulders. His touch was a welcome anchor to Liesel's trembling body. "That is an extreme case reserved for the most notorious criminals these days. Josef hasn't killed anybody. I doubt very much any trial lawyer would ask for such a punishment."

"But people are so zealous! If he were arrested as a traitor, a German American traitor, imagine what a lynch mob would do." She turned away, walking and shaking her head as the awful images played out in her mind. "If Josef has done anything," she called back, "anything at all, we must help him before he gets into any more trouble."

He easily caught up to her. "Help him, Miss Bonner?"

She stopped, confused. "Well, stop him of course."

"Then I can count on you to help me?"

Liesel could not speak. Her throat was so tight she thought she'd never be able to take another breath. How could she agree to work against Josef? This was Josef they talked about, not some stranger.

"I don't know," was all she could choke out.

They turned the block, nearing her parent's house. Mr. de Serre spoke quietly. "I hope that you will decide to work with me, Miss Bonner." His tone was distant, aloof. "You would be paid by the government, of course. Seven dollars a day for an informant's fee. It's a job, after all. Think it over."

Then he turned and left, and Liesel watched him go. For a long while she simply stood there, bled dry of emotion. *Josef. Oh, Josef.*

It wasn't until she turned toward her home that she considered his words and some residue of feeling returned—all unwelcome. Work for the government for a fee? How could she do such a thing? She couldn't, of course. She just couldn't. Informant's fee, indeed. Who would be the Judas then?

CHAPTER *Twelve*

JOSEF rested his head against the cool glass window on the early morning train. The sun barely peeked over the horizon, and the sky was pink, promising rain later in the day. Soon he would be on his way back home again. He'd already been gone longer than he liked. His latest sales trip began in New York two weeks ago and went on to Virginia. Now he was headed back to New York to see one more client, then pick up his Bearcat, and return home at last. His trip, so far, had been a most successful venture. He closed his eyes in repose.

Just two days ago, he'd caught a train from New York and traveled south to Norfolk. The trains between the two stations had buzzed with military personnel. Civilians like himself were at best ignored, at worst bumped to less suitable routes and generally treated as an inconvenience. Posters at the stations challenged civilians with such phrases as, *Are you sure you need to travel?* And the bolder one: *Get out of the way for our soldiers!*

But Josef was hardly deterred. His business was as important to him as transporting all those troops was to the government.

Soon, though, he could go home. He would see Liesel, the one safe and comfortable haven life held these days.

"Miss Bonner! Miss Bonner!"

Liesel heard her name from behind. She stood outside church with her parents and siblings but knew from the voice that it was not a summons for little Greta.

Turning, she saw Mr. Miller wave at her. With a glance to her parents, also looking to see who called, she said to them quietly, "Please wait, won't you?"

Her family loitered just beyond the church grounds as Liesel met Mr. Miller.

"Thank you for stopping, Miss Bonner," said Mr. Miller, out of breath. His spectacles had slipped down his nose during his brief jog to catch up to her, and he adjusted them before speaking again. "I just wanted to ask you . . . that is, I hope you won't mind if I ask you . . ." As he struggled with words between stammers and stutters, he removed his straw summer hat and glanced over Liesel's shoulders at her parents. Liesel turned and caught a glimpse of them as well. Her mother watched them openly, although she was beyond hearing range, while her father spared only an occasional glance as he stood with Greta, swinging their arms back and forth as if playing London Bridge with an imaginary "fair lady."

"The church picnic is coming up next Sunday, Miss Bonner," said Mr. Miller, who found his voice at last. "I was wondering, that is, I was hoping you—and your family, of course—will be there."

"Yes," she replied. "We're planning on it. My mother is in the quilting bee, and they're going to raffle off one of their quilts to raise money for war bonds. And my father is judging the mustache competition."

"Oh, yes, of course. But I wanted to be sure . . . you'll be there, won't you?"

She nodded.

"Then may I, that is, would you mind terribly if I come by to escort you? I haven't a motorcar of my own, but I plan to borrow a friend's for the day. A genuine Pierce-Arrow, Miss Bonner. It'll be quite a ride; I can promise you that."

Liesel shook her head. "I'm sorry, Mr. Miller, but I believe our family friend will be back in town by then. Mr. von Woerner. He'll be escorting me—with the family, of course."

"Oh. Oh, yes, of course." He still grasped his straw hat, rotating it by its round rim. "I understand. But won't Mr. von Woerner's motorcar be crowded, what with your whole family? Are you sure you won't reconsider?"

"No, Mr. Miller. I'm sorry."

"Well," he said, sucking in a deep breath, "perhaps he'll be able to make more room next week by getting rid of those bundles in his trunk."

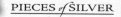

Liesel looked at him, perplexed. "Bundles in the trunk?"

"Yes, Miss Bonner. The bandages the church ladies made for the Red Cross. They must still be in his trunk since the Red Cross never received them."

Liesel heard the words and felt her insides go cold, then hot—so hot she thought perhaps she would faint. But her feet held her upright even though the rest of her quivered. She remembered the day Josef had cajoled her out of delivering the bandages together. "He was to have dropped them off before his business trip, but he's been gone quite some time." Her voice sounded far away, as if someone else were talking for her.

Mr. Miller nodded, but there was something in his eyes that looked as if he didn't believe a word she said. Liesel had the distinct impression he was somehow accusing her or Josef of something. Nonsense.

Feeling compelled to explain, defend, justify, Liesel spoke quickly. "I'm sure he forgot, or perhaps he dropped them off at another Red Cross collection depot on his travels. In any case, Mr. Miller, I will check on it myself just as soon as I can. Thank you for mentioning it."

"Of course." He sounded somewhat smug.

"Good day," Liesel said, then turned and walked briskly away, right past her family. By the time they realized she was finished with her conversation, she was already several paces past them.

"You should have let me drive you," David said to his old friend Mio, who held a single duffel bag over his shoulder, containing the few personal belongings he would take. Behind him waited his family: his wife, Anna, and their boys. They all stood near the train that would take Mio away.

Mio shook his head. "Would have taken you from your job."

Saying good-bye was something neither man did very well. When David had left home for college, they'd done nothing more than wave, though they'd been like brothers their entire lives—even after the death of Mio's father. By the time David had returned home from college, Mio was off to seminary, and for a short time before Mio married Anna, David and Mio had shared a room just outside Washington. On the day Mio got married, their farewell to each other had consisted of another simple wave.

But this was different. Going off to college or to live a new life with his bride was altogether different from going off to a battleground, even if the first stop was training camp, an orientation of sorts for Red Triangles in the YMCA. David felt the sharp contrast from other good-byes and knew a wave wouldn't be enough.

"Mio," he said, knowing Anna stood waiting with the boys, giving them a minute alone. "I just want to tell you. What you're doing. It's a good thing."

Mio laughed and punched David's arm with good nature. "Well, a compliment from the stoic David de Serre! Wish I kept a journal. I'd record the day. Hey," he added, more serious. "I took out a war risk life insurance policy, you know, just in case. Five thousand dollars. You'll help Anna, won't you, and the boys in case. . . . They'll need a man to look up to. You're the one who can fill that bill, my friend."

In that moment, David decided being left behind in a war was perhaps harder than going off to battle: action had a way of using up the energy created by fear. He couldn't get another word out if one tried to choke its way from his tight throat.

Suddenly David couldn't wait to get back to work.

Mio reached out and took David's hand in a firm grasp. "You fight 'em over here, and I'll stand behind those fighting 'em over there, and between us and God, we'll get this business finished. Right?"

David nodded, raising his free hand to clasp Mio's shoulder. "Right."

Anna stepped forward, and Mio turned to embrace her. The two boys, seeing their mother suddenly cry, wiggled in to create a tight little circle, and David watched with a mix of love and awe and a touch of envy at seeing such a composite of family. He'd been single too long.

Rather than going straight home, David went to his office. He didn't have a key to the four-story building, but the department had added another night watchman for security reasons so he didn't have long to wait for someone to let him in. David finished several reports that night, updating events related to the cases in which he was involved. He held the last file in his hands for quite some time. Liesel Bonner. The name was scrawled in his own handwriting on the top.

He was tired. He should go home. Nonetheless, he opened the file and went over once more the information he'd collected. Not one slender thread of evidence indicated she'd ever been involved in von Woerner's work. He knew that now without having to go over the file; he knew it not just on faith but something deeper. Like the way he knew God was there; it wasn't just faith. Something inside him told him the truth. He knew it. So it went with Liesel Bonner. She was an innocent.

So why didn't she want to help? Do her duty? Just in the last week, they had found a witness ready to testify that von Woerner worked at his factory up until that factory went on strike. Von Woerner was more than just a troublemaker; he interfered with the most vital work this nation did, war work. He had to be stopped. Why didn't she see that?

David knew why. She wasn't weak-minded, oh, anything but that. She was in love. The thought was unaccountably distasteful to him. He chose not to ask himself why, concluding no more than the obvious: that anyone in love with a traitor was bound for trouble.

A sudden, unexpected vision of the kind of family Mio had sprang up in David's mind. A family with a couple of kids just like Mio's. That's all anybody wanted, wasn't it? To be surrounded by family? That's all Miss Bonner wanted, too. Only her problem was that she'd fallen for a guy who sabotaged factories and Allied ships for a living.

Well, that was her mistake, and everyone was entitled to make at least one. He didn't care if she loved the guy until her dying day. It was David's job to help her see her duty.

With a glance at his wristwatch, David determined he'd had enough work for one night. And he determined something else. He'd given Miss Bonner more than enough time to decide what was right. Come morning, he had a job to do, a little prodding, a little coaxing. A little coercion, if necessary. After all, he was doing his duty and expected nothing less from every other American citizen. Including Liesel Bonner.

CHAPTER *Thirteen*

LIESEL stepped out into the late afternoon sun and squinted. When she caught sight of her father, she noticed he stood with her two older brothers on the sidewalk. While she rode to and from the office with her father, it was rare to see both her brothers at the same time.

"Here she is, Miss Burnbaum's nemesis," teased Karl as Liesel approached.

Liesel frowned at brother. "What do you mean?"

"Only that rumor has it she's got you locked away in a storage closet and doles out work like crusts of bread to a prisoner."

Liesel couldn't dispute the description but didn't welcome knowing she was the source of talk among the rest of the factory workers.

"That'll be enough from the gossipmongers," her father said firmly. "Liesel, let's go home."

Just as they were about to head in the opposite direction from Ernst and Karl, Liesel saw a familiar but unwelcome yellow spot of color pull up to the curb.

"Miss Bonner!"

Liesel and her father, as well as her two brothers, looked to the man calling her from behind the wheel of the sporty roadster. Liesel wished she could simply melt into the hot cement sidewalk rather than face Agent de Serre under the close scrutiny of her two older brothers.

She stood still as he left his car and came to stand in front of her. Her brothers stayed put, openly watching. Karl crossed his arms in front of his chest; Ernst shifted from one foot to another. Neither one of them made any attempt to move.

"I'm glad I spotted you," David said. "Can I give you—and your father, of course—a ride home?"

"You just happened to be passing by?" she asked skeptically.

"Well . . . not exactly," he said, smiling first at her, then at her father, then back again at her. "I was hoping I'd see you."

With that, Karl stepped forward, followed closely by Ernst. David looked their way as if noticing them for the first time.

"These are my brothers, Ernst and Karl," Liesel said, somewhat reluctantly. To them she added, "And this is David de Serre."

"David de Serre." Karl repeated the name as they exchanged handshakes, openly assessing David. "Not a familiar name, Liesel. How do you know each other?"

"We met through the railroad," David said before Liesel could. "Liesel and I became acquainted, and I'd like to say we're friends now."

She remained silent.

"So you work for the railroad?" Karl persisted. David was considerably taller than Karl, and Karl's suddenly protective stance seemed almost laughable considering Liesel knew he was probably more concerned over Josef's interests than his sister's reputation.

"I work for the government," David said. "And what I'd like to do right now is offer your sister and father a ride home. Can I offer one to you as well, although it'll be a bit crowded?"

"No, no that's all right," Karl said slowly, still eyeing him. "But I'm sure my father will appreciate avoiding the trolley."

Papa laughed, appearing totally at ease even though Liesel sensed more than a little tension from Karl. Ernst added to her discomfort, the way he stared at Mr. de Serre.

"Well," her father said, "I'll like to get out of paying that nickel. Unless you're going to charge me for the ride? I've heard that's how quite a few auto owners make a decent living these days."

David's smile broadened, evidently just as comfortable as Liesel's father. "No, sir. I don't have a license to charge a fare. Not that I would, anyway."

"Well, let's go then! Come along, Liesel."

Papa got into the car, assigning himself to the small backseat. He complimented the upholstery while adding less charitably that they certainly were economical with space in the rear. When Liesel asked if he would like to switch places, he said he was fine, even though his knees were nearly up to his nose.

"Oh, Papa, change places!" Liesel insisted. She didn't want to ride home with Mr. de Serre in the first place and would certainly like to dodge the front seat.

"No, no," her father insisted. "Mr. de Serre, let's go! I feel twenty years younger already just sitting back here. This is quite the jaunty model, isn't it?"

"It's from 1911. Old enough to be an antique as motors go," David said as he started the engine.

"I'll say! Being so old, it's a good thing it's a Packard."

Liesel remembered a law passed a couple of years ago when she'd first started working for Hodges, Pierson, and Deane. "Because of standardization, you mean?"

Both men looked at her as if they'd forgotten she was there, let alone might want to be involved in the discussion. Her father finally nodded.

Talking about cars was perhaps one of the last things Liesel normally wished to do, although today it served the purpose of diverting her growing agitation over Mr. de Serre's apparent ease, as if he were quickly assimilating himself right into her family. "Why so surprised, gentlemen?" she asked. "Can't a woman know anything about the automobile industry?"

"Well," her father said, "you and I have talked about a great many things daughters and fathers don't often discuss. Politics, the war, business. But never the auto business."

As Mr. de Serre drove down the lane, she looked at her father. "I've worked outside the home for a few years now, Papa. I've learned a little on my own."

"Oh?" He looked every bit as surprised as he had a moment ago.

Turning back to face the street rather than her father, she continued, "I know that auto companies have had to use standard parts since 1915 rather than use anything they feel like."

"That's right," her father said. He stroked the leather seat. "I have never been in one of these Packards. They're pricey. Oh, I've ridden in Otto's Peerless—but it's like traveling in a moving room compared to this. This is like riding a wheel, only without the work! Like a Bearcat!"

Liesel didn't miss the reference to Josef's motorcar, although she was sure her father hadn't particularly intended to remind her of Josef. Still, it served the purpose.

All the way home, her father and de Serre chatted about horsepower and chassis and other such things. Liesel hadn't realized her father knew so much about cars, but she shouldn't have been surprised since he had an engineering background and loved machinery. She, on the other hand, had already revealed the extent of her knowledge of the motor industry and had no great interest in learning more. It irked her to see the two men obviously enjoying one another's company. If her father only knew what Mr. de Serre was really about, how friendly would he be?

Such thoughts brought little comfort. Papa might be shocked by what Mr. de Serre knew, but exactly what would he do? Would he help the government stop a saboteur no matter who that saboteur might be? After all, Papa had chosen the American government as his own.

For nearly two weeks, Liesel had denied the very slimmest of connections between Josef and Mr. de Serre. While her job didn't keep her busy, its frustrations certainly kept her mind occupied. But with Agent de Serre constantly showing up to remind her of everything she was trying to forget, it was impossible to ignore the ugly situation. If he would just go away, if Josef would just stay away, then she could dismiss everything associated with this rotten mess.

When they pulled up to the Bonner home, Liesel jumped from the car before David could get around to assist. He did help her father, however, climb from the rather cramped and unsteady tonneau seat.

"Thank you for the ride, Mr. de Serre," Liesel said curtly as she stood back from the car waiting for her father. "We'll be seeing you."

"Yes, as a matter of fact, I'm sure you will. But stay a moment, won't you, Liesel? Miss Bonner? I won't take more than a few minutes of your time."

As her father pulled himself to his full height, he said to his daughter, "It's the least you can do, Liesel, for the ride. I'll tell Mama we're home." Then he turned to Mr. de Serre. "Thank you for the transportation, sir. And if my daughter were thinking, she would invite you to dinner herself. You're welcome to stay if you're hungry."

"Thank you, Mr. Bonner," he said. "But I think I'll need to discuss that first with your daughter."

"Very well, then," he said. "*Liebchen*, take your time. I'm sure Mama won't have dinner ready yet. We're early thanks to missing all those trolley stops along the way."

Liesel watched her father walk up the steps to their porch and go inside. Of course dinner wouldn't be ready, even if they'd been on time. Mama allowed Papa his one luxury, the daily bath after working inside the factory all day. He was given precisely twenty minutes from the time he walked through the door; then dinner was served while his hair was still wet.

Even so, twenty minutes was more than the amount of time she wished to spend with Agent de Serre.

"Would you care to walk?" he asked.

"No."

"Sit on the porch or perhaps back in the car?"

"Neither."

She did not look at him, but she saw from a side glance that he folded his arms in much the same guarded manner Karl had done just a little while ago.

"Look. You can make this friendly or unfriendly; it doesn't matter to me. I expected to hear from you, Miss Bonner. Why haven't you called?"

She raised a surprised face. "You said yourself you can't force me."

"I spoke too kindly then because that's precisely what I'll do if that's the only way to get your help."

"You haven't the faintest idea what you're asking of me."

"I know exactly what I'm asking, Miss Bonner. I'm asking no more of you than I ask of myself or any other American. I'm asking you to do your duty. Nothing more, nothing less."

"Oh, you think it's just that simple, do you? Just why do you need my help, anyway? Perhaps solid evidence against Josef eludes you because there is no evidence to be found."

"Hardly so. Von Woerner was spotted in Norfolk and then disappeared. Norfolk is a dock town, Liesel. I can only hope he didn't cause too much mischief." He paused, but she felt his gaze still on her. "I understand there is to be some sort of social function at which you are expecting his company by Sunday. Does that mean you've heard from him?"

"How did you . . . ?" She didn't finish her statement; there seemed little point. It suddenly made sense why Henry Miller had shown up at her church, why he'd become so interested in her these days. He'd been the only one she'd told about expecting Josef to take her to the picnic. "So, does Mr. Miller work for you now?"

Mr. de Serre seemed genuinely bewildered for the barest moment. "I can only assume you've had a conversation with one of the local boys in the APL. Yes, Miss Bonner, you're being watched. I can't be everywhere."

Liesel folded her hands into tight little fists, her body tingled with anger. "Just what sort of surveillance are we talking about, Mr. de Serre? I thought I was not under investigation anymore."

"Anyone associated with von Woerner is considered a potential subject. When he contacts you, which I have no doubt he will do, then I will be informed that much quicker. And at this point, that's my main concern."

"This is dreadful!" She turned on her heel.

He caught her by the arm, at first firmly but then, when she looked back at him with nothing but anger, his touch softened.

"Must we be on such icy ground, Liesel?" His voice had lowered to a near whisper.

While "a soft answer turneth away wrath," it took Liesel a moment to feel her anger leave. His face, no longer cold or judgmental, was full of concern. There was even a hint of caring in those dark, handsome eyes. His touch was so gentle he could have been holding back a child. Then he let her go and stood looking at her with intensity and interest, no longer as if she were some kind of object from which he might extract clinical information.

"I'm sorry if I've behaved badly," he said after a moment. "I've been rude, and I apologize. It's the war. It's gotten the whole country on edge, and I'm no exception, especially since my job revolves around people trying to stymie what this country is doing. It's hard to find somebody to trust these days, isn't it? I'm sorry if I've taken my frustrations out on you."

Such an apology was entirely unexpected. Liesel lowered her face, suddenly confused and ashamed of her own behavior. Was she wrong to have ignored the truth for so long? Wrong to have tried to stuff all this away, pretending none of it existed? For days she'd vacillated from one end to the other, one moment convincing herself of Josef's innocence, the next uncertain. Since she'd seen that photograph of Josef picketing, the moments of thinking Josef guilty far outnumbered those hoping he could be innocent.

She'd alternately worried and prayed over the whole matter, wondering what God would have her do. She wondered what God thought of Josef's activities. Was Josef wrong, or did the war justify what he did—if he truly believed himself German and not American? But she had no answers, had come to no conclusions. Her search for God's guidance hadn't brought the peace she longed for—especially when she took the matter back into her feeble hands to worry over.

"It's I who should apologize, Mr. de Serre. You're only doing your job, and I've certainly been of no help. I just . . . I just don't see how I can be of much help." She sounded like a whining child, but other words eluded her. "Josef has never given me any of the kind of information you must need. He doesn't talk to me about his trips; I never know where he goes or where he's been. He's not about to start telling me what he's involved in since he's never done so before. And I can hardly play the spy, trying to pry information from him. He'd see through me in a minute. I don't know what you want or how I can help."

She wanted to be strong, didn't want to fall apart, but she was on a shaky bridge leading her straight over a chasm—one she fell into. Turning away from him, ignoring that they were in public, she covered her face with her hands and sobbed.

Gently placing an arm about her shoulders, David led her back to his car. Barely aware of it, she let him assist her inside. He went around to the other side, reached into his pocket for a handkerchief, handed it to her, then started the car and directed it away from the curb.

They had driven three blocks before Liesel regained a portion of her composure. "I can't be away for long. My parents . . ."

He spared her a smile. "Don't worry. The worst they'll think is that I've kidnapped you. And since it's my office which investigates such things, all that would happen is that they'd be directed to me or to one of my associates."

The notion was so ridiculous that Liesel burst into laughter as uncontrollably as she had cried just moments earlier. Then she held up a hand and spoke breathlessly, "Oh, but it would be a disaster, Mr. de Serre. They'll know who you are!"

She laughed again but could tell he didn't share her amusement, and her laughter dwindled away. She didn't know what was wrong. Every time this man came around, she lost all control. Now she'd lost whatever dignity she thought she possessed.

"I'm sorry," she said again, looking at him. She wiped away the last tear, caused as much by the strange laughter that had consumed her as by the pain. Looking at the neighborhood rather than him, she took a deep, steadying breath. "We really ought to return, Mr. de Serre. They might worry."

"We will," he assured her. "Just as soon as your eyes aren't quite so swollen and your nose isn't pink. I'd rather not have them thinking I was the one who inspired your tears."

She glanced at him. "Yes, you're right, of course. I really don't want them to know . . . about Josef, that is. At least not until you've proven his involvement in all of this."

David steered the car off the road and into one of the many parks in Liesel's neighborhood. A stream ran along the land, a tributary of the Potomac. Along the shallow banks, wildflowers grew profusely, and in the river itself, beaver dams sprang up like so many little huts, slowing the flow of the water. Liesel often walked to this park from home.

"I know this is hard for you," he said, "but sometimes God has a way of letting things happen around us, even to us, that make us stronger in the end."

She looked from the creation around her to him, grateful for the second time that, if Josef must have someone after him, at least it was a man of God. "Thank you."

They sat for some time, neither of them speaking.

"Josef's father said he is due back before the end of the week," Liesel said at last. "I don't know where he is." Then she looked at Mr. de Serre, remembering what he'd said before. "But you do. You said he's been in Norfolk."

"That's right."

"You see?" She folded the handkerchief he'd given her, feeling its dampness. She must launder it before returning it. She didn't welcome the thought since that meant she'd have to see Agent de Serre at least one more time, a possibility she realized was entirely probable whether or not he looked for the return of his handkerchief. "I couldn't possibly tell you anything more than what you already know."

"If it's any comfort, Miss Bonner, I'm not looking for your help in trapping him. I just want you to be aware of what he's involved in. Listen to the way he talks with new ears; watch him with new eyes. He may have done any number of things to give himself away before, but you weren't looking for anything out of the ordinary."

"I thought you didn't need me to spy on him."

"I don't. I'm asking you to look at him in this new light for your own good, Miss Bonner, not to tell me everything he says and does."

"You've never told me exactly what it is you do want of me, Mr. de Serre."

"It's just this. Watch him. Don't report every little thing to me, but be aware that he might need help one day. The trunk lines for telegrams around the world are monitored by the Allies. If he's getting any information from Germany, we'll know about it. Things are tightening everywhere against German involvement in this country now that we're officially at war. He may need help sometime soon. If he believes you know nothing about his activities, he may think he can get you to help him in ways that seem innocent. But now you know too much to be fooled."

Liesel nodded, wishing it weren't so.

De Serre smiled. "Who knows? If the German network gets too shaky over here, he may retire."

With brows raised in hope, she asked eagerly, "Then you'll leave him alone?"

"Or he may get bolder and take on new assignments of his own machinations." Her question, evidently, did not warrant an answer since he'd continued as if she hadn't spoken at all. "If he's a true zealot for Germany, that's what he'll do—in which case, he may get sloppy."

"So you don't want me to report his daily activities, just be aware of what he's up to and tell you pertinent information if he lets anything slip."

"Exactly."

Liesel shook her head, aware that her heartbeat was still erratic. Their discussion sounded so reasonable, belying her uneasy thoughts. But nothing was the same anymore.

"And if you know he's about to leave town, you can inform me, as well. It'll save my man from having to scurry at the last minute. I also have a few photographs of others I'd like you to take a look at," he added, "to see if you've noticed any of them in Josef's company."

Liesel nodded silently, but even as she did so, her hands trembled. What was she doing, agreeing to work against Josef? This was *Josef* they discussed as if he were some kind of project!

"I think I'm quite stable enough to go home now, Mr. de Serre."

Without another word, he started the car, and they went back to her house. When he pulled to a stop, he detained her with a touch so brief and light she wasn't sure he made actual contact. But she'd seen his hand near hers, felt something as light as the brush of a butterfly wing tickle the faint hairs on her skin.

"Liesel," he said, and his voice was so soft it was similar to his touch. "This isn't my place, I know, but something compels me to speak. Listen to the Spirit that's inside you. Guard yourself. Not physically, but your heart, Liesel. I know you hold the Bible close. Perhaps that means you wish to follow the Lord with everything in your life. If you do, then think about what Josef is doing. Can his activities be inspired by the same Lord you serve? I don't pretend to know Josef on a personal basis; I certainly can't judge his motives or his faith, if he has any. But the Lord made him an American. Not German. In wartime, many things seem justified, but are his actions? Josef is working against the American government, a government blessed by no less than God Himself. Has this government suddenly gone awry? Is it evil? Can Josef justify under the Lord that working against his own government is right?"

Liesel was mesmerized by these words as if it wasn't de Serre speaking at all but a messenger from God. Surely it mustn't be a coincidence that this man, this man who knew enough to question what God's will might be, had been assigned this case. Mama always told her there were no coincidences.

"If you follow the Lord, Liesel, then don't you want to make sure the man you marry does the same? First and foremost?"

Liesel couldn't speak. She felt herself nod, and that was almost too much. How did he know? How did this man know so much?

"I'm sorry," he whispered. "I spoke too personally."

"No," she assured him, and her voice was surprisingly strong. She felt herself reach out and touch his forearm to bolster her words. But beyond that, she found nothing more to say. She could hardly share with this man all her worries about Josef.

He turned away to let himself out of the motorcar, effectively ending the moment that Liesel could only call spiritual communion. Agent de Serre rounded the motorcar to her side even as Liesel shook away the remnants of that spiritual feeling. She was practical, and her faith was practical. She wasn't sure God spoke quite so clearly though other human beings . . . at least through ones she hardly knew.

"Just one last thing, Miss Bonner," he said as he assisted her to her feet. "I know I've told you before, and I'm sorry to bring this up again. But I can't stress how important it is that you keep this to yourself."

Liesel said nothing.

"I know it's upsetting. It would probably bring comfort to talk this over with someone else. But you cannot. If you must, call me. That's the most I can offer."

He slipped a card from his pocket and handed it to her. She saw it was void of his name or occupation; it simply held two telephone numbers scrawled in bold handwriting, a little *o* after one and an *h* after the other.

"Home and office numbers, Miss Bonner. If I'm not at one, I'm at the other. But," he said with a smile, "if I don't hear from you, you can bet you'll hear from me. Regularly."

She nodded, accepting the card without a word.

"Good night," he said. "Thank your father for the dinner invitation, but I have a former engagement anyway."

"Good night, then."

When Liesel went to bed that night, she took her purse with her. The phone numbers inside seemed to burn their way through the white fabric. They were all she saw, and she wanted to take no chance of having anyone else ask about them if they happened to spot the card.

That night as she prayed, she silently cried out for God's wisdom. Again she prayed, what would God have her do? Would He have her turn in Josef, if such was within her power? How could she?

Agent de Serre's words engraved doubts deep inside. All her life, she'd imagined herself married to a man who revered the Lord as she did. Had she been fooling herself to believe Josef was that man? He went to church every

Sunday. He knew references from the Bible, having sat under the teaching of a godly pastor. But how deep did that faith go? Had she assumed something that wasn't there?

The burden plagued Liesel throughout the days that followed. No longer could she push them away, pretending everything was as it had been before she met Mr. de Serre. Nothing could dispel the thoughts, not even her frustration over Miss Burnbaum's obvious disregard for her. Uncle Otto's ignorance of what was going on didn't help, either. At one point, she felt a measure of compassion for Uncle Otto. Josef was his only son, his only family. What would he think to know the government suspected Josef of such crimes? What if Josef was actually guilty? Uncle Otto had nothing but his businesses, his money . . . and Josef. What comfort would he have if his son went to jail?

But such compassion slowly dissipated. Each day, hearing Uncle Otto speak German more often than English to businessmen who visited or refer to Germany as the Fatherland made Liesel ache. If Josef was involved in all the things Mr. de Serre said, wasn't Uncle Otto every bit as much to blame for raising Josef with more loyalty to Germany than to America?

By Thursday, she was exhausted emotionally, mentally, and physically and in no mood to go home to a big family meal. She'd barely slept more than a few hours all week, was unable to eat and had no energy left to evade Miss Burnbaum's jibes. By five o'clock, she wanted nothing more than her own bed. *Sleep will come tonight*, she thought. It must. Sleep seemed a very seductive escape.

Taking her purse as she prepared to leave for the day, she opened it as she'd done a thousand times that week to see if the card was still in its place. Phone numbers she hoped never to use, numbers that both haunted her and strangely comforted her. Mr. de Serre knew the truth. He was the only one besides herself who suspected Josef of being anything but what he wanted others to believe. If thoughts of Josef drove her any more mad than they already had, she could call one of those numbers. One day, she might do that very thing.

Her feet seemed heavy that night, as if the heels on her shoes were filled with lead.

"Liesel, wait one moment, will you?"

Perhaps, if she'd only walked a bit faster, she wouldn't have heard Miss Burnbaum's call. Liesel stopped, both relieved not to have to lift those heavy shoes and filled with dread at the thought of more time in the company of Miss Burnbaum.

"I've noticed you looked rather peaked the last few days," the older woman said, stressing the word *peaked* with a high-pitched tone. Liesel could detect no concern in the older woman's colorless eyes. "If you're sick, you really shouldn't come in to the office and spread it around. Why don't you stay home tomorrow?"

Liesel looked at Miss Burnbaum, whose lips were bright red and cheeks unnaturally pink. She looked disdainful, as if any illness was entirely Liesel's fault.

"I'm feeling perfectly fine, Miss Burnbaum," Liesel said with a sigh. "I'm sure I'll be here in the morning."

"Very well, although you may want to rest. Otto says Josef is due back, and I'm sure you don't want that young man to see the way you look today." Her bright red mouth slanted into a smile. "We want our von Woerner men only to see the best of us, don't we, dear?"

Something in her tone struck Liesel's curiosity. "I certainly want Josef to see me at my best," she said slowly. "And you, Miss Burnbaum? Do you wish my uncle Otto only to see you at your best?"

Miss Burnbaum's cheeks deepened nearly as red as her painted lips. "I'm sure that's the only way Mr. von Woerner has ever seen me. I've made certain of that for twenty years."

"Yes," Liesel said. For the first time since meeting her, Liesel felt sorry for Miss Burnbaum. Twenty years was a long time to wait to be noticed by someone. "I'm sure I'll get a good night's rest tonight. Good day, Miss Burnbaum."

Sleep did indeed grab Liesel like a vacuum into the bliss of unconsciousness within moments of her head coming to rest on the pillow.

Until the dreams began.

Late in the night, long after Greta lay sleeping in her bed nearby, they came to Liesel in horrifying detail. Josef lighting a fire, Josef setting a bomb, Josef running away as a bomb blew up a dock the way Black Tom Island had exploded a couple of years ago. She dreamed of workers like her father and brothers blasted into oblivion.

She awoke sweating, breathing rapidly. The darkness frightened her, and she went to the window where she could see the stars. Thankfully, Greta still lay asleep in her bed, undisturbed by Liesel's turmoil.

Once again, Liesel turned to God, whispering a prayer. *I need help, Lord! Help me see what I should do and do it with Your strength. I don't have any left of my own. I know You're with Josef, Lord, whether Josef sees that or not. Help him to see You! To see the right thing to do. And help Mr. de Serre, too, to search only for the truth. You've promised to be with us through all of life, the good and bad of it, and I know enough to trust in Your promises. Thank You, Father, for that promise. Just help me to always trust in it. To trust in You.*

The dream sufficiently banished by the sure knowledge of Christ's presence, Liesel returned to her bed. Sleep eluded her for a long time, and she used that time to continue to pray. Something warned her that she would need the strength God promised in His Word. And soon.

By Saturday morning, Josef was back in his Stutz Bearcat, driving toward Washington. The sun was high in the sky, but a line of gray-black clouds loomed like giants along the western horizon. He'd be lucky to beat that rain in his topless motorcar. The roads would turn to muck half a foot deep and slow his progress considerably if he had to drive through a storm.

Rounding a bend, he spotted something ahead and swerved, avoiding a boy and his bicycle. The boy was kneeling beside the bike, his face an odd combination of white and red, his hands covered with black grease as he tried, evidently with little success, to rethread the bicycle chain.

Josef pulled to a stop with a glance at the approaching clouds. A boy on a bike would have a tougher go of it than he would.

"Complications?" he greeted the youth, who looked to be about fourteen—just around the age Josef had been when he'd discovered how far he could get on his own two-wheeler.

The boy didn't look up. His face was dry, but Josef guessed he'd been crying. Josef squelched the urge to scold him for acting like a child, attributing such behavior to the inferior training he must have received so far in life. If he'd gone to a German school, he'd have learned not only the mechanics of the bike, but also to show pride instead of tears.

"Mind if I take a look?"

The boy said nothing; he just backed away.

He had managed to thoroughly snarl the chain, but Josef had no doubt he could fix it. Over his shoulder, he asked, "Come very far?"

"Couple miles."

"Once this bike is back to condition, you'd best make straight for home. These roads won't be fit for any wheels before long."

"Yes, sir."

"Of course, in *Deutschland*, they have a bicycle race where they ride no matter what the weather."

"Where's that?"

"Germany."

"Oh."

Josef caught a hint of suspicion form on the boy's face.

"You from there?" he asked.

"Yep," Josef answered. "You know that race I just mentioned? It lasts six days."

"Six days!" The suspicious look transformed to surprise. "How do they do it?"

"Well, you have to train for it. You have to ride every day for a long time leading up to the race so that you learn to ride almost in your sleep. Holding on to the handles or not. And you have to eat right and work to get strong."

"Sounds hard."

"It is. That's the only thing worth doing, boy. The hard stuff."

"Say, how come you're over here in America if you're a German? You a spy or somethin'?"

Josef laughed. "You think a spy would stop to fix a bicycle chain?" He laughed again. "I'm a salesman."

"What d'you sell?"

"Glass and coal. Need any?"

The youngster grinned. "Naw."

Josef had the bike back in working order just as the first drops began to fall. Only a drizzle, but the clouds were thicker now. They were behind Josef, and if he was lucky, he'd still be able to outrun the worst of it.

"Best get on home, then," he said as he handed the mended bike over. "And think about that race over there, boy. You could do it, too, if you wanted to enough."

"Think so?"

"Sure. You're healthy, aren't you? Not overweight, not some weakling, either. But you have to work at it. Nothing good comes without hard work. Alrighty?"

"Yes, sir!"

Josef left the boy, who unfortunately was headed right into the clouds. Josef saw him ride fiercely, the wind rippling his cotton shirt. He looked every bit as determined as Josef had once been, when he'd first decided he would train himself into racing condition. Of course, he'd never actually raced anybody except Karl, who lost to him every time, but it had been fun going through the disciplines.

The clouds stayed behind Josef, but Washington was still miles away. Josef remembered how hard he'd worked when he was younger. Certainly

Karl had never worked as hard as he had. Karl was so Americanized even though he was a German. Oh, well, Josef couldn't very well change that.

But soon if Germany won the war, German ways would spread here, and everyone would know the value of the German culture. Even Karl, whose father had obviously forgotten.

CHAPTER *Fourteen*

"PAPA, I won't be joining you on the trolley tonight," Liesel said as she and her father walked from the glass factory at the end of Saturday's workday. "I'm going home with Karl."

"Oh?"

"I told Katie I would help her with the costumes for the YWCA play she's working on."

"Isn't Josef due home today? He'll probably come by to see you."

"Oh, is it Saturday already?" she wondered aloud, heart pounding. The sun was hot, but that had nothing to do with her sweaty palms. She knew only too well that Josef was expected home, and she'd set up this date with Katie for the sole purpose of avoiding him. "I'll just see him tomorrow. These costumes must be done. I'm sure he'll understand."

"I can send him round to Karl's, then."

Liesel grabbed his arm before she knew what she was doing. "No! I mean, that's really not going to help get those costumes ready, is it?"

"He can visit with Karl while you two work."

Relief swept over Liesel as she remembered something she had heard Karl say. "Karl won't be home. He's going to his chess club."

Her father grunted. "Bunch of grown men getting together to play a silly game. Whoever heard of such a thing?"

"Oh, Papa, grown men are playing chess all over the world. And believe it or not, I actually think Karl is quite good. In any case, it gives poor Katie a break from having to play."

"Well, maybe Josef would like to go with Karl to this meeting."

Liesel swallowed hard before responding. "Josef hardly ever wanted to play growing up. Why would he want to play now?"

She looked away when her father sent her a rather lengthy gaze. While Liesel wasn't entirely sure Josef didn't like the game, she knew he'd only played it with Karl on rare occasions when they were young. He preferred being active to sitting at a table playing a game, even one involving strategy.

"I'll send Josef on his way, then, when he comes calling."

"I'm sure he'll want to visit with you and Mama for a little while."

"Ah, yes, I can see how exciting such a visit would be for a man Josef's age."

His sarcasm wasn't lost on Liesel, but she was helpless to say anything to dissuade him. Avoiding her father's eyes once again, she ignored his open curiosity.

Liesel did precisely as she'd planned that evening. Two days before when she'd approached Katie about visiting on Saturday, it had been easy enough to persuade Katie to accept Liesel's help with the costumes. And even though Liesel knew Katie could have done the job without her or even asked someone from the Y to help, Liesel was nonetheless glad to have an easy escape from home.

Her visit to Katie's lasted past ten o'clock, which served her purpose well. And Papa didn't send Josef to her, after all. She left Katie's that night feeling somewhat ashamed, knowing she couldn't avoid Josef forever.

Sunday morning brought a hot sun and a breeze so thick with humidity the simple exercise of breathing felt a chore. It was easy to attribute Liesel's tight chest and short breath to the weather.

At church, Liesel avoided Mr. Miller as if she were a deer and he a hunter. A mere glance at him brought a mix of anger and repulsion, and she was determined not to provide him with any more easy information. If Mr. de Serre wanted to know her whereabouts, to whom she spoke, and what she did, then he would just have to come and see for himself.

She was grateful Josef attended a different congregation with his father, allowing her solace and focus during her own church hour. She welcomed the worship time as an opportunity for seeking guidance from above as she never had before.

At home later that morning, she found Mama in the kitchen, gathering napkins and tin plates and the two cakes she'd baked as her contribution to the potluck dinner being held at the afternoon picnic.

"Liesel, will you get the tablecloth from the bottom drawer in the pantry? The pink one with stripes on it."

"I thought that had a stain and you made rags out of it," Liesel commented.

"I intended to, but Papa said we should keep it a while longer. I think it'll be all right for outside. I can put one of the cakes on the stain. No one will see it then."

Liesel found the tablecloth and handed it to Mama, who added it to her collection in a large wicker basket. While she worked, she hummed a new hymn, "The Love of God," and as she listened, Liesel wished she could somehow manage to disappear. Just be taken right up to heaven in that very moment, the way Elijah and Enoch before him vanished so long ago.

"I'm not going to the picnic," she told Mama flatly, and as expected, Mama's hymn stopped mid-bar.

"What?"

"I—I won't be able to go the picnic, Mama. My stomach is upset, and I'd really rather just stay home out of the heat."

"But it is the annual picnic! None of us ever misses the summer picnic."

"I know, Mama, but I just couldn't stand to be outside today. I can barely breathe."

Mama put a hand to Liesel's forehead too quickly for Liesel to avoid.

"No fever," she said. "Why can't you breathe? Is your dress too tight?"

"Of course not, Mama!"

Mama eyed her from head to foot, obviously seeing how the pink floral dress hung the way it always did, as every dress in her closet hung. Loosely, comfortably.

"I don't like this, Liesel," said Mama, her brow furrowed. "You've been keeping to your room too much. And now you say you don't feel well. Perhaps we should send for Dr. Morris."

"No, Mama," she said as if Mama were drawing too much from a simple stomachache. "I'm sure I'll be fine by tomorrow."

"Oh, but I don't want you to miss today. Our family is always there! And Josef, when he came to see you last night, he was disappointed not to find you here. Now he won't see you again today. What will he think?"

Liesel lifted her chin ever so slightly. "He shouldn't think anything at all. I've always been here for Josef every single time he's come calling. All my life I've been here, just waiting for him."

Mama raised a brow as if Liesel had inspired some new idea. "Are you sure it's your stomach, Liesel? And not your heart?"

"Oh, Mama, how you do read things! Don't be silly. I have a simple stomachache. I want to avoid the heat. When you see Josef, tell him just that."

"Just what?" Papa came into the kitchen as Liesel finished speaking.

"Liesel doesn't go to the picnic today." Mama's tone suggested a national disaster.

"What?" Papa said. "Not go! Of course she's going. We're all going together, the whole family."

Liesel shook her head. "No, Papa. I have a stomachache, and I just don't think I can stand the heat today. I'd prefer staying home."

Papa looked ready to protest but hesitated. Mama prodded him closer to Liesel, pulling lightly on the sleeve of his white cotton shirt. Then he shook his head, facing not Liesel but turning to Mama.

"Then that's the way it shall be, Ilsa. If she has a stomachache, she has a stomachache. The heat won't help that." He stepped closer to the large basket on the kitchen table. "Is this ready to go? I want to have everything— and everyone who's going—on the porch when Josef arrives. He said last night he'll be switching cars with his father to accommodate all of us. Still, it'll be a tight fit."

"But Hans! Is that all you say to Liesel? Don't you think she ought to go? She can stay in the shade, bring a little fan, wear a sleeveless dress."

"No, Mama," said Papa as he picked up the basket and headed back to the door. "Liesel is old enough to make decisions on her own. If she wants to stay home, she stays home. Let's go."

Much to Liesel's relief, her entire family was gone within a half hour. She stayed in her room, picturing how Josef pulled up in his father's Peerless and let the family pile in. How he probably inquired after her before Mama and Papa got into the car. Evidently he didn't insist upon checking on her, since she heard no movement within the house.

Another delay tactic executed and accomplished. Liesel was quite proud of herself, having gained a few hours of peace and solitude. Well, solitude at least. She spent most of the afternoon prostrate on her bed, her face awash with tears.

Near four o'clock, the humid breeze coming in from her bedroom window did nothing to dispel an overwhelming feeling of being trapped inside her rapidly narrowing room. She knew her family would not return for quite some time. The annual picnic led to a crescendo of fireworks once the sun set. The Bonner family always stayed until the end. Even though the benefactor who donated the fireworks had been restricted this year because of the war, Liesel knew he'd been able to scavenge quite a few of the colorful sky works. Word had spread throughout the town, and a number of families outside the church planned to attend for the fireworks alone.

Liesel went to the kitchen for a glass of water. She had no appetite but forced herself to eat a couple of crackers and a bit of cheese. Then she went to the bench on the porch in back of the house to catch whatever scant breeze could be found. She liked the familiarity of their well-used yard, enjoyed the view of the trimmed lawn and trees, a peaceful setting that blocked out everything beyond. Before long, she experienced the first peaceful moments of her day and fell sound asleep.

Josef took the half-dozen stairs by two and tapped at the front door. He waited several moments before knocking again more boldly. Then he turned from the door and looked up and down the block, stepping off the porch to look at the second story of the Bonner home. Although he'd never been inside Liesel's room, he'd been in Karl's. He knew from passing Liesel's closed door that her room was at the back of the house. If her window was open, perhaps she would hear him if he called from the backyard.

Rounding the house, he silently thanked Liesel's father for giving his consent to visit Liesel alone. Josef had driven the Bonners all the way to Potomac Park and sat through lunch, trying to think of a way to see Liesel that wouldn't strain the protective nature of Liesel's parents, especially her mother.

He'd been surprised that Liesel hadn't been home the night before, his first evening back in town. She was the first person he visited every time he returned, and he was sure his father had told her he would be home by Saturday. So why had she gone out? Hans had mentioned something about donating her time to yet another worthy cause, and he didn't doubt that was true. But did she have to be away on his first night home, especially after he'd been gone so long?

He had half a notion to find her last night but thought better of it while he'd driven around. He depended on Liesel for a sense of calm and goodness in his life. Without her company, he'd been restless.

And now the picnic. A stomachache, her father had said. When Josef had received the news, his first impulse had been to march inside and demand to see whether she was sick or not. Liesel would never put him off, yet that's exactly what it felt like. But pride, as well as Hans's eagerness to be off, prevented Josef from following his impulse.

Then Karl had spoken to him at the park. It hadn't taken him long to pull Josef aside and ask if he knew anything about a man named David de Serre who worked with the government through the railroad. Josef admitted he didn't, and what did it matter, anyway? That's when Karl had told him this man had offered Liesel a ride home from work one day. Karl had learned from Greta that somebody had come calling the week before, taking Liesel to dinner. Evidently this same David de Serre.

Josef had never considered himself a jealous man, so it was quite a revelation to discover that's exactly what he was. Sure, Liesel was a beautiful young woman and any number of men might dream about spending time with her. But she'd always been faithful to him. They were past the age most young couples married—he in his mid-twenties and Liesel a couple of years younger. She'd waited for him. He had been slow about asking her to wed, but she was so loyal she never brought it up. Because she loved him. Didn't she?

Josef skipped up the few steps to the back porch leading to the kitchen and stopped short. There on the painted green bench was Liesel herself, an empty glass tilted precariously in her lap. Sleeping and as lovely as any legend he could imagine.

Quietly, he took a seat next to her. Taking the glass from her limp hand, he whispered her name and gently stroked her cheek. In a moment, her eyes slowly opened. Her sleep must have been deep, for she had that lost look on her face, one of confusion and disorientation. But when she smiled upon recognizing him, he felt a familiar giddiness in his chest, rendering him as helpless as a little boy. Until her welcoming smile was replaced by a frown.

"Your parents told me you weren't feeling well," he said quietly, sliding close and putting an arm around her shoulders. He wished she would lay her head on his chest, but she didn't. She just sat there, not moving away but not settling in to the closeness he tried to create. "Perhaps I should have let you sleep, but I couldn't resist sitting by you. You can go back to sleep if you want."

"No . . . no. I'm awake now." She shifted to a more upright position. He felt her body stiffen as if she didn't want to accept the support he was eager to give.

"I missed you at the picnic and wanted to see if there's anything I could do to help you feel better. Can I? Do anything, that is?"

She shook her head, not looking at him. Odd, he thought, that she seemed reluctant to meet his gaze. How many times had she looked up at him with those pale blue eyes, and all he wanted to do was kiss her?

"You shouldn't have left the picnic just for me," she said.

"I hoped I could persuade you to come back with me if you're feeling up to it."

She shook her head again, still not looking at him.

Josef could barely stand the downward slant of her face. He put a light hand to her cheek, stroking once softly, feeling the smoothness of her skin, and turned her face toward him. Slowly, she raised her gaze to his.

"Is it anything more than a stomachache, *mein Liebe?*" he whispered.

Her eyes sparkled, but she squeezed them shut before he knew for sure if it were tears he saw there or not. "That's all it is," she whispered back. "Just my stomach."

"Let me make you some tea, then. My father used to get stomachaches, and he took chamomile. If your mother doesn't have any, I'll go to my house and fetch some."

"No, Josef." She touched his hand, then withdrew it, but he captured it in his before she could get away.

"I want to help you feel better." He drew her into his arms and placed her head on his shoulder, stroking her hair, breathing in the scent of her: soap and powder and something else, something sweet in her hair. A scent he could compare to nothing else on earth.

She pulled away, but he breathed once more deeply, catching the fragrance again before she took it away. He watched her stand, looking out at the yard. A croquet game was set up, the wickets and balls looking abandoned in the thick lawn. Ilsa Bonner's roses grew along the back picket fence beyond the shade of the two cherry trees on each side of the yard. The flowers and branches barely swayed in the heavy air. A vegetable garden had recently been planted, and the green sprouts shot up through the brown dirt. Gardens enhanced the smallest yard in Washington to the grounds of the White House itself, all to save food for the soldiers.

But Josef hadn't come to admire the yard. He stared at Liesel's back. After she'd stood for what seemed a long while, she turned back to him with a familiar smile on her face. A smile on her lips, but something else in her eyes. He couldn't tell what; she didn't look at him long enough for him to study her.

"I had a dream while I was sleeping, Josef. It was about your father."

"Oh? Not a bad one, I hope?"

She offered a half smile. "No, but it was very strange. He had the chance to return to Germany without being sick on the boat." She referred to his father's fear of ships, the main reason he'd never returned to Germany after his businesses had prospered and he could easily have afforded to return. "He wanted to stay right here in America. Don't you think it's odd that I would dream such a thing?"

He nodded. "If my father could go back to Germany by any means other than a boat, I'm sure he'd take it."

"That's what I thought. Perhaps I dreamed he wouldn't want to return because of the war, the same reason that prevented you from going to the university there for your graduate work. The German people must be having an awful time of it."

Josef nodded, although he knew the people of his homeland were so strongly unified they would undoubtedly survive the longest, ugliest war.

"I've often wondered at the differences between your father and mine," Liesel went on. "Yet they're friends."

"What differences? My father has great respect for your father. I think he wanted to make him a partner in the business when your father told him to remodel the old beehive ovens to the new byproduct coking furnaces back in Baltimore. But your father wouldn't accept. Something about thinking there's a difference between offering an idea rather than cold hard cash as part of the investment."

Liesel smiled and leaned against the post that supported the roof of the back porch. "I don't think my father knows how to put a price on an idea. Money is too important; ideas are from thin air—and that idea was too simple to be worth as much as a partnership. He might have enjoyed the money a partnership would bring but not if he didn't think he'd earned it with a lot of sweat."

"My father thought he had." He sighed and looked around the porch. "Your father and mine represent the best of *Deutschland*, Liesel. Insightful, hardworking, incorruptible."

He watched Liesel fold her arms in front of her as if she were chilled, which was of course impossible in this heat. "My father has always had ideas," she said. "It's why he came to America in the first place. Because America, to him, offered freedom. Where the people vote—well, maybe someday all the people will, even women—and those votes mean something. He wanted to get away from the kaiser and the ways of a monarchy."

"I've never understood that about your father. *Deutschland* is no dictatorship. Politics have nothing to do with the everyday life of a laborer. Your father worked in the coking factories over there just like he did here before the glass factory. As long as the government runs the country, what does a factory worker care about such things as votes and committees and things?"

"The American government is to serve the people—all of the people, not just those who own land and businesses. It's not a government that simply hands down orders to the factory workers."

"Germany doesn't just hand down orders."

"Doesn't it?"

"Of course not! It serves the people, too. How can it not by wanting what's best for them? I'm telling you, *Deutschland* is freer than you might think. There is freedom of the press, just like here, even bold enough to give our own kaiser a thrashing if he deserves it. Does a heartless dictatorship give its people that power—along with pensions, allowances? Insurance for sickness, accidents, old age?"

"You make it sound like there isn't a single poor person in all of Germany. Yet my father said there are slums there."

"Even Jesus said we would always have the poor," Josef replied. "Still, circumstances for the poor are improving in *Deutschland* with labor laws and insurance. The German people are like no other, Liesel. They all want what's best for the country."

"My father said Germany offers insurance to keep the socialists from overtaking the monarchy. That it's not as selfless as it appears."

"Nonsense. Wilhelm wants to insure healthy army recruits. What better way than to have them well cared for, them and their families? *Deutschland* is a great power, Liesel, getting more powerful all the time. Look at history! The Romans had their chance; the British Empire has had theirs. Now it's *Deutschland*'s turn to spread their ways, their language, their traditions. It's only fair and honorable."

"Is that what this war is all about then, Germany spreading its ways?"

Josef shrugged. "It wouldn't be so bad if that were the outcome, though, would it? There are plenty of Germans right here in America who would welcome a greater German influence in the world. It's the way of order, of the satisfaction of hard work, of discipline and dignity. Wouldn't it be better if everyone knew their place? That's all *Deutschland* wants, to give order to the world."

"But who's to decide that order? A German kaiser? Should we all follow the ways of Germany whether we want to or not?"

Josef's blood pumped faster imagining the way he thought the government should be. He dismissed her apparent disapproval because she was uninformed, simply ignorant of all that *Deutschland* offered. "Perhaps, but it's not oppression over there! There's a constitution and laws, which are observed by everybody—by the ruled *and* the rulers. There aren't any arrests without due process of law. Germany hasn't had a political murder like the rest of the world has—even here, President McKinley was shot down in office. That doesn't happen in *Deutschland* because the people admire their rulers."

"Maybe it hasn't happened because Germany doesn't have the diversity we have here. Or because they're afraid of the ruler's military."

Josef laughed. "Liesel, you sound like your brother Ernst and a little like your father."

"Everyone knows Germany is a military state. That's why all those alliances between different countries crept up over there to begin with. That's what started this whole awful war."

"The alliances may have had something to do with it, but it wasn't *Deutschland*'s alliances. And yes, *Deutschland* is militant! We've had to be; we were made that way by God Himself—by virtue of *Deutschland*'s place in the middle of Europe. *Deutschland* isn't isolated like England or protected by a vast ocean like America. We've had to fight during every generation just to prevent being swallowed up by the ambition of others. And God has not let us down. He's made us the best soldiers in the world. We haven't had a military defeat since Napoleon, and we got him in the end, too! Now it's the Allies. We won't be defeated. Practically speaking, it's impossible."

"You make it sound like Germany welcomed this war."

"This war wasn't *Deutschland*'s fault! All those alliances you mentioned a minute ago made it inevitable. What were we supposed to do, let France and England and Russia surround us and overtake us at the slightest whim? They were so busy building up—Russia with their railroads and Britain with their famous navy—what could we have done but build our own navy? The kaiser had always been friendly to Britain up until the war. Why, Queen Victoria is his grandmother. The Russian czar his cousin! He didn't want war with them. But Germany needs to be a strong central power in Europe. We need new markets for our growing industries; we need cheap raw materials. We need colonies and world influence if we're to get that place in the sun the kaiser talked about a while back. A multitude of places in the sun, so that the sun will never set on *Deutsch* territory."

Liesel looked at him. "Oh, Josef," she said quietly.

He wondered at her tone, at the sadness in it. She must be made to understand the differences between America and *Deutschland*. He'd assumed long ago that by virtue of her pure German blood she would naturally understand. But perhaps she'd listened too long to the liberal Americanized views of her father. If only she'd gone to work for his father sooner. Undoubtedly Josef's father would have set her straight a long time ago.

"Liesel." He left the bench to stand in front of her, close to her. "Liesel, *Deutschland* is a land blessed by God. We have the forests, the beautiful Rhine, the majestic peaks of the Bavarian Alps. It's the land of poets and thinkers! It's where education is cherished and individuals are encouraged to learn. *Deutschland* knows it's the moral duty of the state to educate each and every citizen. It's been so for many years, and *Deutschland* is only now seizing its turn to show the rest of the world how we've become the fittest of all. Yes, it's true! Our people aren't stuck in the thought that we are helpless lambs of God. We are stronger, more intelligent, more cultured than the rest. A people God would never call His slaves."

"I believe the apostle Paul himself wanted to be called a slave of God," Liesel whispered.

Josef gently placed his hands upon her shoulders.

"Perhaps, but that was another time, long before each generation improved upon the last. You've heard of Darwin, haven't you? It truly is the survival of the fittest, and there is no better example of that than within the German race. True Germans strive for improvement. We learn and work hard and are shrewd enough to advance. Through industry, through education, through the military. There are many ways, and *Deutschland* provides them all."

CHAPTER *Fifteen*

LIESEL stared at Josef as if she'd never seen him before. If she'd ever heard him speak of politics to her father and brothers, she'd never heard him like this. He was passionate, convinced of his own insight, utterly committed to his ideas. Ideas she could never embrace. He spoke easily of God, but not of the God she knew.

How could she have known Josef for so long yet not really known him at all?

She shook her head and closed her eyes, stepping down one stair and sinking to sit, to escape the touch of his hands on her shoulders without running away. She didn't have the strength for that. Everything inside her had drained away with his words.

Josef loved Germany more than God, more than anything . . . or anyone.

"Josef, Josef." His name tumbled off her lips in a lament for all that was lost between them. She could not look at him. She bowed her head into folded arms that rested on her knees.

She felt him sit close beside her, felt his arms encircle her, drawing her close. *"Mein Liebe,"* he whispered. "I love you. I've always loved you. I always will love you."

The words that she'd once longed to hear came too late. Far too late. Unbidden but irrevocable, tears spilled from her eyes, and she clung to him

because she didn't know what else to do. "Oh, Josef, Josef." Her tears turned to sobs.

"Tears? But why? Because I've been so slow in telling you how I feel? But surely you knew, *mein Liebe!* I've shown you in a thousand ways that I love you. From our very first kiss."

"No! No, Josef, don't love me!" She pulled away though his arms tried to hold her. She stood, going down the few steps to the grass in the yard. From where Josef sat on the step above, their eyes were level: his staring intently, confused, while hers still flowed with tears.

"What is it, Liesel?" His tone was steady; his eyes watched her closely.

She turned her back to him, wringing her wet, trembling hands. She couldn't look at him, couldn't receive the love he'd declared after so long.

Josef came around to stand in front of her. He placed his hands on her shoulders more firmly as if afraid she might try to leave.

"Liesel, tell me why you're crying." His voice was steady. She spared him one look. His face was solemn.

Breaking away, she turned back to the house. She didn't want his concern, didn't want his love. Not when he loved Germany more than he could ever love her . . . or God.

"I cannot tell you." She heard her voice so shrill from the tears and tried to breathe a steadying breath but failed.

He tried to take her in his arms, but she resisted, pulling away in a jerky, almost violent manner. "No!"

"Liesel, what is the matter? I tell you I love you, and you pull away? I thought you loved me, too."

"Oh, I'm sure you did. Once I thought I did, too. But not now! I cannot love someone who lies. That's what you are, Josef. A liar!"

He looked bewildered, even anguished. "I'm not lying, Liesel. Why don't you believe that I love you? Because it's taken me so long to tell you? Because it's taken me so long to ask you to marry me?"

"Marry you!"

"Of course—that's what people who love each other do, isn't it? I thought it was understood that we would marry."

She backed away from him, but the stairs behind stopped her from getting far. "I know at least one of your secrets, Josef. How you've lied to me—not just to me but to others! And you must stop all of this. You must stop for your own sake and for the sake of what's right and decent. I know you act only out of loyalty, but that loyalty is misplaced. It belongs to your Creator. This lying—this espionage—is illegal and dangerous. You can't pretend to be a loyal American citizen, while in the next moment, you pretend

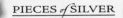

to be Andrew Nesbit. Or persuade munitions workers to strike, or . . . or set ships on fire. If you want to fight for Germany, then renounce your American citizenship, put on a uniform—a German uniform—and fight openly. Not against unsuspecting civilians trying to do the job America expects of them."

Liesel stopped, as much from the stunned look on Josef's face as by the vague conviction that seeped through her incoherent thinking, a conviction that she'd said something that she shouldn't have.

Josef took a step back. "Liesel . . ."

Something came over his face, something like fear showing through that utter and undeniable shock. He looked at her face, then looked behind her as if searching for someone else who had inspired all she accused him of. His gaze took in the whole house, and then he turned around to look again at the yard behind him. At last he turned back to her with a silent look so lost and vulnerable that Liesel wished she could take it all back. Make it all untrue.

He ran from the yard.

Liesel stood unable to move. A moment later, she heard the engine of his motorcar rumble into commission and roar to movement, as if the car couldn't get away fast enough. Then all sounds faded but for the birds that nested in Mama's trees.

Liesel rushed around the house to the front, but he was already gone. She didn't know how long she stood staring at the vacant street. Where had he gone? Should she have stopped him? Could she have stopped him? And then what? Would she have taken him to the Justice Department, turned him over to the hands of the government?

"Oh, Josef," she whispered. She turned back to the house, her head bowed as she looked no farther than a stride in front of her. Josef had proven his guilt. More tears threatened, but she willed them away. She lifted her head as she climbed the porch stairs and went back inside her home. She'd seen his guilt on his face the moment she'd mentioned the word *espionage*.

Inside, she closed the door with a slow but sure thud and leaned against it. Closing her eyes, she saw his face again, so astonished and a moment later so wary, almost as if he'd been betrayed. But she hadn't betrayed him!

Her eyes opened in sudden alarm. No, she had not betrayed Josef. She'd done just the opposite. Sudden sweat sprang to every pore, and her fingers tingled. Blood pumped at her temples. She had not betrayed Josef—she'd betrayed the American government! She'd let slip the very information David de Serre warned her most of all not to reveal. She'd warned Josef, and that's why he'd run.

A moan erupted from deep inside—but no tears. She was far too nervous for such an indulgence. Agent de Serre had warned her not to tell anyone of what Josef was suspected. Not only had she violated that directive, but she'd also told the very person they wanted most not to know. In her rash, naive, utterly foolish way, she'd revealed the one thing the government needed to catch Josef: their secret suspicions. How long would it be before they could turn those suspicions to evidence? How much harder had she made their job because of her impulsive, heedless disclosure?

Treason. Mr. de Serre had warned her if she divulged the information he entrusted to her he would have every reason to arrest her.

The adrenaline tingling in her hands spread throughout her body, spurring her into action. Any action. Thoughtless action. She paced. She went into the kitchen, into the parlor. Finally up the stairs. What should she do? Try to find Josef? He would help if he thought she might be in trouble now, too. . . .

Oh, this is madness! God, oh God! Help me!

Liesel sank to her knees in the middle of her bedroom. For a long while, she was too confused to pray, too inarticulate in her thoughts to utter any coherent plea. She merely rested prostrate before God.

Then without really knowing what she was doing, she found her purse and went back downstairs. She took her hat but left behind her gloves because she doubted she could don them with her hands trembling so. Outside, she knew where she was headed but didn't know what she would do once she got there. She merely trusted that the impetuous act she was about to do wasn't as foolish as what she'd just done.

She walked past the corner grocer because it was locked tight for Sunday and they were likely at the same picnic as the rest of the Bonners. They had a phone, but of course she couldn't get to it. Two blocks farther lived Mrs. Mahler, a middle-aged widow. She was also Dr. Morris's nurse, and because of her job, she needed a phone in her home.

Liesel knocked at the door and waited some time before hearing movement. It would be odd indeed to receive no answer at all. Even if Mrs. Mahler was out on a call, she always left behind Aggie, her maid, to take any urgent messages and tell whomever sought Mrs. Mahler where she could be found.

Aggie answered the door, moving slowly. Her quivering smile and shining bronze eyes were in sharp contrast to her deeply wrinkled brown skin and stark white hair.

"Hello, Miss Aggie," said Liesel. Aggie was near eighty, and Liesel had known her nearly from the day they'd moved to the neighborhood. She marveled at how normal her voice sounded as she greeted the older woman.

"Hello, Miss Liesel. Sorry it took so long to get to the door. My rheumatism is actin' up, and I'm moving kind of slow today."

"Oh, I'm sorry to hear that," Liesel replied. "Is Mrs. Mahler at home?"

"No, Miss Liesel," said the woman, holding open the door with one hand and brushing back a strand of wispy hair with the other. "But you can come in and wait for her if you want. She'll be back in a half hour or so."

"Actually, I only need to use her telephone. May I? It's rather important."

"Oh, sure. Come on in." She opened the screen, and Liesel stepped inside. The house always smelled somewhat of antiseptic, not wholly unpleasant but not nearly as welcoming as the light pine scent Mama used for cleaning.

Liesel knew where the telephone sat in the dark living room. Aggie had explained often enough that Mrs. Mahler didn't want the furniture to fade, and so she kept the windows shrouded with heavy shades. It was a crowded room with a large, puffy couch, two chairs with tall backs, and several tables with curved legs. The telephone sat on a small table in the corner, and Liesel walked to it on limbs that she noticed for the first time no longer quaked. She barely knew what she was doing except that she was trusting, simply trusting. This direction was from God—it must be because she suddenly had the strength to carry through. What she was about to do seemed the only option available, no matter what the consequences.

"I'll leave you to your call, then," said Miss Aggie, and she disappeared from the shadowy room.

Liesel took the card from her purse and held it toward the single, dim shard of light seeping in from the edge of one shade. The numbers were bold and clear, and when she picked up the receiver, she had no trouble reading them for the operator. She chose first the home number, thinking he surely would not be in the office on a Sunday afternoon.

It rang and rang but received no answer. Finally the operator came back and asked if she would like another number since there obviously was no one at home. Liesel gave her the office number but with little hope of a different result.

After only three rings, however, someone on the other end picked up.

"Justice Department."

Liesel nearly gasped, so surprised was she to have gotten an answer. Gulping back that gasp, she asked, "Is . . . is Agent David de Serre there?"

"No, ma'am. This is Special Agent Donahue. Anything I can help you with?"

"Do you know where I can find Agent de Serre?"

"He stopped in here earlier, but I don't think he'll be back until tomorrow. Any message?"

"No. No, thank you."

"Can I tell him your name?"

"No. I'll see him tomorrow."

She hung up.

Liesel fought the urge to sink into one of Mrs. Mahler's precious pieces of furniture and have herself another cry. Instead, she walked from the parlor on legs that still miraculously held her steady, thanked Miss Aggie for the favor, and left.

She went straight home, knowing if her family were there she might not have opted for that destination. But if they stayed for the fireworks, as she fully expected them to, at least she could go to bed and play one more delay game by avoiding them until tomorrow.

And then what? What would she tell them?

Briefly, she considered going to Josef's home, wondering if she might be able to find him. Perhaps he had an explanation for leaving her so suddenly, and not denying all she'd said.

But something inside called her a fool for trying to believe such a thing. If ever she saw guilt on a person's face, she'd seen it today on Josef's. If he were still in town, he'd be at her side, touting his innocence.

Once again, Liesel sought the privacy of her bedroom. It had turned to a prison earlier, but now it was once again a place of solace, of familiarity and family love. A place she'd known for years, a safe place where she'd been happy and sad, healthy and sick, good and bad. Always it remained home.

She thought of Josef and how for years he'd been so good to her, so fun to be with. Why, oh, why had he turned to a secret life? How could he claim to be someone calling himself Andrew Nesbit? She understood to some extent that his loyalty to Germany had been bred into him from the earliest age. But did that excuse going against the law of the land in which he lived? The land to which he was born?

Never before had her patriotism been tested, and she reminded herself that her father had chosen America. She'd been born here because her parents wanted to raise her in a country of freedom. The war may have made everyone aware of just how important was that freedom, but regardless, the issue of freedom went deep because it touched her life, her family, her future. Being an American was like saying she was a woman, something that was a simple fact that couldn't be separated from who she was.

Did Josef think the ways of Germany more valuable, more important than those of America?

She cried for Josef. She may not have loved him in the way a woman should love a husband—how could she, not knowing so much of what he thought and believed? Nonetheless, she loved him as a brother, someone she'd grown up with, someone who'd been a friend to her. Now it was as if he were dead.

Perhaps it would be better if he were. The thought shocked her but didn't go away. How would Uncle Otto take the news when the truth finally came out? How would her own family take it, her parents and Karl? Josef was as much a part of this family as any of them. And she wasn't about to tell them that Josef was probably on the run somewhere, dodging the government because he was a traitor.

By the time dusk settled, Liesel's emotional upheaval had left her sagging with exhaustion. Sleep took her like a sickness, complete and dreamless. Worries over what to tell her family disappeared, and it wasn't until the next morning that she faced reality once again.

Liesel woke to the sounds of Greta dressing.

"Oh! I wasn't supposed to wake you." Greta held one shoe, while the other, which had fallen with a thump, sat on the floor nearby.

"It's all right," Liesel whispered. "I was waking up anyway. Are you going to school early?"

"No, it's nearly nine o'clock."

Liesel sat upright. "Nine o'clock! Why didn't anyone wake me? I'm late for work."

"Papa said you're sick, and before he left, he said he was going to tell Uncle Otto you wouldn't be there today. That's when he told me not to wake you up."

Liesel swung her legs out of bed and reached for her robe. "Well, I'm better now. I'll get dressed and go. . . ." Liesel let her words drift off. Why was she so eager to go back to Uncle Otto's? How could she face Uncle Otto and not tell him what she knew? Did he know anything? Had Josef found his father, told him of the trouble he was in? Worse, had Otto known all along what his son was involved in? Encouraged him?

Liesel donned her robe and headed downstairs. Greta, now fully dressed, followed closed behind.

"You should have been there last night, Liesel!"

"Were the fireworks exciting?" she asked.

"Yeah, but not the ones in the sky." She giggled. "Josef never came back to take us home."

Liesel stumbled on the stair and turned to face Greta, who jabbered without pause.

"We thought Josef had Uncle Otto's Peerless when he left the picnic and didn't come back. He must've walked to his house or sent one of their servants to bring his Bearcat, but we didn't know that. Papa looked all over for Uncle Otto because it was either find him or take a jitney. And you know Papa didn't like the idea of having to pay anybody to drive us all the way home. We probably would have had to walk. But then we found Uncle Otto, and he took us back home in the Peerless."

"Did Uncle Otto know where Josef was?" Liesel's throat was tight, the words hard to form.

"No indeedy! That's the best part. He wanted to ask you where Josef went, since Karl said Josef came here. The house was so dark and quiet that when we got in everybody thought you and Josef had run off and eloped. Oh, it was so exciting! But then I came up here and tip-toed into the room, and there you were, sound asleep. Boy, was everybody disappointed. It would have been really something to have my sister go off and get married just like that."

Liesel fought the lump in her throat, feeling as though she were choking. They were standing in the middle of the stairs, and she heard the kitchen door swing open. Mama stood at the base of the stairs.

"I heard Greta tell you about all the excitement last night," she said, wiping her hands on a towel.

Liesel didn't move. She stood, still holding her robe's belt at her waist. She knew she must get dressed, and quickly, then go to Agent de Serre. She must tell him Josef had gone—because of her.

Liesel was about to do just that when a firm knock sounded at the door. The lump redoubled in her throat. They knew! It was Agent de Serre, Liesel was sure of it, there to arrest her. Would he let her dress first or just haul her off to jail in her robe?

Liesel stood immobile on the step. She was too far up to see who stood at the door when Mama went to answer it, but by the pleased welcome Mama offered, Liesel became confused. A moment later, Uncle Otto stepped into the hallway, hat in hand, halting at the bottom step. Liesel's knees nearly gave out, but somehow she remained standing as she looked down at him.

"Uncle Otto!" Greta exclaimed as she passed Liesel by and flew down the stairs. "You sick, too? You're not at work."

"No, no," he said. He didn't look at Greta. He was looking up at Liesel, appearing distracted. "I came to see your sister."

"Oh, she's all better now. I have to go to school. Do you think you could take me in your big car?"

"Oh, Greta," scolded Mama. "It's only two blocks! You will walk, the same as every day. Now scoot, or you'll be late."

Liesel still did not move. She stared at Uncle Otto, knowing without doubt the reason for the look on his face.

"Come into the kitchen, Otto," said Mama. "Liesel will get dressed, and the two of you can go back to the office. It was so nice of you to check on her this way. Come, come. And tell me, where was Josef last night?"

Uncle Otto covered his face in an ineffective attempt to hide an outburst of tears. Though it lasted only moments, Liesel and her mother exchanged a glance of astonishment. Liesel came down the stairs, sick that she could not address his fears openly and honestly. She simply watched Mama direct him to the parlor, where he sat on Papa's chair.

"Otto, Otto, what is it?" Mama whispered, over and over again.

Otto's breathing steadied at last. He looked at Liesel instead of Mama. Liesel stood several feet away, heart pounding.

"Josef was not at home yesterday," he said in German. "He was not at home all night. He was not at home this morning. And then . . ."

"What?" Mama prodded.

Otto shook his head, still staring at Liesel. "Do you know what happened to my boy? Was he here yesterday? Did he come to see you?"

"Yes, yes, he was here," Liesel said softly.

"When? What time was it? How long did he stay? What happened? Did you fight? Argue?"

"No."

Liesel wanted to tell him but knew she couldn't. And to what end? Would the truth ease his pain?

"He was here around four or so," she said. "He stayed a little while, and then he left."

"And that is all? He wasn't upset or angry?"

Liesel could not hold his gaze, but she managed to say, "No, he wasn't angry."

"Because his motorcar . . . it was found off the road, plowed into a big tree. The police came to me this morning. They said whoever was driving must have been driving crazy because of the tire tracks and gashes in the tree. But Josef, he was nowhere around."

Liesel sank to another chair. "Was there any evidence that he was hurt? Blood?"

Otto shook his head. "No, no, they said whoever was driving must have walked away. But if Josef was driving, why didn't he come home?" His huge hands rubbed his face, distorting his features for a moment. "If he hit his head . . . if he hurt himself . . . he could be wandering about."

Mama, who stood at his side, patted his shoulder. "The police are look-ing for him, *ja?* They know where this happened. He couldn't have wan-dered too far, could he? Of course not. They'll find him, Otto! God above knows just where your Josef is, and He'll bring him home. You leave it in God's hands now, Otto. He'll take care of Josef."

"Yes," Liesel whispered, a thousand thoughts jarring her mind. Josef wandering about, hurt. The police—both local and federal—searching for him. She had to find Agent de Serre before he came looking for her! "I–I must get dressed. Please, Uncle Otto, please stay here with my mother. You shouldn't go in to the office today."

"No, no, I'm not. I'm going to look for Josef. You may come along."

"No!" The word was out before she could stop it. "No, I mean, I will go out on my own. We can cover more ground that way."

Perhaps she could find Josef, although that would take a miracle unless he really had hurt himself and wasn't intentionally dodging the police—and her. But first she must go to the Justice Department and find Mr. de Serre.

Liesel excused herself and dressed quickly. She grabbed the first thing she laid hands to in her closet: a black suit. Appropriate, she thought after putting it on. The color matched everything about the day.

Otto was gone by the time Liesel came back downstairs. Mama must have heard her. She emerged from the kitchen as Liesel reached the bottom stair.

"You must eat before you go, Liesel."

"Oh, Mama, I can't! I just couldn't swallow."

Mama gently held her back. She looked up at Liesel with concern in her eyes. "Liesel, you must not worry too much, either. God will take care of our Josef."

"Yes, Mama. I know."

Liesel grabbed her hat, clutched her purse, and flew out the door.

CHAPTER *Sixteen*

"SOMEBODY called for you yesterday. A woman."

David glanced up from his desk, eyeing Greg Donahue with one brow raised.

"What was her name?"

The man shrugged. "Didn't leave it."

David glanced at his wristwatch. Nearly ten o'clock. "Any reason you waited half the morning to tell me?"

"Slipped my mind," said Donahue, then walked back to his own desk and sat down. "Without a name, it didn't seem important."

David let out a disgusted sigh, then reached behind him for his suit jacket. Who else but Liesel Bonner could it have been? The only other woman who might possibly ask for him was Mio's wife, Anna, and he'd been with her and the boys half of Sunday afternoon.

David had left the city yesterday after his contact told him the Bonner family had gone to the expected picnic—accompanied by Josef but without Liesel. With everyone presumably accounted for, David had taken a few leisure hours. When he stopped by the office on his way home, he found no messages that anyone had tried to reach him. He'd assumed all was well.

Perhaps that wasn't the case.

David headed to the stairs, wishing the Bonner family had a telephone. If Liesel had tried to contact him, he was sure it was no minor catastrophe. He needed to see her as soon as possible.

David rounded each flight of stairs with ease, sailing by the ground floor without pause until something caught his eye. A slim, darkly clad shadow waited by the elevator. Something familiar made him turn and take a second look.

"Liesel?"

She looked up, and he was sure he saw something like relief wash over her face. As if he were the one person in the entire world she wanted to see. He strode over to her just as the elevator opened and the attendant stepped out.

"Going up," said the uniformed attendant eagerly.

"Never mind, Leroy," said David, and the young man lost the welcoming smile he'd aimed straight Liesel Bonner's way. Then he looked back at David and gave another smile, a somewhat sheepish one, David thought. He'd obviously appreciated the pretty girl in front of them. "Sure, Mr. de Serre." Then he got back inside his elevator.

"I was just coming to see you," David told her. He took her hand and put it on his arm, leading her away from the elevator. She didn't seem to mind his touch, at least not until he'd said those words.

"You were?" She stopped walking altogether, looking at him with alarm all over her face.

"Did you call me yesterday?" he asked.

She nodded. The color had drained from her face.

He put his other hand on top of hers. "I was coming to see if you were all right."

"You mean . . . just to check on me?"

He nodded. "Look, are you all right?"

With her free hand, she put a tiny fist to her forehead as if trying to hold back everything in her mind. She closed her eyes so tight that tiny, premature wrinkles sprang up across her eyelids. Then she lowered her hand, opened her eyes, and took a deep breath before looking at him. "I need to speak to you, Mr. de Serre. Do you have some place? An office or something?"

There was an office for interrogations, and that's exactly where he should take her. He should get on that elevator, check Liesel in with Helen, take the appropriate forms, and go into the interrogation room and listen to whatever it was Liesel had to say. That was the appropriate thing to do, the formal thing to do.

David steered her to the front door. "Come on. We'll go for a drive."

His roadster was parked down the street, and he opened the door to let her in, then went around to the driver's side. He started the car and drove down Pennsylvania Avenue without a single thought as to where they were headed.

"What is it?" He couldn't wait to speak until they'd stopped somewhere.

When she shifted in her seat to face him, he noticed her knuckles were white from fiercely clutching the purse in her lap.

"I came to surrender myself to justice."

Now he wished he'd waited until they were parked somewhere or had indeed stayed at the Justice Department. He didn't want to be holding the steering wheel just at that moment. He wished he could reach over, take her by the shoulders, and stop her from trembling. "What?"

"I—I've done something terrible." Her voice quavered. "I didn't mean to do it. I was foolish, irresponsible, impulsive . . . been mollycoddled all my life. I don't know. . . . That's just it; I *didn't* know. I didn't know what I was doing—"

"Liesel, Liesel," he said, "just tell me. Did von Woerner do something to you?"

Her gaze caught his for the barest moment, and she looked surprised by his words. "To me? No! Of course not. I'm the one who's done wrong this time, Mr. de Serre."

"Short of aiding him in blowing up another ship, Liesel, I can't imagine whatever you've done is as bad as you think. Just tell me."

"He's gone! He's fled! He knows you're after him. I told him."

David turned the corner. The river wasn't far, and he headed to a quiet park. Her news wasn't the shock she must have thought it would be. Not that he knew von Woerner had fled but that she'd warned him away. He'd already considered the possibility that she might give away what she knew.

She was crying softly into a handkerchief—his own, he noted, although it appeared as if it had been freshly laundered by the crease down the center.

"Liesel." He said her name, realizing for the first time that he'd stopped calling her Miss Bonner some time ago without being aware of it. She didn't seem to mind or even notice. "Tell me, is it because he's fled that you're so distraught, or because you're worried over your part in his disappearance?"

She raised watery blue eyes to him. "I—I suppose both. Are you going to have me arrested for treason?"

He wanted to laugh but held back. She didn't look to be in the type of humor that could tolerate even a chuckle. "No, I'm not."

"But you said—"

He nodded. "I know what I said. I couldn't very well have you going around town talking about this case, now could I?"

"But that's what I did. Well, I didn't go about town, but the very first time I saw Josef, I betrayed everything. Like a trumpet just waiting to blare!"

"The fact is, Liesel," he said her name again, seeing no reason to return to formalities, "I still need your help. Whatever von Woerner thinks doesn't matter anymore. He may be so worried about hiding that this slows down his activities. Who knows? And when we do catch him, I'll need you to testify. To tell the court exactly what you said to him that resulted in this obvious flight from justice. His actions prove his guilt."

"Testify?" She bit her lower lip, looking as if his words heralded a new set of worries.

"The whole German network is crumbling. We have a couple of their officers in prison. Those left outside are still a strong bunch, but they liked their authority figure close by. Now that most leaders are either gone or incarcerated, the underlings are starting to get messy. It's only a matter of time before we've nabbed von Woerner and his cohorts."

He eyed her, seeing the tears had stopped, but she still looked unhappy and concerned. "Von Woerner knows you know about him. If he needs help, who do you think he's going to run to? His father, who still thinks he's innocent as a lamb? The other German reservists, who are in as much trouble as he is? No, Liesel. He'll run to you. You're the only one he can trust now."

"Because he thinks I tipped him off to protect him," she whispered, her gaze somewhere far away. Then she looked at David. "I didn't, though. I didn't try to warn him. It wasn't like that at all."

He couldn't help himself. He reached over and patted her hands folded in her lap. "I believe you."

She looked perplexed. "You said you didn't trust me, Mr. de Serre. Why don't you think I did it on purpose?"

He couldn't explain all the reasons. He wasn't entirely sure of them himself. "Let's just say I doubt you'd come to me if that's what you did." Then he looked at the park around them rather than at her tear-streaked face. "Did you tell anyone else what you know? Because of being upset by his disappearance?"

She shook her head. "I couldn't. No one in the family will ever believe Josef is a . . . spy. I don't want them to know. And his father . . . well, if he doesn't know already, what good could it do him to know sooner rather than later?"

David didn't dwell on the protectiveness in her attitude. Just whom was she protecting? The family or their memory of an untainted von Woerner?

"Well, they will one day. But not yet. You'll have to keep this to yourself, Liesel."

"All right. I don't want to tell them, anyway. Not even his father."

"How do you know for sure he's disappeared?"

"His father came to my house this morning. He told us Josef never came home last night. The police found his car off the road."

It didn't surprise David that the locals hadn't bothered to contact his office. They rarely worked together. And they were so shorthanded in his office it wasn't unexpected that their sporadic surveillance on von Woerner had let him slip away. "I'd like to see that car. Do you know where it is?"

Liesel shook her head. "But the police do if they haven't already moved it. They're looking for him. Uncle Otto thinks perhaps Josef hit his head and is wandering about in some sort of stupor."

"That would be too good to be . . ." David didn't finish his sentence, catching sight of her frown. He turned to start his car. "Let's go to the locals, then. I'd like to see if Josef left anything behind in that car."

After what turned out to be a lengthy visit at the police station, they were at last directed to an area outside town where von Woerner's car had been located. Because of David's involvement on the federal level, several officers came along. David hardly welcomed them, but whenever a case warranted federal investigation, it often aroused unwanted "help."

The tree looked as if it had received the worst of the collision. The sporty 1917 Stutz Bearcat was built like a ship, solid and sturdy. Only one headlight was smashed. David doubted Josef himself had sustained much harm. Besides, the car was still in running order. The police had left it for the father to claim. No doubt von Woerner had abandoned it, knowing it was easily described and associated with him.

A visual search inside the open car revealed nothing about its owner. Evidently the impact had opened the luggage box at the back, and David noticed Liesel came around to look inside, appearing curious about any contents. But it, too, was empty except for some tools for working on the motor. One other item David found interesting: a recent copy of the *Shipping News*. Interesting, indeed, since it regularly reported ships that had been sunk. Odd that a glass and coking coal salesmen should have such a thing, unless of course he was keeping track of his successes at sea. David took up the newspaper and tossed it on the seat of his own yellow roadster.

He viewed the surrounding area. Von Woerner could have headed to any number of places west of the city. The train track wasn't far. He could have hopped a train to New York, a likely possibility. Or he could have hitched a ride heading in any direction, any direction at all as long as it led away from Washington.

Just then, David caught sight of another motor heading down the road. An impressive Peerless 48-Six touring car. It slowed as it approached the snag of police cars in the road, and an officer attempted to wave it along. Instead, it pulled up behind von Woerner's car, and the two occupants got out. It took a moment, but David recognized them both.

Karl Bonner came to Liesel and took her hands in his, a look of concern in the eyes that were so similar to hers. Otto von Woerner moved slower with his stocky build, but he, too, joined Liesel, who stood near David. David had never met Otto von Woerner, but he'd seen him on one of the occasions he had his son under surveillance.

"We've been looking for Josef everywhere," Karl said to his sister. "Nothing. We found nothing. Uncle Otto said you were looking, too. Did you come up with anything?"

Liesel shook her head; then she looked at David as if unsure how to proceed. Karl's gaze followed. It was obvious he didn't recognize David at first. When he did, he stiffened, and his back went visibly rigid.

David ignored the cool reception. "We're doing our best to locate him, Mr. Bonner." David turned to Otto. "I assume you are Mr. von Woerner?"

"That's right," Karl answered for Otto.

Neither man extended any further courtesy.

There was little David could offer either man by way of comfort, so he stepped back toward the senior police officer, keeping within hearing distance of Liesel.

———

Liesel watched Mr. de Serre step away, wishing he wouldn't leave her alone. Perhaps he thought she welcomed her brother and Uncle Otto, though that was anything but true. She didn't know what to say to them. She only knew that she couldn't tell them the truth.

"What's *he* doing here?" Karl whispered, cocking his head toward de Serre.

"He's helping in the search for Josef."

"You mean you went to him for help instead of going with Uncle Otto to look for Josef? I swear, Liesel, I don't understand you! You go off to some perfect stranger—that is, if he is a stranger. Just what's going on between the two of you, anyway?"

Liesel glared at her brother. "Nothing!"

In the next moment, shadows closed in from both sides. Behind Karl came Uncle Otto, and Mr. de Serre approached from behind Liesel. It was as if an imaginary battle line had sprung up between her and Karl, and secondary forces were on the flanks.

"Perhaps I should formally introduce myself to you, Mr. Bonner," said Mr. de Serre's firm and familiar voice behind her. "You already know my name, but perhaps you don't know that I work for the Justice Department's Bureau of Investigation. The fact that your sister and I already know each other only helps in this case. I intend doing what I can on a professional basis to help find your friend."

"You are a policeman?" Uncle Otto said.

"My department investigates several areas of trouble including kidnapping."

"Kidnapping!" The monocle on Uncle's Otto's left eye dropped to its chain around his neck. "You believe my son was kidnapped?"

David shook his head. "No, Mr. von Woerner. I only meant that we investigate the sudden disappearances of people."

Despite Mr. de Serre's explanation, Uncle Otto repeated the word *kidnapping* several times, shaking his head and mumbling something about ransom.

Liesel stepped closer to Uncle Otto, putting a hand to his solid forearm, barely aware this was perhaps the first time she had ever touched him. "I'm sure Josef wasn't kidnapped," she whispered. "Mr. de Serre doesn't think so, either."

"Then what am I to think? My son disappeared. Where can he be?" In his agitation, he spoke German again. Liesel knew Karl understood as well as she did. She didn't bother to translate for Mr. de Serre. If he didn't clearly understand the words, he must have detected enough about Uncle Otto's distress to get the meaning.

"Liesel," said Karl, "I'd like to speak to you—alone. Would you excuse us?" Without waiting for either Uncle Otto or Mr. de Serre to answer, her brother took her arm and directed her several feet away. Glancing back at the other two, she saw they looked curious but would not hear whatever it was Karl seemed so desperate to say.

"Just what kind of relationship do you have with this guy, this de Serre? I think it's mighty odd that he just happens to be working on this case all of a sudden. I thought you met him at the railroad?"

"We met when he was working on a case and it led him there," she answered, evasively but truthfully. "And there is no 'relationship.' You shouldn't be asking such a question. It wouldn't be any of your business even if there were."

"It's my business if this guy had anything to do with Josef going off like he has. I'm the one who sent Josef home after you. He didn't happen to walk in on you and him, did he? And that's why Josef left to drive off like a maniac, having an accident?"

"Karl!" Liesel could think of nothing else to say. That her brother thought so little of her made her want to shrink from his bold accusation.

Evidently either Mr. de Serre had very sensitive hearing or he could read lips—or perhaps he only read Liesel's sudden unrest, for he was at her side in an instant.

"Is there anything I can help clear up?" he offered.

Karl looked as if he were going to hit him, clenching his fists and swinging one of them back ever so slightly. Instead, he held them at his side while his feet ground into the earth.

"You can tell me what's going on between you and my sister. I don't believe for a minute that you were called to this case coincidentally."

"Of course I wasn't," de Serre agreed. "Your sister came to my office to tell me her friend had disappeared. It's called using the resources at hand, Mr. Bonner. She knew I worked for the Justice Department and would readily help. Besides, the locals eventually would have called in me or one of my co-workers if Mr. von Woerner didn't locate his son before long. I'd say she did the right thing, wouldn't you?"

"And how does she know you well enough to run straight to you, anyway? Just how well have you gotten to know my sister?"

"I would say we've become something more than acquaintances, something less than good friends. What I don't understand, Mr. Bonner, is the accusation in your voice. You sound as if you think your sister or I had something to do with von Woerner's disappearance. If you do, say so."

"All right, I will. Everybody knows my sister and Josef were going to be married. Then Josef goes out of town—on business, as usual—and while he's gone you start coming around. Josef comes back in town, and my sister avoids him. Looks to me like she was going to dump him for you, and Josef found out. That's why he's gone off."

"A broken heart caused by your sister, is that it?"

"Not entirely," Karl said coldly.

De Serre received the shared blame aimed his way without retort. "An interesting scenario, Mr. Bonner. But I wonder why she would have done everything she could to try and find him if she was going to 'dump' him?"

Karl looked from de Serre to Liesel with narrowed eyes. He felt anything but a brother to her at that moment. "A guilty conscience can make us do a number of things."

Liesel turned away. She couldn't bear the sight of Karl's accusing face and Uncle Otto's shock at having heard that accusation. Then she felt de Serre's hand at her elbow, steering her from her brother's company.

When they were well away, he whispered in her ear, "He'll know the truth before long, Liesel. And he'll choke on every word he just said when he's giving you the apology you deserve." Then he squeezed her arm gently. "But we can't tell them yet. I'm sorry."

Liesel nodded, fighting and winning the battle against tears. He was right, and she knew it. Karl acted out of ignorance, something she'd accused him of many times before. But he would understand. Eventually.

Just then a pair on foot joined the group, stopping to talk to one officer. Papa and Ernst.

"Papa!" she called. His strong arms around her brought Liesel her first tangible comfort of the day. "Oh, Papa!"

Tears flowed out uncontrollably; she couldn't help herself. Papa stroked her head and held her close, shushing her with whispers about everything being all right soon. She wanted to tell him, more than anyone, that it wouldn't be. How could it be?

Confusion erupted just then, interrupting the moment of comfort. Karl and Otto descended on Liesel: Otto speaking German about a kidnapping and Karl demanding to know what had happened when Josef had been with her yesterday.

"You're the last one to have seen him, Liesel," Karl said roughly. "What happened?"

"You don't have to attack her, Karl," said Ernst, who stood beside Papa.

"I'm not. I'm just trying to find out what happened."

Liesel faced Karl. "He just left! He drove away. That's all." Her father's arm about her shoulders steadied her.

There was a general upheaval after that, everyone having something to say at the same time. De Serre spoke above the rest, and the family unit all looked to him at once. "Actually, since you were the last to see Mr. von Woerner, Miss Bonner, I'll need to take you with me to answer some questions. It's routine, of course. Would you mind coming with me?"

Liesel could imagine nothing more appealing at the moment. She wanted to get away from all of them, even Papa.

She stepped toward de Serre, but Papa didn't leave her side. He followed.

When they reached the yellow roadster, Liesel spoke to her father. "I don't mind going with Mr. de Serre, Papa."

"No daughter of mine is going to be questioned all by herself," he said firmly.

"But Papa—"

"I assure you this is all quite by the book, Mr. Bonner," de Serre said, halting before getting into his car.

"That's fine," Papa said. "I'll just go along for the ride, then."

Liesel looked from her father to de Serre, who appeared to be looking at Liesel for guidance. She knew then his request for questioning had served as an escape for her, and gratitude filled her for his well-timed rescue. Though she would have preferred to leave even Papa behind, she didn't want to worry him. When she shrugged, de Serre invited Papa to the backseat.

"Oh, Papa, let me sit back there," Liesel said, remembering how crowded he'd been the last time they'd driven together in the little Runabout.

Her father allowed her the tonneau seat, and they drove back downtown to the Justice Department building without a word. Somehow, the fact that the four-story building housed only a handful of offices as compared to the palatial Treasury Department across the street brought Liesel comfort. The situation was intimidating enough without being reminded so formally that she was dealing with the entire U.S. government.

They took the elevator to the third floor. It was late in the afternoon, but offices were still full. De Serre introduced Liesel to someone named Mrs. Lindsey. The only thing Liesel noticed about her was a friendly smile, but even that couldn't dispel a new sort of unease rising within. While she was glad to be away from Karl and Uncle Otto, she knew de Serre still had a job to do, and she would have to answer his questions. What would come of such questioning? Would he believe that she'd only acted rashly and hadn't meant to warn Josef away?

She'd also wondered how de Serre would handle her father—if he would reveal the truth to him. She found she was eager for her father to know. She needed to be able to talk to someone about everything.

While de Serre showed Papa the room in which he would ask his questions, he nonetheless did not offer Papa a chair.

"As you can see, Mr. Bonner, this is official. Mrs. Lindsey will be present the entire time, transcribing what your daughter has to say. You can see she will be safe. I'm afraid I cannot allow you in the room during questioning. Against regulations."

"Oh," Papa said, frowning. "Oh. Then I'll go." He started toward the door but turned back to Liesel, halting awkwardly. "I'll be right outside, *mein*

Liebe. Right outside the door." He looked a little lost, as if he could use a bit of encouragement himself.

"I can direct you to a fine coffee shop right next door, Mr. Bonner," said Mrs. Lindsey. "Maybe you'd be more comfortable there."

Liesel's father shook his head. "No, no thank you. I'll wait here." He looked again at Liesel. "Right outside the door."

Liesel nodded, then watched as he left the room.

She was alone with de Serre and Mrs. Lindsey. De Serre pulled one of the three sturdy wooden chairs up to the oblong table and offered it to Liesel. Mrs. Lindsey, with a pad of paper and a pencil, sat ready to work. Liesel looked around the stark room. It held absolutely nothing to welcome a visitor: no windows, no carpet, no adornment for the walls. A single light hanging from the ceiling provided light. Evidently electricity had been added to the old building, for the wiring was covered by a painted pipe that led to the switch by the door. It was a plain, cold little room, almost as intimidating as the Greek-columned building across the street might have been.

"Mrs. Lindsey will take down everything you say, all right, Liesel?" de Serre said. His tone was gentle, and Liesel noticed Mrs. Lindsey's gaze popped up from her pad as if surprised for some reason. She smiled at the back of de Serre's head and also at Liesel, but Liesel didn't have time to dwell on the older woman's action.

"Wait just a moment, will you, Mrs. Lindsey?" Mr. de Serre said over his shoulder. He leaned closer and spoke in a low voice. "Mrs. Lindsey knows as much about this case as I do. You can be perfectly comfortable talking about all of this in front of her. But first I want to apologize for bringing you straight here. I wanted to get you away from your family because I could see the whole thing was putting you out. You could have used a breather before getting into all of this, and I'm sorry I couldn't provide it for you. Will you be all right with this now, or do you want me to tell your father that we'd rather do this another time? Of course, that would mean your father will want to take you home, and I'm not sure that'll be any easier for you. But I'll let you decide."

She smiled at him gratefully, silently thanking God for sending someone like de Serre to handle this case. And to think he'd once made her cringe! *That* Agent de Serre seemed as remote as the old Josef.

"No, Mr. de Serre, I'll answer your questions. I think perhaps it might help to talk about it. I can't do that at home."

De Serre began his questioning. He was thorough without applying pressure, probing yet not indelicate. He was quick to understand each answer despite her occasional pauses and stutters. Soon she was at ease, discussing the whole thing the way she'd longed to do for quite some time. She told him everything that had transpired the day before, from the extreme political views Josef espoused to the marriage proposal he'd issued.

"He hadn't proposed to you before yesterday?" de Serre asked. He seemed surprised.

Liesel glanced down at her hands. She still held her handkerchief—de Serre's handkerchief. She had intended to return it to him the next time she saw him, all fresh and ready for his own use. But it had been the first thing she'd grabbed out of her purse that morning. "Everyone understood that Josef and I . . . well, we were dating. Our families have been close for years. It was just sort of understood."

"And what did you say to his proposal?"

"I knew I could never marry him—I think I learned that before yesterday. But after what he said about Germany and God and how he molded God into his own image, I learned he thought Germany was more important than God. I never knew Josef, even after all these years."

She laughed a little, though there was no humor behind it. She forgot that Mrs. Lindsey was taking down each word she said. She even forgot Mrs. Lindsey was in the room. "Like my brother Karl. I guess I don't know him, either. I never would have expected him to say the things he said to me this morning."

"Your brother and Josef are good friends, aren't they?"

Liesel nodded.

"Do you think Karl would help Josef, even if he knew the truth?"

Liesel considered the unpleasant thought, but it didn't take her long to shake her head. "I may not know my brother as well as I believed, but I can't imagine if he knew how passionate Josef is about Germany he would do anything to help him that would go against America. My father raised us differently than Uncle Otto raised Josef. My father loves America. Even if Karl feels more loyalty to Josef than he does toward me, I don't think he would betray our country, even for Josef."

Mr. de Serre paused and glanced at his wristwatch. Liesel had no idea how long they'd been there, but suddenly realized her body was stiff, as if she'd sat in the same position too long.

"I think that's about all I need today," he said. "But I'll be keeping in touch with you. As I mentioned earlier, if Josef is in trouble, he'll more than likely come to you. He may trust Karl, but Karl evidently doesn't know about all this, and Josef will come to the one who does. Which means," he added as he stood, holding out a hand for her, "if I do come around, it will only make Karl more suspicious that it was you who drove Josef away. Would you rather I kept my visits a secret? Telephoning you at your job, perhaps?"

Liesel considered the whole impossible situation a moment before answering. "No, Mr. de Serre. I don't think I'll be working for Uncle Otto any longer. It hasn't been a good fit anyway, and after today, I doubt if he'll want me around. Since my family doesn't have a telephone, it'll be difficult enough for you to contact me without having to worry about Karl. Besides, if you don't mind, I'd like you to keep me up-to-date on all of this—anything you find out about Josef."

He led her to the closed door without reply. He still held her hand as if he'd forgotten to let go. "I know you will contact me if you hear from him, Liesel. This time, I'll try not to be too far from my phone."

She smiled, a little bit sorry that the interview had come to an end. It meant having to go back home, where she could no longer be herself.

"I'll call for you at your house." He stood at the door, his free hand now on the knob. "I'll come by tomorrow afternoon, all right?"

She nodded.

"But you'll call me if you need me before that," he suggested, and she nodded again. Then he let go of her hand and opened the door. Papa stood looking tired and worried. He searched Liesel's eyes.

"We're all through now, Mr. Bonner," said de Serre as Mrs. Lindsey disappeared with her full notebook and worn pencil. "I'm sorry it took so long, but these things must be gone over repeatedly so we can find the slightest clue we might have missed the first time."

"I don't know what could have taken so long," Papa said, still looking at Liesel. His voice sounded as tired and worried as he looked.

"It's all right, Papa. We spent some of the time just talking. We shouldn't have done that with you waiting. I'm sorry."

"If it helped you get through this day, *Liebchen*, you could have taken until tomorrow. Let's go now. Your mama will be waiting."

Liesel looked at de Serre, offering a wave before walking beside her father to the elevator. Part of her didn't want to go at all. Somehow, just knowing Mr. de Serre knew everything made her not want to leave his reassuring side.

CHAPTER *Seventeen*

AT the sight of Josef's Bearcat parked outside their home, Liesel and her father quickened their pace. They found the family in the parlor: Mama, the twins and Greta, Ernst and his wife, Helga, along with Karl and Katie. Uncle Otto sat in Papa's chair. Josef was not in the room.

Liesel's mixed hopes deflated even as Papa spoke. "We saw Josef's car in front. We thought . . ."

"Uncle Otto wishes Karl to use it until Josef comes home," said Mama, who neared them. She stopped in front of Liesel, studying her closely. "You were gone such a long time."

The last thing Liesel wanted was another session of questioning, even if de Serre's inquiry had been as pleasant as possible. This one, however, promised to be more of an interrogation—not just because Karl still had a cool look on his face, but because she knew she'd have to juggle every answer. But she had little choice.

Uncle Otto stood. "Is there any word of my son? Do you know anything else?"

Liesel shook her head. "No, there is no more word. The federal investigators and the local police are looking for him."

Otto shook his head, rubbing his hands together. "Where could he be? Why should he have left unless he is hurt?"

Liesel knew she could say nothing. But as her gaze slid from Uncle Otto, it passed to Karl, who stared at her boldly. She didn't want another confrontation with him, particularly in front of the family. She ignored his conspicuous glower.

In spite of her silent wish, Karl spoke. "What kind of questions did they ask you?"

Liesel answered slowly. "About such things as time and the direction he headed and if I had any idea where he might be."

"And what did you say?"

Everyone, not just Karl, looked at her now. "I told them everything I know. I don't know if I was of any help or not."

"And just what is everything you know?"

Liesel raised an inner, grateful prayer for a new surge of strength she felt. Surely it came from God. She held Karl's gaze. "I told them I have no idea where Josef might have gone. Our visit lasted a short time. He left without telling me where he was going."

Mama spoke before Karl could reply. "And you assumed he was headed back to the picnic, of course."

Liesel said nothing.

"We're all worried about Josef," Mama said. "But we must eat. Liesel, I know you are tired, but could you come to the kitchen and help me start supper? It's late, but no one has eaten. We must, you know. Otto, you will stay for supper." It was neither a question nor a command, just a simple statement that Uncle Otto did not dispute.

Katie also followed them to the kitchen, and Liesel was glad to be away from her brother's unfaltering gaze. She knew Karl was worried about Josef. That he thought she was keeping something from them was obvious. She wondered if anyone else felt that way.

Preparing supper was a diversion, especially since no one in the kitchen brought up the subject of the day. With everyone waiting to eat, Mama made a quick meal of boiled kale and sausages, while Liesel prepared a salad and Katie set the table.

Liesel endured the meal, generally not looking Karl's way. She wasn't much more comfortable around Uncle Otto. But before the evening was out, Liesel knew she must find the words to tell her uncle she wouldn't return to his office. She wondered if he would go there himself, at least until he knew Josef's condition.

And then what? How will it be for Uncle Otto, a German citizen living in an enemy country, once it's discovered that his son is a traitor to America? Perhaps she should not leave his factory so quickly. Perhaps she could help him somehow once everything became known. Leaving when she knew things to come would only get more difficult seemed to be selfishly bailing out.

Papa was careful to keep the mealtime pleasant. No one spoke of Josef or of the war. Despite frequent awkward lapses, the meal passed in relative peace.

Liesel's mind kept floating to Josef. Where was he? Would he be safer to come home and face whatever charges the government leveled or better off in hiding? Surely no one was better off hiding!

How had it all become such a mess? She'd loved him, hadn't she? When was the last time she'd felt her love for Josef? She was surprised to realize she'd taken it for granted so long that it was difficult to remember.

One evening did come to mind. They'd gone on a drive one cold December night and somehow ended up on a road she normally took all costs to avoid: it overlooked shantytown. Much to her dismay, instead of continuing on, Josef had slowed the car to a halt. He'd smiled at her and asked if she was feeling brave. If so, he wanted her help on an errand.

She couldn't have imagined what he was going to do, much less would want her help with. But curious, she had nodded. He'd cut the engine and turned off the headlamps near the section of road that rose above the abominable shacks below. With dusk, shadows appeared that to Liesel were preferable to seeing any stark details of how many people lived. She prayed the tithe she gave at church could be spread wide and far to help those in need such as this.

On that night, Josef had shown her his own way of giving. Going around to the back of his car, he'd opened his luggage trunk to reveal a stack of crisp woolen blankets and two large, covered pots. He instructed Liesel to grab the folded covers while Josef himself took the two heavy pots by their handles.

Then he led the way. They might be poor, he'd whispered, but they still had pride. He knew a spot to leave the food and bedding where neither party would have to see a face. No embarrassment on either side, just a much-needed exchange.

"Exchange?" she'd asked. "They're receiving your donation, but what are you receiving in return?"

He grinned. "I get to feel like I've helped somebody go to bed with a full stomach for once under a warm blanket. There's nothing like it. Come on. There are kids and old people down there. When we get back to the motorcar, I flash my lights twice, and someone comes for this when we leave. Simple as that."

Remembering that night, a surge of love for him rekindled over his generosity and goodness. *Josef! Where are you?*

It was late by the time supper ended, almost ten o'clock. Liesel looked around at Mama's half-filled plate, knowing she wasn't the only one with a reduced appetite.

By the time Liesel was finished with the dishes, she hoped she could go straight to bed. Ernst and Karl had already left with their wives. When she passed the parlor, Liesel was surprised that Uncle Otto was still there. He spoke in low tones to her father. Greta and the twins must have already gone to bed, for the two men were alone.

"Good night," Liesel said as she continued on her way.

"Liesel, one moment, please," said Uncle Otto. Liesel stopped and turned back to the parlor. Uncle Otto raised himself from the plush chair and made his way to stand in front of her. Papa did not join them, but Liesel could see that he watched from his chair.

"Liesel, your brother Karl made accusations today," Uncle Otto said quietly in German. "I do not understand why he should say such things if he did not have reason."

Liesel closed her eyes. How tired she was of this day! She looked at Uncle Otto again, prepared to do what she must. "Karl was upset. I don't think he knew what he was saying."

"This man, this Mr. de Serre. What is he to you?"

Liesel was unsure what to say, but after only the briefest consideration she answered. "A friend."

"Did Josef know you and this man are friends?"

Crossing her arms in front of her, wariness filled her at the line of questioning while she reminded herself how distraught Uncle Otto must be. "No, they never met."

"And you never told Josef about him?"

Liesel shook her head.

Uncle Otto put a hand on Liesel's shoulder and patted once. "I don't know what to think."

"I understand," she whispered.

Uncle Otto looked as if he might turn away, but instead he cleared his throat and spoke again. "I will be in the office tomorrow, Liesel. Business must continue, and I will need to carry on. But I think it best if you . . . if you are not there for a while."

"Not there?"

"Yes, Liesel. These next days will be hard for you as well. And if I must return to carry on, you will only serve as a reminder. I must put this out of my mind."

Liesel looked at him, but he did not meet her gaze. His excuse seemed thoroughly implausible. He would not be able to put Josef out of his mind whether she were there or not. How could he? Was he trying to spare her from working while she was so distraught?

Or perhaps he didn't want her there because he blamed her for Josef's disappearance. As Karl did.

"I will do as you say, Uncle Otto," she told him softly. "But if you change your mind, please let me come back. Perhaps we can help each other get through this difficult time. Together. As a family."

"Yes, yes," he whispered, turning away. He went to the door without saying good night to her or to Papa.

———

Liesel was reluctant to go downstairs the next morning, although she woke as early as usual. She helped Greta choose what to wear, brushed the child's hair and styled it into two thick braids, and buttoned the top button of Greta's cotton blouse when she fussed with it. When Greta was gone, Liesel took her time getting dressed. She went into the bathroom and gave herself a sponge bath, then brushed her hair and fashioned it into a bun at the back, the way she used to before getting it trimmed to a bob. It was too long to be considered a bob anymore, and Liesel didn't have the desire to fuss over how her hair looked.

She dressed in a mauve cotton floral. A casual day dress, not quite right for church or the office, but for a day spent staying at home with her mother, it was just right. She hadn't forgotten that de Serre planned to check in on her, a visit she regarded with both anticipation and a hint of uneasiness. She wasn't sure he trusted her yet, and even though he was the only person who knew everything, the fact remained that she was nothing more than part of a case to him. She expected his visit to last no longer than the length of a brief greeting at the door.

Part of her wished it could be different somehow. Different in a way she couldn't—or wouldn't—define. All she knew was that from the moment she first met Agent David de Serre she'd been prey to a wide range of emotions. Emotions she wasn't ready either to sort out or to dwell upon.

She supposed she would have to look for another job. Mama didn't need her help around the house, at least not enough to keep Liesel as busy as she liked to be. And she doubted Uncle Otto would ask her to return, even—or especially—after the truth was revealed about Josef. She doubted Uncle Otto would understand that Liesel was willing to cooperate with the American government against Josef.

Still, Liesel felt the same as ever about working. She needed to do something worthwhile, and she wanted to be part of the great service army. Waiting to find out exactly what was to become of Josef would be intolerable if
she didn't have some activity to divert her thoughts.

In the kitchen, she talked with her mother about plans to find a job.

"Oh, I understand wanting to work," said Mama, kneading bread dough
at the kitchen table. "But you should give Otto a few days, *mein Herz*. He
may want you to come back once Josef returns. And I'm sure he'll be back
soon."

Liesel looked at her mother's face. She looked hopeful but not quite
serene. Mama's face, Liesel thought, was one that had always offered help in
defining Liesel's own thoughts. From the days when Liesel was a young girl,
it was Mama's face she and the rest of the children sought to decide whether
to laugh or cry over a fall or spill. As Liesel grew, it was the approval or
censure on Mama's face that helped form her own opinions. Even now with
Mama's limited knowledge of the facts, Liesel took comfort in her Mama's
hope.

"I don't think Uncle Otto wants me there because of what Karl said,"
Liesel told her. "I think Karl—and Uncle Otto, for that matter—blame me
for Josef's disappearance."

"Don't be silly, Liesel. It wasn't your fault. Why would they think
that?"

She shrugged. "Karl thinks I was going to tell Josef I didn't want to see
him anymore because of Mr. de Serre."

"Is that true?"

Liesel shook her head. It wasn't true, at least not in the way Karl
thought.

"Then he hasn't anything to his notion at all, has he? So put it out of
your mind. Otto will come to his senses. He is only upset and rightfully so.
Soon things will be back to normal. You'll see."

Liesel wished Mama was right but knew she was not. Nothing would
ever be the same again. It would only get worse once everyone learned the
truth. There was no telling how ugly it could get. Once Josef's activities
became known, the whole neighborhood might turn against them for being
Josef's friends.

The morning passed slowly, and as the afternoon hours approached,
Liesel found herself distracted by thoughts of de Serre's impending visit.
Each time she heard a noise, she thought it was a tap at the door. She kept
asking Mama what she could do to help, anything to get her mind on some-

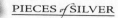

thing else. It was far easier, she determined, to have him come unexpectedly than to be awaiting his call.

When Mama said she needed to go to the corner market for some fresh vegetables, Liesel eagerly volunteered to run the errand. But Mama said she needed to drop in on a neighbor who lived on the way and left Liesel behind with a sewing project instead. Rather than making rags of the stained, pink-striped tablecloth, Mama thought they could salvage much of the material by making napkins. Of course, they did not have another striped tablecloth to match them, but for family use, they would be fine. Liesel welcomed the task but wished it wasn't quite so mindless.

When finally there was a tap at the door—a real one, not imagined—Liesel jumped, jabbing herself with a needle. A spot of blood appeared immediately, and she held up her hand to save the square she was working on until, with her other hand, she located the discarded material and used it to wipe her finger clean. Making a fist to prevent further bleeding, she went to answer the door. Her throbbing finger was exactly what she needed—a distraction from any lingering nervousness.

As Liesel opened the door, de Serre's presence filled the threshold. Liesel knew it wouldn't be proper to invite him inside without Mama there, but she hadn't intended doing that anyway. De Serre was a busy man, surely he wouldn't stay long.

"Good afternoon," he said.

"Hello." The screen door was still between them, and she hoped he didn't notice if her cheeks were suddenly as pink as the stripes on the material in her hand. "Is there any news of Josef?"

He shook his head. "Nothing yet. A vagrant who jumped a train in Baltimore said there was somebody on the same car he was in, but whoever it was never said a word. It might have been Josef from the description."

"Headed where?"

"New York."

"Are you going there?"

"I have two other agents on that trail. I'm coordinating the leads from the office in case that one doesn't guide us to Josef, after all. Another tip might come in."

"Oh."

There seemed little else to say. Liesel looked down at her finger. It was still bleeding, and she pressed the scrap of cloth back to her fingertip.

"Hurt yourself?" he inquired.

She looked up at him. "Not really. I just pricked my finger on a sewing needle. It's nothing."

"I have a bandage and adhesive in my car," he offered.

"No, it's all right."

Neither spoke. Liesel felt awkward and wondered if he did, too.

"Liesel," he said at last. "Will you come outside a moment, sit on the porch with me?"

"All right."

The day was cooler than previous days; the humidity was down. It felt good to be outside. He invited her to the swing, waiting for her to sit before he did.

"I'll want to check in on you on a fairly regular basis," he said. "You may hear from me every day until Josef is found."

"Yes, I expected that."

"Did you?" He sounded surprised.

She nodded. "I know you don't entirely trust me, Mr. de Serre. I guess if I imagined our positions reversed, your caution is justified. You hardly know me. But I assure you I will contact you if Josef gets in touch with me."

With his arms folded in front of him, leaning back on the swing, he looked comfortable. "So you have me all figured out, do you? That I'm keeping an eye on you only because I think you'll lead me straight to von Woerner?"

She cocked her head. That's exactly what she thought. "Am I wrong?"

"Somewhat. As it happens, that's not the only reason. If you are as innocent as you say in all this, then I wouldn't be doing my job if I ignored your safety, at least until von Woerner is caught. He may not want to bring trouble your way, Liesel, but with all his connections, he may not be able to stop it if he comes to you for help."

"So . . . you're here to warn me?"

He leaned toward her. "In a way, yes. Not to frighten you, Liesel, although I'm sure you don't think Josef would do you any harm. But I want you to be aware that if he is involved with a German network of saboteurs, these are real people involved in real espionage, willing to do whatever they think necessary to get in the way of America helping the Allies. Josef may try to draw you in somehow if he thinks he can."

"That would be impossible."

"You speak quickly for someone who was nearly engaged to this man. It depends on how persuasive he can be."

"I assure you I have no intention of being 'drawn in.'" She felt herself getting ruffled, when just yesterday she'd felt so comfortable around him.

He stood, perhaps sensing their once amiable air had disappeared. "I'm only covering all possibilities and perhaps explaining why I find it necessary to make myself a pest. It's as much for your own protection, Liesel."

She stood, too. "I feel perfectly safe in my own home, Mr. de Serre. And that's about the extent of my travels these days."

"So you won't be going back to the von Woerner factory as you thought?"

"Not unless my uncle wishes for me to return. Things are bound to change for him. Not for the better. I don't want to abandon him when he needs friends most of all."

"Your loyalty would be admirable in most cases, but that's just the sort of thing Josef von Woerner will use to get your help."

Liesel didn't care if he saw her suddenly sour mood. "You've made it quite clear you don't trust me, Agent de Serre, and as I've already said, I don't blame you. However, if you insist upon checking up on me, perhaps in the future you won't continue to state the obvious."

He stood inches away, looking as if he would speak. Liesel prepared herself for a backlash—but it never came.

Instead, de Serre placed his hat on his head, said a curt farewell, then left the porch.

David didn't look behind him when he drove his car away from the Bonner home. What a fool he was! He'd gone there today to extend the simplest form of help, to let her know he was still available if she needed to talk. And instead he'd shown up and played the bugbear, citing all kinds of dire possibilities about the entire German espionage network swooping down upon her. What was wrong with him?

He'd felt awkward. He hadn't known what to say. She might have smiled during her initial greeting, but she didn't exactly welcome him inside. Yet what was she supposed to do? Invite him in like he was some kind of friend?

Yes, that's exactly what he'd expected.

David shook his head at his own confused thoughts. His behavior had been immature at best, unprofessional at worst. He had a job to do, and he wasn't about to gum up this case. Maybe part of him *was* looking for reasonable justification for visiting her, but none of what he'd said had been fabricated.

More than duty filled his mind. He remembered the look on her face every time von Woerner was mentioned. She wouldn't be so distraught over his disappearance if she didn't still care for him, traitor or not. Could he blame her if she still loved him? Isn't that what love was supposed to be, loyal no matter what?

He might as well admit it. He could not tolerate the thought that Liesel Bonner—every bit the crackerjack she'd once been described as—could continue to love a traitor. Of course, it shouldn't make a difference to David. He wasn't part of her life. But her feelings for von Woerner did have something to do with this case, and for that reason alone, he considered her loyalty to the man a possible obstacle.

Driving slowly, barely concentrating on where he was headed, he spotted a woman walking down the block, carrying a sack in each hand. David stopped the car. Her face might be shaded by a summer hat, but he recognized her immediately.

"Mrs. Bonner," he called.

She looked up. "Oh, Mr. de Serre! How nice to see you."

"Can I offer you a ride home?"

"But you're headed in the other direction!"

"I can turn around at the corner," he said, getting out of his car and approaching her.

"I don't want to keep you from your business, though." She sounded rather solemn. "Liesel told me how you work to find Josef."

"Yes, but I'm not working on it alone. I can certainly take you the two blocks to your house."

When she offered no further protest, he took the groceries out of her hands, placing them in the back, and then turned to assist her into the roadster. When she was seated, he saw her stroke the sleek leather interior.

"What a nice car, Mr. de Serre. So yellow. I like yellow."

David didn't mention that he personally detested the color, that if he'd chosen the car himself, he never would have picked such a shade. But since he'd long ago sworn off his father's money and the bureau didn't pay enough for him to afford a replacement while he was saving money to buy a house, he had no choice but to keep it.

It had been easy to swear off his father and his money, given that his father barely knew he existed. Between nannies, boarding school, and his parents' love of travel, David had never once felt connected to them. Instead, his family was Mio's. Each person in Mio's life from his mother to his wife had accepted David far more enthusiastically than David's own parents.

David made an easy turn at the intersection without questioning what he was doing. He had the distinct feeling he was a bit too pleased to have a second chance at seeing Liesel, but he ignored that feeling altogether.

"So tell me, Mr. de Serre," Mrs. Bonner said. "Is there any news on Josef today?"

"No, I'm sorry, Mrs. Bonner. Your family—and Mr. von Woerner, of course—will be the first people we contact once we find him."

She smiled. "Then you're hopeful you'll find him?"

"Of course," he said. "Everyone gets found sooner or later."

Her smile faded. "Better sooner than later."

He stopped in front of her home. "Don't worry, Mrs. Bonner. We'll find him."

She nodded, then offered a new smile. "Come inside, Mr. de Serre. I'm sure Liesel will be glad to see you."

"Actually, I just left her," he admitted.

"Oh, well, come inside again anyway."

If that was what David had hoped all along, he suddenly felt uncertain. But he took the two grocery bags and followed Mrs. Bonner inside.

"Liesel," Mrs. Bonner called from the door as she stopped to hang up her straw hat.

"In here," came a strangely muffled voice. "I'm just finishing the last—"

Her voice cut off when David stepped around the archway behind her mother. Between Liesel's lips was an assortment of pins, and strewn before her on the dining room table were odd sizes of material, all striped white and pink. On her face was a look of such surprise he hoped she wasn't in danger of swallowing one of those pins.

She spit the items into an open palm before standing stiffly, as if a soldier at attention.

"Look who offered me a ride in his little roadster," said Mama happily. "In here, Mr. de Serre. I need to put some of that in the ice box."

Like an obedient son, David followed Mrs. Bonner into a spacious kitchen. It was as immaculate as what he could see of the rest of the house— apart from the dining room table, of course. As soon as the door swung shut behind him, it swung open again. Liesel entered, her arms folded in front of her.

"Isn't it nice of Mr. de Serre, Liesel?" Mama said.

"Yes." The tone somehow didn't match the word.

He saw that she watched him as he put the bags on the table.

"Mr. de Serre, my husband will be home soon, and I will be getting supper ready. I want that you should stay here for supper. All right?"

"I'm sure Mr. de Serre is—"

"I would like to stay." His deeper tone covered whatever Liesel had to say. He met her surprised stare with a smile. "My office works around the clock. After a dinner break, I'll head back."

"Good, good!" said Mrs. Bonner. "My husband will be asking you questions about how they search for Josef. Will you mind that?"

"No, not at all. I expect you must all be very concerned."

"Yes, yes, that's true. But we're glad you work on this. If you're already a friend of Liesel's, then you know how much Josef means to our family."

He nodded.

"Liesel, will you help me with the vegetables?" asked Mrs. Bonner. "And Mr. de Serre, you sit right here. I'll get you some cool lemonade, and you keep us company while we make supper."

David accepted the lemonade and took a deep sip but did not sit down. He didn't often cook for himself but was entirely capable of doing so. Having been coddled most of his life by servants, his complete naïveté had been a great liability at college, even though many of his fellow students had come from backgrounds every bit as privileged as his own. Those were not the ones he spent the bulk of his time with however. Instead, he'd passed the five-year program with students who had barely scraped together enough money for entrance or who had attended because of a benefactor. They hadn't let him get away with expecting anyone to serve him. Along with his other studies at school, he'd learned to cook and clean up after himself instead of expecting someone else to do it. He could even mend a tear or sew a loose button, but that wasn't something he revealed to many people.

When he offered to help peel potatoes in preparation for the Bonners' meal, he was met with nothing short of surprise on both women's faces.

"It isn't necessary that you work for supper, you know," Mama said.

Liesel, whose surprise had turned to what looked like skepticism, said nothing and handed him a small, sharp-edged knife, setting the sack of potatoes in front of him.

"Just let the peelings fall on this towel," she said. "We put them on the garden when we're done."

It had been some time since he'd peeled potatoes, but after the first few strokes, he regained his skill, and the rest of the potato peeling went smoothly.

The company went smoothly, too. He learned Mrs. Bonner was friendly and witty. And although Liesel was quiet at first, she gradually relaxed. Soon there was a smile on her face, too.

———————

Liesel enjoyed preparing the meal far more than she wanted to admit, especially seeing the concentration on de Serre's face as he listened to Mama's instructions about the *Kartoffelring*. Mama chopped the boiled potatoes to a fine puree, added the other ingredients with a last bit of nutmeg, then told Mr. de Serre what to do next.

Liesel watched as Mama tried to teach de Serre how to mold the potatoes. At first the ring was lopsided, which didn't appear to bother him. In fact, he looked quite pleased with his creation. But Mama said it wouldn't bake evenly, so she smoothed it out with expert hands, then popped it in the oven, telling the government agent what a fine job he'd done.

Liesel shook her head and held back a laugh.

Papa arrived home only minutes before the twins and Greta, who had been at a friend's house for an after-school visit. No one seemed particularly surprised to see Mr. de Serre, Liesel noticed. They accepted him as easily as they would a cousin or other such relative they didn't see very often. They were a trifle more polite but only at first. It wasn't long before the twins were teasing Greta, fighting among themselves, and revealing just how noisy the entire family could get.

Liesel told herself to stop being embarrassed. There was absolutely nothing she could do to change a family who'd behaved this way ever since she could recall.

Papa asked a few questions about the investigation, but not as many as Liesel might have expected. He also asked a number of questions unrelated to Josef. He asked where Mr. de Serre had grown up, and upon learning his guest had attended Harvard, Papa wanted to know more. He himself had attended the university in Berlin, and the two men spent some time comparing experiences.

By the end of the evening, Liesel had learned a plethora of new things about de Serre. She had suspected for some time that his family was well-to-do, at least enough to have hired those chefs he once mentioned. But he didn't speak of them at any length, only that they lived in Virginia. She gained the distinct impression he didn't see them very often.

She also learned he spoke fluent Spanish, had a law degree, and possessed a rather dry sense of humor. The twins seemed to like him instantly, perhaps because of his job. He was careful not to reveal the portion of his work that dealt with espionage. Instead, he talked about kidnapping cases he had knowledge of and about criminals he'd investigated. They weren't the masked bank robbers the boys asked about; instead, they were crafty criminals who worked out detailed plots to pretend they were bankrupt while they hid their money to avoid paying taxes and debts. While the boys might have started the conversation wanting to hear about gun-slinging bandits, they nonetheless asked a variety of questions indicating they found bankruptcy fraud—at least the way Mr. de Serre described it—almost as exciting.

When Liesel walked him to the door, she found she was sorry the evening was over. It was the first bit of enjoyment she'd had in what seemed like a very long time.

"Good night, Mr. de Serre," she said as he took his hat.

"My name is David," he said. "After all, if I call you Liesel, the least you can do is insist on calling me David."

She smiled and nodded. "All right."

He stood at the door, one hand on the screen and the other holding his felt hat.

"I need to apologize, Liesel," he said, speaking low.

She hadn't expected such words. "Why?"

"Earlier today, I must have sounded like a boogey man with all those possibilities I mentioned. I'm sorry. I handled it badly."

"Perhaps you're right, though," she whispered. "I don't like to think about everything that's happening—that Josef or his cohorts may come to me for help." She said nothing about his challenge to her loyalties.

"Remote," he said. "Very remote. I shouldn't have brought it up. Especially what I said about questioning your loyalty. It's that I apologize for."

Liesel looked away, suddenly embarrassed by his softly spoken words. "You're just doing your job," she whispered. Was it possible he was beginning to trust her?

He opened the door. "If it's all right, I'll stop by again tomorrow. But," he added with a smile, "as enjoyable as the evening has been, I don't expect your family to feed me every night. I'll take you out for coffee if that's all right. Say, three o'clock?"

"All right." She wanted to finish her response by saying his name, but something held her back. How odd that she was suddenly shy.

"Good night," he said, then went out the door.

Liesel watched him drive off, undeniably sorry he was gone.

"Good night, David." But no one could have heard her, not even the birds sleeping in Mama's tree.

CHAPTER *Eighteen*

FOR the next week, Liesel's only reason for leaving the house was to accompany Mama to the market, walk Greta to school, or run an occasional errand. And to have coffee or dinner with Mr. de Serre. David.

She was getting used to calling him that. Each time they were together, Liesel found herself more comfortable with him. They talked about all kinds of things, from the war to politics to sermons they had heard through the years. Liesel liked to hear him talk about the Bible. He was well read, though she sensed humility in him. He had thought about so many things, from biblical arguments against the popular new ideas growing out of Darwin's *On the Origin of the Species* to some of the equally humanistic philosophical trends that left so little room for God. She'd grown to admire so much about David: his faith, his knowledge, and the easy way he articulated both.

Walking home from Mario's after sharing dinner one night, the conversation turned to Josef.

"It's been two weeks since Josef left," Liesel mused. They didn't often talk about Josef anymore, but Uncle Otto's Peerless parked at the curb reminded her. "Uncle Otto seems to have given up. He's convinced Josef is . . . dead."

"He isn't."

Liesel raised a surprised gaze to him. "Do you know that for sure?"

"I'm fairly certain. No one has actually spotted him, but we're pretty sure he's in New York."

"How do you know?"

"We caught another agitator yesterday: Friedrich Luedke. At least, that's who I think he is. He claims to be Alfred Reiner, a simple tailor, but we're pretty sure he worked with Josef, and we arrested him in New York. Josef was probably getting help from him."

"Does that mean Josef may not have anyone helping him now?"

"Well, at least not Luedke. We need Josef more than ever. If he agrees to testify against Luedke, he may get a lighter sentence."

A surge of hope coursed through Liesel. "Why didn't you tell me? About this other man, I mean? And that there may be some hope for Josef if he's caught soon?"

"I was going to," he answered. "Once I knew for sure we had the right man." He looked away as if he had more to say but didn't want to speak. "You know, Liesel, it works both ways regarding Luedke. If he agrees to testify against Josef, *he* may be the one to get a lighter sentence."

Liesel nodded.

They were at her porch. "Uncle Otto may want to see you before you go. Can you spare him a moment?"

David followed her inside. Otto didn't greet them at the door as he had on other occasions when he'd learned that David would be there soon. He simply stood when David entered the parlor, shook his hand, and took the lack of news about Josef the way he had the last few times: with a nod and a thank you. Then he excused himself and left.

David did not stay long after that, and Liesel walked him to the door.

"Call me if you hear anything," he said as he always did. It had become a light, seemingly habitual addendum to his good-byes.

"Yes, I will."

"Oh, I keep forgetting to mention this. If you do call and I'm not there, ask for Weber or Gertz. Or Helen Lindsey. Do you remember her?"

She nodded. "Is there someone I'm *not* supposed to speak to?"

His face softened, as if he'd been trying to keep something back but she'd been too shrewd. "I'd rather you didn't talk to an agent named Donahue."

"Any reason?"

"None I can go into any detail about. Let's just say he's a little too eager for my taste. I want to take Josef in as peacefully as possible."

"That's what I want, too."

"Good night, then," he said quietly, but for a moment he simply stood there.

"Good night," she replied. She smiled, glad he wasn't rushing out the door even if his job demanded his return.

He bent down and kissed her forehead. It was a graze of lips to skin, something he'd never done before. Warmth spread through Liesel as if little bits of kindling ignited everywhere inside.

He left without another word, and when he closed the door, Liesel stood there a few moments, considering his action. She lifted her fingertips to the spot his lips had skimmed, touching her forehead as if she could catch that kiss and hold it a little while.

She stiffened. What was she doing, dwelling on that friendly gesture? She had no right to think of David de Serre as anything other than a man with a job to do.

She turned from the door only to spot Greta standing with arms akimbo and a wide grin on her mischievous face.

"I saw you. He *kissed* you!"

Liesel's pulse sped. "That wasn't a kiss. It was a demonstration of friendship. Like in the Bible where it says to greet one another with a holy kiss. It wasn't any different than saying good night to a brother."

"Then why are your cheeks all red?"

Liesel walked passed Greta with a tug to one of the child's braids and a grin, silently denying her own discomfort. She went upstairs but couldn't help realizing she was glad Greta hadn't followed with her childish teasing.

In her room, Liesel picked up her Bible from the middle of her bed. Mama had given it to her on her thirteenth birthday, with an inscription quoting Paul in his letter to the Philippians: "Those things, which ye have both learned, and received, and heard, and seen in me, do: and the God of peace shall be with you."

She looked at the writing, her gaze dwelling on the word *peace*. Since she'd learned of Josef's trouble, she'd had too little of that. And lately, though she couldn't deny Josef was on her mind less and less, she couldn't claim any more of that precious feeling of tranquility.

Why was that? Perhaps this verse had the answer. She'd forgotten, at least lately, so much of what she'd learned from this very book Mama had urged her to study.

Liesel wasn't ready to replace the emotion she once thought she held for Josef with a new set of emotions for David. Yet part of her felt in danger of doing just that. How could she? David and Josef were nothing alike. Josef was fiery and impulsive; David quiet, cautious. Sure of himself yet in a different way from Josef's obvious self-confidence. Josef could boast with the best of them, extolling not only another's virtues but his own just as easily. David's confidence was the quiet kind that most often diverted attention away from himself.

Yet it wasn't their differences that bothered Liesel so. She was afraid. She'd trusted Josef. She'd believed with every part of her heart and soul that he'd been the man he presented himself to be. Now she realized she only knew the Josef he wanted her to know—a part of him that was real, surely it must have been, but not the whole of him. He was in reality more devoted to Germany than to any faith, and that devotion had led him into danger. And possibly into danger for her, too.

How could she have been so thoroughly fooled? How could she have known him all these years yet not really known him at all?

Maybe she was incapable of seeing the truth. Maybe she wasn't the sound judge of character she'd always thought herself to be. Maybe she could be fooled again.

"Oh, Lord," she whispered, brushing her fingertips a second time to her forehead. "Help me to remember that we're all just human and living in a world full of other fallen humans. That I can truly trust only You, and if I follow You and what You've taught me, then peace will surely follow."

***

By the end of the week, Liesel determined Uncle Otto probably wouldn't ask her back to work and she should look for another job. She could no longer tolerate the long days, and even if she did enjoy Mama's company, she was beginning to feel like a schoolgirl again. It was past time to get out of the house.

During her jaunt from one end of the city to the other, she passed the Justice Department building and was tempted to stop at David's office. It was lunchtime, and whether or not that was precisely what she'd had at the back of her mind all morning, she gave in to that temptation and went into the four-story building. Ignoring her racing pulse, ignoring the thoughts cautioning her against calling on David, she took the elevator up.

The office was nearly empty. Two men she didn't recognize sat at a table with telephones in front of them. She turned away, thinking she'd been foolish to come up anyway. It was just as well she couldn't find him.

"Liesel Bonner?"

She froze, but a moment later, a smiling Mrs. Lindsey greeted her warmly.

"How nice to see you," she said. "And just at lunchtime, too." She threw a smile over her shoulder at the near deserted room. "I'm afraid most of the agents are out on leads or at lunch. Is there anything I can help you with?"

"No. I . . ." She gripped her purse. "I was just passing by and thought I'd stop in."

"I'm sure Mr. de Serre would love to see you. Can you wait?"

She shook her head. "No. I have so many errands, and I haven't lunched yet."

"Oh! How about grabbing a sandwich together, then? I'd love the company."

So the two of them shared the midday meal in a nearby coffee shop. It wasn't exactly what Liesel had expected, but she enjoyed herself. They exchanged secrets of the clerical trade as well as laughter over office fiascos they'd created, avoided, or endured.

The hour passed quickly, and they left the café to return to the Justice Department. As they approached, Liesel spotted David with another man. Mrs. Lindsey must have seen them as well, and despite the mature, maternal picture she presented, she called David's name. The two men turned in their direction.

"Miss Bonner was looking for you, Mr. de Serre," said Helen.

Liesel's cheeks warmed at the announcement, and though she smiled, she allowed only a quick glance David's way.

She was happy to see in that moment that he looked pleased to see her. "Weber and I—oh, this is Hal Weber. Weber, this is Miss Bonner. We just had a meeting over lunch. Is everything all right?"

She nodded. "I was in the area. That's all."

He smiled. "Come up and stay a little while anyway."

She shook her head. "I have an appointment. I started my job hunt again this morning."

If he was disappointed, he hid it well. Maybe he wasn't, or maybe he was aware that their relationship was strictly business—more aware of that than she'd been when she'd stopped in without a good reason.

Liesel noticed out of the corner of her eye Mr. Weber and Helen leaving the impromptu meeting without saying anything. David made no move to follow.

"How long will you be in the city?" he asked.

She glanced at her watchpin. It was two thirty already.

"Perhaps until five."

David dug in the pocket of his serge suit, coming up with paper. "Do you have a pen?"

She reached into her purse. She always carried a self-inking fountain pen when going from office to office, filling out applications. She handed it to him.

In a moment, he returned the pen with the small piece of paper. "This is my address and directions. If you aren't busy, go there when you're through, and I'll meet you. We can share an early dinner."

Liesel's heart seemed to bounce around inside. She should say no. Of course, she should say no. She might not still love Josef the way she thought, but she was hardly ready to spend time with another man. And that's what David was: a man, not an agent. Not someone with one goal, to use her to get to Josef. This was a man she was undeniably attracted to.

It was one thing to have him stop by her house or meet him for coffee or even share a spontaneous dinner at Mario's. But this was different. Planned . . . like a date.

Vaguely, she considered what her mother would say about going unescorted to a man's home, even if only to wait until he arrived and then leave for a public restaurant.

But she nodded before all those thoughts had an influence on her answer. "I should let my mother know I'll be home later than I expected."

"I'll send one of the boys from the office with a note that you'll be having dinner with me. Don't want anyone worrying. All right?"

He smiled so naturally any thoughts of her hesitation disappeared. She nodded again.

"Good. I'll be there just after five."

He turned to leave, and she called after him. "How will I get inside if you're not there?"

"It's not locked. See you later." Then he was gone.

She went to her appointments, filling out applications and hoping as much as ever for some success. Then, just past five, she found her way to David's neighborhood. She was more than a little curious about his home. It proved to be a brown brick apartment building, with wide cement banisters on either side of the six steps leading up to the wood-and-glass entrance door.

A trace of hesitation wriggled in through her nervous excitement. Perhaps she should have refused. Wasn't that what Mama would have wanted her to do, refuse? But Liesel was, after all, twenty-three years old. Just because she'd been living like a schoolgirl the past two weeks or more didn't mean she must return to such schoolgirl restrictions. Her mother respected her judgment. Liesel wasn't about to do anything wrong; she was merely waiting in an empty apartment for a man who had become a good friend to her. All perfectly respectable.

Inside, the corridor smelled of wood wax and was slightly musty. Each apartment was plainly marked with metal letters affixed to a solid door, just above a matching doorknocker. Liesel found Apartment B without any trouble. He'd said he would be a little later than five o'clock, and it was just twenty past the hour now. She put her hand to the brass knocker in case

he'd already made it home. But before following through with the knock, she stopped. From behind the door came the distinct sound of laughter. A child's voice, then more giggles.

Looking again at the address and the apartment number, Liesel was sure she was in the right place. Still, she started to turn away. Perhaps he'd written down the wrong number. However, short of wandering the streets in search of him or returning all the way to the Justice Department in hopes of catching him there, she had little idea what to do.

She tapped lightly at the door. Perhaps this neighbor would know where he lived.

In a moment, a petite, attractive woman stood before her. She was smaller than Liesel, with black hair and eyes every bit as dark. Her face was thin and heart shaped, her large eyes like burnt almonds. She smiled warmly at Liesel, a question in her eyes.

"Yes?"

"I'm looking for David de Serre, and I understood he lives in this building. Do you know which apartment?"

"Why, this very one. Come in, come in!"

A sudden cry erupted behind the welcoming young woman.

"Mama! Mama! Marcus broke my plane."

"Marcus! Hector! Can't you see we have a guest? Come now. Behave like little gentlemen as your papa taught. Be still!"

Liesel watched the picture in front of her as if she were in a dream. The pretty woman took both of her lanky sons in her wispy little arms, still smiling a warm welcome. The boys looked like her, with straight, dark hair and dark eyes. While the family in front of her transformed into an agreeable, smiling trio, Liesel felt her head spin. Why hadn't he mentioned there would be someone here to open that unlocked door?

His family!

In all the time she'd spent with David, she'd never imagined he was married. But why couldn't he be? He was handsome, wasn't he? And certainly not too young to have fathered these two saplings. But the fact that he was married stunned her. It had never occurred to her.

"I—I'm sorry," she whispered, hardly knowing what else to say. Sorry for what? Sorry she'd spent so much time lately with the patriarch of this family, taking him away from them on the evenings he'd been with her and her family? After all, it had been perfectly innocent. She was nothing more than part of a case to David.

"David didn't tell me there would be anyone else for dinner," the dark-eyed woman said. Now that the boys were quieter, she let them go, and they disappeared to a corner of the room, where one picked up a broken wing from a small wooden biplane. "But I always make plenty of food. David is a big eater, you know. Come in to the kitchen. He will be home soon."

Liesel barely noticed the apartment around her except that the kitchen was small and that this dainty, pretty, young Spanish woman seemed to fit right in. The counter was full of groceries, and something bubbled on the stove. If it wasn't for Liesel's suddenly upset stomach, the smell of the meal might have been enticing.

David. Married. Liesel couldn't speak. Nor was she hearing properly, apparently, for the woman was staring at her as if she awaited an answer to some just-issued question. Liesel had no idea what the woman had said.

"I'm sorry," Liesel said again, feeling dimwitted since that's all she had uttered since walking through the door. "What did you say?"

"Only that I hope you like Spanish food. I don't cook with too many spices but a little. Is that all right?"

Spanish food. Hadn't David once mentioned he loved Spanish food? She couldn't remember when he'd said such a thing, but she was sure he had. It was little wonder that it was his favorite. Or that he spoke Spanish fluently.

"Yes. I mean, I don't know. I've never had Spanish food before."

The woman beamed. "Oh! Then I'm especially glad you're here. I am honored to be the first one to introduce you to the food of my homeland."

She pulled out a kitchen chair for Liesel, which she accepted, giving needed rest to her wobbly knees. Then the woman turned back to the stove, stirring something in a pan.

"How long have you known David?" she asked over her shoulder.

"Not long. Just a month or two."

"Oh, but that's plenty of time for him to have told me about you. I wonder why he's never mentioned you?"

"I'm just part of his job, sort of a . . . let's see, I think they call people like me outside help or something like that." An informant is what she should have called herself, since David had once offered an informant's fee. But it sounded far too sinister.

"Outside help? Then you don't work with the Justice Department?"

"No."

She turned to face Liesel fully. "Don't tell me you work with that American Protective League. I heard they were working with the Justice Department, but I—"

Liesel shook her head. "No. I'm not working at all right now."

"Oh." She turned back to the stove. "I should not have jumped to any conclusions. I'm sure that the APL is a worthy organization. You just hear such things about them, about how they go prying into everybody's business. I hate David's group being involved with them. I may be from Spain, miss, but I'm an American since I married my husband. And I do not take my citizenship lightly. I read the newspapers every day. I know what's going on."

She wiped her hands on a towel and came closer to Liesel. "I just called you miss, and I realized I never introduced myself." She held out a small hand. "I am Anna. And what's your name?"

Liesel told her, accepting the outstretched hand. Just then, another commotion erupted between the boys, and Anna went into the other room. A moment later, the noise quieted, and Anna returned.

"Excuse my boys," she said as she returned to the pot on the stove. A flat, unbaked pastry rested on the counter, and she poured what appeared to be a custard, barely cooled, on top. A few moments later, she rolled the pastry and slipped it into the oven.

"We call it gypsy's arm," she said of the dessert. "I hope you'll like it."

Liesel said nothing. She wasn't at all sure she wanted to stay for the meal, although she scolded herself for being so cowardly. Why was it so upsetting that David had married this lovely woman? That he had two rambunctious boys, healthy and vigorous, right in the next room?

The reason was painfully obvious. But she couldn't face this conflict now, not in the presence of his family. She would have to sort it out later.

Liesel needed an excuse to leave, to start that sorting right away. She wished to be gone before David arrived to see how confused and humiliated she felt. But what could she say to excuse herself? Obviously this woman— so inviting, so secure in her happy home—expected Liesel to stay.

Just then, Liesel heard the sound of a door opening and the boys' squealed greeting, followed by a grunt and a growl as if David responded to them by wrestling or some other physical contact. Laughter echoed around the apartment, and as happy as it sounded, it only added to the empty feeling within Liesel. Such a happy home, like the one she hoped to have someday.

Reluctantly, Liesel followed Anna from the kitchen and back into the front parlor. There, as she'd guessed, she found David grappling with the two young boys. David had one pinned to the floor, while the smaller of the two was glued to his back, spindly arms wrapped around his neck.

When he caught sight of Liesel, he stood, but the boy attached to his back didn't budge.

"Give me a ride! Give me a ride!"

David trotted over to Liesel, passing her by. "I see you met Anna and the boys." He looked so happy, Liesel wanted to sink into the hardwood floor.

"Yes."

"Good, that's good! And I smell something scrumptious." He glanced at Liesel. "We won't have to go out, after all. Wait until you taste Anna's cooking. You told me once you've never had Spanish food. Just wait!"

He was getting out of breath trotting around the room first with one boy and then the other.

"We're having *pimentos rellenos*," Anna announced, then looked at Liesel and added, "Stuffed peppers. It's one of David's favorites."

"Oh, I see." She could think of nothing else to say. She wished she were anywhere but where she was just at that moment.

At last David stopped near Liesel, letting the older of the two boys slide to his feet. When the other pounced on David, Anna pulled him away.

"Enough, boys! We're going to eat soon; let's go and wash your hands now."

The boys protested all the way to the bathroom, where Anna followed to supervise.

"I'm glad you met Anna," David said. His eyes shone every bit as much as the rest of his face. "She used to be a nurse, and she's always forcing us into washing our hands. She's swell, isn't she?"

Liesel nodded. This was only getting worse. That he loved the woman should have made her happy. Husbands should love their wives; the Bible commanded it.

He went into the kitchen, where he peeked inside the oven, then looked under the lid of a pan. After washing his hands at the sink, he pulled some dishes from the cabinets and set the table.

"I'm afraid my collection of cutlery doesn't quite match," he said as he took out knives and forks from a drawer. "I don't often have company, especially for a meal, so I never bothered to purchase a whole set. Most of this has been pilfered, I must admit. From Anna and Mio."

Liesel watched him put out the place settings, vaguely wondering who Mio might be.

He turned to the icebox and opened the door. "Milk! Anna must have stopped to get some for the gypsy arm." He looked over at Liesel with the open door between then. "I don't stock much, and when I do, I usually don't get to it before it spoils. It's a good thing there's enough left for the boys." He held up the quart-sized bottle, which held a small amount at the bottom. "But not much for the rest of us. I guess I should have stopped and picked some up, but I forgot they were going to be here today."

Liesel tilted her head to one side. "Be here today?"

"Well, visiting," he said. "Anna's been coming around once a week since Mio left. I was trying to get out there to see them, but with everything happening with the job, I haven't been able to make it. I forgot she was coming today, otherwise I would have . . ."

His words faded as he stared at her. She had no clue what he saw and didn't particularly want to know. Embarrassment engulfed her. That she was relieved, so relieved she wanted to laugh or cry, she couldn't conceal. At the moment, she hadn't any idea who Anna and the boys were, but they could hardly be his family if they were just visiting.

"What is it?" he asked.

Disconcerted, she turned away from him toward the kitchen table, placing her hands on the back of a chair. She knew she was blushing; she could feel the warmth from her hairline all the way to her chest. "I thought . . . oh, it doesn't matter what I thought." She spared a quick glance to his curious face. "Who is Anna?"

"She is the wife of my friend Mio. I've known him all my life. We grew up together. He's a minister."

As he spoke, he closed the icebox door and approached her. She could feel his gaze on her, studying her much more closely than she would have liked. There wasn't a thing she could do about it except try harder to conceal her sweeping discomfort.

"Mio is the one who taught me so much about the Bible," he went on, his voice low, his intense gaze not softening a bit. "He is very wise, and I suppose I shouldn't have let you think I'd learned the things we've talked about all by myself. Just trying to impress you, I suppose."

Liesel looked up at him. He was standing so close. She looked quickly away. "Where is he now? Mio, I mean."

"He volunteered to be a chaplain in the YMCA. He went overseas."

That spurred another glance upward, one of surprise and a bit of concern. But thoughts of Mio, someone she knew of only by name, quickly disappeared as she saw David studying her far too intently. He took her hand in both of his so that hers was enveloped.

"Liesel, did you think Anna was my wife?"

"I . . ." A ready defense disappeared, knowing whatever she could make up wouldn't be entirely honest. Looking at the tiny space of floor between them, she nodded. A moment later she felt his finger at her chin, coaxing her to look at him. His other hand still held hers while he stroked her cheek.

She should look away, break the gaze and the hypnotic hold it had on her. But his dark eyes seemed connected to hers, as if he, too, was unwilling or unable to look away. A moment later, he leaned closer, and Liesel stopped breathing altogether.

Just as he might have spoken, the boys burst into the kitchen, along with Anna. The boys scraped the chairs away from the table and climbed to their seats with chatter about how hungry they were, while Anna stood at the threshold with an odd look on her face, something like pleased suspicion coupled with surprise.

"Perhaps our timing was not so good?" she said with a little grin, then passed them to go to the stove.

Liesel took a step away from David. She looked at Anna. "Is there anything I can do to help?"

"Ah, no, just sit down. I was going to let it simmer a while longer, but if everyone is ready, we can eat now. David, put a towel down to protect the table from the hot dish."

The meal passed in noisy companionship. The boys obviously loved their *Tío* David, and the feeling was noticeably returned. Anna told Liesel about her husband, Mio, about their church, and their home. Of all of them, David spoke the least, although he seemed to enjoy having everyone talking around him.

By six thirty, the meal and dessert had ended. Liesel helped with the dishes, then prepared to go on her way. Although she wasn't accountable to her parents for every minute of the day, she knew they would worry if she wasn't home before long.

When Liesel said good-bye, Anna took her hand and squeezed it tight for a moment. "I hope that you will be here again when I come to see David. And please, if he can ever drag himself away from spy-chasing, come with him to our home. I'm glad that David has met someone at last."

Liesel felt yet another blush, not knowing what to say. She should correct her, make it clear that her association with David was due only to a current case. Instead, she said nothing.

David was busy hauling the two boys around the kitchen table, one in front and one on his back. "We'll have to go in shifts for me to take you to the train and also take Liesel home," he said over the boy's voices.

Liesel neared them. "I can take the streetcar. I don't mind."

Anna came up behind Liesel. "Of course you won't! The boys and I will get back to Union Station the same way we arrived here this afternoon. We know the way, and the boys could use the walk. David, take Liesel home."

Liesel spoke before he could. "No, I really insist—"

David shook his head, prying the two boys away. "We could argue about this all evening. Liesel, if you don't mind the walk, why don't we all go over to the station and then come back to my car, and I'll take you home?"

"Oh, that'll be fine," Anna said. Liesel was not quite so eager to agree. She wasn't sure she wanted to be alone with David, at least so soon after making an utter fool of herself.

"I'd like the walk," she said, silently determining to find a streetcar along the route.

Outside, they enjoyed the warm breeze. At Union Station, the boys waved from the train as if they were going on a long journey rather than a short train trip, and Liesel watched David wave both arms. Fatherhood would fit him.

They left the station, and as expected, several horse-drawn streetcars were headed the right direction. "I'll just get a ride from here," Liesel told David.

"But I was going to take you home in the Runabout."

"I don't want to make you drive me all the way home," she said. "I know you've been working long hours, you should go home and rest. I've taken the streetcar from this neighborhood plenty of times. You needn't worry about me."

"I'm sure you're perfectly capable of finding your way home," he said. "But I want to take you."

Out of the corner of her eye, she saw a streetcar approaching and a group of people waiting at a designated pick-up spot. She was suddenly desperate to be on her own, knowing without doubt he was going to ask about the earlier misunderstanding, but the emotion behind that misunderstanding was something she couldn't explain, not even to herself.

"I'll be fine, David, really."

He stayed her with one gentle touch, a fingertip to turn her face to his. He stood so close she could feel his breath tickle a curl on her forehead.

"Liesel," he whispered.

She had to look up at him; she couldn't help herself. If she thought she should still feel embarrassed, it disappeared at the look on his face. With his gaze aimed so deeply into her eyes she believed in that moment he knew the exact cause of her embarrassment—and every other thought she so hopelessly tried to hide.

His lips came down on hers, and she had neither strength nor will to resist. He was gentle, tentative at first, until he must have sensed her complete lack of resistance. His mouth felt smooth, warm . . . inviting. His kiss deepened, his lips pressed into hers, and his arms closed around her just as hers slipped around him. She couldn't help herself. She clung to him exactly as he clung to her.

"All aboard!"

The call penetrated the fog filling Liesel's head. What was she doing? Publicly kissing a man—not just a little peck on the cheek, but the kind of kiss no one let happen on the street. He was not just any man, but David, the man who'd brought her nothing but havoc since the moment he'd entered her life.

Pulling herself away, she didn't allow herself to look at his face. She couldn't bear for him to look into her eyes that way again.

"I have to go. I—I'm sorry." She waved at the trolley driver and hopped aboard.

She watched David from the rail. He stood still a few moments, then, perhaps realizing he was still in the street, moved to the curb. A moment later, the streetcar turned a corner, and he was out of sight.

Holding the cool, metal railing, Liesel let out a breath after what suddenly seemed a long time without air.

She didn't know when it had started brewing, but she couldn't deny she'd wanted that kiss for some time. Yet how could she have allowed it? No, more than that, she'd welcomed it as if she'd waited too long, had *yearned* for it! What was wrong with her? Barely out of Josef's arms, she flew into David's? The man who sought to arrest him?

She leaned forward, pressing her forehead into her arms. Oh, this was too much to sort out. This situation with Josef was disturbing enough, yet somehow the case had changed into something more. It was something as wonderful as it was horrible. Horrible for all the obvious reasons. Everything wonderful about it boiled down to one thing: this case had allowed her to know David. Until it all came to an end.

And she didn't know how she would handle that day—for Josef's sake or her own.

David watched the trolley navigate the corner, standing there like the fool he felt. So much for keeping his personal feelings in check until the case was closed. He was quite the professional, wasn't he?

He wasn't mistaken. She had been stiff and nervous when he'd first arrived at his apartment before dinner. When he'd guessed she must have thought Anna his wife, he wanted nothing more than to explore the relief on her face the moment she'd learned who Anna was.

He frowned. How could Liesel have thought that he was married, any-way, after all the time they'd shared? Wouldn't he have brought it up before? Certainly he wouldn't have visited her as often as he'd been doing.

Perhaps the reason for her relief wasn't so obvious, after all. She might have thought she'd taken him away from his family, and he knew her well enough to believe she'd be mortified to have played any part in keeping someone from his family even if for business. But it had been more than just business. They both knew that without having exchanged a word about it.

That brought up a whole new set of questions, not of Liesel but of himself. Exactly when had this case become so personal? Was he losing all objectivity? Worse, was he suddenly using this case just to get to know her better? Somehow it had all faded into one thing, this case and Liesel and his desire to know her better. He couldn't think of catching von Woerner without considering the impact it would have on her.

He should have the case reassigned to someone who could be objective, who would contact Liesel only as needed, make sure she was still safe, and assure the agency she wasn't in contact with von Woerner, that he hadn't shown up to coerce her into helping him.

But this case had been his from the beginning, and he wanted von Woerner brought to justice. That it allowed him to know Liesel this way . . . well, he was still doing his job, wasn't he? He needed to keep an eye on her for all the reasons he'd just touched on. Who else would be so thorough? If anyone needed the protection of the government, it was Liesel Bonner. He had no doubt that if von Woerner needed help, the man would run straight to her.

And she would come to David. In spite of everything, in spite of David's personal interest, the job was getting done.

He shook off the accusing thoughts even as new ones filled his mind, emerging more from his soul than his brain. Too much divided his attention these days, the very days he needed his faith most. The war and his work demanded every bit of David's energy. It was too important to shirk. Meet-ing Liesel now, when he needed to be clearheaded, was the worst timing.

But it wasn't just bad timing. His job had demanded so much of him lately that he'd ignored something else. Someone else. The One who could help him to make sense of his personal life.

When David reached his home, he went straight to his Bible. If anyone could help David re-map his priorities, it was the One who'd created him.

CHAPTER *Nineteen*

OTTO von Woerner stared at the man seated across the desk. He looked every bit a vagabond, from his worn derby hat to the scuffed shoes and pants that sported knees in need of patching. Comfortable, unkempt, still lean even at fifty-odd years. Otto had known him a long time, even before the man started going by the name Hank Tanner. They'd met on the boat from *Deutschland* almost twenty-seven years ago, both with dreams of the riches they'd find in the New World. And while Otto had obviously been more successful monetarily, no one challenged that Hank Tanner, baptized Henrik Tahnenheiser, was the best German private detective along the entire East Coast.

They'd been fast friends on that journey so long ago—had to be, since it was only the first twenty-four hours Otto recalled at all. Once they hit the choppy open waters of the Atlantic, seasickness overcame Otto, and he no longer visited with anyone. He spent the rest of that voyage flat on his back, gradually dehydrating and losing all but the skin on his weakening bones. Henrik had been attentive to Juditha, Otto's wife, shielding her from some of the other, bolder second-class passengers. Otto had been grateful to have befriended the man but not as grateful as now. It had taken Otto a week to convince Henrik to devote himself entirely to locating Josef.

"If it had been any building but that one, I'd have said no to breaking in," Henrik was saying. "But that old Justice building is about as secure as a tenement and as easy to get into."

"No matter," Otto said, leaning forward in his seat. "What do you have?"

The man held no files, no papers whatsoever. What he had was entirely in his head, but fortunately for Otto, it was a head he trusted.

"Oh, plenty, but you're not going to like it."

"Is he . . . is he dead?"

Henrik laughed. "He's alive. But he's in trouble."

Otto frowned. He didn't want to have his suspicions confirmed. It was the last thing he wanted, but he had to know.

"Tell me."

"He's in hiding. They have quite a file on your son. From planting bombs on ships to sabotaging munitions plants. He's been working for the Germans for a couple of years now according to what I found in de Serre's desk."

Otto shook his head, finally resting his forehead in the palms of his hands. Those disappearances, those lengthy business trips, the secrecy. The money. He'd known for a while Josef was up to something, but he'd trusted his son's judgment. Trusted that whatever he was involved in, it was something that would make them all proud.

Standing, Otto turned away from Henrik even as the man continued issuing a litany of offenses performed by Josef. There was a window in Otto's spacious office. Below, he could see the street, although the sounds and smells had been shut out. From his office, he could hear nothing of his own factory.

"Whatever my son has done has been for *Deutschland,* then?"

"That's it, but you know the American government recognizes him as a citizen of this nation, even if you don't."

"American law," he whispered. "*Deutschland* recognizes no such citizenship. Even you with your American name and your naturalization, *Deutschland* still sees you as her son. Born a *Deutschlander,* die a *Deutschlander.*"

"That's the kind of thinking that got Josef into this mess, Otto. America is where you live, and American law is what you'll both have to follow. If Josef really is guilty of working for the Germans, he's a traitor, not some wayward German citizen who will be sent home for bad behavior."

Otto turned back to his desk, resting closed fists on the surface. "You must find him, Henrik. Find him before they do."

Henrik shook his head. "No, Otto. I'm finished with this case as of today."

The shock blasted heat from Otto's head to his feet, like standing before one of the gas furnaces downstairs. "What?"

"There are plenty of other investigators you can hire, Otto, and you can afford one with broader connections than mine."

"But I trust *you*, Henrik."

Henrik shook his head. "I may be a German in your eyes, Otto. But I'm an American in mine. And the name is Hank now."

Otto clenched his jaw, staring at the man's apparent betrayal. "You are a fool, Henrik, to turn your back on the Fatherland, especially now. When *Deutschland* wins this war, you'll reclaim your citizenship. I guarantee you that."

Henrik turned toward the door, but he paused with his hand still on the knob. "They had a file on a woman in that office, Otto, one they must think will lead them straight to him if he surfaces."

"Liesel Bonner."

"You know her?"

"Yes."

"You will find him through her."

Otto stared down at his hands supporting his weight on his desk, but all he saw was his son. Hiding. Afraid. Hunted. It was enough to make Otto frantic, but he kept a tight check on his emotions. There was work to be done.

Starting with rehiring Liesel Bonner. If she was the best connection to Josef, he intended having her close at hand.

Otto called Lucille Burnbaum into his office. As always, she entered promptly and with a smile. He'd welcomed that smile though the years because with it came a pliable spirit. Miss Burnbaum was, Otto had long since realized, someone he could convince to do almost anything.

Though she had as much as said Liesel wasn't needed in this office, Otto planned to see just how pliant Lucille could be.

David unlocked the drawer, withdrawing the file on von Woerner. As he did, he noted the file on Liesel and stared at it a moment. One piece of paper was slightly askew.

Carefully pulling it out, he opened the file. Everything was still there, still in the proper order. He looked at the other folders sharing that drawer. All there, all in order. Even the one on von Woerner. However, the corner of that single sheet of paper had been evidence enough. Someone had been in his files.

Donahue. David felt a hint of remorse over the speed at which the other agent's name came to mind. *Lord, help me to see through Your eyes.*

David tried to ignore the fact that he just couldn't stomach Donahue. The zealous agent made no secret of his opinion that David's slower, more meticulous way of bringing people to justice was a monumental waste of time. Had Donahue been looking for names of suspects he could interfere with? Arrange for a quick arrest on his own, regardless that this was one of David's cases?

Guilt reminded David they worked on the same side. Ostensibly they wanted the same thing: to protect the American way of life, apprehending anybody who put it in jeopardy. Surely Donahue wouldn't be so foolhardy as to interfere with David's cases just because he wanted another arrest attributed to his name.

Helen walked nearby with a stack of papers under one arm. David motioned her over.

"Have you seen anybody around my desk lately, Helen?"

"No, is something wrong?"

David shook his head. "No, but if you happen to see anybody lurking around, would you let me know?"

"Of course."

Two hours later, the security manager visited the bullpen with news he suspected someone might have tried to break in the night before. There was evidence of a window having been tampered with, although it was found locked from the inside. He wanted to make everyone aware of the possibility and to check if anything was missing.

While David offered a silent apology for the eager mental accusations he'd made toward Donahue, he added a note to his report on Liesel. Suspicion mounted that someone had looked in her file, and when he finished, he headed to her house.

But even on his way, he questioned his readiness to drop everything so he could check on her. He shook his head, thoughts warring within. Was he going to question everything he did regarding her? His motives? Had he lost all objectivity?

Last night, he'd asked God to guide his way personally and professionally, especially when the two intermingled. Was he allowing God to guide him, or was he just grasping at the first opportunity to see Liesel again?

As he pulled up to her house, he had no answer. And when he learned from her mother that Liesel was not at home, he ignored the disappointment. Job hunting, Mrs. Bonner said. Immediately, he wondered if she would stop by his office for lunch again, but as quickly as the thought came, he dismissed it. She wasn't looking forward to the awkwardness of facing each other again. He wasn't either, even though he'd just flown to her side the minute he had the flimsiest excuse.

Would she avoid him because their relationship had somehow drifted outside the boundaries of business? Because they'd become something more than friends? That's exactly what he'd hoped would happen, but it was easy to see she was hardly ready to accept such a step. Because she still loved von Woerner? Perhaps. Even if she someday accepted the truth about him—that he'd never deserved her love—it would take time to learn to love again. David wasn't normally a dreamer, nor did he usually push anything before its time. Patience and perseverance, the ability to hold on and wait. That was as instinctive to David as faith, and he was willing to do just that.

"Yes, I think we can use you," said the woman seated behind the desk.

Liesel stood in front of the desk, so surprised by the words she could think of nothing to say.

"Do you want to start today or come back in the morning?"

The shock at being hired, even if it was only for a minimal wage and in the front end of a uniform laundry company, made her slow witted. "I'll start whenever you wish."

The girl looked Liesel over, assessing her appearance. "Maybe you'd better come back in the morning," she said. "It's already past noon, and by the time you get home to change your clothes and come back, most of the day will be over anyway."

"Change my clothes?" Liesel was confused. She'd applied for a clerical position.

"Yes," she said. "It gets pretty hot back there. That suit will have you as limp as a wet towel in a matter of moments."

"The office . . . is in the laundry?"

"No, the office is up here," she said as if explaining something to a child. "But you'll have to start out in the laundry. We need somebody back there right away. Ironing."

"But I applied for—"

"Yes, I know you're looking for clerical work. But as you can see, I've already got that job, and I'm all they need. But we do need someone to iron. You've got that job."

"Oh, I see."

"So you come back around seven in the morning, all right? And you can wear whatever you like, something a lot cooler than that suit. Sleeveless is perfectly acceptable, considering the temperature back there."

Liesel nodded. "Thank you . . ." But then she caught her words. She was a stenographer and a mighty good one, too. Trained and experienced. While ironing for a living was no doubt a perfectly respectable way of earning a paycheck, that wasn't what she'd set out to become. "No, I mean, no, thank you. I believe I'll continue my job hunt elsewhere, but thank you for the offer."

She walked out of the building, and the young woman made no attempt to stop her.

That had been Liesel's last appointment, without a single prospect for the following day. As she made her way home, she battled discouragement, fatigue, and an unavoidable sense of failure. It did little to strengthen her against the other matter she battled.

How had it happened? Thoughts of David infiltrated almost every hour of her day. She often wondered what he was doing at any given moment or counted down the time until he would come by. She had even dreamed of him on more than one occasion. And no matter how many times she had relived that kiss in her mind, thinking of it caused her heart to twirl anew.

At first, she hadn't realized she was thinking about him so much. Before when she caught such thoughts, she had easily told herself this whole case was so upsetting that it should come as little surprise that everything about it invaded her mind. But now when she thought of David, it had nothing whatever to do with Josef.

Yet it was sometimes hard to keep separate the fact that she would have stopped loving Josef even if she'd never met David. That these new feelings had materialized for David during this time caused more than a little confusion. At times, she felt guilty about thinking of David, as if she were somehow being unfaithful to Josef. Never in all the years of her relationship with Josef had she struggled not to think about him the way she struggled so hard not to think about David. David's face filled every pause in her day.

When she arrived home, she saw Uncle Otto's Peerless in front of her home. His visits had gradually decreased since Josef's disappearance. It was as if he'd given up all hope, accepted the fact that Josef must be dead. And while Liesel had reason to believe that wasn't true, she knew she could say nothing.

"Liesel! Just in time for supper. Come, sit down."

Liesel followed Mama into the dining room, where the family and Uncle Otto were taking their places. Liesel barely looked up from her place setting.

"Liesel," her father said, "Uncle Otto came to see you this afternoon. He's been waiting to speak to you."

"Oh?" She spared him a glance, but something made her stare a moment longer. There was something different about him, although she couldn't quite define it. At the very least, that empty, lost look was noticeably absent.

"Yes, Liesel," he said. "Do you remember saying that if I changed my mind about having you return to the factory, I should tell you?"

Slowly, she nodded.

"Well, I should like it very much if you would come back. I was wrong to have let you go to begin with."

"Uncle Otto wants you to come back, Liesel."

She should be pleased and wondered if such a feeling would emerge after her surprise wore away. "Yes," she said, nodding at Papa. "Yes, I heard." She looked at Uncle Otto. "I will be happy to return." And she added a quick smile because it seemed to go with the words.

"*Nun gut, nun gut,*" he said. "Lucy will be glad to have you as well."

Liesel looked down at her plate of food that suddenly seemed less appetizing, heartily doubting Uncle Otto's words. Well, perhaps there had been a reason she'd been unable to find employment that day. She knew things would get harder for Uncle Otto. Perhaps God wanted her nearby.

"Tomorrow morning, then, Liesel?" he said, his face nearly beaming. "Or should I say, Miss Bonner?"

CHAPTER *Twenty*

LIESEL walked into the office at precisely eight o'clock the next morning. Commotion and activity resounded. Uncle Otto and Miss Burnbaum were already there along with a pair of workmen busily moving boxes and furniture from the storeroom she had used before as her makeshift office. Glancing again at her timepiece to be sure she wasn't late, she joined Uncle Otto, who oversaw the men loading a long cart.

"Uncle—Mr. von Woerner," Liesel said, "what's going on?"

His brows rose in warm welcome as he saluted her with his monocle between two fingertips. "Your room needed remodeling. We have gotten rid of all those boxes and the hectograph."

"The hectograph?"

"We simply moved it, dear!" said a smiling Miss Burnbaum as she passed with a small lamp in her hands. "So you'll have more room."

Confused, Liesel looked between Uncle Otto and the space being changed into a tidy office. The workers had been busy for some time. They had added a string of electric lights to the single one in the center of the formerly dingy room, lighting the little place as bright as any sunny day. The hectograph was indeed gone, as were most of the boxes. Her desk had been moved to one side, and on top of it sat a typewriter beside her very own telephone.

Liesel eyed Uncle Otto, who seemed pleased at what he saw. What was going on? Why the sudden transformation, as if he suddenly cared whether or not she would be happy working for him?

And Miss Burnbaum. The older woman shot a maternal smile Liesel's way. She was behaving nothing like the Miss Burnbaum Liesel knew.

Liesel pushed away such dubious thoughts. "Well, this is quite a room."

Before her was everything a stenographer could hope for. Miss Burnbaum connected the small lamp to an outlet near the corner of the desk. It added an inviting homeyness to the workspace. Liesel couldn't help but wonder if the pleased look on the other woman's face would disappear as soon as Uncle Otto returned to his own office. Maybe then the old Miss Burnbaum would be back. In a way, Liesel almost hoped so; she knew *that* Miss Burnbaum. This one . . . who could tell where that smile came from or why it was there?

Liesel now had the environment, the equipment, and the energy she needed to keep herself busily working throughout the day. But she had to wonder if actual work would come her way.

As the men rolled away the last of the boxes, Uncle Otto patted Liesel's shoulder. "Let me know if there is anything else you need. I have a document I would like transcribed, so once you've accustomed yourself to this new typewriter—"

"It's a Remington," she noted. "I've worked on one before. I can begin as soon as you like."

"Very good, then," he said. "Lucy, er, Miss Burnbaum, will you bring the document from the corner of my desk for Miss Bonner?"

"Of course!"

Liesel could not believe this was the same place she had been employed at just a few short weeks ago. Miss Burnbaum handed her a hefty, handwritten document.

"It's a ledger full of legal notes one of Mr. von Woerner's associates drew up from meetings he's attended for the past two months," she told Liesel. "While Mr. von Woerner has been made aware of most of this verbally, it needs to be drawn up into formal documents for review and filing. It's quite a task, especially deciphering some of the legal terms used. But Mr. von Woerner told me you're used to working with lawyers, so perhaps it won't be such a chore for you."

"I'd be happy to take it on," Liesel said.

The two left her, and Liesel took off her jacket, hung it on a recently installed hook on the back of the door, and sat down under the glow of the new electric lights. It would be heavenly to be busy in a quiet, well-furnished office such as this, with a new typewriter to top it all off.

She stared at the empty threshold a moment, wondering yet again why Uncle Otto and Lucille Burnbaum had fussed over her return. Odd indeed. What possible reason did they have to want her here this time?

But with the stack of papers to be transcribed beckoning, Liesel put aside such questions. What did it matter, really? She had work to do.

The day went so quickly that Liesel gave barely another thought to either Uncle Otto or Miss Burnbaum. Neither one of them paid her the slightest attention, so she set aside her questions. By five o'clock, she was surprised to hear the whistle from the factory below the offices.

Though she'd worked consistently, she was only halfway through the lengthy document, so she set it aside to continue the next day. Then she straightened her desk, turned off the lamp Miss Burnbaum had personally added, took up her jacket, and emerged from the room.

Miss Burnbaum was not at her desk, but Uncle Otto's door was open. Liesel approached to tell him she would be leaving for the night.

What she saw surprised her. Miss Burnbaum stood not on the normal outer side of Uncle Otto's desk but next to his chair, bending over something on his desk that they both were studying. Their proximity was so close Liesel almost backed away, as if she was interrupting something she ought not see.

But Miss Burnbaum caught the movement. If she was embarrassed, it was too hard to tell through her gleaming eyes. She'd never looked happier.

"Good night, Miss Burnbaum, Mr. von Woerner," Liesel said, prepared to walk away.

Uncle Otto cleared his throat. He stood awkwardly, seeming to relax only when Miss Burnbaum slowly made her way out from behind his desk.

"Oh, just a moment, won't you, Miss Bonner?" Miss Burnbaum called.

Liesel paused, waiting.

"Starting tomorrow, we would like you to answer all the calls. My telephone has so much static on the receiver I can barely hear the other end. I suppose I'll have to place an order for a new one. Tell me first if Mr. von Woerner has a call. You can deal with other inquiries yourself or ask me to come to your office. All right, then?"

Liesel nodded. She'd learned her phone was connected to Miss Burnbaum's, but it hardly rang all day. She'd gone from having too little responsibility to having more than she thought possible while Miss Burnbaum still held her position. It was almost enough to demand of either one of them what was *really* going on.

But she said nothing, too grateful for the day's work. Work that wasn't even finished. She hadn't enjoyed herself so much since she'd been at the railroad with Mr. Quigley.

"Good night, Miss Bonner," said Uncle Otto. He was nearly smiling.

"Good night."

Liesel left, meeting her father for the trolley ride home. She told him about her busy first day back and how much she might like working for Uncle Otto if there could be more days like it.

She'd been so busy she had spent remarkably little time thinking about David. That changed the moment she sat on the trolley and had the slightest moment of free time. His face came immediately to mind. She expected him to visit tonight, since she had not seen him the day before. When she arrived home from her calls yesterday, Mama had told her he came by during the day, saying he hoped he would be able to see her later last evening. But by seven o'clock, he'd sent a messenger stating he wouldn't be able to get away at all and would see her the next day. And as usual, she'd gone to sleep thinking of him after her prayers.

She wondered how awkward it would be when she first saw him again. It wasn't just the kiss, although that would have been reason enough. Had he guessed why she'd been so upset over the misunderstanding about Anna? That she had somehow imagined herself in that very role—as his wife? It was all so humiliating. He must have guessed that. Why else would he have kissed her? And while it was true she'd welcomed that kiss—indeed, thought of little else since—it was also true this was too much, too soon.

When Liesel and her father arrived home, David was already there, helping to set the table as if he were a member of the family. Upon seeing him, Liesel offered the barest smile. "You should go and sit. I'll finish the table."

He caught her gaze. He was neither smiling nor frowning, as if he were too busy trying to read her expression to give her one of his own. He kept the plate. "No, I don't mind."

Liesel took the plate from his hands. "You're rather eager to help out."

"With good reason," he said softly. He was standing entirely too close, and the words tumbled into her ears like a caress.

Looking at the table instead of him, she spotted the last empty spot in need of the plate. "And why is that?" Despite her best effort, her voice still trembled. She moved toward the empty place setting.

Following her around the table, he nearly bumped into her when she stopped to put down the dish. He stood directly behind her. With him right there and the table in front of her, she couldn't move away without brushing directly past him.

"It's the polite thing to do, isn't it?"

Liesel turned to him. "Yes," she said. "But totally unnecessary since you're a guest."

"Perhaps. But uninvited guests should be all the more ready to help out."

"Uninvited?"

"Aren't I?"

"Under the circumstances, it's understood that you will stay if you're here during the dinner hour."

"Yes, well, not a very formal invitation, is it?"

This was the longest trivial conversation Liesel had ever held with David. She looked at him a moment, wondering if he felt as awkward as she did over their last parting and if perhaps that was the cause for his odd behavior. But she didn't consider the idea for long. He looked entirely too comfortable.

"Then I'll get the napkins, and you can place them around the table."

She waited for him to move farther away to let her pass, but he merely stood still, looking at her.

The kitchen door opened, startling Liesel into movement. Heading to the side table, her shoulder did indeed brush against his as she passed. She wondered if he was aware of the contact. Then, taking out the pink-striped napkins, she handed them to David, barely looking at him. She turned to help her mother place a heavy crock in the center of the table.

"I'll get the dark bread, and we'll be set," said Mama; then she looked at David. "I hope you like *Blindhun*, Mr. de Serre."

"I'm not sure if I do," he said, though his voice was optimistic. "What is it?"

Mama's laughter brightened the room. "Why, it is stew, of course! Beans, potatoes, bacon, vegetables—and some apples as well. Not fancy, but filling."

"Smells good," he said. "That's the best start."

They took their places, David next to Liesel across from the twins. Greta sat beside Mama at the opposite end from Papa. Papa prepared to say grace, but Greta spoke up first.

"At my friend Sally's house they all hold hands while they pray," she said. "Maybe we should do that, too."

"All right," said Papa.

Slowly, Liesel slipped her hand into David's. His fingers were smooth and surprisingly cool for the warmth of the day. Liesel hoped he didn't notice how warm she suddenly felt. She hardly heard Papa's prayer.

"I heard some teachers talking about a big suffragette parade in the city today," said Henry after Papa finished the prayer. "A bunch of women got carted off. Did you see any of it, Papa?"

Papa shook his head. "No, we heard nothing of it around the factory."

"It's a good thing Liesel wasn't there," Rolf said. "She'd have been nabbed by the coppers!"

Liesel felt herself blush. Perhaps if life were as calm as it used to be, she might have been in the center of that parade.

"Well, it's a good thing our Liesel is back to work to keep her out of trouble. Those suffragettes, they are getting nasty."

"Nasty!" Liesel repeated in spite of herself. "How can you say that, Mama? They just want the vote, same as you and I."

Mama gave a little laugh. "*Ja*. Well, we may want the vote, but do we stop up all the traffic to call attention to us?"

"How else are they going to make Congress recognize the issue if they don't call attention to it?"

"Ah, you've got her started now, Mama," said Papa with a laugh. "Our own suffragette, right here in the dining room." He looked at David. "And what do you think of all this, Mr. de Serre? About women having the vote?"

David paused before answering, finishing the bread he'd just bitten into. Liesel glanced at him, keenly interested in what he was about to say.

"My views aren't widely accepted," David said slowly, "by most men or most pulpits."

"Then you must be for the women!" Rolf said rather loudly, laughing as if he'd discovered something secretive.

David didn't deny it.

"And why is that, Mr. de Serre?" Papa inquired.

"As I see it, our society judges men by how much money they make and women by the success of their children. Right or wrong, that's the world's way. If women can get a better education for their children, better working conditions for their sons, and adequate child care if they themselves are forced to work, they should be allowed a voice. If a woman doesn't have a vote for or against the people making those laws, then this society isn't allowing her to do her best at the very thing it wants her to do."

Papa nodded in agreement.

Liesel stared at David, astounded by his succinct logic and eloquence. She couldn't have said it better herself, and it made her almost sorry she'd missed that suffrage parade, arrests or not. But then she shook away such a ridiculous notion. She had had one run-in with the government already this year and didn't need another. Although looking at David just then, she was undeniably grateful for this government run-in.

When dinner ended, David insisted Mama go and sit with Papa in the parlor while he and Liesel took care of the cleanup. Liesel was both eager

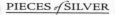
and reluctant to do that. Eager to be alone with him ... reluctant that it might give her yet another opportunity to make a fool of herself.

She washed the dishes, and he dried. Liesel made every attempt to keep what little conversation they shared on a strictly casual basis, hoping he had forgotten her embarrassing behavior of the other day.

"Perhaps you should go into politics," Liesel said. "If women are ever to get the vote, it's going to take people with your opinion in a place that counts."

He laughed, and she was caught for a moment—once again—by his handsome good looks. Brown eyes with a light of warmth and happiness. White, strong teeth added to the appeal of that smile. "Politicians talk too much," was all he said.

They were quiet after that, and she felt a strong sense of awkwardness sweep over her. Polite conversation seemed impossible. But even as she wondered what to say next, she couldn't wish him gone. In a rather twisted way, she enjoyed each torturous moment.

"Would you care to go for a walk when we're done?" he asked. "There's something I need to tell you."

"All right. But we can talk here, too. This kitchen is a million miles from the family when there are dishes to be done."

"It's about Josef."

"Oh," she looked down, feeling a splash of conflicting emotion. Was he captured or nearly so? Surely David would have told her that already. "Is there something new in the case?"

David nodded. "Luedke's singing like a bird. He's named several counterparts. Josef is one of them."

Liesel swallowed hard. This should come as little surprise. Hadn't she already prepared herself for Josef's guilt?

"Tell me," David said softly when she did not speak, "in all of the time you spent with Josef, did you ever hear him say the word *Patria*—or see it written on anything in his possession?"

She shook her head. "Is it some sort of code?"

"We think so."

"So you finally have all the evidence you need?"

"All we need now is the man."

Liesel took a deep breath. The truth was still difficult to accept even after all this time. Her heart weighed heavy as fears for Josef's future bombarded her. Fears she couldn't dwell on, not if she wanted to maintain at least a facade of well-being.

They finished the last of the dishes, but neither one moved toward the door to rejoin the family.

"Mind if we walk?" David asked gently.

She looked up at him, welcoming his tone of voice. She followed him out.

It was nearly nine o'clock. The summer sun was just setting, and as they stepped out into the yard, Liesel's attention was captured by the sky. Some streaks were as deep a red as Mama's roses, with a shock of purple slashed here and there. But the brilliance of color wasn't enough to steal her glance for long. She looked at David, seeing an odd look on his face. He stared past Mama's roses too intently.

"Something wrong?"

"Thought I saw something."

She followed his gaze to where the bushes grew thick and met foliage from other plants. Nothing appeared unusual.

"What did you see?"

He shrugged, leading her away from the back porch and apparently dismissing it. They went around the house to the front sidewalk. As they walked down the street, Liesel caught the scent of Miss Corretta's honeysuckle bushes, reminding her of the romance of summertime. Parks were full of strolling pairs; traveling circuses drew not just children but also handholding twosomes. Moon and starlight seemed to beckon couples outside. It was impossible not to be affected, and Liesel found herself wishing David would take hold of her hand. But of course he did not, and she recanted the wish.

They walked one block, then another without saying a word. When they seemed aimlessly headed back toward Liesel's home, David spoke at last.

"Liesel." His voice was quiet in the dimming light. She held her breath. "The other day when I sent you to my home to wait for me, I should have told you Anna might be there. It slipped my mind that she'd be visiting."

Liesel expelled her breath slowly. "That's all right." She looked at the sidewalk instead of him.

"I'm sorry for the confusion," he went on. "It must have been a shock to think I might be married after all the time we've spent together."

She said nothing, didn't even nod an admission.

David stopped, lightly touching her elbow in an invitation to turn to him instead of walking on. Liesel looked up at him. It seemed as though he searched for something on her face, and she wished she could turn away, to hide everything she felt. Surely if he studied her long enough, he would guess at that moment she wanted nothing more than another kiss.

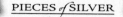

For the briefest moment, Liesel thought that wish might come true. He edged closer, lowered his face nearer hers. But in the very next moment, he turned away, looking down the street.

"Shall we go back?" he asked politely, stiffly.

Liesel paused, unwilling to do as he asked. Part of her wanted to stay right where they were and confront the feelings that were undeniably there. But were they there for him? Had he held himself back from kissing her because he knew it would be a mistake? Because it was only the moon and the starlight making him want to kiss her?

Liesel could hardly believe her own thoughts. Here she was wishing for another kiss, when for the past two days, all she could do was berate herself for allowing him to kiss her in the first place. It was too soon, she reminded herself almost cynically. Too soon after Josef.

In front of her parents' house, they paused. He turned to her, his back to the house, preventing the completion of their stroll by standing in her pathway.

"Liesel."

She looked up at him. Waiting.

"I owe you an apology. Again."

She looked away but not before shaking her head.

"I do," he insisted. "For two reasons. First, I have no right to rush you into something you're probably not ready for. I know you think your feelings for Josef have changed because you've learned some things you never knew about him. But maybe it's not so easy to change how you feel. Only you can decide when you're ready to move on to someone else, and I shouldn't be rushing you."

He'd put into words all she'd thought, which should have endeared him to her. Instead she felt embarrassed and a little short-tempered that he'd said it instead of her. Evidently part of her was ready before he thought she should be—ready to have enjoyed his kiss and to even want another.

"And the other reason?" she asked.

"I don't want to lose my objectivity on this case," he said. "I need a clear head, and I don't seem to have that when I'm around you."

Her brows raised, but she said nothing. She wanted to hear more.

"I need to get this case closed. Not just because it's important, but because with it still open, there are . . ." He paused, as if hunting for the right word. "There are issues that can't be resolved. Between us. I've come to value your company, Liesel. But it's taking away my edge on this thing. I've got to step back a little, at least until this case is finished. Do you understand what I'm trying to say?"

Unsure but unwilling to appear the clinging woman she was evidently becoming at that moment, she nodded. "Of course. It's a timing issue."

"I know you'll contact me if you hear from Josef, and I'll still be in contact with you, of course," he said. "One way or another. Only I don't think I should spend evenings here."

She nodded, still looking at him closely. He looked almost as unhappy as she felt.

"Will you come inside to say good night to my parents?"

He nodded. Liesel watched him, wondering how long it would be before any of them saw him again. He gave nothing away, only thanked Mama for another excellent meal and shook Papa's hand. He appeared his old self again, confident in a reserved sort of way, quietly self-assured.

She walked him to the door, resisting the urge to follow him outside at least as far as the porch.

"Good night," she whispered.

"Good night."

Then, in the comparative privacy of the alcove, David bent his head and kissed her cheek, barely touching the corner of her mouth. It was unlike the brief graze to her forehead so long ago but certainly nothing like the kiss at the trolley stop.

Then he was gone.

David heard the door close softly behind him and stopped. What he wanted to do was turn around, thrust open that door, and take Liesel in his arms. Forget the case—let someone else take over. Liesel was more important.

One foot turned as if to lead him on that very path. But something from across the street caught his eye. A tall shadow slipped inside the moonlit outline of one of the houses. For a moment, David resisted, still wanting to go back to Liesel. But the very foot that would have taken him to do that now led him after the silhouette.

He found no one, and even in the blue glow of moonlight, he could see no footprints suggesting anyone had been there lately. The sturdy grass was dry and trimmed so short it would have been difficult to detect prints even in the best of light. He stood still, listening. Nothing.

David started back to his car, then remembered something. When they'd left for their walk, they'd taken the back door, and David was sure he had seen the glow of a lit cigarette sail quickly to the ground, only to be snuffed out before he could be certain of what he saw. The incident had been easy to ignore, thinking it was most likely a neighbor banished from the house for a smoke. Being in Liesel's company made it all too easy to forget that it had happened. He frowned. He should have investigated anyway—but he'd wanted too much to have his walk alone with Liesel.

In that moment, he determined it wasn't Liesel taking him away from this case; it was his own selfish desires. He'd passed up looking into something potentially important because of what *he* wanted to do, ignoring what was best.

Of course, no one was there now. Not a trace that he could find in the dark, not even a burnt cigarette butt. It probably hadn't been a neighbor sent outside to smoke; there would likely be evidence of such a habit, at least with an area of crushed grass or an ashbin. So who had it been?

Looking to the house, the view from the bushes through the Bonners' unshaded windows included the dining room and kitchen. If someone had been watching them, he would have tailed them once they embarked on their walk.

David crossed the street, finding the best view of the Bonner house. This time, he studied the ground not for footprints but for something else. Before too long, David spotted something. A cigarette butt burned all the way to its cork tip. David stuffed it into his pocket. It was the only one to be found, which was good. Still, he could be following a wrong lead; this could be nothing more than the homeowner's overlooked trash.

As he drove home, he wondered if he was just imagining it all because of an overprotective attitude about Liesel—or maybe he was blowing it all out of proportion in order to deny just how useless he'd been lately.

He shook off the doubts and the reasons for them. If he was going to do his job and do it well, then he must treat all leads equally whether they went anywhere or not. If someone was secretly watching Liesel's house, it could be Josef. David didn't think he had the habit of smoking, since in all his surveillance of the man, David had never seen him do so. But he might have taken up the habit while in hiding. If it was Josef watching Liesel's house, it wouldn't be long before he made contact.

The thought made David want to turn around, go back to Liesel's, and camp out on her front porch until Josef made his move. That urge wasn't just his desire to catch a criminal. The man was dangerous. David didn't want Josef anywhere near Liesel.

The fact was, if Josef planned to contact her soon, David shouldn't be as visible as he'd been lately. Nonetheless, he was loath to go home. Instead, he drove around the city, stopping now and then, attentive to anyone on the road or in trolleys heading the same direction as he. Perhaps he was the one being followed, not Liesel. If so, he was only too happy to give the culprit the opportunity.

However, after more than an hour of making himself available, David detected no sign of anyone following him. If anyone was being watched, it was Liesel.

He turned his Runabout back in the direction of Liesel's home. It was late, well past eleven. As he approached her neighborhood, he found it quiet and dark. David parked his car at a corner a block from her home. He didn't want the sound of his engine to alert either those in the houses or anyone lurking around outside.

He walked slowly, heeding movement and sound. He heard a cricket, a frog, was startled by a cat stalking nearby. But other than the natural sounds of the night, David heard nothing, nor did he see anything unusual. After two passes down Liesel's street, he determined he had either mistaken benign neighbors for something sinister or whoever had been watching was gone for the night.

David made his way home, determining he would stop by the von Woerner factory in the morning to warn Liesel to be on the lookout. Better to warn her early. Besides, he added to reassure himself, seeing her briefly at the factory wouldn't be compromising his intention to keep his distance. This was business.

CHAPTER *Twenty-One*

JOSEF woke with a start, thrashing the covers that bound him immobile. Run! He had to get away before they caught him. He saw no faces, but they were closing in. The hunter breathed the name again and again.

Patria. Patria.

Throwing off the sheet, his feet hit the cool wooden floor, and in a daze, he stumbled and fell. Only then did he realize it had been a dream.

They might be after him, they might even know he was Patria, but no one knew where he was—yet.

Wiping sweat from his brow and the back of his neck, he sank to the floor and leaned against the bed, breathing deeply. The sun had barely risen; he could tell by the light filtering through the two small windows high on the wall of the bedroom.

Standing, he went into the kitchen, knowing he wouldn't find anything there. Habit, mainly. He'd drunk the last of the milk days before, eaten the last of the bread sometime after that, the last crackers yesterday morning. His stomach growled again. He'd have to go for food; he couldn't wait any longer. Not even a tin of beans could be found.

It was no use to wait, anyway. Friedrich had been gone for days, and Josef had little hope he'd be back. Either he'd found his way to *Deutschland*, as many in the organization were trying to do, or he'd been nabbed. Even if Friedrich had left him behind without help, believing his compatriot had made it to safety gave Josef hope that he could do the same.

Whatever might happen, Josef knew he had to do something—and quickly. He had no money or contacts left, and he would have to leave the house he currently occupied within the week. It was driving him crazy to be cooped up in a place that must appear unoccupied—no fire in the stove, no lights at night, no noise. Friedrich had known the man who usually lived in this house, and while he was gone, the house was safe enough if no one knew it was being used. Friedrich had said the owner would offer no help beyond shelter, and once he returned from the business that kept him out of town for the rest of July, he would be of no further help. Josef had no intention of finding out if he could press for anything more. Friedrich had been only too clear on that.

Josef looked down at his appearance. He was thin, he knew. Not just hungry but weak. Since he'd left Washington, he'd grabbed sporadic sleep and caught what little nourishment could either be begged or stolen, finding his first shelter in this house after he'd caught up with Friedrich. At first, it had been more than Josef had hoped for: a roof over his head and food, which, although sparse, was more than he'd gotten on the street. And enough safety to get the first steady sleep since he fled.

That would all change now. He'd have to go back to the life of a vagabond. A frustrated moan escaped him when he thought of his home in Washington: his huge, downy bed, enough food to chase away the slightest hint of hunger, all the comfortable, clean clothes he could want. And money. All he needed and more.

He ran a hand over his face, cursing the day he'd been found out. But Liesel had no part of that curse. She was his one hope. She'd warned him, hadn't she? Told him the government was on to him. Still, he didn't like to think of that day. There had been something in her voice, in her eyes, her mannerisms that revealed more than what she'd learned of him. It had haunted Josef for the weeks he'd been gone. He had had time to dwell on every minute detail of the conversation. She might not have wanted to judge him, but she had—and harshly. He'd seen it in her eyes. She didn't approve of a single thing he'd said that day.

Yet she had helped him. Without her, he might have stayed in Washington too long—long enough for the government to finish whatever case they had on him and walk right up to his door and arrest him. Yes, he thanked Liesel for what she'd done.

He didn't want to contact her solely because of that judgment he'd seen. But he told himself that judgment had only been there because she didn't understand. Not yet. Once this war was over, he could take her to *Deutsch-*

land with him. Together they would see how happy everyone was, and he could make her happy there, too. Surely she hadn't stopped caring for him, even if she didn't yet understand his loyalties and politics.

For now, he needed her help regardless of whether or not she understood. She could go to his father and ask for the money he needed, and Josef could find his way to *Deutschland* on his own. It was too dangerous for Liesel to travel with him yet. She could join him there later.

The thought of his father and the money Josef's escape would cost made him frown, but not for long. It wasn't the time to be dwelling on such sentimentality. His father, of all people, would understand once this was over. Finally, Josef would be able to tell him what he'd been up to. And finally, his father would notice him. Maybe he'd even take a day off work to spend some time hearing all the tales Josef could tell.

Perhaps Josef would be able to convince his father to take the chance on another sea voyage and meet him in *Deutschland* with Liesel. Josef might have gone directly to his father and left Liesel out of the money transaction for her own good, but Liesel was the one who already knew the truth. He wouldn't have to explain anything to her as he would to his father. Besides, with his father's staunch German ways, Josef didn't want him knowing too much. If Josef was caught, his father would be a likely target—if not by the government, at least by the neighbors. It would be best for him if he knew nothing.

Today is the day, Josef determined. He had little choice but to return to Washington right away and contact Liesel that afternoon. Soon this nightmare would be over.

———

David admired Liesel's office, comparing it with his paltry desk in the bullpen. "Private industry!" he said with a low whistle. "New desk, new typewriter. Even gets you your own telephone."

"Yes, well it hardly ever rings, which is probably why they let me have the responsibility of answering it."

He looked at her as if curious. "What does that mean?"

She shrugged. "Only that once it was hard to get a lot of work around here." Her eyes returned to the report on her desk. "Not today, though."

"I'll let you get back to it, then," he told her. "I just came to tell you to be on the lookout, make sure you're not being followed or watched. I can't go into more detail because I really don't have much evidence. Josef may contact you soon if he's back in Washington."

"Does this have anything to do with what you saw in my yard last night?"

He nodded. "Maybe it was my imagination, maybe not." *Maybe I'm just imagining this whole thing to give me an excuse to come here and see you. Maybe I'm just a dunce.* "Be careful."

She nodded. "I won't see you later, then?"

"I could give you and your father a ride home," he said before he'd considered the words. Then he felt compelled to add, "I can't stay for dinner, though."

He would have left then, but Liesel held him back. They spoke quietly in case anyone was outside her office. Out of propriety, she'd left the door slightly ajar.

"If it was Josef you saw last night, what shall I do?"

"Bring him to me."

"Just that easily?"

"If he contacts you, tell him you'll meet him at a certain place at a certain time. That's all you need to do."

Liesel rubbed her hands, one on top of the other. "I'll want to talk to him, David. Tell him he should testify against this other person you're holding. Anything at all to help him."

He watched her closely, noting the nervousness in her demeanor. "Yes. Of course."

Turning abruptly back to her desk, she said, "I need to finish the project I'm working on."

"All right. But I'd like to get the number for your telephone before I go."

Liesel wrote it down and handed it to him.

He didn't move, still eyeing her. "I'll see you at five, then. You and your father."

She nodded, and the smile on her face seemed genuine. At least he chose to think it was despite her plea a moment ago to do all she could to help Josef.

David left her office on feet that were, as always, reluctant to take him from her side.

———

Liesel watched him go until she could see him no more. A moment ago, confusion flared in her like sulfur on a matchstick. She wanted to help Josef, yet the moment the words were uttered, she felt as if to do so would be to betray her country . . . and David.

She hadn't known what she thought or felt at that moment about Josef or about David. If she'd let him look at her face, in her eyes, he might have guessed what she felt before she could figure it out for herself.

Determined to put both men out of her mind, Liesel worked hard after that, resolutely attending to her work. Since Miss Burnbaum and Uncle Otto once again ignored her for most of the morning, she forgot about their odd behavior of yesterday. Maybe Miss Burnbaum finally had enough work to feel Liesel might be a necessary addition. Liesel enjoyed every legal term in the document, each scrawl just waiting to be deciphered. She took only a short break to eat lunch at her desk.

Just as she took the first bite of her sandwich, the loud ring of the telephone startled her.

Swallowing quickly, Liesel picked up the receiver on her desk. "Von Woerner's," she said briskly.

"What? Von who?" The woman on the other end had a high-pitched, shrill voice.

"Von Woerner's Glass and Bottle Company," Liesel clarified.

"Oh, that operator. Hang up, girlie, will you? She rang up the wrong number. Clear the line. Clear the line!"

Liesel hung up, only too happy to stop the piercing voice from traveling to her ear. She stared at the phone as she finished her lunch. In the two days since Liesel had been back, the phone had rarely rung. Uncle Otto was never out of the office and took the few calls he received. Miss Burnbaum received no calls. Liesel remembered the phone being busier the last time she'd worked there and wondered if Uncle Otto might purposely be keeping the line clear in case someone from the police department tried to contact him with news of Josef. Or perhaps he kept the line open for Josef himself.

If Josef did call, she knew what she must do. Not simply hand him over to Uncle Otto—he knew nothing of Josef's involvement, and even though Uncle Otto would be relieved to find out his son was still alive, it wasn't as simple as that. That was one phone call she mustn't pass beyond her own desk.

If she had any doubt she would be able to do such a thing, she wouldn't allow herself to dwell on it. She'd thought it all through, prayed unceasingly about it, and knew she must stop Josef from getting himself into any more trouble. He might not see it as a favor, but she knew she had little choice but to do the right thing.

After lunch, Liesel returned to work, glad to rescue her mind from unpleasant images. She marveled that hours could easily slip away when she kept herself occupied. While she had little hope she would be able to keep this job once the truth was known about Josef, especially considering the part she might be forced to play in bringing him to justice, she would allow herself to enjoy it for the moment.

The phone rang twice more that afternoon. The printer left a message that a job ordered a week ago was ready to be picked up. The other caller hung up.

After that second call, Miss Burnbaum came in to Liesel's little office. Liesel was so engrossed in her work she thought perhaps the older woman might have been standing in the threshold several moments before being noticed.

"How is the work going, dear?"

Liesel kept her unwelcome reception of Miss Burnbaum's endearment hidden. Though the woman had been far friendlier since Liesel had returned to her job, Liesel still detected no trace of genuine affection from her. "I'm nearly finished. It's been easy until this last section where the writing gets disjointed. I may have to contact Mr. Haushaven if I can't figure it out."

Miss Burnbaum looked at the writing and, with remarkable ease, translated the section for Liesel.

"Why, you're familiar with these legal terms, after all!" Liesel observed. "You could have done this quite easily."

"Yes, well, Mr. von Woerner made it clear he wanted to keep you busy."

"So I've gathered," Liesel said. "I've wondered about that."

Miss Burnbaum's brows shot up. "Have you?"

"Yes, Uncle Otto . . . Mr. von Woerner . . . and you . . . seem to think I might be of actual use around here now."

"Of course! You're a very competent worker, Miss Bonner. That was obvious from the start."

Just then the phone rang, and Liesel quickly excused herself. Another click.

"The caller hung up," Liesel said. "That's the second call like that this afternoon."

"Ring for the operator," Miss Burnbaum said immediately. "Inquire as to who might be trying this number."

Liesel did so, curious about Miss Burnbaum's obvious interest in what appeared to be an ordinary nuisance call.

"We've just received a ring at this number," Liesel said to the operator, "only to have the caller hang up. Can you identify who tried to reach here just now?"

"No, ma'am. There are a number of operators working these lines."

"Well, couldn't you ask the others? It's the second time it's happened in a short span of time."

"If you want to file a complaint, I can direct you to that party, ma'am. But I'm afraid there's no way for me to track a caller without proper authority. Sorry, ma'am."

"That's all right," Liesel said, then replaced the receiver and repeated the conversation for Miss Burnbaum.

"So the caller just before I came in here hung up, too?"

Liesel nodded. "And a wrong number earlier. The only legitimate call I've received all day was from the printer, which I told you about."

"Yes, well, Mr. von Woerner discourages much telephone usage. He's depending on his managers downstairs to take most of the calls, and they're on another line entirely."

"Oh? Is that a new policy?"

"Why do you ask?"

"Only that it seems the telephone rings a bit less than the last time I worked here."

"Well, Mr. von Woerner hasn't been himself lately. He reduced his work schedule. I'm sure you understand, what with Josef's disappearance and all. You seem to be holding up rather well, I must say."

"I'm grateful to be working, Miss Burnbaum. Being busy helps to keep my mind off of the situation."

"Yes, that's precisely what Mr. von Woerner hoped."

Miss Burnbaum turned away, leaving behind only one thing on Liesel's mind, a question as to why the woman had visited at all. Just to inquire about how the work was going?

It was near four o'clock when Liesel finished the document that had kept her busy for almost two full days. She skimmed it once again, set it into a neat pile, and put it into a folder with the original handwritten pad. Then she delivered it to Miss Burnbaum.

"Finished already?"

"Yes. It was really quite enjoyable. I hope you and Mr. von Woerner will have more work for me just like it."

"Oh, I'm sure we'll be able to keep you happy," Miss Burnbaum replied, accepting the document just as the phone rang.

For a moment, Liesel stood still, expecting Miss Burnbaum to answer it on her own extension since she appeared ready to do so out of long habit. But then she glanced up at Liesel. "Would you mind getting that, dear?" she whispered, as if the caller on the phone might hear if she spoke too loudly.

Liesel returned to her office, noticing the time. Still an hour left to the workday. She wondered briefly if she would have anything to fill that hour.

Liesel picked up the receiver. "Von Woerner's."

Nothing.

Liesel repeated the salutation.

Still nothing, although through the receiver she heard outside sounds like children in the distance and the song of birds chirping nearby. Someone was still on the line.

"Speak up, will you?" she asked rather loudly.

"Who is on the line?" The male voice sounded muffled, with a slight accent, perhaps English or Irish.

"This is von Woerner's Glass and Bottle Company. May I help you?"

"Your name?"

"I beg your pardon, sir?"

"It's your name I'm wanting, girl."

There was something familiar in that faraway tone, something that made her heart skip a beat. "Miss Bonner," she said, suddenly lowering her voice.

"Very good," the clipped voice said.

Liesel spoke. "Who is calling?"

"A friend. Only a friend."

The muffled quality was gone along with any trace of an accent. She had no doubt of the caller's identity. "Oh . . ."

"Say nothing. Someone might hear you."

"Are you hurt? Are you well? Where are you?"

"You do care!" He sounded sweetly surprised, overjoyed, in fact. It made Liesel's heart sink with sadness. "I knew you wouldn't stop caring for me, *mein Liebe.*"

"Yes, of course I do."

"Is anyone nearby? Where is Lucy?"

Liesel glanced behind her to be sure she'd closed her door. "In her office."

"Can she hear you?"

"No."

"And my father?"

"In his office."

"Is he well?"

"Worried, so worried."

"Is he?" he asked. "That cannot be avoided." His tone had grown colder. "I need help, Liesel."

"Where are you?"

"I cannot tell you."

"But for me to help you—"

"Please, just let me talk, *Liebchen*. I need money. Lots of it. You will have to go to my father; he'll give you everything I need."

"But how, without telling him . . ."

"Tell him nothing, Liesel. Only that I am alive and that I need money. Ten thousand, at least. He'll cooperate. He trusts you."

"But without knowing? He'll ask questions."

"Tell him *nothing*. I have to go; we can't speak any longer. You must go to him right away, to give him time to get the money together. I'll be there tomorrow, Liesel. I need it by then. By Thursday. Meet me when it's dark. Ten o'clock behind the scaffolding of the new monument, the one of Lincoln. Bring the money in a bag, a shopping bag or a sack that won't be noticed. I need you, Liesel. Without your help I will . . . I don't know; I may die."

"Let me come to you now. Are you hurt? Are you hungry? You've been gone so long—"

"Tomorrow, Liesel. Thursday. Ten o'clock."

The line went dead.

Liesel hung up. Seeing her hands shaking so visibly only added to the turmoil inside. Her heart pounded all the way up to her temples; her chest felt as if pressed beneath a heavy weight, limiting her breaths. She forced herself to sit still until regaining at least a portion of control.

The conversation reverberated in her brain. *Money. Tell no one. Ten thousand dollars. The new monument. Tomorrow.*

How could she wait that long?

She sprang to her feet, aware of some new source of strength. She paced the little office just once before coming to her decision. She knew exactly what she must do. And she must do it now.

Her purse was in the bottom drawer of her desk, and in it she found David's telephone number. Five after four. He was probably still at his office. He wouldn't leave to pick her up for more than half an hour. Liesel leaned over, reaching for the telephone. And then she stopped.

What was she doing? Would she really turn in Josef just as easily as that?

Oh, God, she prayed, *tell me what to do!*

She had no choice. She'd grappled with this too long to start questioning what was right or wrong. Josef had proven where his allegiance lay, and it was neither with the land of his birth nor with God. If she could get him to cooperate with David, testify against this other man being held, he might come through relatively unscathed. That was the only way to help Josef now.

She reached for the phone.

No operator answered her clicking.

"Hello?" she said into the receiver. "Is someone on this line?"

"Yes, Miss Bonner." It was Miss Burnbaum's voice. "Will you come out here, please?"

Relief swept through Liesel at having learned Miss Burnbaum was on the line before she'd made contact with David. For the other woman to have overheard would be a disaster.

Hanging up the receiver, a vague sense of caution pricked at Liesel's mind. Staring at the phone, she realized Miss Burnbaum's line had been as clear as her own. No static.

Confused, Liesel stood. Why, exactly, had Miss Burnbaum given Liesel the task of answering the phone if there was nothing wrong with her own?

She might as well ask outright what was going on. Right now.

But Miss Burnbaum had on her hat and held her purse and gloves in her hand. Liesel glanced again at her timepiece, assuring herself it wasn't yet quitting time.

"I was just going to telephone a neighbor," Miss Burnbaum said before Liesel could get a word out. "I was calling for help, actually, but I've had a better idea. I'm afraid I have a great favor to ask of you, Miss Bonner." She held her free hand to her forehead, pressing on it as if it pained her. "I have a frightful headache, and I need to go home immediately. I've suffered these headaches before, and they really are quite unbearable. They terrify me. I've fainted from them, you see, and I'm afraid I can't make it home on my own. I hope you won't mind if I ask you to accompany me. Just to my door? I live only a few blocks away; it won't take long."

Liesel squelched a moan and a quick refusal. She had far too much on her mind to worry about Miss Burnbaum's headache. Nonetheless, the woman did look as if she were in pain.

"I can send for one of the errand boys downstairs to take you," Liesel offered, "so we won't leave the office unattended."

"Oh, don't be silly. You'll only be gone a few minutes. I don't live far." She began walking toward the door, her pace steady even as she continued to press a palm to her forehead. "Come along, Miss Bonner."

There seemed little else to do but accompany Miss Burnbaum and return immediately to the office. Liesel eyed the older woman again. Miss

Burnbaum didn't seem the fragile type, one who would let a headache stand in the way of completing a workday for Uncle Otto. Yet why would she be doing that unless she was in a great deal of discomfort?

Liesel pushed down her frustration and grasped her timepiece once more. Maybe she could call David right now, before taking Miss Burnbaum home.

"I—I need to stop back in my office for just a moment—"

"Really, Miss Bonner, I must ask you to take me home right away."

Liesel turned anyway. To her dismay, Miss Burnbaum followed, moving quickly for someone who appeared so debilitated.

Knowing the call was out of the question with Miss Burnbaum hovering near, Liesel retrieved her purse from a drawer instead.

David would arrive to take her and her father home before long. She wasn't going to meet Josef until tomorrow and until then hadn't the faintest idea where he could be found, anyway. There was time, she assured herself. For the next twenty-four hours, all she had was time.

She approached Miss Burnbaum. "But what will you do once you're home? Won't you be there alone?"

"I'll call on my neighbor to check on me from time to time." She looped her arm firmly through Liesel's, as if she couldn't walk without assistance. "Thank you so much for this, Miss Bonner. I really can't tell you how much it means to me."

"That's all right," Liesel said, belated sympathy forming in her breast.

"Oh, this is just awful, dear," said Miss Burnbaum as they left the office. "I can barely tolerate standing up."

"It came on rather suddenly, didn't it?"

"Always does," she said, somewhat feebly.

Miss Burnbaum told Liesel she normally walked home but, because of the pain, suggested they take a trolley despite the short, three-block trip. Besides, the trolley would speed Liesel's return to the office.

Liesel thought she felt the woman's hand tremble and wondered how severe the pain must be to make a woman normally self-possessed so weak. A moment ago, Liesel had been hesitant to believe anything was wrong with the woman, but it was obvious something was agitating her.

They walked from the trolley stop to Miss Burnbaum's small home a few doors down. Taking the three steps up to the door, Miss Burnbaum searched her purse for a key, coming up with it moments later to unlatch the door with some difficulty. The door open, Liesel prepared to depart.

"Please come in a moment, will you? Just long enough for me to take my medicine?"

Liesel was developing a headache of her own, the urge to speak to David was so strong. She must do it, get it over with. It was hard enough to contemplate the impact of what she intended to do without having this delay create time for her to reconsider.

Yet she pushed such thoughts away. She knew what she had to do and would do it. Just as soon as she returned to her office and met David.

But that would have to wait at least a few minutes more as she followed Miss Burnbaum inside. The front door opened into a parlor, sparsely furnished, meticulously clean. It smelled of lavender oil. A small dining area lay behind the parlor, which heralded a wide window overlooking a yard full of trees. Next to the dining area, Liesel glimpsed an archway to a kitchen, toward which Miss Burnbaum headed.

"Please, follow me," she said. The kitchen was small yet able to hold a round table and two chairs in the corner. There was a wood-burning stove, an icebox, and a wall of cabinets. Two doors led out of the kitchen; one was open to a back porch, and the other, from the looks of the dark, stone-encased stairway, led to a cellar.

Miss Burnbaum retrieved a small bottle of some sort of medicine from one of the cabinets, then looked in the icebox with an empty glass in hand.

"I always take this with cider," she said. "The medicine is a powder, you see, and tastes quite deadly in plain water. Oh!"

"What's wrong?" Liesel was more impatient than ever to leave. The moan irritated her.

"No cider up here. And the prospect of taking those stairs makes my head pound to think of it. Oh, dear, my only cider is on the shelf down there."

"I'll get it," Liesel said quietly, but once on the cellar stairs she was anything but a cheerful giver. She just wanted to get the deed done and leave. "Where is the shelf?"

"Under the stairs, down there. Here, take a candle with you."

The woman took a candle from the counter and matches from inside a drawer. Liesel noticed Miss Burnbaum's hands trembled so fiercely she could barely light the wick before placing it unsteadily inside a pewter holder to catch falling wax.

"There," she said, handing it to Liesel. "Just go down the steps. You'll find two clay jugs on the bottom of the shelf. Bring one to me."

The stairs squeaked as Liesel descended. The kitchen window let in ample light, although farther down she was sure she'd welcome the candle in search of the cider. The stairs were sturdy despite the creaking, and the walls were of such thick stone and mortar she guessed if the house were hit by one of those bombs she heard they used on the battlegrounds overseas this cellar would sustain little damage.

But she had neither time nor desire to study the architecture. At the base of the stairs she held the candle high. The cellar wasn't large, at least what she could see of it, hardly more than a hole in the ground. She saw low shadows in the dim light, something large and square shoved to one corner, but little else on the cement floor. Around the stairway and below the steps was a shelf full of bottles, barrels, and cans. Liesel saw nothing that looked like a clay jug.

"Miss Burnbaum," she called, "I'm not sure which—"

A door slammed, and what little light shone through the slats of the open stairway suddenly disappeared.

Liesel went around to the base of the stairs and looked up.

"Miss Burnbaum," she called. "Miss Burnbaum?"

Nothing. No sound. No light.

Liesel rushed up the stairs. In her haste, the candle dropped out of its holder. It fell to the rough cement floor, snuffing out the meager glow it had provided.

"Miss Burnbaum?" Liesel tried the door. To her horror, it was locked tight. "Miss Burnbaum!"

If the woman heard Liesel's cries, she did not answer.

"Miss Burnbaum, open the door! Why have you closed me in here? Open this door!"

Ominous silence answered. Seconds passed like an eternity. Liesel listened. She heard a door opening and closing, the scrape of a chair against the floor, another door opening and closing.

"Open this door!" she demanded again, and much to her amazement, someone did. But it was not Miss Burnbaum.

CHAPTER *Twenty-Two*

UNCLE Otto took a seat at the small kitchen table, the glass Miss Burnbaum had held just moments ago now in his hands. It was filled with water, and he sat in the chair as if for an amiable afternoon visit. Miss Burnbaum was not in the room.

"Uncle Otto!" Stark suspicion struck Liesel the moment she saw his calm face. "What is going on?"

Instead of answering, he took a sip of his water. She noticed with growing unease that his thick fingers shook.

"Nothing to be concerned over, Liesel. You'll see."

She had no intention of waiting around to "see." She took a step past him, but Uncle Otto, as solid as he was, stood quickly into her path.

He laughed, and the sound was nearly as strange as the situation. He sounded so friendly, friendlier than he ever had. "Sit down, Liesel, sit down. And calm yourself." He smiled as he wiped away the moisture from the edge of his Bismarkian mustache and abandoned the glass on the table.

"I really think—"

"Sit down, Liesel."

This time his tone left no room for disobedience. Liesel approached the kitchen table but did not sit. What was happening? It was as if she was exactly where he wanted her, and he'd used Miss Burnbaum to get her here. But why?

All she knew was that she must leave. She had to get to David.

"Uncle Otto," she said, forcing her voice to remain quiet and calm, "I must return to the factory to meet my father and go home. He'll be waiting for me."

"Nonsense, Liesel. It's just past four thirty." He spoke slowly, almost soothingly. "Now sit down. We must talk."

Liesel took the edge of the empty seat opposite Uncle Otto. "Where is Miss Burnbaum?" Liesel spared a cautious glance around the kitchen to the archway behind her that connected to the dining room.

"It's likely she is on her way back to the office."

"An amazing recovery from her headache," Liesel commented. She eyed Uncle Otto, wondering why Miss Burnbaum had lured her here under false pretenses. "What's going on?"

Uncle Otto's face shadowed with such a serious look Liesel thought perhaps he might not be able to speak. He seemed ready to cry, his eyes moistened, and he took another drink that steadied his suddenly trembling lips.

"I have been forced by circumstances beyond my control—and yours—to detain you." He spoke in German, which indicated whatever he had on his mind took all of his concentration, demanded too much of him to be able to sort through it as well as translate. That fact frightened Liesel.

"What do you mean, detain?"

"Nothing more than to be able to talk to you undisturbed. We have a dilemma, Liesel, a dilemma that we share, you and I. We both love someone in trouble. Isn't that true?"

"I . . . don't know what you mean."

He offered a brief laugh, or perhaps it was a moan, Liesel couldn't tell. "Come, come, Liesel. Keeping up this pretense disturbs me. It makes me think perhaps we aren't on the same side, after all." He leaned forward, setting aside the water and folding his large hands on the table. "You love my son, Liesel. You have always loved him from when you were children. You were to be wed. Have you forgotten?"

Liesel looked at him, unsure how to answer. "Josef never asked me to marry him. Not until the day he left."

"*Nun gut*, there you have it. We all knew his intentions, and you were not unwilling to receive them. Were you?"

His tone challenged her, and she eyed him a moment before answering. "No."

"Josef is in trouble. We both know the kind."

Liesel raised a surprised gaze at him. "What do you mean?"

"No need to hide it any longer, Liesel. I know what the government suspects of my son."

"You . . . you knew? All along? You knew what Josef was involved in?"

He shook his head. "I only know what they *think* he's done. Josef needs our help. He telephoned you a little while ago, asking you to contact me for money. He wanted to protect me by not coming to me directly because he must think I don't know the truth. But I do know. And you, Liesel, must know I will do anything to help him find safety."

A ready protest formed on her lips, but she swallowed it back. "Yes, we both want what is best for Josef."

Uncle Otto stood, going behind his chair and placing his hands on the top rung, leaning forward as he continued. He stared at her. "I am not certain you can be trusted anymore, Liesel. That is most unfortunate, since you have known me—and Josef—all your life. Far longer than you've known this David de Serre."

"What has he to do with this?" she whispered.

Uncle Otto laughed again. "*Guter Himmel!* Do you think me a fool? How long has my son been gone, and already you allow another man to take his place?"

Liesel said nothing.

"It is because of him that you can no longer be trusted. Before this man came into your life, I would have given you the money and entrusted you to take it to my son, along with my greetings and love. I would have arranged for both of you to go to *Deutschland* or a *Deutsch* colony. Or you could have stayed here with me while Josef sought safety alone for a time. Either way, I would have done everything I could to keep you happy and to keep Josef safe. As it is, I can only do the latter now. While I wish you no harm, of course, since I have always considered you family, I cannot trust you with the information you have of Josef's whereabouts until after tomorrow. So I am afraid until then you must stay here."

"What?" Shock and confusion tumbled in her head, like a knot growing ever larger, tying up every thought.

"*Natürlich*, I cannot allow you to contact this man de Serre. Even if you were to tell me right now that you have no intention of telling him where he can find Josef, I could not afford to trust you. My son's life is too important."

Liesel sprang to her feet. "You intend keeping me here against my will?"

He nodded. "*Ja*, Liesel. It is necessary."

She shook her head in disbelief. "How can you even consider such a thing? This is—this is kidnapping! Don't you think my family will look for me if I don't come home tonight? Don't you think David will?"

"Ach, your David!" He ground out the words in anger. "You trust this man too much, Liesel. Don't you know this is all just a case to him? That he spends his time with you only in hopes of finding my son? Did you know he has a file in his desk on you, too? That he has considered you a suspect? You are nothing more than a lead to a man he considers a criminal."

"Josef *is* a criminal!" she insisted, refusing to listen to the accusations about David's reason for becoming such a part of her life. "He is a traitor!"

"*Du Esel!* He is nothing of the sort! He is a loyal *Deutschlander* only doing what he believes best for *Deutschland.*"

"But he is an American citizen. If he wanted to work for Germany, he should have gone over and joined their army."

"He is no American. He is a *Deutschlander!*"

Liesel leaned over the small table and stared boldly into Otto's eyes as she'd never done before. "You are to blame for Josef's trouble. You and the way you've taught him all these years, with your pride and—and *arrogance.* You should have gone back to Germany years ago."

Suddenly he raised a hand as if to strike her, catching it back only when she lifted her hands in defense. He turned his back on her, pulling out the chair and taking a seat, still not facing her. He leaned down away from the table, putting his forehead in his hands and shaking his head. That his thoughts tormented him was only too obvious, yet Liesel could not stand there and watch. She felt no pity.

What she felt instead was a desire to escape. Sparing little more than a glance in his direction, she took a few steps back, closer to the arch that led to the dining room. Then, just outside the kitchen, she turned on her heel and rushed to the front door.

A piercing grip caught her by the wrist, long fingernails pressing into her skin. Pulling Liesel back to the kitchen, Miss Burnbaum's face was every bit as harsh as it had been when Liesel first knew her. The Miss Burnbaum Liesel knew was back.

"You'll have to stay, my dear," she said through clenched teeth. "Come along."

Liesel saw that Uncle Otto had collected himself. He stood, once again resting his hands on the back of his chair. He smiled grimly Miss Burnbaum's way.

"You have proven invaluable to me yet again, Lucy." He looked at Liesel, and any hint of a smile disappeared. "This is foolishness, Liesel. Sit down."

Miss Burnbaum put a firm hand on Liesel's shoulder until Liesel took the seat.

"I mean you no harm," Uncle Otto said. "You must know that. But you have proven that you cannot be trusted. Yet because of my son's love for you and because you have always been like a daughter to me, I still want you to be comfortable while you stay. Miss Burnbaum has generously collected a number of books for you to enjoy and to keep you occupied. You will not be hungry or thirsty; I guarantee that. She has even moved a soft mattress and pillow for you to rest upon. You will be quite comfortable downstairs, Liesel. And it is, of course, only temporary. A day, that is all."

Liesel shook her head, eyes narrowed. "Do you think you will succeed, Uncle Otto? Do you think nothing will come of this even if you do help Josef? That I will just go home after all of this and forget that you've held me here against my will? You are protecting a criminal by your actions." She cast a quick glance Miss Burnbaum's way. "And what about you? Do you think I won't press charges once you let me go?"

Uncle Otto approached, brushing aside Miss Burnbaum and laying a heavy hand to Liesel's shoulder where Miss Burnbaum had held her down.

"I assure you I mean you no harm." In spite of the words his tone was harsh. "You will be comfortable here. There is no reason to be afraid."

"If you are inviting me to stay of my own will, I refuse. Let me go."

"That I cannot do. You will stay." Suddenly he smiled. "And when it is time for you to go, you will return home as if nothing has happened. You will see."

"And why would I forget about all of this?" she asked incredulously.

"Because I am your uncle Otto." Any trace of weakness he'd once shown was now gone.

She managed a laugh. "Even if I were to forgive you, Uncle Otto, what do you think my parents will do when they hear of this? They'll be frantic with worry even if I'm only gone a few hours, let alone an entire night. When they find out you are responsible, they'll want you to learn that you cannot go about breaking laws and taking away another's freedom simply to suit your own illegal purposes."

"Illegal?" He laughed. "I am a *Deutschlander,* as is my son, and I am protecting a *Deutsch* citizen in a time of war. American law means little to me. As for your parents, I'm sure once you tell them how well you've been treated, and they are assured you were perfectly safe and unharmed, they will forget the whole thing in time."

She stared at him. Had he completely lost his mind?

He continued, his tone relaxed. "Especially since it is my factory which employs not only your father, but your two older brothers as well. How easily do you think they will find employment if hard feelings cause them to lose their jobs? We've all heard about the difficulties you've had trying to find employment because of your German name. How will it be for three Bonner men of somewhat limited talents to go about locating work?"

"Limited talents!" she spit back the words. "If it wasn't for my father's engineering talents, you'd still be in that stinking coking coal! You've said so yourself many times."

"Your father is sixty years old, Liesel. An old man, even if he was at one time quite a help to me. Who will hire an old man, an old German? And your brothers have families to worry about. Without me—or with me in jail, if you think you can send me there—you have the capacity to ruin three more families, Liesel. Forgiveness might come a bit easier if you consider all of this."

Liesel shook her head. The incredible fact that Uncle Otto held her prisoner made everything else too much to handle.

"Come now, Liesel. Back downstairs. It's quiet down there, where you won't be disturbed."

"Don't you mean where I won't disturb anyone?" she asked.

"Yes, that, too. You may make all the noise you wish, Liesel. Fortunately for the neighbors' peace of mind, they will not hear you. Come now. My dear Miss Burnbaum has chosen a variety of reading material, and she has some magazines right here."

With a smile as friendly as it was obviously false, Miss Burnbaum held up a current *Ladies Home Journal* and *Harper's Bazaar.*

"If there is anything else you request to read," Uncle Otto added, "just let Miss Burnbaum know."

Liesel stopped short, turning to Miss Burnbaum, who followed so close behind they collided at the sudden stop.

"How about a Bible, Miss Burnbaum? Or don't you have one?"

"I . . ." She fumbled just a moment, losing that smile. She looked away from Liesel's gaze. "Yes, I have one. I'll get it."

Uncle Otto stepped aside to let Liesel pass. She stood on the top step, awaiting Miss Burnbaum's return.

"You are wrong to do this, Uncle Otto. What Josef has done is illegal, and he must know that since he is so eager to leave the country. Both of you are wrong."

"I need take no life lessons from you."

She shook her head. "I don't expect you to." Just then Miss Burnbaum handed her a family Bible, large and unwieldy, yet Liesel held it up in one hand. "I know you own one of these as well, Uncle Otto. Go home and read it, and let it teach you some life lessons."

"Go downstairs," Uncle Otto said, somewhat sadly, it seemed. "I will hold open the door until you get to the bottom. There is an oil lamp behind the stairs. Get it, and I will light it for you. Then I will close the door."

Liesel knew she had no choice. With each step downward, she felt her heart and hopes sink with her. Was it all beyond her help now? Was Josef bound to stay free with his father's help? That would be hard for David to accept after all he'd done to bring Josef to justice.

But Liesel knew one thing as she clutched the Bible to her chest. God reigned. She had to remember that. And He'd taught her to trust Him.

"So, have you ever seen one like this before, Weber?"

Weber held up the cigarette butt David had collected the night before. David had told Helen to let him know the minute Weber returned from testifying in court on another case.

"Sure. It's a Philip Morris Original. Cork-tipped to keep the tobacco from sticking to your lips. Supposed to be a Turkish blend, but the Turkish leaf hasn't been available since the war. Taking up smoking, de Serre? I wouldn't have guessed it."

He didn't answer the question; indeed, it hadn't been meant for one. Everyone knew Weber was the resident expert on smoking, although he personally didn't have the habit. He'd gotten to know everything about the industry during the four years he'd worked on the anti-trust case against the huge American Tobacco Company. The case was considered a great victory, since the Supreme Court had ultimately decided the company had to break up their monopoly.

"It's a British company, in fact they're His Royal Highness the king's tobacconists. But they opened an American branch back in 1902 up in New York. You know, to avoid all the tariffs on luxury items like short smokes, cigars, cigarettes."

"Any other brands have this cork tip?"

Weber shook his head. "Nope. They've got a patent on it."

"I've never seen one like this around here. How big of a market share do they have?"

"Oh, not big. Single digit percent nationally. Probably less than 5 percent. Pricey, you know. Import. Didn't lower their prices once they opened up here."

"What kind of packaging do they come in?"

"Last time I checked it was a little brown cedar wood box. Nice packaging, like you'd expect for the price. No paper wrappers like the penny-a-smokes. What's up?"

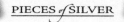

"I'm not entirely sure . . . yet."

"They sell 'em down at Union Station if you want to see for yourself."

David glanced at his watch. Four forty-five. No time for that now. He had to pick up Liesel.

By the time he reached the von Woerner glass factory, it was five minutes after five. He parked the car, seeing that most of the employees were already well down the street heading away from the factory. He didn't see Liesel or her father among them, although he did see Karl.

"Karl!"

The man turned at the call, and David noticed the immediate scowl. It was gone, however, by the time David caught up to him.

"Have you seen your father and sister?"

"My father was waiting for her over there," he pointed back toward the door. "But she must be caught up in something. He went up to the office to see if he should wait or head home without her."

"Thanks," David said, then turned to go into the plant.

Karl detained him. "Any news on Josef?"

A few feet away, David turned back to him. "No."

Karl made no move to leave. He stared at David as if pondering whether or not to speak again, crossing his arms in front of him. His lunch pail dangled below one arm.

"You've been spending a lot more time with my sister than necessary, I think," he said. "Just what are your intentions toward her, anyway? Now that Josef's gone, you just move right in?"

"Not exactly," David said coolly.

"Yeah, well, when Josef comes back, I don't think my sister will have much time for you anymore."

He turned and walked away.

David watched him for the barest moment, then turned to the factory. There wasn't time to dwell on Karl's views, but it was hard to shake the thought that Liesel might do that very thing if Josef wasn't in so much trouble.

He found Hans Bonner in the office David had visited earlier, talking to the pinch-faced Miss Burnbaum. She was fidgeting with some papers on her desk as she talked to Hans. Liesel was nowhere in sight.

"Liesel's gone home, David," said Hans. "Miss Burnbaum said Liesel had a headache and they sent her home on the trolley an hour ago."

Immediate tension stiffened David's spine. "She left without telling you?"

Hans lifted his shoulders and hands simultaneously. "Evidently."

"Must have been some headache," David said loud enough for Hans to hear. Silently he cautioned himself against immediate panic, against revealing the adrenaline coursing through his veins.

Outside, David led Hans to his Runabout. He walked fast, but Hans kept up. "We can make it to your house in twenty minutes."

David was already starting the motor as Hans sat down. "Ja, this is most unusual for her. She's never come home early before. She doesn't get headaches."

Soothing Hans was the last thing David felt like doing, but he knew he had to try. "These have been unusual times, plenty of reason for a headache." Even as he spoke, he liked the situation less. It was obvious Hans was concerned. If David told him there might have been someone tailing his daughter, at least since yesterday, how much deeper would that concern be?

He drove to the Bonner home in record time, safely yet faster than he'd ever driven down city streets before. What he wanted to do was hop from the car and run to the front door, leaving Mr. Bonner behind because age slowed him from such fast movement. But David squelched that urge. It wouldn't do to let on just how concerned he felt. Not yet, anyway.

He waited for Mr. Bonner, and the two of them walked up the steps as if there was nothing at all to worry about. They would open the door, and Mrs. Bonner would tell them Liesel was upstairs sleeping or resting to rid herself of her headache. David would see if she was up to his company, and if she was, he'd stay a while in spite of the deal he'd made with himself about not spending so much time with her. If she was too sick to see him, he might stick around the neighborhood to see if anyone showed up who didn't belong in the area. When they'd pulled up moments ago he'd noticed kids playing down the block, and a woman sat on a porch swing. Two young girls sat on the sidewalk, talking conspiratorially. Nothing amiss.

"Ilsa!" Hans called when at last they reached the doorway.

Mrs. Bonner was just coming down the stairs. Perhaps she'd been up there with Liesel. She smiled when Hans greeted her with a kiss.

"Ah, David," said Mrs. Bonner, "you've come for supper, I hope?"

David ignored that his heart was suddenly pumping as if he'd run a race. "Mrs. Bonner, is Liesel well enough for a visit?"

Mrs. Bonner looked at him with a question in her eyes. He didn't welcome the sight. "What do you mean? Where is she?"

Hans spoke up. "They said at the factory that Liesel came home early with a headache. Isn't she here?"

"No," Mrs. Bonner said. "She never came home early. Who said she came home?"

"Miss Burnbaum said she left around four o'clock. With a headache."

David heard the concern building in Hans's voice. Panic solved nothing. David knew that. Yet he not only saw it looming on both Bonner faces, he felt it in his heart.

"Now, just a minute," he said, holding up one palm. "Let's wait a moment before we get alarmed. She could have stopped to pick up something at the apothecary. Or she may have thought a bench in the park was just the place to get rid of a headache. I'll go and look for her and bring her right home."

"Yes, David," said Mrs. Bonner, taking his arm and all but pushing him from the house. "You find her right away. She's our Liesel, David. You must find her." Then she dropped that hand from David's arm and turned to her husband with a sob. "Oh, Hans! Where can she be? She would have come straight home if she is not well. It's Josef all over! She's gone, too!"

"Now, Ilsa," Mr. Bonner said, patting her back, but over her head he looked at David with every bit as much concern in his eyes. "We will find her. It's only five thirty. She hasn't been gone long. We'll bring her home."

"If you go, then I go, too!"

"No, Ilsa. There isn't room for all of us in David's car once we find Liesel." He patted her shoulder again. "You go to Karl's. Bring Katie here. Tell Karl to go on the trolley line between here and the factory and ask every driver in between if they saw Liesel. Tell him to take her picture to identify her."

"Oh, Hans!"

"Go now, Ilsa. Send the twins for Ernst, too, and he can help Karl. We'll find her, Ilsa. Don't you worry. She'll walk in the door any minute, and we'll be the gooses for getting upset over nothing."

David was already heading to his car and saw Hans move to follow. He didn't have the luxury of time even to comfort Mrs. Bonner.

When they were both in the car, David drove as he'd never driven before. He followed the path of the trolley, searching with a desperate gaze both the trolley cars and the sidewalks. He stopped at the two apothecary shops on the way, inquiring if anyone matching Liesel's description had been in within the last hour or two. No one had seen her.

They stopped at every park that lay between her home and the factory. While a small number of people were enjoying the sunny weather, Liesel was nowhere to be seen, and those Hans and David questioned had not seen her.

They went back to the factory, but it was empty except for the night crew watching over the furnaces. When Hans told them they were looking for Liesel, a few of them volunteered to help, but Hans refused to let them leave the furnaces untended.

David heard Hans speak in a surprisingly calm voice. "We're not sure she's missing," he told them. "She left early and could be anywhere. Maybe we're making something out of nothing."

"Can't be too careful," said one of the men. "Not since the boss's son went off like that."

"Yeah, what about that, Hans? Maybe she went off with him."

David eyed Hans, who smiled with what appeared great difficulty. "Ja, maybe it's one of those elopements," he mumbled. "We'll let you know as soon as we learn anything."

David left Hans and headed alone up to Liesel's office, finding it locked. He picked the latch free in moments, a talent he'd learned as a child when he broke into his father's study on numerous occasions. Although seldom home, his father spent his time in the study when he was in town, going over records of the money his ships brought in. When he was gone, David always used to break in and sit at his desk, pretending his father was with him.

Liesel's office was dark, and David pulled the string to light the bulbs above. The desk was neat, as it had been earlier. He opened the desk drawers one by one. Nothing. It appeared she had left everything in order.

A moment later Hans spoke behind him.

"What they said down there," Hans began, "about Liesel going after Josef . . ."

David didn't prompt him for more. He didn't want to think about it, wanted even less to talk about it.

"She didn't go after him."

David looked from Liesel's desk to the older man. "Why do you say that?"

"She didn't. I know it."

David didn't press him.

"We'll go to Otto's," Hans said after a moment. "He may know if she said anything about stopping on her way home. In any case, he'll want to know she's missing. If she is."

David didn't know whether to shake the man or cling to the same hope he obviously grasped. Of course she was missing! He might not have many tangible reasons, but he knew something was wrong. She would not alarm her family this way.

While her family didn't hold her accountable for every moment of her day, this was different. If she'd gone somewhere, she certainly wouldn't have left work early under the pretext of a headache. David didn't want to consider all of the possibilities. But one prospect had bothered him since the first moment of doubting her whereabouts. What if that figure he'd seen lurking about last night had been Josef?

A flood of new worries coursed through David's mind. Any number of things could have happened if Josef had made contact. He might have guessed Liesel wanted to turn him in. He could be holding her against her will at that very moment. Or worse.

He shook his head. In all the surveillance of the man, Josef had never been considered a danger to anyone personally. In fact, it was almost the opposite. In the explosions David believed Josef responsible for, Josef always made sure the firebombs were placed in cargo holds containing no explosives that would sink the ship before the crew could get to lifeboats. Or he put the bombs in holds that could be flooded, saving the ship itself but ruining the ammunition the ship carried below. It was all to stop the armaments, not to kill people; that much had been obvious. Using firebombs might mean he was bold about what he believed, but Josef wasn't a killer.

More than likely, he'd never hurt Liesel. That created a whole new set of concerns. Suppose he'd contacted her and somehow convinced her everything he was involved in was a noble thing to do? He must believe that himself. Was he persuasive enough to convince Liesel? She'd loved him not so long ago. Perhaps she still did. Was he even now convincing her not to turn him in? If that was the case, Liesel had every reason in the world to avoid all contact with David. Perhaps she wanted to be alone, deciding what to do about Josef. Or perhaps she'd already decided to go away with him.

David shook his head, rejecting the thought, but it persisted. He had to face that possibility. He knew the thought of turning in Josef had never been easy for Liesel to accept. Perhaps when put to the test, it had been too much for her. Perhaps her ultimate decision had been to help Josef, after all.

If the latter was true, going to Otto von Woerner was exactly the thing to do. Under Hans's unnecessary direction, they were there in minutes.

Otto lived in one of the most fashionable sections of Washington. The house, a three-story mansion, boasted an expansive, weedless lawn and perfectly trimmed hedges. In the shadow of the tall home sat a combination stable and garage, the latter looking as if it had been added in recent years. Hans walked up to the porch, passing a pair of padded wicker chairs on either side of a glass-topped table that held a hearty bouquet of fresh-cut flowers. It was the kind of house David had seen on the rare occasions his parents had allowed him to tag along to the homes of others they associated with in Virginia. David was impressed by none of it.

Hans seemed to notice nothing, probably out of familiarity, as he rang the bell, then rapped on the door. In a moment, a servant answered Hans's knock.

"Is Otto in, Zo'?"

The pretty young maid in a black damask dress stepped aside with a curtsey. "Yes, sir. He's in the parlor. I'll announce you if you wait here."

They did so, and a moment later the maid reappeared with Otto behind her, a look of concern on his ample face.

"Hans? What an odd time for a visit!" He eyed David with a frown. "Good afternoon."

David received the coolness without flinching. He hadn't seen von Woerner in a few days, and his first thought was concern that the older man might think he'd come with bad news of his son. That would be one reason for his visit. Yet von Woerner said nothing.

"It's Liesel, Otto," said Hans. "Miss Burnbaum said Liesel left early with a headache, but she never made it home."

"Oh? Oh, yes, I remember Miss Burnbaum mentioned something to me. I'm afraid I've been busy and barely noticed when anyone left. Did you speak to Miss Burnbaum?"

"Only at the office. I'd like to speak to her again if you could tell me where she lives."

"Well, now, come in, settle down for a moment, Hans. Zo'! Bring some tea for our guests."

"Otto, Otto, we don't want tea."

Ignoring the words and the obvious emotion behind them, Otto walked back into the room from which he'd just emerged, which proved to be a large sitting room. In the center of the far wall was a massive fireplace, unused now, but surrounded by a carved wooden mantle. The wood stretched out to enhance a wall full of shelves boasting exquisite china, small sculptures, and glasswork. The rest of the furniture was perfectly matched in upholstery and trim, with intricately stitched doilies at each headrest. Several tall plants grew here and there, all lush and adding a deep shade of green.

"Sit down, Hans," said Otto. "I'm sure Liesel is fine. It's early evening yet; you have nothing to worry about. Sit and have tea."

"No, Otto. I only came to ask you if Liesel said anything today which might have indicated she was stopping anywhere on her way home. Did you speak to her at all this afternoon?"

Otto shook his head. "No, no not this afternoon. I spoke to her this morning about some work she was doing. I thought she looked quite well. No sign of a headache."

The maid entered with a silver tea service and china cups and set about to pour. Neither Hans nor David accepted the refreshment.

"If you don't mind, Mr. von Woerner," said David. "We'd like to go to Miss Burnbaum's and ask her if Liesel said anything about stopping anywhere on her way home."

"Oh, I'm sure she didn't. Now that you bring it up, I remember Miss Burnbaum telling me she sent Liesel straight home on the trolley. But that doesn't mean she didn't get detoured. I'm sure she's all right, Hans."

"How can you be so calm after what happened to Josef? Now it's happened to Liesel."

Otto visibly stiffened at Hans's words. "No, Hans. Liesel is not gone. You mustn't worry like this."

"Then where can she be? What's happened to her?"

"We'd still like to question Miss Burnbaum," David persisted. "And maybe a few other employees, to see if anyone saw her leaving."

Otto looked between the two men, then turned toward the front hall. "Very well. Come with me, although I assure you this is needless. I have a telephone in my den, and you may use it to call Miss Burnbaum. I insisted some time ago she have a telephone installed. That will be the fastest way of contacting her. She can answer your questions right now."

David and Hans followed Otto across the front hall and through a double set of carved wooden doors. This room, like the other, was abundant with plant life, all leaning toward the window like an audience straining toward the stage. The huge oak desk that sat in the center was neat, covered by a leather pad. Behind the desk were more wood shelves, these full of books.

Otto picked up the phone and asked the operator to ring a number. In a moment, he spoke again. "Lucy, it is Otto. I have Hans here and David de Serre. Do you remember him? They have told me Liesel isn't home yet, and they are concerned." He paused to hear Miss Burnbaum talking. "Yes, they plan to ask you a few questions. They want to see if anyone saw Liesel leaving and when. Do you understand, then? It isn't only you they'll be questioning?" He looked over the phone at David and whispered with the mouthpiece covered, "No need to upset her."

He handed the phone to David.

"Miss Burnbaum?" David said. "This is Agent David de Serre, from the Justice Department Bureau of Investigation. This isn't an official call; I just want you to know why I'm so familiar with asking a lot of questions. I'm worried about Liesel Bonner. You said earlier that she left the office before quitting time. Do you know the exact time?

"Oh, yes." Miss Burnbaum sounded breathless. "She left at four o'clock. I know precisely because I walked her to the trolley myself."

"You left the building together, then?"

"Yes, that's right."

"And that was at four o'clock?"

"Yes."

"Did she say she was stopping anywhere?"

"No, she didn't." Her voice was still uneven, as if she were breathing oddly. "But of course, she had quite a headache. Maybe she stopped to buy something for it. They can be quite nasty, you know, those headaches."

"Yes, well, thank you, Miss Burnbaum. Now tell me, might she have said anything earlier in the day to indicate she wouldn't be going straight home? An errand of some sort?"

"Oh, perhaps," she said. "I don't know. She's mentioned the public library to me on other occasions. She likes it there."

"The library," he repeated. "Very well. Anything else? What about her behavior? Did she seem upset at any time?"

"Why, no, Mr. de Serre. She was busy as a bee working the whole day."

"What about any visitors? Other than myself, did anyone come to see her today?"

"No."

"Did she receive any phone calls?"

"No, sir. I answer all the calls at von Woerner's, and she didn't receive any calls today."

"You answer all the calls?"

"Well, it's my job, you know. She helps out when she can, of course. But it's my job."

"All right, then, Miss Burnbaum. Thank you for talking to me. But I may want to come around the office in the morning and talk to you again if Liesel doesn't make it home."

She gasped as if the notion were unheard of. "Oh, I'm sure she'll be home by then, Mr. de Serre. Where else could she go?"

"Yes, well, thank you again."

He hung up.

David's gaze met Hans's for a brief moment, seeing his own concern reflected so vividly. He said nothing, could think of nothing to say that would ease the man's worry.

"Let's go, then," he said.

"Where are you going?" Otto asked as he trailed them.

David heard Hans answer as he continued to eye the surroundings. He had doubted Josef would contact his father rather than Liesel, yet if Josef was back in Washington, even if he had Liesel with him now, he might need Otto's help as well, especially if she wasn't cooperating. Even if she was willing to help Josef, it made sense that he would need his father's money and resources, especially if he was trying to leave the country.

The bureau didn't have the resources to tag Otto von Woerner continuously before, but if it was true Liesel was missing, then a surveillance of the man was in order now, no matter how short-handed they were.

"We'll keep looking, of course," Hans was saying.

"What can I do? I will send my driver out to look, and I will come along with you."

"No, no, Otto. Besides, we don't have enough room in David's motorcar. If you want to help, you can pray. And maybe go to the house. Ilsa is beside herself."

"Yes, yes, I'll do that."

Hans was so shaken by the situation that he dropped the hat he held in one hand, and when he stooped to pick it up, he nearly toppled one of the plants sitting at the threshold. It tottered unstable on the tall, narrow stand, and David was just in time to save it from what might have been a rather messy fall.

"Sorry," Hans mumbled, then put his hand to the brass door handle, opened it, and walked out.

David righted the plant, but not without noticing a cigarette butt stuck into the sandy dirt at the base. With a quick glance to make sure he was unobserved, he pulled it out and slipped it into his palm. Placing his hat on his head, he tipped it von Woerner's way and followed the same path Hans had taken.

Behind the wheel of his car, he opened his palm and studied his find. Cork-tipped.

"What's that you have there?" Hans said.

"A cigarette butt."

"Where did you get it?"

"In that plant by the door, just now."

Hans looked back at Otto's house, and David's gaze followed his. The door was closed; the house looked as it had when they'd shown up. "Otto doesn't allow anyone to smoke in his house. He says it isn't good for the plants."

"Somebody didn't want to bring it any farther than the threshold."

David stuffed the used cigarette in his pocket, then started his motorcar, and they took off down the road, both sets of eyes automatically searching the street.

"Any reason you swiped it?" Hans asked after a moment.

David didn't answer. He drove.

"I know something is going on," Hans said quietly, looking straight ahead rather than at David. "My daughter is missing, and I know you and she have been something other than friends. Josef didn't just wander away; you didn't just happen to meet my daughter."

David took a deep breath, still hesitant to speak. "How long have you had questions about all this?"

"Long enough. When you took Liesel to your office to question her, I looked around while I waited in that hallway. It wasn't hard to guess your division isn't limited to kidnappings—or bankruptcy fraud. Still, I didn't think much of it. Not until that afternoon you brought Liesel and me home from work. You made her cry on my front sidewalk, and for someone who is supposed to be a casual friend, I thought that strange."

"Why didn't you ask us, then?"

Hans sat still, hands on his knees. "I thought she would come to me." The sadness was so apparent on his face, David had no doubt of its depth. "She always did, you know. Before."

"That's my fault," David hastened to say. "She couldn't. And I can't. At least, not yet."

"David, she's my daughter."

"You're better off not knowing."

"It can't be worse than my imagination."

This time he shook his head. "Don't let your imagination get the best of you. It's serious, but I believe she's safe. Besides, she may even be home right now. I think we should go back and check before we keep looking. I just have one stop to make in between."

Hans didn't ask more questions after that, for which David was grateful. He had so many thoughts to sort through, he doubted his ability to answer Hans very well. Perhaps it was time to tell him everything—except David had to know where Liesel was. If she'd willingly gone off with a spy, a wanted criminal, David needed to know that first.

He made his one stop, to a corner store that had a telephone. He contacted his office, asking for Weber or Gertz, and got Weber after Donahue handed over the call.

"I need you to tail von Woerner."

"Is he back?"

"No, I mean the father. Otto von Woerner." David gave him the address. "Josef von Woerner may be in contact with him. And he may have Liesel Bonner with him."

"Huh?" He sounded instantly surprised. "Liesel Bonner? Isn't she the one I met?"

"That's right. And could you spread the word around to the others to be on the lookout for her?"

"I won't ask questions now, but I'll have plenty later," he said.

David hung up and rejoined Hans, who waited in the car. The man looked as if he'd gained a few years since they met at the factory that afternoon.

"We'll find her, Hans," said David. And he meant it.

CHAPTER *Twenty-Three*

THEY found Ilsa Bonner surrounded by her children. The twins and Greta sat on the floor. Katie and Helga, Ernst's wife, were there as well, huddled in a tight little group with similar expressions of worry on their faces. It took only a moment to guess Liesel wasn't back.

When Ilsa saw her husband, she thrust away the hands that had held hers and rushed to meet him.

"Have you found her? Where is she, Hans?"

Hans shook his head, his expression somber.

Ilsa Bonner turned to David. "You must find her, David! You must call your office and tell them. I will call the police here, and—"

"I've called my office already, Mrs. Bonner. But I think we should wait a little while before we call the locals."

"But why? We need all to help! Everyone! Ernst and Karl are out now, and the twins were out, too. They only just got home. I think the rest of us—"

"We need to wait the evening, Mrs. Bonner. She may yet come home."

"No, no! She's been late before but not without telling me. And she's never left work early, never, *never*. Something has happened. Oh, my Liesel! Something like Josef!"

Hans took his wife in his arms, patting her gently, shushing her quietly. But he had no words of comfort. And David knew he couldn't keep the truth from them much longer.

Just then, a knock sounded at the door, and in unison, everyone rushed to the front hall. Hans opened the door, only to deflate every hope upon sight of Otto.

David frowned. He was willing to tell the Bonners what he knew but not Otto. Not yet.

The family trickled back into the parlor, no one talking except Otto, who took Ilsa's hand and told her she should not worry. Everything would be fine soon. He sounded so sure of himself, he was even getting Ilsa to nod. Perhaps it was a good thing he'd come, after all. Besides, if Otto stayed with the Bonners, it would free Weber to help search for Liesel.

David would have slipped away unnoticed but for Hans, who seemed to be watching him closely and stayed behind while the others left the front hall. At the door, David spoke.

"I'm just going to take a look around outside," he said evasively.

"No, David. You must tell us the truth now. All of it."

David turned to him and put a hand on the man's arm. He was willing to do that but not here. Not with Mrs. Bonner so upset she might repeat every word he spoke. And that wouldn't do with Otto von Woerner around. "Go and get your wife, Mr. Bonner. When I return, the three of us will go out and look for Liesel together. Just the three of us."

Hans nodded, then David left.

He walked down the block and spotted Weber's familiar motorcar, a black Tin Lizzie that provided quite a bit more privacy than David's Packard. Before David got close, Weber emerged, and the two walked around the corner.

"I'll keep an eye on Otto," David said. "I think he's here for the evening."

"Good, I have someone else I'd like to tag." Weber sounded agitated and spoke in low tones despite their relative privacy. "I saw a young guy come out of the back of the von Woerner house after Otto left."

"Josef?"

Weber shook his head. "No. But not a servant, either. And he was smoking. I got a look at the pack, and it looked like the brand you mentioned earlier. Morris Originals. I can't be sure, and he didn't leave anything behind, but that's my guess."

"Good," David said, mystified by who the person could be. "How will you pick him up again?"

"I saw the car he drives, and he was following von Woerner until we turned down this block. I can probably find him again if I go right away."

David nodded, calling after Weber as he went to his car. "Keep in touch through the office. I'll check in as often as I can."

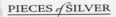

"Right."

David found Ilsa and Hans just inside the door.

"We're ready, David," said Hans.

Briefly, David looked over their heads toward the parlor. No one else could be seen through the archway. He wondered exactly what they'd said to the others, hoping it wasn't too obvious that he wanted to speak to them alone. He wasn't sure of all the facts yet, but the feeling was mounting that he had to be especially cautious around Otto von Woerner.

As they walked to the Packard, David asked Hans the details.

"I told them just what you said before, that the three of us are going out to look. That's what we're doing, aren't we? We can talk and look at the same time?"

Nodding, David assisted Mrs. Bonner inside while Hans climbed to the back of the tonneau seat. He wished he had a Tin Lizzie of his own just then. At least it had a backseat worthy to be called that.

"We'll go by the park," David said.

"Oh, yes," said Mrs. Bonner hopefully. "You know the one, the one she likes?"

"Just down the street?"

Ilsa Bonner nodded. "She goes there all the time, ever since we moved here. Her, and Karl, and Josef . . . all of them loved that park." She sobbed after speaking Josef's name. Josef and now Liesel sharing the same apparent fate, at least in her mind.

David wasted no time. It was approaching the dinner hour. The park was empty, the forest beyond quiet. For a moment he considered what he would say, unable to deny he wished he could talk to Hans alone. At least he was prepared. Would Mrs. Bonner even believe that Josef could be involved in the things of which David accused him? Would she be able to go back to the Bonner house and put on a stoic facade in front of Otto? More variables than he liked working with, yet he knew what he had to say would ease her worries somewhat.

A stone gazebo sat not far from the street. David parked the car and waited until the others got out.

"We're stopping here? But I don't see anyone, David," Mrs. Bonner said.

"We'll go to that gazebo and wait a little while there."

"But I really think we should keep moving, David!"

"Ilsa, come. Sit down," said Hans, and the three of them went to a bench seat in the gazebo. Mrs. Bonner sat, but upon her face was a look of annoyance, as if the last thing she wanted to do was sit quietly on a park bench.

David remained standing, eyeing the area. The only thing to see was the setting sun torching the sky to colorful flames. Swallowing once, he knew the best thing to do was simply state the facts. He didn't know how else to do it, how else to prepare them.

"There is a possibility, Mrs. Bonner, that Liesel has gone away of her own volition." The words barely made it out of his mouth. He hated to say them, hated the meaning behind them. Hated everything about this case just at that moment. He'd gotten too personally involved, and now he paid the price. Even that he stood here telling them things he should perhaps put off, spoke loudly of just how personally involved he'd become.

"What do you mean?" Liesel's mother asked quickly. She looked up at him, both hopeful and skeptical.

"She may have gone with Josef," David said.

"And where would that be?" Hans asked.

Mrs. Bonner spoke at the same time. "With Josef! But we don't know where he is, either. And why? Why should they disappear like this?"

"Let him talk, Ilsa!" said Hans quietly but firmly enough to end her questions.

David looked between the two of them as he spoke. "What I must tell you will be . . . unpleasant, but—" He held up a hand to stay Mrs. Bonner's interruption. "Maybe the truth isn't as unpleasant as your imagination. What I have to say is to be kept right here, to go no further. Do you understand?"

Hans, who had taken a seat beside his wife, stood. He put a hand to David's shoulder. "Tell us, David. She is our daughter. We'll do nothing to endanger her. Whatever you can tell us, even if there is some kind of trouble."

"Trouble!" Mrs. Bonner seized the word. "What do you mean? Our Liesel isn't in any trouble. At least, not of her own doing."

David wanted to agree, how he wanted to believe her. But if their daughter was in Josef's company willingly, she was in a great deal of trouble. Running off with him would only make charges of aiding and abetting stick.

Hans spoke. "You said she might be with Josef. Do you know where?"

David shook his head. "No, not yet. But we will find him, especially if he's here in Washington."

Mrs. Bonner stood, too. "I don't understand any of this. If Josef is in Washington, he would come home."

"I have been watching Josef for two years now. The reason he has run off is because he is working for the German government as a saboteur."

"Saboteur!" she repeated the word as if it, by itself, were poison. She raised a confused gaze David's way. "How can this be?"

"I have quite a bit of evidence of his involvement with a German espionage network. That is why I first contacted your daughter, to see if she might corroborate some of my suspicions."

"Suspicions? Is that all it is?"

He shook his head. "No. Josef's disappearance proved his guilt, especially considering the evidence I've compiled. Plus, we've arrested some of his cohorts, and they're naming Josef as one of their members."

The couple sat down, staring straight ahead as if in a daze. At last Mrs. Bonner blinked and looked at her husband. "Could this be true, Hans? Could Josef be a—a spy? Our dear Josef?"

Hans looked up at David sadly. "I don't know why David would make any of this up. And we both know how Otto has always been, the way he raised Josef. What has Josef done, David?"

"He's caused plenty of trouble, I assure you of that. But as much trouble as Josef has been to us, he's shown a certain civility. That won't be forgotten at the trial."

"Trial! Oh, Hans." Mrs. Bonner stood again, a look of pure anger on her face. "And you think our Liesel has gone off with him? If she knows what Josef is involved in, she would not go with him. She would not!"

Hans stood, too, putting his arm around his wife. He was rock still, staring at David as if he'd suddenly accused them and their daughter of all he'd accused Josef of doing.

"I've known your daughter for these last couple of months, Mrs. Bonner. I have no reason to believe she's been involved in any of the activities we suspect of Josef. But her disappearance can mean one of two things: either she's gone off with him on her own, or he has taken her—which is unlikely, since he has enough trouble without taking an unwilling partner along."

Mrs. Bonner sank down to the bench as if exhausted. "But if she's gone off with him . . ." She looked at David. "That would mean she is in trouble now, too, just because she has chosen to be with him. Or help him."

David didn't want to think that was true, but he could not deny her conclusion.

Hans shook his head. "No," he said. But he said nothing more.

Mrs. Bonner reached up to clutch Hans's arm. "You don't think she is with him?"

Whether or not he heard his wife was questionable at first. He simply stared ahead, looking beyond the gazebo shading them from the sunset. "No," he said again, as if he spoke to the sky. "She would not do this if it means betraying America. She would not."

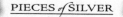

"But Hans, perhaps she hasn't looked at it that way." Mrs. Bonner spoke with an unsteady voice. "If she thinks only of Josef—"

He shook his head again. "No, she would not go with him like this."

"Oh, Hans!" She burst into tears, and her husband sat beside her, pulling her to him, raising her face to look at him as he shook his head. She leaned against him, allowing him to hold her close.

Hans spoke again, his voice covering the sound of her tears. "Think of how she's been behaving lately, Ilsa. Remember how she was even before Josef disappeared? She wanted to avoid all contact with him, remember?"

She sniffled and nodded. "She missed the annual picnic." Mrs. Bonner reached into her pocket for a handkerchief.

Hans nodded. "She was not behaving like some love-blind girl. She has been loyal to him, yes, of course, but to the point of betraying what we've taught her? Of God, her family, her country?"

"Yes, well," David began, not totally convinced, "love can make us do all sorts of things we wouldn't normally do."

"She would not abandon her family. Nor would she go against the authorities of her country so long as they didn't compromise her faith."

Mrs. Bonner stood. "You are right, Hans!" She looked at David. "I know my daughter. And I do not believe she loved Josef so much that she would do that."

David wanted to believe her. But the facts said otherwise. He wasn't sure what to think.

"I'm sure you'll have new worries because of what I've just told you," he said, "but at least you know as much as I do. I thought it would help ease some of your fears, at least narrow some of the uncertainties."

Hans stood and held out his hand. "Thank you, David. It's done that."

"I'll take you back to your home now, but Otto has no idea that we suspect his son of this sort of activity."

"Oh, you must tell him, David! He's been so worried about Josef. At least you can tell him he's alive."

David shook his head. "I cannot entirely trust Mr. von Woerner just yet, Mrs. Bonner. If I let him know what kind of trouble his son is in, he may try to help him. And he certainly has the resources to do all he can if he thinks his son . . ."

Suddenly it hit him. Otto must know. Why else had he been so calm upon learning Liesel was gone, when to anyone else it probably would have been like reliving his nightmare of Josef's disappearance? He *must* know Josef was still alive. Otto von Woerner had any number of resources to have learned it all. Perhaps, like David himself, Otto had sent a man to track Liesel in hopes of finding Josef! And perhaps that very thing had happened—Liesel had led him to Josef!

But he denied that thought. If Liesel had already led Otto to Josef, Otto would be with Josef as well. Certainly Otto wouldn't force Liesel to go off with Josef.

Suddenly he had a great deal of questions for the man Weber had seen with von Woerner. If he wasn't Josef, he might have been a man hired by von Woerner.

Without wasting time, David returned to the Bonner home. He sprinted ahead up the stairs ahead of Hans and Ilsa, going inside as if it were his home. The family was still gathered in the parlor, but instead of Otto sitting in one of the two front chairs, Karl Bonner sat there.

"Where is Otto von Woerner?" David inquired quickly.

"He left. His driver returned for him just a few minutes ago."

"Was he headed home?"

Standing so that he was just a few feet from David, Karl replied, "No. He said he was going to look for Liesel. I offered to go along, but he said my mother might need me."

David didn't have time to answer the questions Karl had written all over his face. Passing Hans and Ilsa on their way in, he raced out the door, calling over his shoulder. "I'll be back. If Otto von Woerner returns, make sure he waits until I return." Looking straight at Hans, he added, "Make sure of that, all right? And say nothing about what we talked about."

Hans nodded, and David drove away.

He headed straight to his office, wasting no time in getting to the telephone table. There was always an agent on duty to relay messages and take calls even in the middle of the night. David ignored his chagrin at the sight of Donahue sitting at that desk.

"Did Weber check in?" he asked without bothering to waste time with a greeting.

"Not directly, but a few minutes ago Gertz called in about him. They spotted each other while the guy Weber is following stopped for gasoline." Donahue's gaze was full of curiosity.

"Where is he?"

"Headed south out of the city toward Virginia."

David scooted out the door, ignoring Donahue's questions. He raced through the city streets, following the direction Weber indicated through Gertz. It was dark, and the streets were quiet. There was no sign of Weber's Tin Lizzie.

———————

Liesel rapped on the door again, ignoring the pain to her knuckles. She'd alternated her left hand and her right and back again for the last half hour. All to no avail. She heard the phone ring for the second time and was quiet as she listened to Miss Burnbaum's muffled voice, but since she was unable to make out what was being said or who might be calling, she continued knocking, hoping the noise could be heard by the caller. Miss Burnbaum ignored her.

Finally, fingers bruised from her efforts, Liesel stopped and leaned against the locked door. She wanted to cry, but she was too angry. How could Uncle Otto have done such a thing? How could Miss Burnbaum help him?

The latter was easy enough to figure out. Miss Burnbaum would do anything to help Otto von Woerner if she thought it might gain his attention and gratitude. Renewed anger at Miss Burnbaum gave Liesel an idea. She went down the stairs to retrieve a tin of vegetables to serve as a doorknocker. She was sorry she hadn't thought of it earlier. It made far more noise.

After five minutes of bruising the door rather than her skin, Liesel finally heard footsteps.

"You stop that right now!"

The door opened so unexpectedly Liesel almost fell face-first to the floor. As it was, the can in her hand tumbled, landing on the stair next to her and rolling down each consecutive step to the cellar below.

"Look what you've done to that door!"

Liesel squinted at the light, meager though it was. The lamp had gone out, and she'd sat in darkness for what seemed hours. Struggling to her feet, she found her limbs stiff from her odd position, her arms and hands numb from banging on the door.

"I wouldn't have done it if you'd just answered me," Liesel said. Then, seeing the door that led to the dining room and freedom beyond, she looked at Miss Burnbaum. Could she make a dash for it?

Miss Burnbaum must have guessed her thoughts the moment Liesel looked her way, for she slammed the door before Liesel could even raise one stiff leg to the top step. She was cast into darkness again.

"Miss Burnbaum," Liesel cried, feeling a hot tear slide down one cheek. "Let me out. Just let me out!"

"Absolutely not, missy, and you better stop damaging the door. This isn't my house, and you've got no right to leave any marks behind!"

Liesel caught the words, although she hardly cared. Nonetheless, she asked, "Not your house?"

"Well, for all practical purposes it is. I take care of the place. The owner is in an institution for the aged. Belongs to my aunt and uncle, but it'll be mine soon enough. And I *don't* want to have to replace that door."

Liesel moved on unsteady limbs to hobble down the stairs. By the time she found the discarded tin, blood was running smoothly in all her veins, and she raced back up to the door, banging harder. "Let me out, and I'll stop! Let me out!"

More footsteps, retreating.

Liesel called after her. "Wait, Miss Burnbaum! Wait!"

The footsteps halted.

"I'll stop if you talk to me."

"I have nothing to say to you."

"But you do, if you'd only answer some of my questions. Please. Just stay and talk."

"I cannot answer any of your questions." Her voice wasn't so harsh; instead she sounded matter-of-fact.

"All right, then just listen. I know why you've done this, Miss Burnbaum. Because you'd do anything for Otto."

"Don't be ridiculous—"

"It's all right, Miss Burnbaum," Liesel interrupted, even though she could tell her guess was correct from the tone of Miss Burnbaum's agitated voice. "You've worked for him all these years, been a loyal employee, taken care of him in so many ways. I'm sure you feel part of the von Woerner family. And Uncle Otto is . . ." She searched for the right words, choking back her disdain in her efforts to find complimentary terms to describe the man who had kidnapped her. "He is a powerful man, running that business so successfully all these years. You must have great respect for him."

"Of course. Everyone who works for him does."

"It only makes sense that you would care for him since you've been so close to him all of these years."

"I really don't see why you should be interested one way or the other."

"Please, just allow me to speak, Miss Burnbaum. This detention is giving me plenty of time to think."

"What does it matter? You'll be free to go home by tomorrow night. It's only a few hours of your life and for a worthy cause."

"Worthy?"

"Otto is trying to save his son, which is exactly what you should have done yourself. You should be working with Otto to help Josef, not trying to stop him."

"Do you know what Josef has done?"

"I know that he is in trouble with the government. They think he's a spy, of all things. It's ridiculous. Not a shred of truth to it."

"That's what I thought, too," Liesel said, more softly. "But they have evidence against him. They've tracked his whereabouts, placing him at spots just when the trouble mounts. And they have a man in custody who says Josef is guilty of everything the government suspects of him."

"They would take the word of a criminal against Josef, the son of Otto von Woerner?"

"He's put bombs in ships, Miss Burnbaum. Destroyed property. Don't you think Josef should learn that's wrong, or at least be stopped?"

"If, and I do mean *if*, he's done anything wrong, I'm sure he'll stop doing all that now that his father is aware of it. He won't tolerate anything less than what's right."

Liesel laughed. "He would believe what Josef has done *is* right. To him, Josef is only acting the way any young German man should act in defense of his country. And his country isn't America. It's Germany."

"Otto is a German citizen." Miss Burnbaum's voice sounded defensive.

"Josef isn't."

"To Otto he is."

"So you agree that he should ignore his American citizenship? That what he's done is morally acceptable?"

"What I believe is no concern of yours."

"It is if deep down you think they're wrong. If you think American law is worthy of respect. I know you're German, Miss Burnbaum, but you've chosen to live in America for some reason. You must realize that by letting Otto help Josef you're going against the American government. You're committing treason yourself."

"What nonsense! I'm only helping Otto help his son. I have no political views whatsoever; it means nothing to me."

"That's not how the government will look at it once they realize you helped a traitor. It makes you every bit as guilty."

"Ridiculous! I don't have to listen to this." Liesel heard footsteps again.

"Miss Burnbaum—don't go. Wait!"

No answer.

Liesel raised the can again and pounded on the door once more. She wasn't about to give up.

CHAPTER *Twenty-Four*

A sudden noise behind him roused David with a flinch, and he jerked his head from the cradle of his arms on the telephone table.

"Hey, what are you doing here so early?"

David rubbed his face in his hands, glancing at the wall clock that hung on the far end of the bullpen. Six forty-five. He'd been there for an hour and been asleep for nearly as long. Gertz stood behind him.

"I thought Donahue had the overnight last night," Gertz said. "I was supposed to relieve him at seven."

Turning to Gertz, David said, "I sent him home. I'm waiting for Weber. He hasn't called. Have you heard from him since yesterday?"

"Nope. We were told to be on the look out for von Woerner— "

"I'm pretty sure he's back in Washington." Grogginess gave way to the familiar panic he'd felt the night before while searching the streets of Washington for Weber and the man he'd been tracking. David had then gone to the von Woerner home, boldly knocking at the door despite the midnight hour. The same maid who'd shown him in earlier answered in a robe and nightcap, only to say Mr. von Woerner was not at home. David had staked out there until an hour before dawn, when he'd given up on the possibility of von Woerner coming home. If he was with Josef or involved in some way with Liesel's disappearance, he obviously did not want to be found for questioning.

After several hours spent in vain, David had returned to the office in hope Weber had called. David had sent Donahue home, and then called Stewart, another agent, to take up the lookout at the von Woerner home for its missing owner and, with the local police's help, to bring him in for questioning.

"You should go home," Gertz said. "I'll call you if I hear from Weber. You look pretty bad."

David shook his head, standing up. "I've got to go, but not home. I'll get to a phone and check back every quarter hour. If someone needs to reach me, I'll be at the Bonner house, but they don't have a phone so you'll have to send someone."

David stopped in the department bathroom to wash his face and comb his hair; then he left for the Bonners.

Before he'd even knocked at their door, Hans Bonner opened it. If David had any hope that Liesel might have returned on her own, it evaporated at his first sight of the older man. He looked as unkempt as David felt, still wearing what he'd worn the day before.

"Do you have news?" he asked before David had reached the top step.

David spotted several more heads peeking from behind. Mrs. Bonner, Karl, Ernst, and the rest of the family, with Greta making her way to the front. No one looked rested.

"I just wanted to check if she'd come home on her own." David's voice sounded as hopeless as he felt at the moment. "My department is working on this already, but I think it's time to bring in the locals. They can help go house to house, at least in the vicinity of the von Woerner factory, to see if anyone saw anything."

"Should have done that yesterday," said Karl from the back of the hall.

David didn't reply. He started walking to his car to find a telephone. Hans came up behind him.

Without exchanging a word, the two of them got into the car. Hans pointed ahead to the corner grocer. The store wasn't open yet, but Hans's firm knock roused someone from the back.

"Sauder," Hans said, calling the man through the glass, "I need to use your telephone. It's an emergency."

The man let go of the string on the shade he'd pulled halfway up, then unlocked the door and let Hans and David inside. The corner store boasted three rows of goods, one on each wall and one down the center offering everything from bread to candy. Near the door stood a wood counter and on that, a cash register and telephone.

"It's Liesel, Sauder," said Hans. "She's missing, and I need to call the police."

"Oh, no. Oh, no," the man said. "Not Liesel! Like Josef? Such a good girl. Yes, yes, call. And then I will go and help you search. Edith and I will both help."

David saw Hans nod and continue to talk to the other man, his face more somber than David had ever seen it. He picked up the phone, asked for the local police precinct, then identified himself as being from the Justice Department. It was too early for the captain to be in, but David felt confident whoever was in charge would start things moving immediately.

He gave the police a description of Liesel, from her height and approximate weight, to the color of her eyes and hair and the clothing she was wearing. He wanted the beat cops to be on the lookout and wanted someone to go door-to-door in the vicinity of the von Woerner factory to see if anyone had seen anything suspicious the previous afternoon. He gave the Sauder's telephone number to reach him, and the Bonner's address for them to send anyone in person. Someone would be out to start the paperwork, and the captain would be notified to come in early.

David made one other call, to his office. Gertz answered the phone.

"Heard anything yet?"

"Not yet. Nothing on either end from Weber or Stewart."

Before hanging up, David gave Gertz Sauder's telephone number.

"I'm afraid I'll have to stick around here for a while," David said to Mr. Sauder after he hung up. "In case someone tries to contact me."

"That'll be fine, fine. Anything to help. Let me go tell my wife—"

Just then, a stout, older woman came into the storefront from a door at the back. She was tying an apron around her ample middle. Mr. Sauder made introductions; then Hans prepared to leave.

"I'm only just down the block," he said to David. "Come and get me if you hear anything."

David nodded.

The telephone rang three times within the first hour, and each time David answered it with a surge of anxiety, only to hand it over to Mrs. Sauder, who had stayed behind in case she could be of assistance to David. The third call was yet another customer, and Mrs. Sauder took down the lengthy order. At the end of the call, David spoke up.

"I'm going to have to ask you to cut short your calls, Mrs. Sauder. I know you have a business to run, but until we have some information, we just have to sit and wait. I'd hate to lose the time it'll take my man or the police to have the operator cut in."

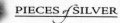

"Yes, yes," she said, her brow furrowed. "I'll do as you say."

He took the phone and clicked for the operator. "If anyone from the police or the Justice Department tries for this line, you are to break in immediately. Is that clear?"

"Yes, sir, that's standard procedure, sir."

David had known that; he just wanted to make sure whoever was on duty knew it, too.

He paced the storefront. Before this, he'd always been grateful that waiting never had the power to drive him crazy the way it did some of the other agents. They would be edgy, short-tempered, hard to be around. Not David. He knew waiting was part of the job and had enough self-discipline to get through it with his temper intact.

Not this time. People came in and went out of that little grocery as if it were any other day. Some eyed him; a few even tried to strike up a conversation, to which he couldn't muster the decency to reply. Mrs. Sauder kept people away from him as best she could, although he was sure his marked effort at ignoring everyone was hardly very appealing.

By mid-morning, quite a bit of traffic was moving through the grocery, and David knew word had spread that it was being used as some sort of headquarters. Everyone wanted to come in for a look, even if it required some nominal purchase. He wanted to throttle each and every one who looked his way, but with a prayer for control, he was able to keep his displeasure to a scowl until at last he was about to close down the store entirely.

Then the phone rang.

"Weber! Where have you been?"

"On a wild goose chase, I'm sorry to admit."

David felt his heart fall to his feet. "No connection to von Woerner?"

"Oh, I wouldn't say that. He's connected, all right. But he's good for a young guy. He must have known I was following him, and he led me so far afield I didn't know where I was half the time. His car had a bigger tank, and he knew it. That's the only lame excuse I have. Anyway, I lost him in the process and had to walk to a phone."

"Go to von Woerner's. Stewart is there. Maybe the father has returned. In any case, that's the only place we have to start for either your man or von Woerner."

"Already on my way," Weber said, then hung up the phone.

David turned to Mrs. Sauder. "I'm going to the Bonner home. Send someone for me if this phone rings again for me. I'll be back shortly."

David didn't bother to knock at the Bonner home; he walked inside. Hans must have spotted him from a window because he was already in the front hall when David closed the door behind him.

"Anything?"

David shook his head. "Has anybody here heard from Mr. von Woerner?"

"Otto? No, no. He never came back, not since yesterday. He's probably at work by now."

Mrs. Bonner came to the hall, followed by others. Despite the fact that it was Thursday, neither Karl nor Ernst had gone to work. Even the children were there, but David guessed the school year must have ended, so where else would they be . . . especially now.

"What's all this interest in Uncle Otto?" demanded Karl from over his father's shoulder. "Do you think Liesel ran off with Josef?"

"It's a possibility."

Karl laughed briefly. "Not much of one. It doesn't make sense with Josef gone so long already."

David didn't reply. He looked instead at Hans. "I need someone to go to the factory to see if everything seems to be as usual. Someone who wouldn't be out of place."

"I'll go," Hans said, but David shook his head before he'd even finished.

"No, von Woerner will expect you to be at home, waiting." David looked at Ernst. "I want you to go."

"Sure," Ernst said. "What am I supposed to do?"

"Go up to the office, see if Otto von Woerner is there, and make sure everything is as it should be. Call Sauder if von Woerner is there. Be obser-vant. Note anything at all that might seem out of place, even if you think it's trivial."

"I've only been up in his office once or twice, but I'll do my best."

"Come back to me at the Sauder's store. I noticed Josef's Stutz Bearcat is outside. Is your family still using it?"

Karl nodded, pulling the keys out of his pocket.

"Take that, Ernst. It'll be faster than the trolley."

"All right, but what'll I say to Uncle Otto?"

"Nothing. Only that you wanted to see if somehow Liesel had showed up at work, that we're running out of places to look, and we're going back over original territory. Anything *except* that I sent you to see if he's there. Then find the nearest phone, and call me at the Sauder's store with whatever you find out."

Ernst nodded. He looked like he might want to ask another question but refrained. He took the keys from Karl, then went out the door.

David turned to follow, but Karl's hand on his arm delayed him.

"I want to know what this is all about with Uncle Otto."

David looked at Karl, then at Hans, and back to Karl. "I have reason to believe he's connected to your sister's disappearance."

"Oh, no!" cried Mrs. Bonner. "You said Josef, but not Otto, too!"

Karl looked around, his face full of confusion. "What are you talking about? Josef and Uncle Otto?"

David eyed him closely. He obviously knew nothing of what Josef was involved in. Yet he was perhaps as loyal to Otto as Josef and couldn't be trusted.

"I don't have time to discuss it now, Karl," he said, heading out the door once again.

"You do if I come with you."

David stopped. "No, Karl. I can't go into detail just yet."

David was out the door when he heard Karl speak to his father. "You know more about this than you're telling, don't you, Father? What's going on?"

David turned back. "Karl, if you want to help, why don't you go down to the local precinct and wait for any news from the door-to-door questioning?"

He folded his arms at his chest. "Won't they call you at Sauder's?"

"Yes, they will. But they won't call your parents. You can come straight here with the news and save me the time of trying to tell them something."

That must have seemed feasible, at least enough to leave his questions unanswered. Karl left with David, going in opposite directions once they reached the sidewalk.

Lunch passed, and David went through more hours of endless waiting, his hopes alternately rising and falling. How much longer could they go on without knowing where she was? Even if she'd originally gone off with Josef willingly, she wouldn't keep her family worrying forever, which only made the situation more serious.

David stared at the phone, willing it to ring. He had finally demanded that the Sauders close their store, so all was quiet in the little grocery. At last Ernst called and said Otto von Woerner was not at his office, but that everything else seemed perfectly calm. Ernst had used the phone on Miss Burnbaum's empty desk.

David asked if Miss Burnbaum's day off had been expected by other co-workers, and Ernst inquired of a clerk filling in, who said if Mr. Von Woerner was on vacation or out of town on business, Miss Burnbaum often planned a day off as well. Something about the office being too quiet for Miss Burnbaum without her boss present. Miss Burnbaum had arranged for her absence late yesterday. When asked where Mr. von Woerner might be, the clerk had no idea.

David rubbed his chin. Coincidence for both to be out of the office on this particular day?

David asked Mr. Sauder to bring Hans to the store. Liesel's father arrived a few minutes later, his face drawn with worry.

"Hans, do you have any idea where Miss Burnbaum lives?"

"I only know she lives within walking distance of the factory—how far or in which direction, I have no idea. Why do you want to know?"

"Just a hunch," he said with a casual shrug. "Probably nothing."

"I will go to the office," Hans said. "Somebody there must know."

David shook his head. "I'll call my office. It might be quicker."

Liesel looked up from the dimly lit pages of the Bible. *Oh God, how much longer?*

Liesel still had her timepiece pinned to her lapel, and, from a narrow shaft of light at the base of the door where she'd held the Bible to read ever since the oil in the lamp burned out, she had enough light to see it was past noon. Miss Burnbaum had brought her breakfast long ago, along with a sandwich wrapped in a napkin, ostensibly to be kept for lunch. It lay untouched somewhere at the bottom of the stairs. Before opening the door to give her the food, Miss Burnbaum had told Liesel to go to the base of the stairway or she wouldn't open it at all. Liesel, heart thumping, only went as far as the middle of the stairs in hopes that she could make a dash once Miss Burnbaum opened the door.

But the light nearly blinded her eyes, accustomed as she was only to the darkness. She tripped on the second stair from the top, hurting her wrist in the process. Miss Burnbaum dropped the tray and slammed the door before Liesel had even righted herself.

Liesel tried to talk to Miss Burnbaum again. She told her not to trust Otto von Woerner. Was her loyalty so deep she was willing to get herself into trouble? If she wanted to trust someone, she should look to God for direction. "Look to your heart, Miss Burnbaum," Liesel had said. "You know it's true. The one we should trust first is God. I learned that myself through Josef."

But all of Liesel's arguments fell into silence.

Not long after that, she heard a door opening and closing, and she believed Miss Burnbaum had left the house. Liesel leaned back against the door, suddenly overcome with exhaustion. The only time worry had been forestalled was when she was deep in prayer. She began to pray again and for a time found peace in a light sleep.

When she woke, it all came back like a tidal wave, an uncontrollable influx threatening to overcome her. She pounded on the door again, but after a while, her energy spent, she put down the can and burst into tears, collecting herself only after exhaustion overwhelmed her again.

Then she heard footsteps.

"Who's there? Miss Burnbaum, is that you?"

Nothing.

"Miss Burnbaum!"

Still nothing.

Pressing her ear to the door panel, she stopped breathing altogether, listening for the slightest sound. Nothing. She peered through the opening beneath the door but couldn't see anything, not even the bottom of a pair of shoes.

Yet she was certain she'd heard something. A creak to the floorboards, a pattern to the steps heading toward the kitchen. She hadn't imagined it.

"I know you're there," she called. "And I know you can hear me. Let me out."

No one answered.

Liesel looked at her timepiece. After four o'clock. The twenty-four-hour mark had come and gone. In a few more hours, Josef would be waiting for her at the monument, but she would not be there. Instead, he'd be surprised to see his father, but happy enough when Otto handed over the money and provided Josef a way to freedom.

Liesel closed her eyes to the vision. "Oh, God," she prayed, "this is in Your hands. I ask for justice, but I accept Your will. I know that sometimes justice must wait for eternity, but I pray that Josef will turn to you before then. Let him see Your will for his life, Lord, not Germany's."

Then Liesel prayed for her family again, knowing they must be frantic over her absence. Certainly David must be looking for her as well. What must he think? Would he believe, even for a moment, that she intentionally hid from him in hopes of helping Josef? If only she'd had more time with David, more time to let him get to know her without the tension this case had brought. More time to help him trust her. He wouldn't doubt she'd do the right thing.

But then she shook her head at her own thoughts. She'd had a lifetime to know Josef, yet she hadn't really known him at all. Could one person really ever know another? Why should anyone trust another?

The sound of a door opening again stirred Liesel to a standing position. She heard quiet voices, confirming her suspicion that someone had been there the entire afternoon, no doubt making sure she stayed where she was. A man, judging by the low tone of the other quiet voice and the heavy creaking in the floorboard. Not Uncle Otto, though. She believed they spoke English. But as quiet as Liesel remained and as intently as she tried to listen, she could not hear more than a few inconsequential words.

Then she heard footsteps again. From the sound of heels tapping on the floor, she knew it was Miss Burnbaum.

"Miss Bonner," said Miss Burnbaum, "how are you this afternoon?"

Liesel didn't answer.

"Miss Bonner, answer me," she called a little louder. "I know you're in there."

"I'm fine," she answered quietly.

"Do you need anything? More food, something to drink? A fresh bed pan, perhaps?"

Liesel scowled at the ease with which the woman referred to the embarrassing necessities associated with her captivity. They had certainly thought of everything.

"Who else is there with you?" Liesel asked after a moment.

"No one."

"Someone was here all afternoon."

"Oh? And how do you know that?"

"I heard him."

"Well, that shouldn't concern you, dear. Can I get you another book, perhaps?"

Liesel didn't answer; instead, she said, "Have you thought about what I said earlier?"

"I'm afraid I wasn't listening, dear. How about dinner? You must promise no antics, though. I won't have you trying to escape, or you can go without eating. Now, about dinner?"

"Remember that I talked about treason, Miss Burnbaum. Do you really want to finish this out? It's not too late, you know. If you let me go, you can still prevent a crime. And not be part of it."

"I was going to heat a vegetable stew, Miss Bonner," she said as if she wasn't listening to a word Liesel uttered. "I don't eat meat myself, you know. Can't tolerate it. But Otto said you are to be satisfied, so I can send for something if you like. A hamburger, perhaps?" She laughed and it sounded odd, shrill. Perhaps she was nervous. "Do you know the local café is calling them 'liberty burgers'? Because of Hamburg in Germany? They hate us, you know."

"Yes, I've felt that, too."

"Have you?" She sounded interested for the first time.

"Yes," Liesel said, anything to keep the conversation going. Whether it was because of her forced solitude or because she still held hope that Miss Burnbaum might help, she could not decide. She only knew she must keep talking and get Miss Burnbaum to talk, too. "I searched for weeks to find a job before coming to Uncle Otto's, and he only took me on because he's German, too. No one else would give a German girl like me a job."

"I know it's like that," said Miss Burnbaum. "They turn away Germans even if they need someone to work. They refuse to serve Germans in some restaurants in town, did you know? No longer welcome, they say. And even if you don't talk, even if you try to sound American with no accent, they know. Somehow, they know." She sighed. "I have worked since I was twenty to overcome my accent, but still, they know."

"Yes," Liesel said. "It's wrong. Very wrong. But not everyone is like that."

"Enough of them!"

"It only seems like a lot because those who aren't that way don't say anything."

"And they are wrong, too."

"Yes," Liesel answered. "But they're afraid. The ones who speak their hate are very loud. It's frightening for everyone."

"Knowing all that, you are telling me it's wrong to help Josef? Even if he is guilty, he's one of our own, isn't he? And we've been treated unfairly. He deserves to go home to Germany."

"But what he's done is wrong, no matter whose law it is. He has to know that."

"By bringing him to a judge who will find him guilty only after hearing his name? That's hardly fair. You're German. How can you want to turn him over to a government who sees him as the enemy?"

"Not everyone is like that. Maybe that's our job—to find someone who can make sure Josef will be treated fairly. He's been raised to believe Germany is somehow better than the rest of this world and anything he does for it is right. But that's not true, Miss Burnbaum. Germany is full of people just like everybody else, sinners who must look to God. To follow the Christ who came to forgive sins and to allow us God's loving mercy. If Josef has committed a crime, he'll have to face justice—American justice because he's American and that's where he committed the crimes. But I know someone who will make sure he's treated fairly."

"Yes, I know you're about to name the man who's taken Josef's place in your life. Don't waste your time trying to convince me he is the answer. This conversation is over."

Liesel heard the tap of heels taking Miss Burnbaum out of the kitchen again.

Around dinnertime, the solitude once again drove Liesel to pound on the door. She knew it would bring Miss Burnbaum sooner or later.

———————

Almost nine o'clock. It would soon be dark. David sat in a chair behind the counter at Sauder's, not far from the register. The store was empty, permeated with unfamiliar shadows as the sun sat so low behind the building. The Sauder family had left him alone after an invitation to share their dinner, which he had refused.

He felt like he'd missed something, as if the answer to Liesel's whereabouts could be figured out if only he saw whatever it was he'd missed. If only he could find Otto or Josef or even Lucille Burnbaum. Oddly enough, even she seemed to be part of the puzzle. Public records had an incorrect address for her, an apartment not far from the von Woerner factory that turned out to be rented to someone else—someone who hadn't a clue as to who Lucille Burnbaum might be or where she currently lived. Frustrated over the lost time, he'd sent Ernst back to the von Woerner office to try and find a correct address. Ernst had to threaten a clerk, but it turned out the office had the same old address. Another dead end.

David stared ahead. Twice that day he'd nearly lost any shred of sanity, and he felt close to losing his tenuous hold once again. He knew someone had to be headquartered, collecting the information that many out there could gather. He served the case best right where he was. Yet it was driving him mad.

A tap at the door interrupted his disjointed thoughts, and he saw Ilsa and Hans Bonner through the glass. Mrs. Bonner had a tray in her hands. He let them in, finding a light and turning it on.

"You must eat," Mrs. Bonner said.

"No, but thank you."

She set the tray on the counter. "I'll leave it for you, then."

"What can we do, David?" Hans said. His eyelids hung low as if ready to shed tears. "This sitting, this waiting, we cannot tolerate it much longer."

David wanted to shout that he felt the same way, that waiting was the last thing he wanted to do. Did they want to be out there, using up this awful energy in another way than just worrying? That's what he wanted. Did they want to go door-to-door, running, shouting, organizing every last able-bodied person available? That's what he wanted. Yet the only thing they could do was wait. This was part of it. He'd done it before in dozens of other cases. It was the waiting that led to worrying, the worrying that led to madness. He'd never understood that until this case.

"There is nothing else to do," he said softly.

Then he turned away because he didn't want them to see just how hard that waiting had been on him, too. He pretended an interest in what was beneath the pink-striped napkin. But touching it, he remembered that day he'd seen Liesel sewing those napkins, and he almost moaned out loud. Instead, he dropped the corner and stood still, hands clenched at his sides.

He spotted Hans watching him closely, then managed a short laugh. "Waiting isn't easy for any of us."

Hans nodded and put a hand on David's shoulder. David welcomed the contact.

"Karl has been going back and forth from the house to the precinct all day, but no one has reported anything unusual or seen anyone who fits Liesel's description. They've been going around again this evening to check the houses that didn't answer earlier."

David nodded. He already knew that. He'd been calling the precinct and his own office all afternoon.

"How is the family doing?" David asked, mildly interested. For once, it seemed better to talk than to be silent. "Is Karl asking more questions about Josef and Otto?"

"No, no," said Hans. "He is worried like the rest of us. One thing is odd, though. Otto hasn't been seen all day, here or at work."

David nodded.

"But you knew," Hans said. "You knew that already. Katie has been at church all day, praying for Liesel. We kept the children home and told them not to say anything to their friends who came calling. Katie and Helga are with Ilsa now, and so is Ernst. We try to pass the time, to read from the Book, or to play a game, but . . ." He let his words drift off, and David nodded in response. He knew.

"The sun will set soon," Hans noted as he turned to the window.

"Oh, Hans!" Mrs. Bonner said, and a sob slipped out after the words. "Not another night without our Liesel."

Hans put an arm about his wife's shoulders, and she put her head on his chest, pulling out a worn handkerchief and pressing it beneath her nose.

The phone rang, and the three of them jumped at the sound. David tripped over his own foot getting to it, pulling it to the edge of the counter and raising the receiver to his ear.

"De Serre."

"Yeah, this is Sergeant Williams over at the precinct. We got an officer here said he heard somethin' odd at one of the houses a few blocks from the factory. Could be something, or it could be nothing, but you told me to call no matter which."

"What is it?" David didn't care if the man thought it was the most trivial clue; anything at all was better than nothing.

The sergeant gave David the address. "Our man said it was his second visit. Got no answer this morning. It was quiet then. But this time a woman was home. She said she didn't see anything, cooperated with all the questions. The odd thing is, though, our man said he heard some kind of banging in the background. He asked about it, and he says the woman got nervous. Said it was her brother building a canning shelf in the cellar. But he said it didn't sound like a hammer. Too slow, had a rhythm to it. Nobody bangs a hammer that way."

"Got it," David said, then hung up. Immediately he clicked for the operator. "Get me the Justice Department."

To his annoyance, Donahue answered the phone.

"I need to know who lives at this address," David explained. If they had a phone, they would be listed in public records, and that was the fastest list to check. David prayed they had a phone. "And Donahue, get on this right away. Call me back as soon as you've got it."

When David hung up, he turned to the Bonners, who looked at him with anxiety.

"It might be nothing," he said. "It's just something we've got to check, to make sure. They'll call me back in a few minutes with more information."

If David thought the last twenty-four hours dragged, it seemed every bit as long before the phone rang again.

"What do you have?"

"Yeah, David, it's me, Weber. I'm here at the office. Donahue told me you were checking on an address. It belongs to the Wenzel family, Max and Elsie Wenzel. Want me to get over there?"

David's hopes both soared and plummeted within a matter of moments. "Get over there, Weber," he said in spite of the facts sounding innocuous. "Just go and take a look."

David hung up again, shaking his head at Hans and Ilsa. He had nothing to give them. Yet.

CHAPTER *Twenty~Five*

LIESEL ignored the spasms of pain throbbing through her arms. She could barely hold up her head she was so tired, yet she kept pounding. *Thump. Thump. Thump.* Slow, one right after another. Like a clock ticking away the longest seconds in time.

"Stop it, stop it!"

Liesel heard Miss Burnbaum's voice but kept pounding.

"Stop it, I say! Stop!"

Liesel kept pounding, only faster, spurred on by Miss Burnbaum's obvious agitation.

"Just stop, and I'll talk to you," said the older woman's weary voice.

Liesel stopped. "Tell me who was at the door a while ago."

"No one."

"I heard someone knock."

"That was your own pounding."

"No, I heard someone at the door," Liesel insisted.

"It was a salesman."

Liesel didn't believe her, but there was little she could do to prove her case. "Tell me what Uncle Otto is doing. Does he have the money ready for Josef?"

"I expect so," Miss Burnbaum answered. "Why so interested in the man you're eager to turn in?"

"I was never eager to turn him in," Liesel defended. "But I knew it was the right thing to do."

"Go ahead, pound away! It's better than hearing you rant about right and wrong."

"The only reason you're bothered by what I'm saying is because you know I'm right." This was like having an argument with Karl. He only got offended when she was closer to the truth than he was.

"Even if I thought you were right," Miss Burnbaum said after such a long moment of silence Liesel thought she might have left again, "there is nothing I could do now. It's too late."

Liesel couldn't see her timepiece from where she sat. She bent down to catch the narrow band of light from under the door. It was almost nine o'clock.

"It's not too late! There is over an hour before I was to meet Josef. If you go to the Justice Department right now—"

"No, Miss Bonner. I'm not about to turn myself in. Or Otto. Not after coming this far. I've heard about those Justice Department fellows. They'll arrest a person just for being German."

"No! Not David de Serre. He's a good man, Miss Burnbaum."

"So, he's here as God's avenger, is he? Your Mr. de Serre?"

"No, of course not, but he does want justice."

"Otto was right that you let this man take Josef's place in your heart."

"Josef stepped out of his place quite on his own," Liesel said. "We don't believe in the same things. I wasn't looking to replace him."

"Lucky for you that you have such a pretty young face to snap up someone else so quickly."

Liesel heard the envy right through the door, as if an invisible sword pierced through the wood panels separating them. She leaned against the stairway railing. "You once said the von Woerner men are very dedicated. I think you're right about that. Josef to Germany, Uncle Otto to Germany and to his businesses. They have no room for women in their lives—or even each other, really. Perhaps that's why Uncle Otto's wife died. She simply gave up trying to find a spot in her husband's life. It would have been the same for me if I'd loved Josef. I waited for him, you know. But I think I would have had to wait my whole life before he finally had time for me. Just as you're waiting for Uncle Otto."

Miss Burnbaum said nothing.

Liesel shook her numb arms and hands, bringing life back into them. She'd stopped hoping she could penetrate Miss Burnbaum's sense of right and wrong; she didn't know why she kept trying.

After a few moments, Liesel went down the stairs if only to stretch her legs. She couldn't bear to take up that pounding again. If it rattled Miss Burnbaum, it did no less to Liesel herself. Her arms—and ears—couldn't take it anymore.

She tried sitting on the mattress that had been provided and had gone unused the night before. But restlessness set in once again. Closing her eyes, she prayed that God would send her deliverance, that she would keep trusting Him no matter what happened, that He might use her to serve some measure of justice.

Still restless, she went back up the stairs. She spotted the tin can that had served as her mallet but couldn't muster the strength or desire to start pounding again. So she pressed her ear to the door, listening for any movement.

She heard nothing.

"Miss Burnbaum," she called. Perhaps she was in the kitchen.

Hinges on another door squeaked, and Liesel stopped all movement in hope of hearing something else. Had Miss Burnbaum left? Was she going to Uncle Otto, to accompany him to meet Josef? Liesel doubted that. Besides being too early, it seemed unlikely Uncle Otto would permit the unnecessary risk of taking Miss Burnbaum along.

Liesel heard the clip of heels on the floor again. Miss Burnbaum was in the kitchen.

"Did someone come in?" Liesel asked.

"No."

"Was someone at the door, then?"

"No."

"I heard something, Miss Burnbaum."

"It was nothing. Don't concern yourself. No one knows you're here, and no one ever will. Not until Otto comes back to take you home. Just a couple more hours, and then you'll be free."

"After Josef is safe."

"That's right."

Liesel sank to the stair again. *Oh, God, help me to trust. Just to trust.*

———————

"De Serre," David said into the telephone.

"It's Weber. I went to the house. A woman lives there. I've never seen her before, but she wears a lot of lipstick."

"So?"

Hans and Ilsa Bonner were still with David. They seemed reluctant to leave, at least until David had anything else on the tenuous lead. They

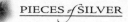
watched him, as if sure the telephone call would reveal something about their daughter.

"So, she didn't smoke the cigarette I found outside her house."

David's heart leapt to his throat. "Cork tip?"

"You've got it."

"I'm on my way."

David grabbed his jacket, rounding the counter and heading to the door. "Stay here, Hans, and take any calls. I'll contact you as soon as I—"

"Oh, no, you don't. I'm coming along!"

David didn't have time to argue. "Somebody has to stay here and take messages."

"I will do that!" Mrs. Bonner said quickly. "And I'll send Sauder to fetch Ernst. He will be here, too, if you need him."

"He can stay with you," David said over his shoulder as he neared the door. Outside, he ran down the street to his motorcar. He started the engine, and the car lurched forward, only to pull over again to get Hans.

"This could lead to absolutely nothing," David cautioned, and Hans nodded. In spite of his words, the tires on the Runabout screeched as David sped away.

The street with the correct address was dark. David shut off the electric lamps on his motorcar as he approached the front of the house, then killed the motor. Without a word, he got out of the car. Hans followed.

"Stay by the motor," David said quietly. "I'll call if I need help."

David was relieved when Hans did as he asked. He spotted Weber in a few minutes, lurking somewhat closer to the house.

"The woman who lives here is still in there, even though she hasn't lit any lamps. I saw her through the window."

David nodded. "Let's go."

They went to the door and rapped soundly.

No answer.

"She didn't leave," Weber quietly insisted.

David knocked again. Still nothing.

"I know you're in there, ma'am. Better come to the door. We only want to ask you some questions."

"I'm calling the police!" The voice was shrill but clear nonetheless.

"Go right ahead, ma'am. We're with the Justice Department Bureau of Investigation. The police will be able to verify that."

"I want you to leave my property," she said again, her voice wobbly. "I want no trouble here."

"We're not here to cause any trouble, ma'am," said David. "We only want to talk to you."

"About what?"

"We want to know if you've seen anything unusual in this neighborhood."

"Somebody was here earlier asking a bunch of questions, and I told them everything I know. Which was nothing. Now go on, get off my property."

"Are you Mrs. Wenzel?" David inquired.

"Why do you ask?"

Keep talking, he thought. Was there something familiar about that voice? "Isn't this the home of Max and Elsie Wenzel?"

"Yes."

"And are you Mrs. Wenzel?"

"No. I only take care of the place for them. Mr. Wenzel passed on."

"And Mrs. Wenzel?"

"In the home for the aged. But I've got a right to be here. They're relations of mine."

"And what's your name?"

"I don't want to talk to you anymore. You leave here now. I'm not answering any more questions."

"If you don't answer my questions, ma'am, I can get a court order to allow me inside. Is that what you want?"

"I want you to leave."

She was getting nervous, he could tell. It made her voice less familiar.

"An officer heard some strange noises coming from inside. Do you have any idea what that might have been?"

"No, I don't."

"Why don't you open the door, ma'am? Maybe there is something we could help you with."

"I don't need any help!"

"We just want to make sure, ma'am."

Weber put a hand on the door, which was locked. "Go around and see if there's another entrance," David whispered. Then he turned back to the door and spoke louder. "I won't leave until I make sure everything here is safe."

"I'm telling you it is. Why don't you believe me? You have no right to harass me in this way."

"I told you I'm from the Justice Department. Have you called the police yet? I encourage you to do so, or come to the window, and I'll show you my identification."

"I'm not doing any such thing!"

"It might help to calm you down, ma'am. Or you could call a friend and have them come over to be with you. A neighbor."

As he spoke, David stepped back, assessing the house.

"David, can I help?" called Hans quietly.

David shook his head.

If there was trouble ahead, the last thing he wanted was for Mrs. Bonner to have to deal with a hurt husband on top of everything else.

The roof of the house was low with one gabled window in the center that probably led to an attic, judging from the height of the house. There were also several windows on the first floor, a pair on each side of the door. Breaking his way inside through one of them would be quicker than trying to break down the doorframe, even with Weber's help.

David listened for Weber. He'd been gone more than enough time to round the small house. David looked from corner to corner, seeing no one, hearing nothing. He went to one side of the house.

He found nothing. Returning to the front in case Weber would show from the other side, David went to the opposite corner. There, in the setting sun, he thought he saw something disappear around to the backyard. David trotted to the back of the house.

There lay Weber in a heap. David crouched low beside him, scanning the area as he did so. He saw no one.

"Weber!"

He was out cold, but he wasn't dead. A quick view of the rear of the house revealed another door just beyond where Weber lay. David stood and reached it. Locked.

David stayed close to the shadow of the house. Someone had dragged Weber, judging by the track in the dirt and flowerbed. A rustle came from around the corner. Slowly, barely breathing, he rounded the edge in one effortless move.

Nothing.

Stiff with tension, David straightened, then breathed once, wishing he had a gun. But only the locals were licensed to carry weapons. David's department did the investigating; the locals made the arrests. It hadn't mattered so much to David until tonight. There wasn't time to get the locals here.

Turning back to the yard, he stopped short at the moonlit reflection of the very kind of weapon he wished he had—a gun, pointed straight at his heart.

"Looking for me, mister?"

David eyed the young man in front of him. He was built solidly, multiplying the intimidation of the weapon.

"You the one who knocked out my partner?"

"That's right."

"Then I guess you're the one I'm looking for," David said.

"I think you better take your pal and come with me for a while."

David wasn't about to follow willingly.

The sound of banging distracted them both. The man looked away, and David lunged for the gun. The man quickly backed off, still gripping the weapon. David regained his footing, holding out his hands cautiously.

"What's that noise?" he asked.

"I don't hear anything."

"The banging. What is it?"

"I don't hear it," the man said, but his smile belied his words.

"Sounds like somebody trying to send a message. Somebody in trouble."

"You got quite an imagination, mister."

"I am a federal investigator, and so is the man you knocked out. If you want to avoid trouble for yourself, you'll put down that gun and cooperate."

The man laughed. "Looks to me like you're the one with the trouble, bein' on that end of the gun."

"I don't know what kind of business you're in, sir," David said. "Or who might be paying you. But is it worth a federal offense? Is it worth going to jail?"

"Who's going to jail?"

"You are."

He laughed again. "There you go with that imagination again. All you need to do is come with me, and we'll have a nice friendly chat for a while. No crime, no harm."

"Then why the gun?"

"Oh, this here is my persuader. You know, in case you're not in the mood for visiting. You either come inside for a while or haul your friend out of here and don't come back."

Over the man's shoulder, David saw movement. Another hulk? Or a roused Weber? He hoped the latter. There was no way to tell. David only knew if he kept the man talking, the other person might find a way to disarm him.

"I hope he's paying you enough," David said, conversationally.

"Who?"

"Whoever's paying you. I hope it's enough."

"Oh, it is."

"Tell me, is he paying you enough to keep you smoking Morrises? They're pretty pricey."

His smile widened. "Oh, yeah, I'll be smoking Morrises the rest of my life."

The dark figure lifted a piece of wood, cut to fit in a wood stove. It came down hard on the head of the man in front of him. His gun went off. David instinctively ducked, even though he knew the bullet would sail over his head. The man in front of him grunted at the impact from the wood. It didn't knock him out, but it dazed him long enough to make him drop the gun.

David pounced on it. Without taking his eyes from the man, he pointed the gun at him. From the corner of his eye, he saw Hans drop the wood. David spared him a glance. "Good work, Hans!"

"*Ja, Ja,*" he murmured. He looked every bit as stunned as the man he'd clobbered.

A shriek came from the back of the house, followed quickly by a door slamming. David sped past Hans and the other man, who had sunk to a sitting position. Hans didn't follow, he picked up the wood again and held it high, as if he'd hit the man again if he tried to move.

The back door was closed, and Weber was where he'd been a moment ago, still immobile.

David beat on the door, noting the pounding from inside the house had stopped.

"Open this door!" he demanded.

"I heard a gun!" the woman cried.

"Your henchman's."

"There's a man outside this door. Is he dead?"

"No. Just knocked out. He'll be needing a doctor, though."

"Oh my, oh my! This is just too much! Oh my!"

"Open the door, ma'am," said David, more calmly.

It took a moment, but the door slowly opened, and David finally placed the voice with the face.

"Miss Burnbaum!" Why was he surprised?

She stepped back, a look of pain on her face. The back door opened to an enclosed porch, offering a table and chairs. Another door led to the rest of the house. David went to it.

"Where is she?"

The woman burst into tears, pointing inside the house. David ran in, hearing more footsteps behind but too intent on the task to turn around.

"Liesel!"

He called her name frantically, passing a kitchen and entering a dining room. He called her name again and turned in all directions but saw nothing.

Then he heard a call.

"Help me! I'm in here!"

David caught sight of a door in the kitchen.

"Liesel!" David rushed toward it, finding it locked. Still clutching the gun, he went back to Miss Burnbaum and took her by the collar. "The key! Where's the key?"

She pointed toward the countertop.

David thrust her away and grabbed the key, pushing it at the lock. He fumbled. It wouldn't go in.

"David?"

"Liesel! I'm coming!"

With an effort to calm his trembling fingers, he managed to unlock the door. There she stood, disheveled and squinting from the kitchen light, but as lovely as he'd ever seen.

"Liesel!"

She leaned toward him, and his arms automatically wrapped around her. He pulled her up to the kitchen floor in the tight circle of his arms. Then his lips were on hers, completely and firmly, in a kiss he'd dreamed of often enough. He felt her acquiescence and didn't want to stop. She was warm and soft, and he wanted nothing more than to be close, stay close, and never let her go.

"David," she whispered.

Hans entered the kitchen, and David knew he had to let her go. Her father swept her up into his arms.

"*Liebchen, Liebchen*," he said, again and again, and they both cried. Slowly, David remembered he still had a job to do. Weber was out cold, there was a staggering criminal outside no doubt trying to flee, and neither Josef nor his father were anywhere in sight. David *wanted* to wind his way in between Liesel and Hans and brush Hans aside altogether, but knew he couldn't. David searched the house, finding neither Josef nor Otto but spotting a phone that he used to call the locals.

Suddenly he heard Liesel's frantic voice. "What time is it?"

"Nine forty five," he heard her father say.

"There's still time." Just as David reentered the kitchen she shouted, "David! We've got to get to the monument. The new one they're working on."

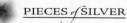

Then Liesel was outside her father's arms, pulling at David's hand. She looked like someone else, determined, almost hard. David didn't ask questions. They made it to his motorcar in seconds.

"Go, David, go!"

"Wait for me!" It was Hans, calling from the curb.

"No, Papa! Stay here! I love you!"

"Help Weber!" David called. "The police are on their way. Tell them to go after the guy who ran from the yard. And send some men to the Lincoln Monument." Then David sped off.

There were a myriad of questions in David's mind, but he asked none of them. That she'd been held against her will was obvious. That von Woerner and Burnbaum had worked together was also plain. And that she wanted justice was every bit as clear. Suddenly he was ashamed of himself, of the doubts he'd harbored about her loyalty to everything he knew she believed in: God, her country, her parents. Answers to questions could come later.

The ride to the vicinity of the monument took only minutes. David parked well out of sight, and they walked silently closer. Because of ongoing construction, the area was roped off to the public. It was quiet.

"Ten o'clock," she whispered. "He is supposed to be behind the monument at ten o'clock."

David still had the thug's gun. It was against regulations to use it, and he hoped he wouldn't regret not taking it out of his pocket immediately. But to protect Liesel, he'd do anything he needed to do.

"Otto is here somewhere. He was going to bring Josef money to get out of the country."

"Alone? Or for both of them?"

"I—I don't know."

"I think you had better stay behind," David said. "Go back to my motorcar and wait."

Liesel shook her head. She had that look on her face again, one of determination and of immovable stubbornness. She filled him with as much anger as admiration.

"I don't want you in the middle," he persisted.

"I already am."

They made their way up the slight hill and around tall, steel platforms. The monument was near completion, the seated figure of the sixteenth president stoic and peaceful just inside the tall pillars.

The closer they came, the faster David's heart beat. Not for himself but for Liesel. He didn't know what to expect and hated having her here.

Vulnerability would only make his job harder. Stepping over boards and around scaffolding, he drew her wrist into his hand.

"I'm asking you once more, Liesel, go back to the car."

"You might as well let her stay, Mr. de Serre. No use now."

David swiveled on his heel toward the voice behind him. Otto von Woerner stood barely visible in the shadows, a gun in his hand.

"Uncle Otto! Put that gun down. This has gone far enough."

He laughed, and the monocle fell from his eye. The gun's barrel shook just a bit, but it was still aimed their way. "Oh, not quite far enough, Liesel. I mean you no harm. Either of you. I just need to put you off a little longer. Then you may do with me what you like. It won't matter. Now if you will please leave, Mr. de Serre, no one will get hurt."

David remained still except for slipping his hand into his pocket. He thanked God that he knew how to shoot, thanks to Mio's uncle. The bureau offered no such training.

"If that is a gun in your pocket, Mr. de Serre, I suggest you leave it where it is. I will shoot you if you do anything to interfere. I have nothing to lose. Nothing I care about."

"Please, David!" Liesel whispered, whose gaze went to the hand in his pocket.

David moved his hand away.

"A wise decision," Otto said.

"Uncle Otto, will you give up the rest of your life for Josef? He wouldn't want you to." Her voice trembled as unsteadily as David's heartbeat. "But you will go to jail because of Josef and what he's done."

Otto opened his mouth, but a voice sounded from behind them instead. "He's not doing it for me."

Josef von Woerner's voice echoed off the marble around them. David didn't see him at first, but he was there, somewhere.

"My father is doing it for *Deutschland*."

Evidently it was the first Otto had seen of his son since Josef had disappeared. David saw his eyes widen and his mouth open, as if to say something, but his mouth closed with a twitch to his full mustache. He must have remembered his position and the gun in his hand. He still held it firmly and returned his gaze to David.

Otto held a dark cloth sack in his other hand, which he threw to the ground off to the side, closer to Josef.

"There is what you need, Josef. Now take it and go. I will detain them long enough for you to get away. Go!"

David couldn't see Josef; he didn't want to take his eyes off Otto and his gun. He heard Josef's footsteps on the pavement come up behind Liesel.

"You came here with him?" Josef asked softly. He stood so close that David tore his eyes from the gun, unable to look at anything except Josef as he whispered into Liesel's ear.

Liesel did not respond.

"You betrayed me?"

"Josef—"

"I knew you didn't approve," he said. "I saw it on your face that day I left. I told you how it will be. It *will* happen, Liesel. *Deutschland*'s day in the sun is coming. You would have been happy with me. I would have made you happy."

Liesel said nothing. Her head was bowed. She didn't look at him.

"You loved me," Josef said. "You loved me once."

To that, she did look up. Tears stood in her eyes—David saw their reflection in the moonlight—and she met Josef's gaze. She didn't deny his words.

"Come with me now, Liesel. I can still make you happy. And I will do as you ask; I will go to *Deutschland* and fight as a soldier. Only come with me."

"Enough of this nonsense, Josef!" cried his father, stepping closer. "She was going to turn you in."

David saw his opportunity. In his impatience with his son, Otto had taken his eyes from his quarry. David lunged. He knocked the gun from the older man's hand, and it soared up and then came to the ground with a docile *thwack*.

"Run, Josef!" Otto yelled, even as David fended off his fist.

Confusion erupted from all directions. Angled headlamps of a motor-car on the hill shot two beams of light, illuminating and shadowing the scaffolding and monument. Someone shouted, footsteps clattered, unseen faces called through the beams of light. David turned to Liesel to see that she was safe and in so doing caught Otto's jab to his jaw.

"Run, Josef!"

David thrust Otto to the ground with a shove. The man hit the ground hard, but David couldn't stop to assess damage. Josef had Liesel by the hand, running toward the dark side of the monument. He grabbed the bag his father left for him.

They were out of sight from David, but eerie voices echoed off the monument.

"No, Josef! You mustn't run." Liesel's voice sounded firm. "And I won't go with you if you do."

David rounded the corner to see Josef drop her hand and take flight on his own.

"David!" Liesel cried, grabbing him by the arm. She pointed toward other agents, one of whom had Otto by the arm and another of whom swooped down to pick up Otto's discarded gun. The man rushed past them in the direction Josef had fled.

"He has a gun, David! Don't let him use it on Josef!"

David had no time to assure her. He looked at her tormented eyes. Did she really want the man protected, after all? But he couldn't stop now. He thrust her away, racing after Josef. To his horror, he saw it was Donahue who'd picked up the gun. David bolted for them.

Josef wore dark clothes, but the moon was bright, and the dark hat he wore flew off, revealing his light hair. He was easy to spot. The Potomac wasn't far, and he ran in that direction.

But Donahue had a head start. And he had the gun poised to shoot.

"Back off, Donahue!"

"This is war, de Serre!" Donahue shouted back. "Not for cowards!"

Donahue was gaining on Josef. David pressed on, his breath slicing his throat.

They heard a splash, and the moon slipped behind a thick cloud, casting the area into darkness. At the river's edge, both David and Donahue waited for the hunted to surface for air. David rushed downriver, guessing Josef would allow the current to aid his flight. Donahue must have had the same idea; he sprinted along the bank.

Then David saw Josef, popping up for air.

David dove into the water.

He heard a shot followed quickly by a scream. David paddled water and shouted to Donahue.

"Hold your fire!"

But then Josef rose again. He didn't look like he was swimming anymore. He might have been hit. David dove after him. He knew the river well enough to remember its depth and that the current grew stronger up ahead. The river itself would carry Josef beyond reach if David didn't catch him quickly. And if Josef was hurt, he might not be able to make it ashore. David swam harder just as the current picked up. Suddenly he spotted Josef again, and David lunged at him, his hand outstretched.

"Take hold!" David shouted, but there was no response. That hand simply slipped from David's reach without flight or fight. Without any movement of its own.

David swam faster, but in the next moment, he lost sight of Josef altogether.

"Josef!"

Water lapped and splashed in response. The moon emerged, illuminating the river. But David saw no sign of Josef.

Frantically, he treaded water, going under, but it was too black to see anything. He shot up and scanned the area, seeing nothing. Donahue searched from the shore.

At last, David swam to the edge, heaving himself out of the water. Clothes heavily soaked and shoes slippery on the grass, he stumbled into a run. Josef might be farther downstream than they thought. David knew it would be a miracle if Josef made it to shore, and he prayed for that miracle.

Donahue caught up. David wanted to throttle the man for shooting. They might be after a spy but not the kind who would have received—or deserved—a death penalty. And as far as David knew, Josef had been unarmed.

Donahue pointed downriver. "There he is!"

Josef was easy to spot in the bright moonlight. He looked like a rag doll floating face down, bobbing along the murky path. He hit a rock and didn't flinch. If he wasn't already dead, he was at least unconscious. David raced forward, thankful for only one thing. If Liesel really had loved this man, she couldn't see him now.

"Josef!" He heard her cry, nearly a scream.

David didn't stop. He'd get to the man if only to answer that call. He would bring Josef to her if that's what she wanted.

Josef went under again.

David ran toward the spot, plunging back into the water. If he could reach Josef, David would scoop up the man and throw him to shore.

He swam the width of the waterway, but Josef had disappeared again around a tree-lined bend. At least the water was calm. David went back and forth, then back again along the inlet. He was sure that was where the current had aimed the body. He went deep to see if Josef was caught below. He found nothing.

After a while, David heard Donahue's call from the bushes on the opposite shore. The moon disappeared again behind a line of clouds so thick the area was in near total darkness.

"He's gone, de Serre. We'll have them dredge the river with nets for the body in the morning when we can see something."

His tone was dispassionate, cold. David looked around for Liesel and knew she'd heard it as well. She came up behind Donahue, fists clenched at her sides. David swam ashore.

"You killed him! You killed him!"

She flung herself at Donahue, small, ineffectual fists pounding against the agent's massive chest.

"He didn't deserve to die!"

David caught her from behind, pulling her away. Putting two steady hands on her quaking shoulders, he bent low enough to match her eye level, his gaze demanding hers. At last she looked at him, eyes still wide and tormented, but in the deep breath she took, he sensed the beginning of a diffusion of all that railed inside of her.

Then David turned on Donahue and landed a punch Liesel couldn't have delivered had she used every ounce of her strength. Donahue stumbled back and raised his own fist, but David ducked and turned away, unwilling to fight anymore. He'd never given in to anger in such a physical way and had no intention of giving that anger more fuel. He drew Liesel into a wet embrace and led her away from Donahue, who stood rubbing his jaw.

"I'm sorry," David whispered to Liesel.

"Josef!" she cried. "He didn't deserve to die. Not to die!"

"No," David said. "He didn't deserve that."

Her body trembled with sobs, and he held her close. Over his head, he saw Donahue look on in disgust, and David turned from the sight. He felt no small amount of that emotion himself.

Hardly aware of David leading her, Liesel followed him away from Donahue. Away from where she'd last seen Josef.

Josef. Flashes of him in the river, facedown, played vividly in front of her.

"Oh, David, David," she said, holding back a new onslaught of tears.

He pulled her closer, and then he turned her away from the sight of the others. She felt a chill from his wet clothes even as she was comforted by the embrace.

"Do you want me to take you home?"

She nodded, then shook her head and tried to catch another sob by pressing her fist against her mouth. It was as useless as trying to hurt Agent Donahue a moment ago. "I—I don't know. I can't think."

"Wait here, then." They were downhill from the monument, far enough from the river and far enough from those standing by the scaffolding so that they would not be bothered by either. "I have to talk to the others. You'll be safe here, and I'll be right back."

"I'm fine." But she wasn't, despite the facade she tried to erect.

He seemed hesitant to leave, as if he didn't believe her lie.

"Go," she said. As welcome as his arms had been, she suddenly liked the idea of being alone.

He waited a moment longer, eyeing her. "I won't be far. Just up there where I can see you."

She nodded.

Then he turned and headed back toward the monument.

Liesel felt a breeze and shivered, though the night was warm. She noticed part of her skin and blouse was wet from David having held her.

Her gaze scanned the river again. They'd walked far from where Josef had disappeared, and she looked in that direction. She wanted to go back to that spot to see if she could find him. Perhaps he'd made it after all and only needed help.

She looked up toward the monument lit once again by moonlight. She could see David talking to three others. One was Agent Donahue; she could tell by his posture. He held himself with a stiff back. She turned to the river.

Liesel started walking. She retraced her path, the one she'd frantically followed when she first saw Donahue, then David, chasing Josef.

By the time she reached the spot, she was shivering though she wasn't cold. Every part of her trembled, from the tips of her fingers up to her lips and down to her knees. She could hear the lap of water, but it sounded odd. Nothing seemed right just then, not the hot breeze or the shifting moonlight or the nearby crickets and frogs. It all sounded too loud, unfamiliar. Or was it just the way it sounded in her ears? As if everything was near, then far, faint, then full, in a rhythm that matched the unsteady beat of her heart. It warred with the sounds around her, muffling, then magnifying.

She stared at the water and saw the rocks, the very ones that had battered Josef's limp body. For a moment, those rocks became an enemy, too. Why were they there, where anyone who fell into the water could be hurt by them?

But her thoughts were confused, incoherent. It wasn't the rocks that had killed Josef. It wasn't David or even Donahue. It was her. She'd been the one to betray him. And Josef knew it. "You betrayed me?" he'd said.

She had.

Then she saw it, just a flash at first. Something glimmering in the crossing moonlight. Whatever it was, it was caught between a low hanging branch and some rocks below.

She ran to it, growing more agitated when she saw it was the buckle on a bag, smooth and dark.

Holding her skirt high, she stepped into the water. It felt shockingly cold beneath her feet, but she hardly noticed. The river ran fast even along the edge as it swished around scattered rocks. She climbed on to one in an effort to keep dry, but the rocks were smooth and slippery, offering nothing to grab. The tree branch was too high to reach this close to shore.

Slipping, Liesel fell to a crawl and inched toward the branch where it was stuck on the trapped bag. If she could just slide a bit farther . . . stretching, pulling, aching to touch it. An unexpected wave crashed up, spraying over her head. She sputtered, swallowing and choking against the fountain of water. But the water jet carried what she sought and she leaped forward, latching on to the sack before it could be taken away.

She landed on the group of rocks that only moments before had snagged the sack she now held firmly against her.

Otto's bag. Partly relieved and partly repelled, she held the inanimate object. She wanted to throw it back, as if its very existence reminded her of everything else for which she was to blame.

Another shift in the current splattered her. Despite the disparaging thoughts aimed at Otto's possession, she clutched the bag and scooted backward, but only far enough to feel secure. Scanning the area with a gaze as intense as any huntress, she waited for the light of the moon to aid her search.

It wasn't long. Clouds parted, and a full moon lit the area with a blue so bright she could see the other side of the wide river. Trees, shrubs, and grasses soon took shape out of the blackness around her. And the water itself twinkled here and there as lovely as a sheet of stars. She hated the sight, because what she sought could not be found.

There was no movement but of a rustling branch and running water as it splashed its dance before her. Nothing that should not be here. No Josef.

She looked behind her, wondering if he'd somehow made it to shore. But the ground was undisturbed along the banks except by her own footprints. Scanning the shore farther down, she wondered what distance a current could carry a limp body if he'd made it beyond that inlet. Perhaps a search of her own wouldn't be a bad idea.

Standing, she turned around on the rocks and faced the shore. The quest for the bag had taken all of her concentration, and she hadn't realized she was so far out. Knowing she would need two free hands, she hurled the bag ashore and tried to reach the branch that had snarled the bag minutes before. She'd always been better at climbing trees than swimming. If she could grab hold, she could use the tree to get back to shore, safe and dry.

Without the bag pulling down the branch, it was now too high to reach even from out here. Kneeling, she made her way to the farthest edge of the rocks where the branch curved to its lowest angle and nearly touched the water.

A little farther . . . she reached out and could touch the leaves with her fingertips. In a desperate grab one leaf came off in her palm. If only she could reach just a bit . . . she could grab hold of the twig that leaf had been attached to and pull the rest of it toward her.

Another splash of water spewed over her, obscuring her target. Coughing, she caught her breath, then spotted the branch again. The water was so unpredictable she didn't know when to expect another gush. With a reckless burst of fear and energy, she vaulted from the rock and strained for the branch.

For the barest moment, she had it in her grasp, and she clung to it with all her might. But it was more pliable than she'd expected, and it swayed precariously downward, so low that she sank deep into the moving water. Then the branch sprang up, but it wasn't strong enough to carry her. The water dragged her down, filling her shoes, soaking her skirt. The branch shot away with a snap, and all that was left in her hand was a fistful of leaves.

Before she knew it, she was swept up with the current, the water carrying her away.

CHAPTER *Twenty-Six*

"WE caught him two blocks from the scene of the crime," Weber said. "The pounding Mr. Bonner gave him must have gotten the best of him. The guy was passed out cold."

David eyed the other agent, who was sporting a lump of his own on his forehead.

"And how's your head?"

Weber grinned. "Guess I've got a thicker skull than the guy working for von Woerner."

David put a hand to Weber's shoulder. "You did a great job tonight. Now why don't you take off and go home?"

Weber didn't move. Some of the other agents were dispersing from the monument, but a few still remained.

"I'll check out the area again with you if you want."

David shook his head. "If you don't want to go home, go back to the office and call in a couple of Jake's men to help with a preliminary search by boat tonight. I don't think we have to wait for daylight to get started. Lanterns will help."

Weber nodded. Donahue had already left. *Probably had enough of me for the night.* The guy would be lucky not to go to jail after the inquest David was ready to initiate.

"And let's keep the trains, borders, and shipyards looking for him," David added. "Just in case he made it."

But even as he heard his own cautious words, David knew better. His touch had grazed Josef long enough to know he'd been at best unconscious. There was no way an unconscious body could survive that dunking unless he'd somehow been washed ashore. And given their search of the area, that had not been the case.

No, he was fairly certain Josef von Woerner was dead.

"I'm taking Liesel—Miss Bonner—home," David said, "but I'll be back." He glanced around the area. "Looks like you'll be the last to leave."

"I'll come back with Jake's men," Weber said. "Won't get any sleep tonight anyway."

"Then I'll see you in a bit."

David turned anxiously back to the river. He'd seen Liesel wave several minutes earlier, a forlorn gesture if ever he'd witnessed one—as if she were trying to reassure him she was all right. He knew she was anything but.

David followed the pathway she'd taken, guessing where she was headed. She must want to see for herself if he was really gone. Did David blame her? It would have been hard even for him to accept, if he hadn't felt with his own hand that Josef didn't have the strength to fight for his life in the deep water. David didn't know where Donahue's bullet had hit Josef, but he was sure it had knocked him out if not killed him. The rocks and water would have finished him if the bullet hadn't.

With the moonlight so sporadic, David's view of the shoreline was intermittent at best. Now and then a bush or tree got in his way as well. He kept walking, having misjudged the distance in all of the excitement. Surely she wasn't much farther.

The sound of gently drifting water gradually modified from peaceful lapping at the shore to an increased flow. More bushes and trees grew along here, closer to the water's edge.

He wasn't sure what made him look from the shoreline out to the water. Maybe it was the moonlight suddenly illuminating everything in front of him. Or maybe it was one of the trees. An overhanging limb bounced oddly from its tip into the rocky river.

"Liesel!"

Without knowing for certain what he'd seen, he knew someone had fallen—or jumped—into the water. David dashed to the water's edge and leaped in downriver in hopes of blocking passage.

"Liesel!"

He shouted her name, and a slender arm shot above the water. He heard a cry, and with a howl of his own, David called back to her. He reared against the deep water as if it was nothing more than a puddle, rushing at her just as she was swept below the surface.

Her body wrenched toward him, pelting him with a wave. He fought the river for control of her as the current sucked at her clothes. Grabbing hold of her arms, he flung her over his shoulder, barely above the surface. In a few steps, the water became shallow again, and he lowered her in front of him, carrying her like a child out of the running river.

Safe on the shore, he placed her on the high grass, kneeling beside her with a prayer already on his lips.

"Oh, God, don't take her now! Liesel!"

He turned her over to her stomach, prepared to pump water out of her, but the shift in her position was enough to start deep, sputtering coughs intermingled with raspy gasps for air.

"Slow down," he said after a moment, kneeling beside her and gently rubbing her shoulders and back. "Breathe. Just breathe. You're all right."

Knowing that she was safe, he wanted to shake the rest of the water out of her. What had she been doing? How had she ended up in the water? Had she fallen?

Her breathing calmed, but she was crying. He wondered if they were tears of relief—or sorrow that he'd saved her. Her shoulders trembled, and she tried to sit up, but her body was shaking so badly, he offered immediate help. He pulled her up into his arms.

"Liesel, Liesel," he whispered, not knowing what else to say. If she had jumped, there could have been only one reason.

Sudden anger filled him and an unbearable need to show her that a lost love didn't mean her own life was gone along with Josef's. To David, her life had taken a turn long ago, far away from Josef, a new direction that was intricately enmeshed with David's own. Hadn't she seen that?

But his anger melted when he turned her face toward his. She was lovely. Her face sparkled with moonlit water droplets; her eyes welcomed him without a trace of the emptiness he would have expected to find in someone who'd just tried to end their life. And her mouth . . . it was as if she was on the brink of a smile.

His lips came down on hers before he could see that smile. He couldn't stop himself. So many impressions and thoughts warred in his head that he could obey only one, the urge to show her what he'd wanted to show her so many times before. That she didn't belong with a man who loved his father's country more than he loved his own, who loved that country more than he could ever love her or the God who'd created them all. She belonged with David, and he with her.

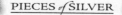

David pulled his lips from hers only to cover the rest of her face with little kisses. Her skin was cool and damp, but when his mouth returned to hers, she felt warm and inviting. Her trembling stopped altogether as her arms closed around him. It was suddenly he who wanted to tremble, and he kissed her deeply, hoping to steady himself.

"David." She whispered and laughed his name like a caress. "David."

He kissed her again, and he pressed closer. Their clothes were wet and stiff and cold, but he didn't care. The heat from his body was enough to warm them both. She didn't look chilled. He saw only gladness in her eyes, an intimacy he'd struggled often enough not to imagine.

"Don't let me go," she whispered.

"I won't. Not ever."

And then he kissed her again, her mouth, her cheeks, her ears, her neck, tasting the cool water speckling her skin. He wasn't sure what was happening, except he knew this was more than simple relief she hadn't drowned. More than grasping at life after nearly losing her own.

A new, different sort of trembling emerged. Her breathing grew uneven, her hands, when he moved one of his toward hers, quivered. With another kiss, he realized her unsteadiness matched his own.

"Liesel." He said her name, and his voice sounded different, almost flustered. "I don't want to lose you. I could have just now."

She shook her head, and one of her palms rested on his cheek. "No . . . no . . . you saved me. You saved my life."

"If I hadn't seen you jump in . . ."

"Jump in?"

He looked at her, suddenly unsure. "I thought you were trying to go to him. To join Josef."

He felt her stiffen. It was as measurable as his own increased heartbeat.

"In . . . death?"

His silence answered for him.

Liesel pulled away, and he knew he was every bit the idiot he feared himself to be. They were still on the ground, still close, but there could have been a chasm between them as wide as the river itself the way he felt just then.

"I'm sorry," he whispered. "It all happened so fast. I haven't thought it through. I should have known you wouldn't try to take your own life."

"No, I wouldn't. Not for any reason. And certainly not for Josef."

He sat back and pulled up his knees, folding his arms on them. He looked at the river they'd just fought. "You loved him," he said quietly.

"Yes." She rose to sit beside him.

His insides grew colder, matching the wet clothes that, without the two of them together, felt suddenly chilly. He sat quietly, wishing he could think of something to say, but words had never been his strong suit.

"I did love him," she whispered. He didn't look at her. Her tone of voice was enough. She was trying to be kind, to gently tell him her love for Josef could never be replaced. Then she went on. "But not the way I should have."

He looked at her curiously.

"I loved him . . . comfortably," she said. "And I've learned that love isn't necessarily supposed to be comfortable. At least, I don't think it's supposed to start out that way."

David didn't move. He held himself in firm control, knowing if he was going to keep himself from being a fool again, he had to keep his mouth shut.

"I loved Josef like a brother. My love wasn't right for him, and his wasn't right for me, either. He loved me somewhere around third place, I think. First he loved Germany, then he loved his father's business. Then me. And God . . . God never even placed. I didn't know, I never guessed because I was just too comfortable with him to see the truth."

As the words took meaning, the coolness that had seeped into David's heart dispelled. In its place warmth began to spread. Tentatively, he took one of her hands. "Liesel." He ignored former caution. "You deserve a man who goes to God for his priorities—for your sake and for the sake of the children you'll bring into the world someday. I can't tell you I don't get my priorities confused sometimes, because I do. But God has mercy on me and loves me anyway."

"I know that," she said. "I think I knew it that first day I met you when you quoted the Bible to me."

David squeezed her hand. "Josef gave you reason not to trust him. I won't."

She held his gaze, and he knew she believed him.

"I'm sorry he's gone," David said, and he was. "You cared for him; your whole family cared. And in spite of the things he did, I have to believe he was probably a good guy. He had to be if you cared for him." He let out a long, slow breath. "It was my case. I'm responsible—"

"No, no." She put a finger over his mouth. "It wasn't any of us alone, you, or me . . . or even that agent who shot him. Aren't we all responsible for our own actions? Doesn't Josef bear some of the responsibility with his actions, too?"

David nodded but didn't say what he thought. One day she might blame him. Only time would reveal that, and he wasn't ready to face that yet. What he wanted to do was pull her back into his arms, tell her he loved her, and hear her tell him the same. Yet he didn't want to rush things. They'd shared kisses and hopeful words, but they'd faced so much in the last few hours that maybe she hadn't time to know what she really felt. Maybe she'd welcomed his kiss only as a celebration of life, as a natural reaction to having just witnessed death and come so close herself.

"Just how did you end up in the water, anyway?" If he didn't keep the conversation going, he'd take her in his arms again.

She pointed upriver. "Josef's bag. It was caught on a branch, and I fell in trying to get it. I threw it ashore. It's down there somewhere."

"Brave of you," he said, "but I wish you'd come to me instead of risking your life for it." He looked at the river as the thought of nearly losing her crossed his mind again.

"David," she said quietly, almost shyly, "don't you want to know how I learned so much about love, about how it's not supposed to be comfortable at least in the early stage?"

He issued a lopsided smile. If she wasn't going to hold off on the topic, then neither would he. "Yes, I would like to know."

"I learned it from you. From everything I've felt when I'm with you or thinking about you or when someone just mentions your name. Comfortable has never been among the emotions I've felt."

"I love you, Liesel." He pulled her into his arms, wet clothes and all. He felt her shiver when her clothes pressed to her, and he laughed to cover a shiver of his own. She laughed, too, and the sound tickled his heart.

"And I love you," she said.

"We'll be all right," he whispered. "For the rest of our lives, we'll be all right. Do you know why?"

She waited for him to answer.

"Because we've put our trust in God first."

He watched her smile widen, and he held her gaze but only for a moment. Then his lips came down on hers, and smiles were lost in their kiss.

"Liesel!"

"Liesel!"

Her name echoed from every direction, and they rose from the tall grass, still holding hands. When David saw the dark outlines of Liesel's parents followed by several more shadows not far behind, he was grateful for the distance between them. Perhaps they hadn't seen the reason for his delay in getting Liesel back to them.

"My," Liesel said, obviously as surprised as he was by her family's sudden appearance.

"Where did you say Josef's bag was?"

She pointed forward, nodding as if she understood his plan to cover what they'd been doing the past few minutes.

Just as Hans and Ilsa Bonner swept their daughter up in a family embrace, David nearly tripped on the canvas sack.

He turned and watched the Bonner family one by one pile around Liesel in a huddle. They laughed and cried, tears of joy followed quickly by ones of sadness for their lost family friend. But the family circle stayed intact—opening only long enough to let David inside.

CHAPTER *Twenty-Seven*

HANK Tanner closed the door of his apartment quietly, shifting the bag of groceries in his arms to lock the door behind him. His neighbors who knew him as the reclusive loner were either too old to hear or, at least the younger ones, too busy with their own lives to bother with his. That was exactly why Hank had chosen this flat. He wasn't the kind to fraternize and had made sure his neighbors figured that out soon after he'd moved in so many years ago.

He placed the bag on the round wood table that sat to one side. The kitchen was little more than an alcove tucked into one corner, open to the rest of the room. Hank hadn't cared how small the apartment was until last night. Now he wished he had a separate bedroom. But all he had was the one room, his bed right in the middle of it.

On that bed lay one sick young man. The vomiting had stopped at last, and his fever had broken that morning, which was why Hank had taken the chance to go out for food. The boy would probably wake up soon, and if he really were on the mend, he'd be hungry.

"Who are you?"

Hank turned to the sound of the voice. He was mildly surprised by the firmness in the tone when just twenty-four hours ago, Hank had feared the boy might die.

Hank told him.

"Where am I?"

"This is my place."

"But where? In what city?"

"Don't remember much, do you?"

The blond-haired, blue-eyed young man looked away. Hank couldn't tell if he was just groggy or if he really was as confused as he looked.

"How did I get here?"

"I brought you here."

He tried to sit up, but his head must have sent him a warning not to move because he sank quickly back to the pillow, one hand reaching tentatively to touch his bandaged forehead.

"What happened to me?"

"You fell into a river and hit your head on a rock." Hank didn't mention the fact that first a bullet had skidded across that hard, youthful forehead.

"You . . . saved my life?"

Hank shrugged. "Maybe. Maybe you would have made it without my help."

The man did not take his eyes from Hank's, and the action spurred an odd feeling in the back of Hank's mind. The depth of the emotion surprised him.

"I guess I'll just have to ask," the man said slowly, "since I don't seem to recall much. . . . What was I doing in a river?"

Hank wasn't about to tell the young man the truth, especially if God had miraculously—and mercifully—removed his memory. Hank wouldn't tell how he'd been following the boy for weeks despite the fact Hank had refused further services to his client once federal crimes had been revealed. Without Otto's knowledge and by the grace of God, Hank had known this man's every step.

He served a merciful God, one who'd given Hank a second chance to help this boy, after all.

Instead of answering the question, Hank asked, "What do you remember about last night?"

The boy was quiet for what seemed a long time. He started to shake his head, but that movement, too, must have hurt because he stopped. "I don't remember anything. Not even . . ." His gaze traveled back to Hank's as if the moment revealed something unexpected to him. "Not even my name."

Hank frowned. He was no medical expert, but he knew that wasn't a good sign. And he knew there wasn't a thing he could do about it.

"Well," Hank said softly, turning away so the boy wouldn't see his sudden uncertainty, "it'll probably all come back when you're feeling better. For now, you'd better eat a little."

He didn't object, for which Hank was silently grateful. Hank helped him sit up, and soon he was sipping broth and getting back some color.

"I'm sorry I don't know who you are or why you helped me, but I guess I should thank you, anyway. Maybe I wouldn't have made it out by myself, and you really did save my life."

Hank didn't reply.

"Were we boating or swimming or something?"

Hank shook his head.

"Okay," the young man said slowly, "I don't know you, but do you know me?"

Hank nodded.

"That's a relief. Then you can fill me in on the details until it comes back. Like, for instance, my name?"

Hank hesitated, but not for long. Maybe this was a gift. Undeserved, but nonetheless a gift. A second chance not only for Hank but for this young man. A chance to be the man God intended him to be, not the man Otto von Woerner had molded him into.

"Josef," Hank said, in a low voice. "Your name is Josef."